BACK FROM THE DEAD

The girl was familiar. So familiar . . .

Becca stared at her hard, putting a physical effort into it.

Is she someone I know?

Becca struggled to remember. Who was she?

Distantly, she felt the light-headedness, the clammy warning that she was about to pass out.

"Who are you?" she called, but the rising wind threw the words back into her throat.

The phantom girl took a step forward, the tips of her boots balanced over the edge of the cliff. Becca reached out an arm. He mouth opened in protest.

"Stop! *Stop!*"

Was she going to throw herself to her death?

Becca lunged forward just as the girl turned to face her. Instead of a profile shot, Becca caught a full-on view of her face.

"Jessie?" she whispered in shock.

Jessie Brentwood? Her missing classmate? Gone for twenty years . . .

Books by Lisa Jackson

SEE HOW SHE DIES
FINAL SCREAM
RUNNING SCARED
WHISPERS
TWICE KISSED
UNSPOKEN
IF SHE ONLY KNEW
HOT BLOODED
COLD BLOODED
THE NIGHT BEFORE
THE MORNING AFTER
DEEP FREEZE
FATAL BURN
SHIVER
MOST LIKELY TO DIE
ABSOLUTE FEAR
ALMOST DEAD
LOST SOULS
LEFT TO DIE
WICKED GAME
MALICE
CHOSEN TO DIE
WITHOUT MERCY
DEVIOUS
WICKED LIES
BORN TO DIE

Books by Nancy Bush

CANDY APPLE RED
ELECTRIC BLUE
ULTRAVIOLET
WICKED GAME
UNSEEN
BLIND SPOT
WICKED LIES
HUSH

Published by Kensington Publishing Corporation

LISA JACKSON

Wicked Game

NANCY BUSH

ZEBRA BOOKS
KENSINGTON PUBLISHING CORP.
http://www.kensingtonbooks.com

ZEBRA BOOKS are published by

Kensington Publishing Corp.
119 West 40th Street
New York, NY 10018

All Kensington titles, imprints, and distributed lines are available at special quantity discounts for bulk purchases for sales
promotion, premiums, fund-raising, educational, or institutional
use.

Special book excerpts or customized printings can also be
created to fit specific needs. For details, write or phone the
office of the Kensington Special Sales Manager: Attn. Special
Sales Department. Kensington Publishing Corp., 119 West
40th Street, New York, NY 10018. Phone: 1-800-221-2647.

Zebra and the Z logo Reg. U.S. Pat. & TM Off.

ISBN-13: 978-1-4201-0338-0
ISBN-10: 1-4201-0338-5

First Printing: February 2009
10   9   8

Printed in the United States of America

Special thanks to Terry of Iron Station, North Carolina, for supplying the character name for Butterfinger, the cat in this book.

Prologue

St. Elizabeth's campus
February 1989
Midnight . . .

Mother Mary, help me!
Oh, please . . . save me!

The girl rushed headlong through the maze and rising mist. She stumbled, her face grazed by a poking branch.

"Damn." Clapping a hand to her cheek, she instantly felt the warmth of blood welling against her fingers. It spurred her onward. She kept running, moving, breathing hard. Her calf muscles ached, her lungs burned, and still the midnight rain washed over her, cold and cruel.

This is wrong. Oh, God, so wrong.
It shouldn't be this way! Couldn't!

Glancing over her shoulder, she listened hard, deafened by her own heartbeats. She wasn't lost. She knew where she was. She knew the twists and turns that would take her to this maze's center, and once there, she believed there was another exit—maybe two—though it had been so long since she'd seen them. She thought for an instant that she might be leading him to her own doom, to a trap of her own creation. She just had to keep moving, recalling twists and turns . . .

But it was so dark.

And he was getting closer. She could feel him. As if his breath was already brushing across her skin.

Fear clutched at her throat and she nearly slipped around a corner of shivering laurel. He knew about her and now was running her to ground.

How had he known? When she'd spent so many years— her entire life, it seemed—learning the truth herself!

Then, foolishly, she'd goaded him. Dared him. Brought to the maze by her own invitation as she'd hoped to learn more; to expose him. She'd believed she could turn the tables on him, avert the very doom she now faced. But things weren't going as planned, she thought, her shoes slipping on the long grass. Somehow the hunter had become the hunted.

But how could he know about her . . . unless . . . unless he was *one of them*?

Oh, Jesus!

She heard something. A noise . . . a sibilant hiss . . .

The hairs on the back of her nape lifted.

What the hell *was* that?

She froze in place, hands up, as if to ward off danger, body quivering, poised on the balls of her feet, softly panting. *He was here!* Close! He'd already entered the maze. She could hear him now easily, as he was making no effort to disguise his approach.

Her heart knocked painfully against her ribs.

Was he alone? She thought he was alone. He *should* be alone. She'd set this up so he *would be* alone, but now she didn't know.

Didn't know anything.

That's where the fear came in, because she *always* knew.

That was her gift.

And maybe her curse.

That's why they hadn't been able to keep the truth from her. That's why she'd found out who they were, and who she was, even though they'd tried hard to keep her from learning.

For her own safety, they'd said.

And now . . . now she was beginning to understand what they'd meant.

Because of him.

She strained to listen, her heart quivering, her fear mounting. He was walking through the maze. Unhurried. Undeterred. Making all the right turns. Was there more than one set of footsteps? Someone else? She couldn't be sure.

And she couldn't stay where she was. She glanced upward over the tall hedge and saw, as the clouds shifted over the moon, a shaft of the palest light. It threw the bell tower of the church in stark, ominous relief, and near it, just to the south, the roof line of the convent.

She'd seen those landmarks a hundred times before.

Heart thudding, her bearings now intact, she slipped through the hedges. Stealthily. Edging onward, around a bench and a sharp angle, toward the center of the maze, toward the statue.

She'd always been slightly leery of the ghostly Madonna, but now she wanted to reach it with all her heart. Her need to find it was like a hunger, something she could almost cry out for if she dared on this dark, evil night.

Sanctuary.

Safety.

Or so she prayed. Her veins were filled with ice, freezing her so thoroughly it felt as if her blood might solidify.

Silently rounding a final corner, she stopped suddenly as the statue of Mary abruptly appeared, its arms uplifted, greeting her in pale white. Accompanied by the quake of the branches and the musty smell of dead leaves and mud, the statue shimmered ghostlike.

At the sight of it she drew a sharp breath and stumbled backward, nearly falling. A tiny stick snapped beneath her shoe.

She glanced backward fearfully, crouched, poised like a hunted animal. Had he heard? Behind her, through the night-dark maze, she heard his progress. Steadfast. Onward. Skirting corners without hesitation. His footsteps echoed the beats of her own heart, knelling her doom. Swallowing, she licked her lips nervously as she forced her legs to move forward. One corner . . . a length . . . another corner.

Where the hell was the exit?

Had she missed it?

She wanted to cry out in fear and frustration as she was forced to backtrack, knowing he was nearer, feeling him close enough that her skin quivered.

There was no opening, no parting of the thick branches.

Panic tore through her. There had to be a way out, a place to hide, a way to get the upper hand . . . Oh, God.

And still he came.

Nearer.

His footsteps loud against the muddy ground. Determined.

Where? Where the hell was the opening?

She hurried along each of the back walls of shrubbery, running her hands through the leaves, searching . . . searching . . . Head pounding, heart thrumming wildly, her ears seemed filled with the roar of the ocean, the battering of the ocean against distant cliffs . . . though she was nowhere near the ocean in this closed labyrinth. But it had always been this way. She had always heard these oddly familiar sounds, always sensed a remote place with thick salt air . . .

But here she found no opening. No escape. Nothing but thick, unbroken branches.

She swallowed hard against her fear. This was it. There was no escape.

Kneeling at the statue, she mouthed, "Mother Mary, save my soul . . ."

She hadn't been good.

Oh, God no.

But she wasn't all bad, either.

Behind her she heard him move ever forward. No rush, no rush at all.

He *knew* he had her. Terror crawled up her spine.

She kept silently, desperately praying, again and again, *Mother Mary, save my soul*. And then another voice. Deep. Rough. Echoing hollowly through her skull: *She can't help you. You have no soul to save*.

Were they his words? Was that *his* cruel voice inside her head?

She thought with sudden clarity: *I'm sixteen years old and I am going to die*.

How stupid she was to have goaded him—teased him. *Dared* him.

What had she been thinking?

This was the crux of her problem: Not only could she see the future, she sometimes tried to change it.

And now he was going to kill her. In the middle of this maze, in the cold of winter, he was going to end her life. Desperately she slipped one hand into the pocket of her jacket, curled her fingers over the jackknife hidden within.

With all her strength she prayed for her life, her soul. Above her pulsing heart she heard the hunter's footsteps. Nearer. Relentlessly closer. She rose, turning, facing the yawning opening in the thick shrubbery, the only means of escape. From the depths a dark figure appeared.

Tall.

Menacing.

Lucifer Incarnate.

Her beginning and her end.

"Leave," she ordered, holding up the knife.

He kept walking.

"I swear I'll kill you."

A slow, self-satisfied smile slid across his face. *You think you invited me here, whore, when it was I who found you, who hunted you, who will do the killing*. He didn't say a word, yet his voice reverberated through her brain.

"I'm not kidding," she warned, brandishing her small blade, the jackknife she'd stolen from her father's drawer.

Nor am I.

She lunged. Driving the knife downward, intending to slice into his abdomen.

Quick as a snake, he coiled strong fingers around her wrist. "Ah!"

Stupid cunt.

He bent her hand backward.

Pain screamed up her forearm. She cried out and fell to her knees.

Her gaze clashed with his.

Strong fingers bent her wrist back.

"Stop!" she yelled.

Breath hissed through his teeth. With a sharp twist he snapped the bones in her wrist.

She cried out softly. The knife fell from her nerveless fingers. His dark eyes were lasers as he snatched it up and drove forward, jamming it between her ribs. "No more," he rasped.

She clawed at him but it was no use. Meeting his gaze, she whispered, "This is just the beginning . . ." and saw his face contort with rage as he shook his head violently, thrusting the knife deeper.

The night swirled around her. She crumpled to the ground at the base of the statue, aware that her attacker was staring down at her, his teeth bared, his breath visible in short puffs that dissipated as she gazed upward, the lifeblood pooling out of her.

Then she lay still as death beneath the Madonna. He backed out of her ever-narrowing vision. Clouds shrouded the moon. Few stars were visible. The Madonna's arms stretched upward to the heavens. Somewhere, far in the distance, it seemed a bell tolled.

I am a sacrifice, she thought.

Then darkness descended.

* * *

St. Elizabeth's campus
February 2009
Midnight . . .

Kyle Baskin held the flashlight under his chin, beaming its illumination upward, highlighting the planes and hollows of his face.

"Bloody Bones entered the house," he whispered in his deepest, most ghoulish voice. His eyes darted around the circle of boys seated on the ground at his feet, their scared faces turned up earnestly. "Bloody Bones crossed to the stairs. Bloody Bones looked up and could see the children through the *walls*."

"Like X-ray vision?" Mikey Ferguson squeaked.

"Shut up." James, his older brother, threw him a harsh look.

The branches overhead shivered. There was a moon but it wasn't visible over the height of the maze's hedge. Only the faintest trickle of light wavered through the leaves.

"I'm on the first step," Kyle intoned, hesitating for maximum effect. He gazed across the beam of the flashlight at the kids he and James had brought to the center of the maze. They were supposed to be babysitting, but that was boring as hell. "I'm on the second step." He drew a shaking breath and said slowly, "I'm on . . . the . . . third step . . ."

Mikey shot a look of terror over his shoulder and edged closer to James, whose smirk was fully visible to Kyle.

Tyler, that little pissant, started to snivel.

"I'm on . . . the . . . *fourth* . . . step . . ."

"How many steps are there?" Mikey cried, clutching at James's arm.

"Shut the fuck up." James tried to shake him off.

"I wanna go home!" Tyler wailed.

"I'm on . . . the *fifth step*!"

"I'm calling my dad." Preston, the overweight prick, clambered to his feet, his normally toneless voice quaking a bit.

"The phone's in the car, moron."

"I'm on the *sixth step, I'm on the seventh step, I'm on the eighth step*!" Kyle declared in a rush.

The boys leapt to their feet as if yanked by strings, crying, heads jerking around, searching vainly for escape but the hedges loomed, branches sticking out like skeletal arms.

Kyle's voice dropped to a whisper. "I'm on the ninth step . . ."

James started to worry a little. They couldn't have these dumbasses charging off in all directions in the dark. "Siddown!"

"I'm on the tenth step . . . and now I'm walking down the hall . . . I'm outside your door . . . I'm pushing it open . . . *cree—eeaa—kkk*!"

It sounded sorta dumb, James thought, the way Kyle did it, but it sure as hell did the trick. The kids started scattering like cockroaches, shying away from the dirty old statue of that lady, screaming and blubbering. James and Kyle started laughing. They couldn't help themselves. That ratcheted the boys to near hysteria, and Mikey stumbled right into the statue—the idiot—and knocked the damn thing to one side. The bulldozers had been at the site. The school was being razed and they were taking down the maze as well. That's why Kyle had come up with the idea in the first place. One last spooky hurrah where they could scare the snot out of the little kids.

"Moron, you knocked over the old lady," James said in a long-suffering tone.

He went to pick up his younger brother while Kyle corralled Tyler and Preston, who were crying like the babies they were. Mikey had practically turned to a statue himself. He stood frozen, staring. He slowly lifted one hand as James approached, pointing toward a mound of earth that had humped up when the statue tilted.

"Bloody Bones," he whispered, his finger quivering.

James looked in the direction he was pointing. From the ground a skeletal human hand lay upturned, its bones both dirty and oddly white, its fingers reaching upward, as if for help.

James's eyes bugged out. He started shrieking like a banshee and couldn't quit.

Kyle gazed on in raw fear. "Shit," he quavered.

Little Mikey grabbed James's hand and hauled them both out of the maze. The rest of the gang thundered behind them. They all ran for their lives, the cold touch of Bloody Bones feathering their napes all the way.

Chapter One

I feel it . . . that change in the atmosphere, subtle but strong, like the slight tremor of a gentle earthquake with its aftershocks. I know what it means.

I knew it would happen.

Was waiting.

Flinging off the covers of the old bed, I listen to the howl of the wind as it rushes from the west, driving inland, churning up the water. I don't bother with clothes as I open the door from the old keeper's quarters that lead into the lighthouse itself. Quickly I take the circular stairs, running up their rusted steps, ignoring the metal as it groans against my weight.

Faster! Faster!

My heart is pumping and all the restlessness I've tried to contain, the impulses I've kept at bay, are now set free.

The stairs curl more tightly as I ascend to the landing where the once-vibrant beacon lies dormant, its huge lens giving off no illumination, warning no sailors of the impending shoals.

I fling the door open and step onto the weathered grating. Rain spits from clouds roiling in the heavens, wind tears at my hair, and the night is dark and thick with winter. A hundred and thirty feet below the surf churns and boils in whitecapped fury around this small, craggy island that has been abandoned for half a century.

No one inhabits the island.

The lighthouse is off-limits to the public, guarded judiciously by the Coast Guard and a tired, twisted chain-link fence as well as the dangerous surf itself.

A few have dared to trespass.

And they have died in the treacherous currents that surround this sorry bit of rock.

Even in the darkness, I turn and view the mainland. I know they're there. I've taken as many as I can. Their fortress can be breached, though I bear the scars of battle and I must be careful.

Tonight, no lights glow from their windows. The forest covers them.

As I face the sea, I tilt my head, lift my nose to the wind, but I smell nothing other than the briny scent of the Pacific crashing a hundred feet below. I close my eyes and concentrate. As the wind tosses my hair into my eyes and my skin chills with the frigid air, the blood in my veins runs hot.

I imagine the scent of her skin. Like a rain-washed beach. Tantalizing . . .

I can almost smell her. Almost.

Even without her scent, I now know where she is. I've learned of her by another who has unconsciously shown me the way.

Good.

It's time, once again, to right an age-old wrong.

This time, there will be no mistake.

*   *   *

A frisson slid down Becca Sutcliff's spine. She inhaled sharply and glanced behind her. The girl at the counter of Mutts & Stuff slid her a look from the corner of her eyes. "You okay?"

"Someone's walking on my grave, I guess," Becca murmured.

The girl's brows lifted and Becca could practically read her mind: *Yeah. Right. Whatever.* She rang up Becca's purchases and stuffed them in a bag. Thanking her, Becca shifted the packages she was already carrying to accommodate them. Yes, she was filling a need, shopping like it was an Olympic sport, a result of the messy, lingering aftermath of unsettled feelings that still followed from her split with Ben. And now Ben was dead. Gone. Never to come back. And it all felt . . . well . . . weird.

She headed back into the mall, slightly depressed by the cheery red and pink hearts in every store window. Valentine's Day. The most miserable day of the year for the suddenly single.

Okay. She wasn't completely unhappy. She'd known for a long time that she and Ben weren't going to make it. They'd never been in love. Not in the way she'd wanted, hoped, planned to be. When she'd learned he was seeing someone else, she was angry. At herself, mostly. She couldn't really even recall what had triggered their marriage in the first place. What had she wanted? What had Ben wanted? Had it just been timing? A sense that, if not Ben, then who?

Then she learned he'd died in the arms of his new love. Heart attack.

Gone, gone . . . gone.

She was still processing. Still getting used to the fact that he'd left her for another woman. Left her . . . when she'd still believed that maybe, just maybe, there would be that chance for them. That chance to start a family. Have a child. A child of their own. A child of *her* own . . .

The window of Pink, Blue, and You, a combined baby and maternity store, materialized in front of her. She'd stopped into it earlier and picked out a gift for a pregnant coworker. It was a fine torture to be inside. She wanted a baby. She'd always wanted a baby. Her insides twisted with the memory that she'd lost an unborn baby a long, long time ago.

Yet, at times like this, the pain returned, as fresh and raw as when she'd miscarried.

Tears hovered behind her eyes. But she wasn't going to break down, for God's sake. Not now. She'd grieved far too long as it was. She held the stupid tears at bay, turning her face away from the display of pastel pinks and blues and lemony yellows. Was that why she'd married Ben? To have a baby? To replace the one who'd been taken from her?

Becca told herself to get over it. She'd asked herself the same question countless times, had toiled and fretted over the answer. But it was all moot now. Ben was gone. And he'd left his twenty-two-year-old new lover pregnant, something he'd never wanted with Becca.

"I don't want children," he'd said. "You knew it when you married me."

Had she? She didn't remember that.

"It's just you and me, Beck. You and me."

Maybe she *had* married him to have a child. Correction. To *replace* a child. Maybe she'd made up the "I love you" parts. Maybe she'd just wanted the whole thing to be so much prettier than it was.

"Damn it all." She had no time to walk down this lane of self-pity. It was over. O-V-E-R! She turned away from the window. No need to torture herself further. No need at all.

A food court was on her left and she glanced over as she headed the other way. But as she tried to hurry on, her vision grew blurry, forcing her to slow down and finally stop short. Her pulse was suddenly rocketing. Damn. She was going to faint. She'd been down this route before, more times than she'd like to admit. But it wasn't really fainting. No. More like . . . falling into a spell. A wide-awake dream. But it hadn't happened in years. Not for *years*!

Why now? she asked herself a half-second before a sizzle of pain shot through her brain. She staggered and fell to her knees, packages tumbling from her arms. Becca bent her head, instinctively hiding her face from curious onlookers, one last moment of clarity before the vision overcame her.

In a transformation that was both familiar and feared, Becca was no longer at the mall, no longer feeling the wrench of loss of her baby. No longer in the real world but in a watery, insubstantial one, a world that had plagued her youth yet had been curiously missing and distant for most of her adult life . . . until now.

In front of her, a short distance away, a teenaged girl stood on a headland above a gray and frothy sea, her long, light brown hair teased by a stiff breeze, her shirt and jeans pressed to her skin from its force, her gaze focused across churning waves toward a small island, blurred with rain. Becca followed the girl's gaze, staring past her to the island as well, a forlorn, rocky tor that looked as inhospitable as an alien planet. The girl shivered and so did Becca. The cold burrowed beneath her skin and gooseflesh rose on her arms.

The girl was familiar. So familiar . . .

Becca stared at her hard, putting a physical effort into it. *Is she someone I know?*

Becca struggled to remember. Who was she? Where was she? Why was she pulling Becca into her world?

Distantly, she felt the light-headedness, the clammy warning that she was about to pass out. No, no, no! Caught between the two worlds, her body failing in one, her mind desperately searching for answers in the other, Becca focused on the girl.

"Who are you?" she called, but the rising wind threw the words back into her throat.

The phantom girl took a step forward, the tips of her boots balanced over the edge of the cliff. Becca reached out an arm. Her mouth opened in protest.

"Stop! *Stop!*"

Was she going to throw herself to her death?

Becca lunged forward just as the girl turned to face her. Instead of a profile, Becca caught a full-on view of her face. "Jessie?" she whispered in shock, her head reeling.

Jessie just stared at Becca and Becca, powerless, stared back. The wind danced through Jessie's hair and around her small, serious face. Becca's heart pounded painfully.

Jessie Brentwood? Her missing classmate? Gone for twenty years . . .

Except now, in Becca's vision.

"You're too close to the edge!" Becca warned.

The phantom girl lifted a finger to her lips, then mouthed something at Becca.

"What?" Becca tried to clear her mind. *"What?"*

In the gathering mist the girl's image began to fade. Becca pushed forward but it felt as if her feet were mired to the ground.

"Jessie!" she cried.

The girl melded with the rain and the watery world dimmed into endless gray.

Becca sensed tears on her lashes and a dull throb in her head. Somewhere, a male voice was saying, "Hey, lady. You okay?"

With difficulty, Becca opened her eyes. She was in the mall. Sprawled on the tiled floor. Packages tossed asunder. No more ocean. No more wind. No more Jessie.

Oh, God, she looked like a fool!

Tucking her legs beneath her, Becca tried to pull herself together. It was difficult to come back to reality. It always was after one of her visions. The damn things. She'd thought they were behind her. A symptom of her childhood. She hadn't had one since high school, and she was now thirty-four years old.

But she never forgot. Not completely.

"I'm fine," she said in a voice she didn't recognize as her own. Clearing her throat, she fought the blinding stabs of pain that flashed through her head. Another unwelcome part of the visions. "I tripped."

"Yeah?"

The young man bending over her wasn't buying it. A small crowd of "tweenagers" had gathered, small enough that Becca figured she hadn't been out that long, maybe mere seconds. One of the girls was looking at her with huge, round eyes and Becca could still hear the reverberations of the girl's scream as she'd watched Becca go down. She was holding a soda from the nearby food court. Vaguely Becca remembered glancing their way just before she was overtaken by her vision.

"You were, like, having an attack," a different girl said. This one wore a hat that smashed her bangs to her forehead and she peeked out between the strands of blond hair. They all looked ready to jump and run. Briefly, Becca thought about yelling "Boo!" and sending them stumbling over themselves, away from the crazy lady.

Click. Click. Click.

Becca heard the snap of a cell phone being shut. One of the guys had taken a series of pictures of her fainting spell. That did it! Stupid punk kid. Becca climbed unsteadily to her feet and gave the boy the evil eye. He looked torn between bravado and fear. Becca was about to give him a piece of her mind but was saved the effort when a heavyset woman in a dusty blue uniform steamed toward them.

"Back off," she bit out at the boy who attempted to swagger toward his friends, even though he was boiling to escape. They all half ran, half loped toward the food court and an exit door.

"You all right, ma'am?" the security woman asked.

Flushing with embarrassment, Becca nodded, collecting her packages. She was definitely not all right.

"You look kinda pale. Maybe you should sit down."

"This happens to me. Not enough air getting in. Vagus nerve, you know. Shuts down the whole system sometimes."

It was clearly mumbo jumbo to the security guard, and it

was a flat-out lie to boot. Doctors had once rubbed their jaws, speculating what caused Becca to faint and have visions. They ignored the visions, concentrating on the cause of her fainting, and had postulated and supposed and theorized to Becca's parents, Barbara and Jim Ryan, but there had never been any satisfactory explanations.

"I'm fine," she reassured the guard one more time, hanging on to the shreds of her dignity with an effort. Before she could be questioned further, Becca headed out the mall exit and ducked through a drizzling rain to her car, a blue Volkswagen Jetta wedged into a spot between two oversized SUVs. Feeling a twinge in one shoulder from her fall, Becca squeezed through the driver's side door and tossed her bags into the passenger seat, then climbed in. Her body was still tingling, too, as if her muscles had been asleep. She dropped her forehead to the steering wheel and took several deep breaths. This vision had been different. Almost touchable. She'd actually *reached* for the girl. That had never happened before.

Was it Jessie? *Was it?*

Becca shoved her rain-damped hair from her eyes, silently told herself to get over it, then lifted her head only to gaze blankly through the windshield at the mall's cream-colored stucco walls. A twentysomething woman was standing under the portico near the doorway while smoking a cigarette and talking on a cell phone, but Becca, lost in her own thoughts, barely saw her.

Becca hadn't had a vision since that last year of high school. Not once. She'd managed to convince herself over the years that she wasn't odd. Some kind of freak. That she wasn't losing her mind.

But this vision of Jessie had been stronger than anything she'd experienced before. And a helluva lot more frightening.

What did it mean?

"Nothing! Face it, you're just a freak," she muttered under her breath. What she did not need now in her life, absolutely did not, was any kind of eerie visions or attacks or whatever you wanted to call them. She'd hoped they had died a quick and lasting death.

Trying to shake the weird sensation clinging to her, Becca drove from the parking lot, her wipers slapping at the rain. The sky had darkened, night dropping quickly. One of her packages had tipped over and the baby gift she'd purchased was spilled on the seat, a bright, whimsical mermaid puppet sewn in silver lamé and pink and green sequins.

That old sadness threatened to overcome her again, but she wouldn't have any of it. Driving with one hand, she stuffed the puppet back into the shopping bag and headed purposely for the condo she'd once shared with Ben. Now the two-bedroom unit was all hers—all nine hundred square feet of "charming midcentury" architecture, as the literature boasted. In layman's terms this meant an apartment building constructed in the late fifties and converted to condos with a little updating in the late nineties. But it was home. Even without Ben.

By the time she pulled into her designated slot, Becca had managed to push the damned vision and her own case of the unwanted blues aside, but dusk was gathering quickly and the clouds opened up again.

Rain tossed around her in shivery waves as she headed for the front door, fumbling with her keys. The evening paper was in a plastic sleeve on the stoop and she reached down and grabbed it, juggling it with her packages, as she spilled through the door. She dumped everything she was carrying onto the drop-leaf table that stood in the small foyer, then shrugged out of her dampened coat and hung it in the closet as the ticky-tick of Ringo's nails across her oak floors heralded her dog's arrival.

"Hey, bud," she said as the curly haired black and white mutt furiously waved his tail, gazing at her ‘expectantly. "Look what I got you."

She held up the blue collar with its little white dog bone motif, but Ringo kept his eyes on hers. If it wasn't food, he simply wasn't interested.

"Okay," Becca relented as she headed to the kitchen. She pulled out a jar of small, dog-shaped treats. Ringo barked twice, happily, as Becca unscrewed the lid and fished out a couple of biscuits, tossing them to the dog, who leaped up and caught them in his jaws, one by one, then raced back to his bed and snuffled and chewed them.

"We'll go for a walk in a minute," she said, adding some of his regular dog food to his bowl. Ringo quickly finished his treats and hurried to his bowl, munching on his meal with the same enthusiasm as the biscuits. He was not a picky dog.

She gazed out the kitchen window, which faced the back of another condo across an expanse of grass. She could see right inside to the other kitchen, which was festooned with red and pink foil hearts. A young girl was seated at the table, licking the icing off a cupcake decorated with candy hearts.

She recalled last year's Valentine's Day. She'd been waiting for Ben. Though she'd sensed—known, really—that their marriage was in its death throes, she'd spontaneously bought a cake and a bottle of champagne. The cake had been heart shaped with white icing, and in red gel script, it read: *Be Mine*.

Ben had never come home that night and Becca had opened the champagne alone, drunk half a glass, and poured the rest down the drain in the kitchen sink. Calls to his cell phone and text messages had been left unanswered until late in the night when he'd simply texted back: *Something came up. Don't worry. I'm okay*. She would have panicked and called the police, but deep in her heart she'd known what was coming. He'd shown up the next day to break the news that he was in love with someone else, and that the someone else was pregnant.

Despite telling herself that she'd suspected something like this, Becca had tried not to be shocked, hurt, and upset, but she'd failed on all counts.

Suspecting him of having an affair was one thing.

Having that affair *and pregnancy* confirmed was quite another.

"You told me you never wanted kids," Becca reminded him, trying to keep from screaming at him at the top of her lungs.

"I guess I changed my mind," he responded, turning away from her accusing face.

"You guess?"

"Look, I'm sorry. I didn't mean for it to happen."

"If you didn't mean for it to happen, you should have used a condom."

"Who says I didn't?"

"Did you?" Becca demanded. Did he think she was a moron?

He almost lied to her. She could see him thinking whether he could make her believe him. But he knew her almost as well as she knew him. "It wasn't supposed to be this way," he mumbled, heading for the bedroom and his suitcase.

She followed him, too betrayed to let him just go. She yanked down another bag and stuffed it full of his clothes. Her outrage, her all-consuming fury, helped her cram his Brooks Brothers button-downs into small wads. "Take everything. Everything. Don't come back. Ever."

"Becca, you're just upset. I've gotta come back and get—"

"Don't be reasonable, Ben. I swear to God. Don't be reasonable or I'll scream." She glared at him, but all she saw was the baby. The one he was having . . . with someone else. "If you can't carry it now, it'll be on the front porch."

"Don't be ridiculous!"

"I'm ridiculous?" she demanded, dropping one of his white shirts onto the bedroom floor.

Ben, the coward, couldn't hold her gaze. In tense silence

he snatched up the shirt, finished packing his bag, and stormed out. She tossed the other suitcase after him, not caring whether he picked it up or not. It sat on the porch for two days while she stacked other items beside it, crowning the pile with his most prized golf trophy. She half expected the homeowner's association to complain about the mess, but Ben managed to sweep everything up before that happened. He came when Becca was away, so there were no more angry words. In fact, there were no more words at all for several months. Becca had just determined to open the lines of communication again, preparing for the inevitable divorce, when she got a call from Kendra Wallace—the someone else—who between sobs, shrieks, and tears explained that Ben had died in her arms of an apparent heart attack. At forty-two.

For a good ten minutes Becca heard nothing else. Nothing past the fact that Ben was dead. She surfaced to finally understand that Kendra's wailing was along the "poor me, what am I going to do" line. "The baby," Becca said, moving from shock back to reality. Ben was going to be a father . . .

"The baby is mine!" Kendra snapped sharply, as if aware of Becca's desire to have a child of her own.

"Do you have family?" *Someone to help you?*

"What's that got to do with anything?"

"You need someone—"

"I need Ben and he's dead!" she said, sniffing and sobbing. "And . . . and . . . you'll be hearing from my lawyer."

"Your lawyer? Why . . ." Then it hit her. The divorce wasn't even final, the arrangement for separating their finances not quite nailed down. Oh, Jesus.

Kendra slammed down the phone.

Becca was left staring into space. She was aware Kendra was going to come after her financially, but if the child was Ben's, so be it. Then when, after two months, she received no call, she dialed Kendra on the number that Caller ID had coughed up and learned it belonged to Kendra's mother, who told Becca that Kendra had moved to Los Angeles with her new boyfriend. "What about the baby?" Becca asked, and was told, in a chilly voice, that Kendra's boyfriend was adopting the little boy and it was none . . . of . . . her . . . concern. The lawyers would handle everything.

And they had. As it turned out, Kendra's child had ended up with a trust account, funded by half of Ben's life insurance proceeds and set up by Becca's lawyer, who had been a friend of Ben's. Becca accepted that as the child's due, but if Kendra wanted to come after her for more, the fight was on.

Now Becca hugged Ringo briefly, fitted him with his new collar and clipped on his leash, then slid her arms through her favorite rain jacket. Twisting her hair into a knot with one hand, she crammed a baseball cap onto her head as Ringo danced at the door.

Outside, the night was black with rain and cold as they strolled around the condo's grounds. Ringo waved his tail at several other dogs, but he didn't bark. Apart from a woof or two when food was coming his way, he was pretty quiet. Rarely did he growl or make any noise. On walks, he was content to bury his nose or lift his leg on any and all interesting tree trunks.

Today was no exception. There were fewer pedestrians, probably because of the rain. Head ducked into her collar, Becca walked a few blocks toward the river, then back again, giving Ringo time to take care of business.

About a block from her front door, the dog suddenly stopped, planted his feet, and growled low in his throat. Becca tugged on the leash, but Ringo couldn't be moved. "Come on," she said as the hairs along the back of her neck lifted. Un-Ringo-like behavior, for sure.

The dog stared into a space about a hundred yards away where a thick grove of firs, branches waving like beckoning arms, stood tall and dark in the slanting rain. Becca's pulse jumped. Something was wrong. She glanced around jerkily, half expecting the bogeyman to pounce on her.

Ringo gave a sharp bark and lunged, tugged at the leash.

"You're freaking me out, dog," Becca rebuked and bent down quickly, sliding the wet animal into her arms and hurrying toward her front door. Ringo's head swivelled to keep sight of the trees. She could feel the low *grrrrrr* that rumbled through his body.

Inside, she slammed the dead bolt into place, unsnapped the leash, grabbed a towel she kept in the front closet, and tried to towel Ringo off, but he shot to the nearest window, rising on his back legs, nose pressed to the glass, lips pulled back in a silent snarl.

"Stop that," she ordered as she headed to the kitchen and filled a teakettle with water. *It's probably just a squirrel. Or the fat yellow tabby cat who's usually perched on the upper unit's deck. Nothing more sinister. Get over yourself!*

She shook a shiver away, then rummaged around in the cupboard. No champagne this Valentine's Day. Tea would be just fine.

When she returned to the living room Ringo was sitting on his haunches, but his eyes were still fixed on something outside the window.

Becca tried to woo him to sit on the couch beside her, but when she went to pick him up, he sidled away and paced in front of the glass. Unnerved by his behavior, she picked up the paper and slid it from its plastic sleeve. Her eye fell on a picture of statue. The Madonna inside the maze at St. Elizabeth's. The bold headline read: BOYS DISCOVER HUMAN SKELETON INSIDE MAZE.

Her lips parted in shock.

The teakettle shrieked and Becca gave an aborted scream. Ringo flew into frenzied barking. It took long moments before she could calm the dog and her own rocketing pulse enough to actually read the article about the body found on the grounds of the private high school she'd attended, a school now being razed.

When she was finished, she counted her still-accelerated heartbeats and stared at the rivulets of rain running down her window, her thoughts far from this miserable Valentine's Day, her deceased husband, and whatever had spooked Ringo.

Her mind slid easily into the past and those days of high school. She knew the skeletal remains belonged to Jessie Brentwood, the girl from her vision, the friend from high school who'd disappeared without a trace, the girlfriend of Hudson Walker, Becca's own secret crush and the father of Becca's unborn child, had he but known it.

Jezebel "Jessie" Brentwood. Sixteen when she disappeared.

She'd come to Becca in a dream today.

Jessie had said something. Something important. While the wind had tossed her hair and she'd eased her toes over the edge of the cliff. Her whispered words meant something. Something Becca needed to understand, yet didn't.

"Jessie . . ." she said aloud, her gaze dropping to the newspaper and the ghostly image of the Madonna statue. "What happened to you?"

Chapter Two

Sam McNally stood hatless in the rain, examining the taped-off areas the crime scene technicians had painstakingly combed over the last twenty hours. The crowd had thinned, the press long gone, most of the officers either home or on duty elsewhere. Tonight the area was a dark, soggy, muddy mess. The bones had been removed and the techs were doing what they could with them. Preliminary findings said the bones were from a girl, around fifteen or sixteen years old. If these remains weren't Jezebel Brentwood, he would eat a kangaroo, something his son had said too often to count back when Levi was a toddler.

He glanced around the overgrown maze where berry vines wound and grappled their way through the once-tended hedges. There had been talk years ago, rumors, that the maze had been planted by a rogue priest at war with the bishop and archdiocese, that there were secrets hidden in the verdant labyrinth, but they were largely disputed and laughed about. An urban legend that just wouldn't die, held by conspiracy theorists. But then there was the very real murder of a student years before, a boy by the name of Jake Marcott who literally took one through the heart—at the Valentine's Day dance, no less. A perfect irony. Killed in this very maze over twenty years earlier.

And now these bones.

A girl, in her mid-teens. The techs had found her pelvis, but some of the other bones had been scattered, the skeleton not intact, fragments missing or in the wrong place, as if animals had dug through the shallow grave and pulled her apart. One of her ulnae had been located six feet away, under the hedge, pulled from her right arm. There were other scattered bones as well, and what was left of her had been hauled away in bags to be reassembled in the morgue. A gruesome job, but one he thought he might have the stomach to observe.

Who are you kidding? Just the thought of her beautiful body being torn apart churns your stomach.

He scowled into the darkness. "Damn it all to hell," he muttered and glanced at the excavation site, a shallow grave at the base of the statue of Mary. What kind of sick bastard killed and buried her with a private marker?

Had he buried her here so he could return and relive the killing? Or pay penance? Leave flowers on her unmarked grave? It had happened time and time again; even now there were dried remnants of roses that had been placed at the base of the Madonna, roses now saturated with rain and mud and carted off to the lab.

You son of a bitch, he thought, *I'm gonna find you, and I know just where to look.*

"Hey, Mac!" One of the techs waved him over to the base of the statue. The Madonna was tilted, still serene, arms uplifted to the heavens, well, now . . . kind of skewed, but you got the idea.

Rain slipped icy fingers down his neck, but he ignored it as he picked his way over the sticky clods of mud. His boots weighed double their usual amount, they were so caked with the gooey dirt.

"Yeah?" No one called him Sam. No one ever had, or probably ever would, he guessed.

"You think you found her, huh?"

In the shadowy weird, eerie illumination cast by the klieg lights, Mac gazed at the man coolly. It had been a thing around the department for twenty years—his need to learn the truth about Jessie Brentwood's disappearance. And though it generally didn't bother him much, he found it incredibly annoying that his interest in the case even had the techs pausing in their work to theorize and jaw and wonder. Pissed him off no end.

Not that he didn't understand it. He didn't like to admit it, but he had been obsessed about the girl. It had eaten at him in a way he'd never experienced before or since.

"You got something for me?" Mac asked. "Or you just want to talk?"

"You could be right, is all. Sure looks like it might be that girl. Jaime."

"Jessie."

"You said right from the start that she was murdered. Killed by that group of boys, then covered up. Twenty years . . ." He shook his head in wonder. "Twenty goddamn years."

Almost to the day, Mac thought, but didn't add fuel to the fire.

"What are you gonna do now?"

Mac moved away from the curious technician. "Not really my case," he said with a shrug.

"Bull-fucking-shit. Been your case from the beginning, man."

Yeah, well . . . Mac headed back to his black department-issue sedan, switched out of his boots to shoes that weren't quite so caked with mud, then climbed in behind the wheel and backed away from the crime scene. In the distance, the prehistoric outlines of heavy construction equipment were black against a faintly lighter sky. St. Elizabeth's was being torn down. Even without the kids who'd stumbled upon Jessie's grave, her skeletal remains would have inevitably been discovered.

He shoved the car into Drive and rolled out of the pock-marked parking lot that separated the convent from the school. A few lights still shone in the windows of the nuns' quarters, which were to be saved from the developer's bulldozers. The convent was still owned by the church and was to remain that way, at least until a better offer from a developer landed on the archdiocese's table.

Driving past what remained of the gymnasium while the police radio crackled and the rain peppered his windshield, Mac did a quick mental inventory of himself, an exercise he performed automatically, something he'd learned from the ridicule and exposure he'd received after he'd insisted that the group of boys who made up Jessie Brentwood's friends were involved. He decided he was okay. He wasn't nuts and never had been, and that group of boys—the Preppy Pricks, as he'd dubbed them—were the real ones with problems.

They'd all known Jessie. They'd all insisted they were innocent in her disappearance.

He remembered them with surprising clarity. Christopher Delacroix III, a filthy-rich kid who had hidden behind Daddy's money. The Third, as the others called him, seemed to be a ringleader. Now he, like his namesakes, was a Portland attorney and a son of a bitch. Mitch Bellotti, the heavyset football player, had been a smart-ass. He was still around and rumored to be a helluva mechanic. Scott Pascal was a weasel if there ever had been one. He and a buddy—Glenn Stafford—had opened a fancy restaurant together. Most of the others were around as well, and their names and faces ran through his head: Jarrett Erikson, Zeke St. John, and Hudson Walker.

He liked to check his own emotional temperature. He'd learned restraint. He'd learned how to keep things to himself.

But he'd never stopped believing one of the Preppy Pricks, or several working together, were responsible for Jessie

Brentwood's disappearance and death. Maybe there were some guys involved outside of their core group, too; Mac had certainly harassed others who were also friends or acquaintances of Jessie. But the Preppy Pricks were at the top of his list. He'd made their lives hellish twenty years ago; he could admit it now. He'd been twenty-five, full of his own self-importance; brash, cocky, and a real pain in the ass. But he couldn't break them. Hadn't been able to poke holes in their stories. And he'd ended up being the laughingstock of the police department. He'd damned near been demoted from missing persons to some nondescript desk job. It had taken years to become a respected homicide detective, and even to this day some of his superiors regarded him with a baleful eye and most of his partners left him as soon as they could. The Jezebel Brentwood case—his obsession with it—had put its stamp on him.

And now . . . her bones had been discovered.

If they were Jessie's. And he believed with all his heart that they were. His headlights reflected on the wet, crumbling pavement and reflected off the eyes of a lumbering racoon that scuttled into the surrounding shrubbery skirting the abandoned school's main entrance.

Checking his feelings, Mac expected to experience some kind of satisfied "I told you so" building up inside. Maybe there was a little of that, but mostly he sensed his curiosity about the case, a long-slumbering beast, stir from its resting place and lift a nose to the wind.

He pulled onto the highway running through the canyons that carved the west hills of Portland where tall firs flanked the road and elegant homes from the early 1900s were cut into the steep hillsides.

What had happened to Jessie? he wondered. A prank gone bad? A lovers' quarrel that had escalated out of control? An accident? Or was it murder? The cold, calculated snuffing out of a pretty girl's life.

Bile rose in his throat, the way it always did when he was

dealing with the abuse or death of the young. Of the innocent. Though, from what he knew about Jessie Brentwood,
she was older than her years and far from innocent . . . an intriguing underage woman who was as manipulating as she'd
been alluring. One of those females who knew intrinsically
all of her attributes, how to use those wide hazel eyes and
turned-up smile to get what she wanted, even if it meant
playing with fire.

And he asked himself the question that everyone else
seemed consumed with: Why was he so fascinated with this
case? A simple missing persons case, they'd all said. Why
did Mac care about this one so much?

He still had no answer. Maybe he'd been a little in love, a
little in lust, with the beautiful, mysterious girl he'd never
met. He'd handled dozens of cases where kids disappeared,
but this one was different. *She* was different. He'd followed
all the leads he could, dreamed about her, even. Fantasized
about her, for God's sake, and he'd taken a lot of heat for it.
At the time his friends on the force thought he'd gone around
the bend. She was a sixteen-year-old runaway. He was an up-
and-coming hotshot detective who was obsessed by a ghost.

In retrospect, maybe they hadn't been that far off the mark.

Now, twenty years later, a single father working homicide, Mac knew he'd definitely mellowed. He didn't really
want this case now. Old wounds. And problems.

But those Preppy Pricks were still out there. He wondered
how they felt, knowing Jessie's body had been discovered.
One, or several of them, must be sweating bullets now.

Mac smiled thinly. Well, maybe this was the way it should
be after all. Him, heading up a homicide case, a cold case
that put all the smug bastards on the hot seat.

It was sounding better by the minute.

Becca set the newspaper on the coffee table and sank
back on the couch, still staring at the folded pages as if they

were Satan's diary. She felt cold inside and out. What was this? What did it mean?

Ringo circled her feet, tail down, a soft, nearly inaudible growl emanating from his throat.

"Stop it, there's nothing out there," she said softly, as much to soothe her own jangled nerves as to calm the dog.

Jessie Brentwood had disappeared twenty years earlier when she'd been sixteen and a student at St. Elizabeth's, the private Catholic school that had gone co-ed only a few years before. Becca had attended St. Elizabeth's, too, though she was a year behind Jessie, a freshman. But she'd been friends with Jessie's crowd, and she remembered all too well how she'd secretly yearned for Jessie's boyfriend, Hudson Walker, with his dark, longish hair, slow, easy smile, and cowboy drawl. He'd been different from the others, a boy who seemed a tad older somehow, one with a cynical sense of humor and a distance to him that had made him all the more interesting. It was as if he'd known everyone for what they were, had seen through their teenaged façades, and had been amused by all their foolish antics.

Or maybe she'd just fantasized that he'd been more mature and intelligent and innately sexy than his peers. All she knew now was that she'd been crazy in love with him and had hidden it for years.

But that changed, didn't it? Once Jessie was gone . . . then you made your move. You, Becca, were as calculating as she was.

Oh, God . . .

Becca pressed her palm into her flushed cheek, embarrassed and guilty anew, aware that she'd used Jessie's disappearance and Hudson's confusion and grief to her own advantage. Sure, it had been much later, after Hudson and Becca were out of high school and Jessie had been missing for years, but Becca now knew her own motives had not been pure. She'd been in love with Hudson. And when the opportunity arose for her to have her shining moment with him, she'd grabbed it with both hands and had vowed never to let go.

How foolish it all seemed now and yet, after all the years that had passed, over twenty since she'd first laid eyes upon him, those old feelings could rise to the surface in an instant. She'd read somewhere that first love never truly disappeared, that it always lay just under the surface, lingering there, waiting, like dry tinder that only needed the touch of a match, a spark, to ignite.

Did she still feel some of that? She hoped not. She hoped her first love was long behind her.

Yet she couldn't stop thinking about Jessie. And Hudson. And her schoolgirl infatuation that she'd believed was true love. She'd harbored her feelings for years, then had seized her chance to make fantasy a reality.

It had been the summer after high school for Becca; the summer after his first year of college for Hudson when opportunity knocked. She'd ostensibly "run into him" one hot evening, although she'd driven by his parents' home enough times to learn Hudson's schedule and then had followed him to Dino's, a pizzeria that had popped up that year, a place frequented by teenagers and the newly graduated.

Hudson had been meeting Zeke St. John at the pizzeria, as it turned out, and when Becca blithely swept through the swinging doors, she'd managed to hide her disappointment that Hudson wasn't alone behind a bright smile. Zeke and Hudson had been friends in high school and apparently still were, Becca assumed, although she learned later that the friendship was barely on life support.

But when she sailed inside the pizzeria that evening, she only knew that she wanted to connect with Hudson. Her pulse ran light and fast, and though her grin was wide, she was trembling a bit. If she wasn't careful her lips would quiver in a kind of excited fear, and she couldn't have that. She sensed that she'd been treated as an afterthought with his group. Hudson's twin sister, Renee, had barely looked at her, and it was only a carefully cultivated friendship with another girl,

Tamara Pitts, that allowed Becca entry into their tight circle. Being a year behind them was like having a demerit—or worse yet, a scar that said "nerdy underclassman" burned into her forehead. So that night she needed to be confident, in control, and friendly.

She pretended not to see Hudson and Zeke straightaway, striding up to the counter and staring overhead at the listings of traditional and exotic pizzas. She ordered a small pepperoni pizza and a Diet RC, paid, then with her plastic number in hand, looked around for a table. She made eye contact with Hudson and let a surprised smile of greeting cross her face. Hudson lifted a hand back, then waved her over. As she neared, he indicated the chair next to him.

"Thanks," Becca said gratefully. "This place is always crowded."

Zeke St. John was maybe more handsome than Hudson, at least in the classic sense, with dark hair and grayish eyes and a chiseled jaw. He didn't smile when Becca appeared, but the look Hudson sent her was warm. Amused. As if he could damned well read her mind.

Which was ridiculous.

She couldn't really recall what she said after that. It was idle chatter on her part, though she asked a few pertinent questions, then soaked in the information Hudson offered about himself to dissect later. She learned that he had just finished his first year at Oregon State University in business, as had Zeke. They were both heading back to school in a couple of months, and Zeke was spending the summer working for his dad's auto parts business, while Hudson was working on his father's ranch near Laurelton, one of the far western suburbs outside Portland.

Becca herself was playing gofer at a law office, delivering coffee, making photocopies, answering the phones during lunch hours. She was due to start school at a local community college because she didn't have enough money to leave home just yet.

After their "chance" meeting, Hudson called Becca. She could still remember how sweaty her palms had been on the telephone receiver. He asked if she wanted to go with him to see some mindless comedy at a local movie theater, and she jumped at the chance. All she recalled of the film was Hudson's profile and some equally mindless conversation about the staleness of the popcorn, the lack of fizz in the sodas. And the fact that he called her out.

"You followed me to Dino's the other night," he said as he drove her to her parents' house.

She shook her head violently and tried like hell not to blush, to give herself away. Oh, Lord, she just didn't have the flirting thing down yet. Maybe she never would. "I don't know what you're talking about."

"Sure you do." He flipped on his blinker and turned the corner at the end of her block.

"No, really—"

One side of his mouth lifted in that grin that alternately made her want to kiss him and shake him senseless.

"I just wanted a pizza."

"You passed three pizzerias on the way from your house to Dino's."

So he knew where she lived. That warmed her inside. "I wanted a special kind."

"Pepperoni is pretty special, all right."

"Dino's is the best. And your ego's running away with you."

He had the audacity to laugh as he pulled into her driveway and cut the engine, leaving the silence broken by crickets and voices emanating from the neighbors' backyard where, from the sounds of laughter and conversation and the thin layer of burning charcoal drifting over the fence, they were hosting a barbecue.

"You're right, okay?" Becca admitted. "I knew you'd be there."

"Glad we got that straight."

"So now you think I'm a stalker."

"I think . . . it was an excellent ploy."

"God. Ploy." She cringed inside.

"I'm sorry I didn't think of it first. I could have been learning all your favorite spots and following you around instead of having to wait for you."

"Are you making fun of me?" she asked, narrowing her eyes.

"No."

"Did you tell Zeke you thought I was following you?" she asked with sudden horror.

"I don't tell Zeke much," he assured her.

"Renee, then."

"I don't confide in my sister, either." He reached across the car to touch her nape. Tiny tingles of anticipation ran up her neck and she knew she was in trouble. "What kind of guy do you take me for?"

"I really don't know, do I?"

"Wanna find out?"

They stared at each other for long moments. Becca could feel her pulse beating slow and strong. "Maybe . . ."

Then she climbed out of the car and hurried into the house before she could make a bigger fool of herself. She told herself the ball was in his court and it was up to him now—dreadfully afraid he would let her down. But he didn't. He called before she fell asleep that night and made a date with her for the next day.

Two weeks later he kissed her good night outside her door and she was lost all over again, telling herself that she was falling in love and not trying very hard to fight the rush of adrenaline that slipped through her bloodstream whenever she thought of him.

She thought about making love to him. About what it would feel like. And she knew she couldn't wait long.

She was right.

A couple of nights afterward they came together on a

blanket laid out under the stars, far from the lights of his parents' ranch house, kissing and touching and sighing and then the heat . . . the incredible heat and desire that caused her to throw away any lingering doubts as easily as stripping him of his T-shirt and jeans. Even now, almost twenty years later, she remembered that first time, the tautness of his body, the strain of his muscles as he moved over her, the firm warmth of his lips as she opened to him. What little pain there had been when he'd first entered her had quickly disappeared in the rapture and need of her first time. Her first love. It was glorious. Heart-stoppingly incredible. She wrapped herself around him and squeezed her eyes tightly shut and swore she would make him hers forever.

Now, thinking back, her tea cold, the dog asleep on the couch near her, the picture of the Madonna statue still starkly visible on the folded page of the newspaper, Becca knew what a fool she'd been. A schoolgirl creating silly fantasies of a perfect life with a perfect man. On this Valentine's Day, she knew the folly of the whole perfect-man thing. Come on. How naive had she been? "Pretty damned," she told herself while she scratched Ringo behind his ears and he made happy little grunting sounds without raising an eyelid.

That summer had raced by with the heat and intensity of a prairie fire stoked by hot winds. Becca and Hudson spent every night they could making love: on the sandy shores of the creek while their fishing poles and bathing suits were strung forgotten on the banks; on a blanket in the hayloft with the horses snorting in their stalls below; in the backseat of Hudson's car or in his bed when his parents were gone and the window was open to let in the soft summer breezes and thrum of bats' wings.

They couldn't get enough of each other as the months bled together. They spent time with other friends, of course, and Zeke, Hudson's best friend, seemed to always be hanging around, though as the weeks passed, he became distant and the relationship between them seemed strained. At the time, Becca had thought her relationship with Hudson had somehow made Zeke uncomfortable. Later she learned that it was Jessie's disappearance that still affected the one-time best friends.

Jessie, always Jessie.

Now Becca picked up the paper again gingerly, as if its very touch could harm her in some way. She scoured the article once more. There was no mention of the sex of the remains. Nothing more than the bones' discovery. But they had to be Jessie's, didn't they? Had to be.

You should call someone.

She put her hand on the phone. Picked up the receiver and pressed it to her ear. It rang in her hand and she nearly dropped it. For a wild moment she thought it was Jessie, calling from her opened grave.

For the love of God, Becca, get a grip!

"Hello?" she said, clearing her throat, determined to shake off her case of nostalgia and nerves.

"Becca? Rebecca . . . Sutcliff? Rebecca Ryan, in high school?"

Her fingers clenched around the receiver. She knew his voice. Damn, but she'd just been thinking of him! *Hudson Walker*. Her lunatic pulse jumped as it had all those years ago and she inwardly chided herself. "Yeah, Hudson, it's me."

"Good. Uh . . . how've you been?"

"Great," she lied. "Fine." As if he'd called to inquire about her health. Oh, yeah, sure. After all these years. "I take it you saw the news."

"I turned it on after I got a call from my sister."

In her mind's eye Becca conjured up Hudson's sister—tall and thin, with dark hair that had, in high school, feathered around large eyes as brown as her twin's were blue. Renee had never liked Becca much and had made no secret of her feelings. "So she was calling about what those kids found in the maze at St. Lizzie's? The bones?"

"Yeah." His voice lowered a bit and she imagined his dark

eyebrows pulled together in a knot, just as they had years ago whenever he'd been disturbed.

"You think it's Jessie." There was no reason to pull punches. After all, he was the guy who'd wanted things honest way back when . . . well, at least until things had gotten tense between them. Then where had the honesty fled?

"Maybe."

"And you called me?"

"I got your number from Tamara. I take it you sometimes still hang out?"

Tamara, with her curly red hair, porcelain skin, and belief in all things mystical, was one of the few people with whom Becca had kept in contact. At St. Elizabeth's Tamara had been a couple of steps outside of mainstream, but she'd still been a part of Hudson's crowd, even putting up with the constant teasing from some of the other kids, including Christopher Delacroix, the richest kid in the school at the time and the only one who had numerals after his name, as he had the same name as Daddy and Granddaddy. Hence his nickname of The Third. As Becca remembered him, The Third was a privileged kid who got his kicks out of embarrassing others. In short, a dyed-in-the-wool jerk. He had constantly needled Tamara.

"Tamara and I keep in touch. See each other once in a while," Becca admitted.

"Renee is pretty freaked out about the discovery of the skeleton and she wants us all to get together," Hudson said, sounding not quite certain about the wisdom of that.

I bet she doesn't want me, Becca thought, but kept it to herself. She was trying her best to concentrate on the conversation at hand and not on eighteen-year-old questions she wanted to ask him. She hadn't spoken to Hudson in years, had only run into him twice since that summer of their affair. But both of those times she'd been with Ben, and nothing more than a few polite hellos had been exchanged between them.

Which was probably just as well.

Let sleeping dogs lie, Becca. No need to bring up the past that you've worked so hard to bury.

"What does she think will come of that?" Becca asked as Ringo, opening his eyes, stretched on the couch.

"I don't know. She thinks the bones are Jessie's."

So do I. That's why I had the vision. "What do you think?"

"I always thought she ran away," Hudson stated. "She had a history of it."

"I remember."

This was surreal. Her first phone call with Hudson, and they were talking about Jessie again after all these years.

"Renee's a reporter for the *Valley Star*."

Becca knew as much. The *Star* was a local paper; not exactly the big time that Renee had always talked up years before. Even in high school, Renee Walker had ambitions that had been far reaching, a lot farther reaching than the circulation of a second-rate newspaper.

"She's already talked to the kids who found the body, even though their parents were cautioned by the police. But you know her, she gets what she wants."

Except that dream job.

"Anyway, Renee's been doing some follow-up. She wants us all to get together at Blue Note on Thursday."

"The restaurant? Why?" The request seemed to come out of left field.

"To find out if anyone can remember anything that might help identify the bones."

"You mean if they're Jessie's."

"Well, yeah, that would be the first supposition."

Becca wasn't sure getting the old gang together because of a shallow grave and remains up at the school was such a good idea, but she said, "Okay."

"Scott and Glenn own Blue Note. It's in Raleigh Hills. I've got the address . . ." He rattled off the street address and she remembered the area in the west hills, only a few minutes' drive through a tunnel and into the heart of Portland.

"Scott Pascal and Glenn Stafford own a restaurant to-gether?" she asked, thinking of two of the boys she'd known at St. Elizabeth's. She hadn't heard that they'd gone into business together and she didn't recall them being particu-larly good friends in school, but that had been a long time ago. Things change. And business partners didn't necessarily make the best friends or bedfellows.

"Not just Blue Note. They have another restaurant in Lin-coln City, I think."

"I wouldn't have guessed," she said. *But then I wouldn't have guessed that you would call me after all this time, or that a body that could be Jessie's would be discovered at the school . . .*

"Renee wants everyone to meet Thursday after work, around seven, if they can make it." Becca heard a bit of hes-itation in his voice, as if he was second-guessing his sister's plan.

"I can be there."

"Good."

"Is it?"

Again a bit of hesitation, then he said, "Who knows? Renee seems to think none of us have gotten over it."

"'It' being Jessie's disappearance."

"Yeah."

Have you? Becca wondered and doubted it.

Hudson added, "She thinks there's maybe some course of action we should take to find out if it's Jessie."

"Like going to the police?" Becca said dryly.

"The police weren't exactly our friends," Hudson agreed.

Becca leaned back against the couch and glanced out the living room window. The night was dark. Thick. Rain still ran down the windowpanes. Absently she rubbed Ringo's furry head and thought back. The police had subjected them all to hours of interrogation in the wake of Jessie's disap-pearance. The guys had suffered the brunt of the authorities' scrutiny, but the girls had been interviewed as well. Though the general consensus at the school and police department had been that Jessie had run away again, there'd been one cop who'd insisted she was murdered and he put Hudson and the guys in their group through the wringer, interrogating them over and over again until The Third's father, a Portland lawyer who owned several buildings near the waterfront, had threatened to sue the department for harassment. The cop had backed off a little, or so it had seemed, but Becca had felt that he'd had a personal vendetta to fulfill.

Between Christopher Delacroix Junior's threats, lack of evidence, and a missing body, the case had gone stone cold.

"I'll see you Thursday," Hudson said, breaking into Becca's reverie.

"Will Tamara be there?"

"Think so."

"Good. Hey, before you hang up, what was that cop's name? The one who wouldn't believe Jessie ran away?"

"Sam McNally," Hudson said, a distinct chill to his voice.

"Mac," Becca said, remembering. Though the cop, only about ten years older than the kids he was interrogating, had mostly left her alone, he'd haunted their days and nights long after Jessie disappeared. "So now do you think he was right? About Jessie being murdered?"

"I don't know." He was terse. Suddenly distant again. "I sure as hell hope not."

"But if she's still alive . . . where's she been all this time?"

"Somewhere else."

"Yeah . . ."

"I've got to call a few more people, see if they'll join us."

"Okay."

He hesitated a second, then said, "Good talking to you, Becca," and hung up.

Becca carefully replaced the phone. "Good talking to you, too," she said softly to the empty room.

Chapter Three

Hudson glanced around the stable, checking the horses one last time. They were all in their stalls, settling in for the night, nothing disturbed, nothing as it shouldn't be. He snapped out the overhead light, shut the door, and dashed, head bent, across the expanse of gravel that separated the barn, stable, and machine shed from the house. The security lights gave a bluish tint to the night and overhead, through the rain, he thought he spied an owl soar into the higher branches of the old willow tree that he and his sister used to climb.

"Come on, Renee, don't be a chicken," he'd called to her and she, never one to turn down a dare, had struggled up the interlaced branches that he'd scaled with ease. It had pissed her off that her brother, her *younger* brother by nearly four minutes, was stronger and more athletic than she could hope to be.

But she'd been smart.

Had sailed through school while he'd been uninterested in classroom assignments, at least until college. She'd proudly waited for each report card to arrive in the mail and had beamed as their mother had seen the row of As next to the subject matter. Hudson had done all right, though he hadn't really given a crap, except for the comments by the teachers. "Doesn't work to his potential" or "Tests well, but doesn't apply himself in the classroom" or his favorite, "Isn't a team player." Yeah, well. That much was as true today as it had been when his mother had read the remarks aloud in the old kitchen, some twenty-five years earlier.

Tonight, as he ran past, the willow was devoid of leaves and the owl moved to better shelter, flying through the open hay loft window to his perch high in the rafters of the barn, a structure that had been in the Walker family for over a hundred years. Hudson passed the tree and another memory sizzled through his brain, one filled with heat and passion and only the slightest worry that he and Becca would get caught making love beneath the lush, drooping branches and canopy of fluttering leaves. God, he'd had it bad for her.

Maybe worse than you had it for Jessie?

He hurried up the back walk and onto the porch, shaking drops from his hair, as a cloudburst released more slanting rain that battered the old shingles of the roof and gurgled down the gutters. He didn't want to think about Jessie and hoped to hell that those bones found at the school weren't hers, that she was living somewhere far away and was still as intriguing and mysterious as she'd always been.

But his gut told him differently.

He stepped into the house and it felt oddly empty tonight, more so than it had before.

"All in your head," he told himself as he hung his jacket on a peg in the mudroom, kicked off his boots, and in stocking feet, stepped onto the worn linoleum he swore he'd replace this summer, along with the roof and changes to the bathrooms and this old kitchen. The house was starting to look worn. Tired-looking. The same as it had been for the past thirty years. His parents had "updated" it in the early seventies, and now it needed a full remodel.

Spying the phone, he remembered his short call with

Becca, how the sound of her voice had taken him back in time to that summer after his first year at Oregon State. Man, he'd been horny and she, well . . . his groin tightened at the thought of their affair. "Too hot to handle," he said aloud and reached into the refrigerator for a beer.

Funny, when Renee had insisted "the old gang" get together and had finally convinced Hudson that she was going to arrange a meeting whether he liked it or not, he'd offered to call Becca. Not Zeke, nor Mitch, nor Glenn, just Becca. And Renee had known that Becca would be the lure. Her eyes had actually lit with smug satisfaction when he'd reluctantly agreed and offered to call her.

"I bet Tamara has her number," Renee said, tossing him her cell phone, Tamara Pitts's name and number listed on her display. "Give her a call."

She hadn't added *I dare you*, but it had been there just the same. They both knew it, and no, it wasn't a twin thing. Renee just knew how to manipulate people. "She's not married, you know, her husband died last year and get this, he left not only a widow, but a girlfriend to boot, a pregnant girlfriend. Becca didn't even have time to divorce the bastard before he kicked off. A real gem, that Ben Sutcliff."

He didn't ask how she'd known all the dirt on Becca's husband. Renee didn't explain. It was part of her nature, what she liked to call "reporter's instincts," but Hudson thought it had more to do with being a snoop and a busybody.

"So, call her. See if the widow can make it," Renee said, her lips curling knowingly. "You know what, you never really got over her. Or Jessie. I'd call that pathetic, but considering my current marital state, that would be a little hypocritical." She hadn't elaborated and Hudson knew better than to prod. As far as he was concerned, Renee's husband, Tim, was useless. But then he'd always thought so.

"I just wonder, if that skeleton does happen to be Jessie's, what the hell happened to her?"

Hudson hadn't let his mind travel down that dark and

twisted road. He'd always assumed Jessie was alive; that she'd just taken off. Again.

He hoped he was right.

"I'll call her later," he'd said, writing down Tamara's number. He wasn't about to have Renee listen in to a conversation between him and Rebecca Ryan.

Now, in the kitchen his parents had once owned, Hudson twisted off the cap on his bottle of Budweiser and tried not to think about either Becca or Jessie.

Two women he'd thought he'd loved.

Two women who had altered the course of his life.

Two women he might have been better off never meeting.

There was no sleeping. Not with the rain peppering the windows and tree limbs swaying like frantic beckoning arms outside Becca's window. She watched, eyes open in the darkness, Ringo curled up beside her, snoring softly. She'd been uncertain about the dog when Ben suggested they get a pet, then had fallen in love with the mutt, rescuing him from a pet store where lots of puppies tumbled around, noses pressed to the cages. Even though the dog had been Ben's idea, he'd been lukewarm on Ringo. He'd wanted to pick out the dog. Becca hadn't realized it at the time, but she now knew it wasn't about the pet, it was about Ben being able to pick out what he wanted, whether it worked for Becca or not. He'd done the same thing with the furniture, and her car, and this condo. The only choice that had been totally hers was Ringo. And Ben hadn't liked it.

She hugged Ringo now and he let out a long doggy sigh. She tried not to think about the phone call from Hudson, but his cool voice played like a tape in her mind, looping over and over again.

Becca? Rebecca . . . Sutcliff? Rebecca Ryan, in high school?

Squeezing her eyes closed even tighter, Becca fought back

traitorous thoughts. She was too old for romantic ideas about Hudson Walker. That was all part of a long-ago past. And even though she would be reconnecting with some of her old friends—even though she was about to physically see Hudson again, now . . . now that she was a widow and therefore free—it didn't mean she should have even one romantic notion about Hudson. That affair had been all about high school. She was over it, and yet there it was, streaming into her consciousness, taking hold and not letting go.

Even now, in her darkened bedroom, with the dog snoring beside her, Becca remembered the months after she'd graduated from St. Elizabeth's as being a turning point in her life. That blasted hot summer with Hudson had been one of those magical times when everything was working right. Becca had Hudson, and though he might not be proclaiming his undying love for her, he truly liked her and she was head over heels about him. From a few stolen moments, their relationship quickly exploded into a daily/nightly routine where as soon as they were off work they would find each other, ending up in each other's arms, making hot love on a blanket underneath bright stars on the Walker ranch, or in his bedroom, sneakily, after his parents were asleep, or anywhere they could find to be alone.

In September Hudson prepared to go back to OSU, which was located in Corvallis, about an hour and a half down I-5 from Portland. Becca didn't see his returning to college as a problem, but Hudson started growing more distant as the summer wound to a close. Where once he'd been as enthusiastic as she, calling her day and night, he'd started to cool as the shimmering heat of August had slipped into a cooler September.

And then there was the pregnancy.

A skipped period she'd barely thought about, and then another that had worried her. She'd always been irregular, but she felt different, and when she finally worked up the courage to buy one of the home pregnancy tests, she'd sat on the edge of the bathtub at her parents' house and prayed she was wrong—only to see the evidence of the child growing within her, a child she'd always wanted.

But Hudson?

Oh, God. Her throat had turned to sand and tears slid from the corners of her eyes before she could take control again, wrapping all the evidence of the test kit in a brown paper bag and burning it in the wood stove before her parents arrived home from work. Neither Jim nor Barbara Ryan would welcome an unplanned grandchild from an unmarried daughter.

Becca had sniffed back her tears and only told her old cat, Fritter, a tortoise-shelled skinny stray that had attached itself to her, about the pregnancy.

Afraid, desperate, sensing something had changed with Hudson, Becca tried hard not to cling to him. She'd practiced telling him about the baby. Over and over again in the car, when she was alone, or whispering to the cat in her bedroom, but she wanted to wait for just the right moment, didn't want to spring it on him. After all, he'd been the one who had the condoms . . . well, most of the time.

Finally, as a harvest moon hung low in the night sky, she'd told herself it was now or never, she had to tell him. He *deserved* to know. It was his right. But before she could force the words over her tongue, he mentioned that he'd known he'd been a little aloof, that it hadn't been her fault, but he'd been plagued with thoughts about Jessie.

Once again . . . Jessie.

He told her when she was seated next to him on a porch swing at his parents' ranch. He was in jeans, a work shirt, and boots, and there were bits of straw in his hair. He'd been drinking a lemonade when Becca pulled into the drive, and his mother, a tall woman with dark hair shot with gray, asked if she wanted a lemonade, too. Becca politely declined and sat down beside Hudson on the swing. Beneath her skin anxiety ran like an electric current. Something was wrong. She didn't know if she had the courage to tell him. She *had* to tell him about the baby. But she couldn't bear for him to think she'd deliberately trapped him. Couldn't bear to think that maybe she had, a little . . . to have his baby.

Though she was near him, they didn't touch. She sensed there was an invisible barrier between them. Maybe he knew she was pregnant and didn't want to be saddled with a child? But she'd told no one, *no* one, and she'd even purchased the pregnancy kit from a huge store in Portland, not the local pharmacy where someone might recognize her.

Hudson finished his lemonade. There was a heavy pause as they swayed gently on the swing and the sun slanted late-afternoon heat waves at them. A breeze ruffled her hair and pushed a few dry leaves across the walkway. Hudson was silent. Not moody, just not really there, his mind somewhere far away. He stared into the middle distance and Becca had the feeling he'd forgotten she was sitting next to him, just a hairsbreadth from his body. How, when she was so aware of him, wanted to kiss him and hold him and tell him she loved him, could he act as if she were invisible?

It hurt and, in truth, it bugged her.

They were having a child together!

"What's wrong?" she asked him, when she finally found her courage.

Before he could answer a car bounced down the long lane, its engine thrumming, his sister behind the wheel. Renee slammed on the brakes and the sedan, screeching, jerked to a stop a few feet away, dust from its tires wafting in a cloud their way. Renee stepped out of the car and tossed her short, dark hair. A small notebook stuck out of her purse and Becca remembered she was taking some kind of journalism classes. Probably acing them. She flew up the walk and scarcely looked at Becca as she hurried up the porch steps. But then she'd acted as if she'd barely noticed Becca all summer. They hadn't been great friends in high school, but when they were classmates at St. Lizzie's, Becca hadn't felt quite the resentment she now sensed.

Or was this feeling of dismissal, of invisibility, just her overactive imagination?

A product of her crumbling relationship with Hudson?

"Goddamned brakes," she muttered, almost to herself. "Hey," she said, spying Hudson. "You think you could fix them?"

He shook his head. "You'd better call Mitch."

"Bellotti? That moron?"

"He's pretty good with cars."

"Yeah, he'd probably think I'd go out with him or make out with him or—" She gave a mock shiver.

"He's engaged."

"Send the girl my condolences. No, I'm not talking to Mitch. Great idea, Hud. Real helpful."

"You asked."

"Well, forget it. I'm not owing that fat-ass, has-been jock any favors. I heard he already flunked out of OSU. Big surprise." She opened the screen door and nodded toward Hudson's glass and the few remaining drops of lemonade settling near the bottom. "Any more of that left?"

"I think so."

She brushed inside, never once acknowledging Becca. But then Renee always had been a bitch. An ambitious bitch.

Hudson set his empty glass on a table beside the swing. He gazed at her through the shadows but she couldn't read his expression. Finally, he said, "You know, you remind me a little of Jessie."

Becca stared. "What?" she demanded, her voice shaking. The comparison stung, and it hurt far more than Becca wanted it to. Obviously she'd been kidding herself about her affair with Hudson, wrapping it up in love and romance when he'd been harboring feelings for Jessie all along. She understood instinctively that there was no way to fight Jessie's memory.

Jessie Brentwood had been missing for over three years, but she was still very much here.

"I'm not Jessie," she said carefully.

"I know."

"Do you? Why would you say . . . ?" Her throat closed and her face grew hot with embarrassment. Who had she been kidding? She'd suspected, no, make that *known* Hudson had never gotten over Jessie, but to compare Becca to the missing girl . . . or even worse, *fantasizing and pretending* Becca was like Jessie was just sick.

Her stomach, not great anyway, began to roil and she thought she might throw up.

Hudson said, "I don't know. Sometimes I think . . ."

"I don't think I want to hear this," she whispered, all her dreams turning to dust.

"Look, Becca, I'm leaving for school in a couple of weeks. I was talking to Zeke and we're heading down together." She felt a flash of rage at Zeke, sensing he'd been instrumental in Hudson's current, sober self-reflection but couldn't say so. "We talked about Jessie, the other day. We never really have much." He leaned forward and sighed, his hands on his thighs, his foot stopping the swing's arc. "I'm just wondering . . ."

Becca pressed her trembling lips together. A long pause ensued while she waited, dying inside.

"I just think we should take things slower. Work through some stuff. What do you think?"

What I think is that I'm pregnant with your child and you're sitting here next to me grieving over the love of another girl, one you can never have. So now you've somehow twisted everything around. What I think, Hudson, is that I'm a fool, a damned, stupid fool who fell in love with the wrong man. She gazed into his blue eyes, seeing herself reflected. A lonely girl clinging to a dream. Pathetic. She squared her shoulders, refused to cry, and managed to say in a calm voice, "Maybe you're right. It has been a whirlwind."

He nodded. "I don't want to rush this."

"No." Her voice was brittle. She was furious; at herself, mostly. But she couldn't help saying, "We could see each other next time you're home."

"Right."

Misery. Bone-deep sadness and despair. It dragged her down inside, but she managed to make up some excuse about having to get home. Holding her dignity intact, she didn't remember the drive, not one second of it, but somehow she got home that night. Only later, when she was in the bathroom with the shower running to hide the noise, did she break down. As Fritter sat on the ledge of the small window over the toilet, Becca cried and cried and cried. Tears poured from her eyes. Sobs wrenched from her gut. She was sick . . . sick . . . sick . . . Pregnant and shatteringly sad.

Yet, there was hope.

There was a life inside her, waiting to be born. She couldn't tell Hudson now. But maybe next time they saw each other. In a few weeks. When he came home, or called. Until then, she'd pull herself together. She refused to be one of those weepy, wimpy, weak girls she'd always detested.

But he didn't call. And time passed. And Becca was overwhelmed by a feeling of impending disaster, a dark cloud that resolved itself into her final vision, her last one until she'd passed out at the mall this afternoon.

It had been the November following their breakup, as she was driving home from Seaside, her car buffeted by strong, blustering winds. As she gripped the wheel, trying to keep the car in her lane, she was suddenly blinded by an image of thundering surf pounding a rocky bluff. It was all she could do to herd her car to the side of the road before the pain in her head exploded and the vision overtook her completely.

Once the car was idling on the narrow gravel shoulder, she saw an image of an angry, storm-tossed sea and above it, perched high in a tower, loomed a dark, malevolent force without figure or form, the embodiment of pure evil that caused her skin to crawl. She couldn't see the monster's face, didn't know if it had one, but she was certain to the bottom of her soul that whoever it was, *whatever* it was, it surely meant to do her harm.

And her baby's life was in jeopardy.

She heard nothing save the rush of the wind and the roar of the surf pounding against a rain-washed shore, but the threat came to her, echoing through her mind. A warning to her and her baby.

I am here.

And I will destroy you both; make certain the unholy chain is broken.

I smell you, Rebecca.

You are so near . . .

Becca had come to with a cry of fear emanating from her throat, blinking, her hands gripped around the wheel, her knuckles blanched white as bleached bones, her head dull and thundering.

"Oh, God. Oh, God. Oh, God."

She couldn't panic.

Wouldn't.

The vision was nothing. *Nothing!*

But her insides were trembling and she knew that she had to leave, to find her way home, and fast. That was it. She would throw some water over her face, figure out what she was going to do, how she would care for the baby, if she would ever tell Hudson, what she would tell her parents . . .

Gingerly she stepped on the gas.

The road was empty and she could have sworn that the harsh winds that had just been battering the car had died. No birds called, no insects hummed, no sounds of distant traffic reached her ears. Even the car's engine was muted. Still.

And then she heard it.

An engine.

Loud.

Rumbling.

A truck of some sort, traveling fast, coming from around the bend behind her. She didn't dare accelerate onto the pavement until it passed. And yet . . .

Her heart was a tattoo, her palms wet. Something was wrong. Seriously wrong!

It's the vision. It's got you all hyped up. That's all.

The engine roared more loudly.

And then a dark pickup careened around the corner at breakneck speed, its wheels nearly coming off the pavement.

"No!" she cried as the driver apparently lost control.

In a split second, the truck bore down on her, its huge grate magnified in her mirror.

She stepped on the gas, but it was too late.

The truck careened off the pavement.

She screamed. The pickup slammed into her car, nearly broadside, crumpling the back end and door of the Toyota. With a horrible shriek, the metal wrenched. Glass shattered. The driver's door was wrenched from its hinges as the car folded. Pain screamed through her body as she saw the truck tear away, hardly slowing at all. The vision returned . . . a dark angry sea, a large looming form, and a deadly threat as she went in and out of consciousness.

There had been policemen and EMTs and gawkers as the car had been opened with the Jaws of Life and she'd been extracted from the wreckage. People had shouted or whispered or talked into walkie-talkies, but it was all a blur as she was carried into a waiting ambulance.

Please let me keep my baby, she prayed to the ceiling of the ambulance as the siren screamed, resounding. *Please. Please!*

She'd woken up in the hospital, her parents worn and raw, her mother's eyes red-rimmed and teary as she sat in a bedside chair, a wadded tissue in her fingers. Her father, appearing to have aged a decade in the past ten hours, stood near his wife's chair, a big steadying hand on Barbara's shoulders.

"The baby?" she asked in a voice that sounded a million miles away. She felt empty inside, oddly at war with her own body as an IV leaked fluids into her wrist, and outside the private room, through a door slightly ajar, she saw a large, curved desk—the nurses' station.

Her parents had looked at her and shaken their heads. Tears leaked from her mother's eyes and her father's lips pressed flat together.

Her prayers had gone unanswered and a somber-faced doctor only a few years older than she had explained that the force of the accident had caused her placenta to rupture. The baby could not be saved and Becca was "lucky" to have only sustained a broken clavicle, bruised ribs, and facial contusions from the flying glass.

Lucky? When my baby died?

Despair coiled over her heart. Becca's parents took care of their distraught daughter, who refused to tell them the baby's father's name, though surely they could have guessed. She'd never introduced Hudson as her "boyfriend," had usually gone out with a crowd that included several boys, as far as her mother and father were concerned, but surely they could guess.

They just never asked after the first initial weeks.

Her mother confided in her months later that "it really didn't matter" who the boy was. Obviously Becca didn't care enough about him to even give him a name or tell him about his child.

Becca had winced inside but held her ground, never once mentioning Hudson Walker. She recovered slowly, consumed with the worry that the accident might cause her to never be able to have children. Her collarbone finally mended, her ribs and face healed. She was assured that she was fine. That what had happened was just an unfortunate and tragic accident. There was no reason that she couldn't have other children.

The police never located the driver of the truck, and as Becca had no image of the person behind the wheel, and no license number, and no local body shops had reported a truck coming in with the kind of damage it should have sustained in the accident, no citations were issued.

Never admitting to her "vision," Becca went back to school winter term and tried to put the pain of losing her baby behind her. Hudson didn't call, nor did she phone him. She thought about it, but told herself to let the past die. A few months later she moved into an apartment and continued her job in the law firm, never intending to make it a career. But time passed and Ben came to work at the firm and . . . and it felt like the years had suddenly telescoped, as if it could still be that fall when she and Hudson broke up and the automobile accident robbed her of her child.

She'd blocked most of the past. Blocked it on purpose. She'd never told Hudson about the pregnancy. Never really had a chance to toil over whether she should or shouldn't before it was over. She'd forced herself to look forward, not back.

Eventually, she'd married Benjamin Sutcliff. They'd dated, grown close, married, and she'd hoped for a family, that, as it turned out, he didn't want. But that section of her life was over, too.

And now this part of her past, the part with Hudson and Jessie, the part that she'd steadfastly buried and covered with concrete, had suddenly come to life, broken through all of her careful barricades and reared its painful head.

Now, unable to sleep, she shoved her hair from her eyes and snapped on the bedside light. She couldn't, *wouldn't* dwell on the past. If it took every ounce of grit she had, she wasn't about to travel down the thorny path that was her own life's history. No, damn it, she was going to concentrate on her life as it was. As it had become. Reality. She was a widow. An almost divorcée. After Ben's rejection, she'd spent the rest of last year and the beginning of this one in a strange exercise of forced forward motion. One foot in front of the other. Keep going. Push on. Fight your way through and hope to come out the other side stronger, wiser, and maybe even better off.

It had been a tough fight. Her secretarial work at Bennett, Bretherton, and Pfeiffer had tapered off with the decline of the law firm's clients—an aspect of a decline in health of one of the senior partners and disinterest in the others. Now Becca worked mostly from home, using a fax machine to receive her eldest boss's hand-scratched notes, or using e-mail and the Internet to download drafts of contracts, legal notes, letters, and memoranda before rewriting, polishing, and sending the finished product back via the Internet. It was a disembodied way to work, and there wasn't really enough of it to sustain her much longer. The firm was tightening up—keeping their information "in-house" due to confidentiality issues.

Becca was at a crossroads. Choices were going to have to be made. Maybe her earlier vision of Jessie was a result of the low-grade stress she wasn't acknowledging. Or maybe it was that she was a weirdo and just couldn't admit it.

"Damn it all to hell," she said, flipping off the light and yanking the covers to her neck.

Sighing, Ringo stretched his legs and pushed against her with his paws.

And beneath everything she'd thought about tonight was the image of Jessie on that cliff, her hair caught in the wind, the sound of the surf blocking out her words. What had she mouthed so desperately? What had she wanted Becca to know? Was it her own subconscious trying to tell her something, or was it something more?

Becca squeezed her eyes shut, but the image of the girl on the cliff remained, as if permanently etched on her eyelids. Was the skeleton that had been discovered in the maze Jessie's? She kind of thought so, and it left her with an all-consuming feeling of dread.

Something bad was about to happen.

She feels me . . .

As I drive through the rain, watching the road shimmer darkly under the beams of my headlights, my blood boils with anticipation. I've had to bide my time. Wait in seclusion.

But now another has led me back here. One that will have to be taken later, but her interference has given me what I seek: The woman! Missing for all these years because I could not smell her. But now . . . I know where she dwells . . . I can find her.

And she senses me, too. I can almost feel the thud of her heartbeats. Taste her fear.

This should have been over long ago but has lingered. Because of the mistake.

My jaw clenches so hard it hurts as I think back on it, and when I check the rearview mirror, I almost witness my own failure on the road behind.

But I won't think of the time I failed when last I was called . . . Though the woman survived, her demonspawn did not, my mission only partially fulfilled.

Now is the time for second chances, to right that error.

I will not fail.

Not this time.

Not ever again.

If anyone gets in my way, they, too, will be laid to waste.

There is no room for error.

The tires of my car sing across the wet pavement as I regretfully draw away from her. I have been close, but must pull back to plan. But soon . . .

"Rebecca." Her name comes easily to my lips and I feel heat in my veins, the anticipation of release to come when, at last, she will breathe no more and her heartbeat, the one I hear pounding in my ears, will be stilled forever.

"Rebecca . . ."

Chapter Four

Becca pulled her car into the parking lot through driving rain. Her wipers could scarcely keep up with the deluge, and as she turned off the ignition she watched the neon script lights that read BLUE NOTE blur into an indistinct azure haze. So Scott Pascal and Glenn Stafford owned this brick building on the outskirts of Portland in the area known as Raleigh Hills and uncomfortably close to St. Elizabeth's campus. She still found it odd that the two had teamed up. In high school Scott was a bit of a show-off, all swagger and winks, a flirt, always hinting of something racy or naughty or indecent, while Glenn . . . she barely remembered him. He did belong to the group, she decided, but he was on the fringe, always hanging close to The Third, like a little lost puppy, hoping to be noticed. As for The Third, he'd always been a pain, had always rubbed her the wrong way; even his nickname had bothered her.

But it was Hudson who had really occupied her thoughts ever since he called. Maybe it would be good to finally see him, to put that old nostalgia and sense of regret behind her once and for all. She didn't think he was married, at least he hadn't said so, but who knew? He could be fat and balding and have had three wives and eight or nine children since she'd last seen him.

Somehow she doubted it.

She figured he was probably one of those men who got better looking as they aged, and as for wives, exes, and children, she'd never heard that he'd been married. *So now's your chance to find out.* Her hands gripped the wheel. She seemed to forever be waiting in a car, almost afraid to take a breath, conscious that something unpleasant or just plain bad lay ahead of her. This time she was about to meet her old high school friends. Her "gang." Her buddies.

Her lover.

Becca inhaled a long breath, held it, let it out slowly. Hudson Walker hadn't been hers. Yes, she'd made love to him. Yes, she'd wanted him. But he'd been Jessie Brentwood's right from the start, and after Jessie's disappearance he'd been Becca's only briefly, and only because Jessie was gone.

She needed to keep reminding herself of that fact.

Pocketing her keys, she stepped out of her Jetta, locked the door, then flipped the hood of her coat over her hair. Walking rapidly through the rain, she headed for the main entrance of Blue Note while traffic streamed by on a nearby arterial that ran east to west. Three steps across the lot and her feet were soaked through her black pumps. Four more steps and she lost feeling in her toes.

What a night.

Shouldering her way through the double doors, Becca headed toward a small maitre d's podium. A young woman wearing a body-hugging indigo dress and a bright smile greeted her. "Welcome to Blue Note."

"Thanks." Becca pushed her hood off her head. "I'm meeting a group of people here, kind of a reunion. We're with Glenn and Scott, the owners? I think Renee Walker organized it?"

"You mean Renee Trudeau."

"Right." Becca had known Renee was married, but she'd forgotten her last name.

"They're in the private dining room. Right this way." The hostess led Becca across a polished herringbone floor and through several "rooms" that were really curtained-off sections of a larger space, which added an intimacy to the restaurant, making it seem more luxurious than Becca would have believed possible. The tables were mostly empty on this Thursday night; the votive candles flickering in crystal holders were welcoming despite the lack of patrons to enjoy the ambience. Soft jazz emanating from discreet speakers was wasted on the lonely chairs while outside wind threw rain against the windows that banked one wall.

"Right here," the girl said, pushing on the bronze levers to a set of frosted French doors. Inside was a long, distressed black table with heavy carved legs. Around the massive table, seated on taupe armchairs, were Becca's high school friends, every one of whom turned and looked at her as she entered. Water glasses, a few wine goblets, and a couple of short old-fashioned glasses littered the table.

"Becca!" Tamara called, but Becca was still taking in all of the faces. She saw them in a rush of memories, a dizzying kaleidoscope not unlike one of her visions. It was all she could do to murmur a hello to their chorus of greetings and fumble her way to a seat.

"I wondered when you'd get here," Tamara said, a friendly smile stretching across her face. Tan in the dead of winter, Tamara was crowned with the same wild red hair she possessed in high school. *Flamboyant* was the word Becca would use to describe her, then and now. Her arms jingled and glittered with rows of bracelets, her hair curled around a face that showed little aging in the twenty years since she'd been a pain in the neck for the nuns and lay teachers at St. Elizabeth's.

"Becca Ryan. God, it's been a while," a man with blond,

short-cropped hair said before Becca could do no more than murmur a hello to Tamara.

Her heart sank. She'd know that voice anywhere even if she didn't recognize the sharp features of Christopher Delacroix III. The Third hadn't changed much in the twenty years since Jessie's disappearance. Older, a bit thicker, maybe, although it looked like all muscle, he still possessed the leadership quality—or should she say "belief that they should all do his bidding"—that had made him their unofficial but indisputable ruler. In the past Hudson hadn't paid attention to The Third's despot ways, but he hadn't challenged him for the role, either. Hudson hadn't been interested in those group dynamics. A part of the group and yet not. Even then, he'd been his own person and had told The Third to "shove it" more often than not. Somehow, despite his disdain for authority, or maybe because of it, he'd been allowed to stay. And Becca had loved him for it.

"It has been a long while," Becca admitted. "And it's Becca Sutcliff now."

"That's right, you're married." He snapped his fingers as he remembered. "You're with Bennett, Bretherton, aren't you?" The Third was a lawyer at another firm, and Becca had spoken on the phone with him a couple of times.

Already Becca was regretting attending this meeting. Two minutes with The Third and she remembered what she'd hated about high school. "I'm widowed, actually." She didn't add anything else, didn't want to expose herself. Let them think what they wanted.

He snorted, intense blue eyes focusing on her. "Divorced, here. Don't know why I ever thought I could be married to anything other than my job."

She forced a smile and dared a glance around the table. No sign of Hudson yet, though his sister Renee was seated at the end of the table, her dark hair in the same short style Becca remembered from high school. She gave Becca a tight return smile, but Becca sensed it wasn't anything personal. Renee seemed her usual uptight, disinterested self.

But she called the meeting, remember? According to Hudson, this get-together was her idea. On the table in front of Renee, near an untouched glass of wine, was a stack of papers—along with a neatly folded newspaper with the picture of the Madonna statue.

Tamara said to the group at large, "Is Hudson going to show?"

"He'll be here. He's always running late." Renee met Becca's eyes, and for the first time in her life, Becca definitely did *not* feel invisible to Hudson's twin.

"Well, of course he'll show," the woman at the other end of the table stated emphatically as Becca took an empty chair between Tamara and a man she recognized as Jarrett Erikson, another one of The Third's buddies. With dark hair and a swarthy complexion, he, along with The Third, had loved mercilessly teasing Mitch and Glenn, referring to Glenn as a "nerd with a complex."

"We all had to show, didn't we?" the same woman said. She was petite, blond, and nervous, and clung to the hand of the man seated on her left. Beneath the pendant lights suspended above the table, a huge diamond glittered on her left hand. "Kind of a command performance." She shot a dark look toward Renee.

Becca took a second to remember her: Evangeline Adamson. "Vangie." She was seated next to Zeke St. John, who greeted Becca with a silent nod. As Becca remembered, Evangeline had always been chasing Zeke, but Zeke hadn't seemed to want to commit to a relationship. It appeared now, after over twenty years of clinging to a dream, that she'd finally gotten her wish, as there was no question the ring she was wearing was for an engagement. Zeke, meanwhile, looked a little worse for wear. His chiseled jaw had loosened with age, his athletic build was softer, and his once-dark hair was shot with silver.

Hudson's best friend, who, when he'd been nineteen, hadn't given Becca the time of day.

Renee pushed back her chair, its legs scraping over the dark hardwood. "Let's get to it, okay? We don't need to wait for Hud."

"You're pretty hot about that skeleton those kids found up at St. Lizzie's," The Third observed. "That's what this is about, right? You think it's Jessie's."

Leave it to The Third to cut to the chase and ruin all of Renee's drama. Becca and the rest of the group turned their collective eyes toward her. "Yes," she said, but before she could go on, Evangeline cut in.

"It can't be Jessie. I mean . . . she ran away, right? She was always running away. She *told* me she was going to run away."

Vangie had been one of Jessie's closest friends, an inner circle among the larger clique, Becca recalled.

Jarrett Erikson's dark eyes gazed coldly at Vangie. "It's not like we forgot what you told the police."

"What did I say?" she demanded, affronted.

"Just that. You were her best friend and Jessie told you she was running away."

"I wasn't her best friend."

"We were all good friends," Renee put in brusquely, intent on pulling the conversation back to her own agenda. "I was a good friend of hers."

"Yeah, but Vangie acted like she and Jessie were like this," The Third said, crossing his fingers.

"I don't know why you're picking on me!" Vangie sniffed.

"Hard to believe it's Jessie," Zeke cut in. His gaze fell on the way Evangeline's hand clung to his and he moved it to his lap, as if embarrassed.

A cell phone chirped. The Third reached into his pocket, withdrew a sleek BlackBerry, checked the number, then clicked the phone off. "Sorry."

Renee said tightly, "Okay, so if it's not Jessie, then whose bones are they?" She glanced around the table, but no one responded. "Come on. Whether we like it or not, we all know that the body up there is Jessie Brentwood and it'll only be a few days, maybe even shorter, before the police put two and two together."

"Is that what this is all about, going to the police?" For a split second, The Third seemed unnerved. He grabbed his short, near-empty glass, jiggled the ice cubes, and took a last swallow before cracking one of the melting cubes between his teeth.

Renee shook her head. "No. But they're bound to come to us again. It's what they do." Her gaze skated around the table, to the faces staring at her. "Come on, we all know this thing's been eating at us for years. Everyone of us has said, 'I wonder what happened to Jessie. Where she went.'" Renee took a sip of her wine. "Now it looks like she's been found. Part of the mystery solved."

"Nothing's been eating at me," The Third pointed out, and he seemed relaxed again. An act? Or for real? "And I don't know what the hell you mean about a mystery. Vangie's right. Jessie ran away."

"Are we all going to order something, or what?" Scott asked, his now-bald pate gleaming in the subdued lighting. Becca realized he scarcely had any hair left and apparently chose to shave it off completely. "How about a couple of bottles of wine? Looks like we could use some refills and a few new glasses. Glenn . . ." He glanced pointedly at his business partner.

Glenn Stafford looked like he'd been enjoying the fruits of his own kitchen. Once thin to the point of being gaunt, he'd packed on the pounds over the years. His shirt stretched a little tight around his middle, whereas Scott was as lean as he'd been in high school and his face was remarkably un-lined. Glenn, on the other hand, had deep furrows dug into his forehead, as if the worries of the world lay on his shoulders. His hair was still its same medium brown shade and it was close-cropped and neat. He sent Scott a black look, then pushed back his chair and headed toward a wooden swinging door that presumably led straight to the kitchen.

"Are we ordering food, or just drinks?" Mitch Bellotti asked cautiously.

"Oh, sure." Scott nodded emphatically. "Glenn, how about a couple of appetizer sampler plates, show everyone our specialties. That way maybe they'll come back."

Glenn managed a scowl as he left the room, and Mitch seemed satisfied. The ex-lineman was even thicker around the middle than Glenn, but then he'd always been on the heavy side. He'd had a love of cars that had translated into a career as a mechanic. He'd also always had a love of women and was twice divorced, according to his own admission. Becca could feel his appreciative eye fall on her, but she ignored it, as much to give him the message as to keep The Third and Jarrett Erikson from exchanging amused glances. In high school, Mitch had been the group's resident clown, always joking. The Third and Jarrett Erikson had referred to him as the Village Idiot behind his back, and Becca sensed their disparagement of him hadn't changed over the years.

She slid a sideways look at Jarrett, seated on her left. His black hair and black eyes under beetle brows made him seem as if he were hiding secrets. He'd been the least easy to read in high school, and it looked like nothing had changed.

There were a couple of others who had been part of their group, but more peripherally, and they hadn't been invited to this command performance, apparently, as the only chair unoccupied was waiting for Hudson.

This group of friends, their core, was made up of the people most affected by Jessie's disappearance.

But Becca still didn't get why Renee had so wanted this meeting. It wasn't like they could do anything about Jessie now. She glanced again at the notes so neatly stacked on the black table in front of Renee. Hudson's twin. And direct opposite.

The door opened, letting in a whoosh of air that touched the back of Becca's neck.

"Hey." Hudson's voice washed over her and her muscles tightened reflexively as she waited for him to move into her line of vision.

"About time, Walker," The Third said, gazing Hudson's way, his eyes assessing him carefully.

Becca attempted to ease her stiff shoulders, afraid she looked as tense as she felt.

"Traffic snarl on Sunset," he answered.

"You're coming from the west," Jarrett said as Hudson walked around the table into Becca's view.

Faded jeans. Tan suede shirt. Thick, dark hair that brushed his collar. I-don't-really-give-a-damn attitude still intact.

"Shouldn't be any traffic that way." Jarrett eyed him carefully.

"You think I'm lying?"

Jarrett backed off with a shrug. "Just think you're late."

"Okay, now that the bull rams have locked horns, can we get over this?" Renee asked.

"After we say hello," Tamara said. She turned to Hudson and added, "Hudson Walker. You haven't changed a bit."

"Oh, there have been some changes, all right." He took a chair next to Zeke, directly across from Becca, and when his gaze touched hers, Becca remembered all too vividly how those blue, blue eyes could dilate in the dark. There was just something earthy and male about him that couldn't be missed. Of course, as she'd guessed, he looked even better than she remembered, and she kicked herself for noticing, for the sudden rise in her pulse.

"Hey, Becca."

"Hi." She smiled a greeting, hoping she'd hidden her true

feelings as he greeted everyone else. Pretending to be unaffected, which was damned hard. He seemed to have grown an inch or two, which was probably all her perception. But along with a cynical, "just dare me" smile, he still had that tall, rangy cowboy style going for him. And it was sexy as hell.

Great.

She'd hoped to be immune to him.

But this more mature, more relaxed, more confident Hudson was even more intriguing than he had been two decades before, as sexy a man as she'd ever want to meet. Whereas Zeke's good looks and appeal had diminished, Hudson's had increased.

Renee said, "The thing is, I'm doing a story on the discovery of the remains. A piece about high school and what it's like when one of your friends disappears and how it can affect you. We've all dealt with the same questions for twenty years. Where's Jessie? What happened to her? Did she leave on her own, or was she taken from us? Now maybe we can find some answers."

Evangeline stared at her in horror. "You're not serious!"

Jarrett breathed noisily through his nose. "What a bunch of bullshit. Until you know who's been rotting in the maze at St. Elizabeth's, you're writing fiction. I don't think the *Valley Star* is big on conjecture."

"I can theorize, put my spin on it," Renee said. "I've already talked to the kids who found the bones. Great story. Older brother and friends were trying to scare the littler kids by telling ghost stories in the maze, and then one of the kids sees this bony hand reaching upward."

"Oh, for the love of God." Evangeline pressed her lips together. "You're trying to profit from this?"

Renee regarded her coldly. "I want a purge. I want this behind us all. My way is to write about it. I've kept in contact with Jessie's parents all these years because I *was* a good friend of Jessie's," she said directly to Evangeline, "and I think she died in the maze at St. Lizzie's and I want to tell that story. For Jessie, and for us all."

Scott said, stunned, "To your paper?"

"Don't count me in!" The Third stated, glaring. "Jessie ran away, okay? I don't believe those bones are hers. And I've had more than enough wrangling with the police about it. Those bastards wouldn't leave us alone."

"McNally wouldn't leave us alone," Mitch corrected.

"Who gives a shit? I'm not doing any of it again." He reached for his glass, then realized it was empty and let it sit on the table.

"The police will figure it out," Renee went on. "Those are somebody's bones, and I'm guessing they're Jessie's. It's all over the news. If I don't write this piece, somebody else will."

"Oh, yeah. You're our savior." Jarrett was sardonic. "You're writing the damn thing to make a few bucks." He waved away her arguments. "Gain some attention. That's what this is all about, and it's crap."

"I'd like to know if the body the cops found is really Jessie." Hudson met Jarrett's eyes. "And if so, then I'd like to know what happened to her."

Renee bit back a hot retort and seemed to relax a bit when Hudson came to her aid. "I've been thinking about Jessie a lot lately. Remembering what she said. Doing some research."

"What kind of research?" Becca asked. The vision she'd had of Jessie on the cliff felt very close. It was all too much of a coincidence, and she was starting to feel claustrophobic.

"The Brentwoods never left the area after Jessie disappeared. They wanted to be where she could find them when she returned, but now they think the bones are hers, too. I told them what I wanted to do and we talked about Jessie at length. I think they want closure, too." Renee looked thoughtfully at Evangeline. "They remember you and Jessie being tight."

"Wow. Everybody's telling me how it was. Funny, I don't remember it that way." Evangeline pulled her gaze from Renee's and looked around the room, obviously trying to distance herself from the missing girl. "Can I get a glass of wine or something?"

Scott nodded, appearing irritated as he glanced at the door to the kitchen. "Glenn should be back any minute."

Renee wasn't sidetracked. "Before she disappeared . . . Jessie was on a search herself. Kind of obsessed about it. Kind of looking into who she was. Trying to figure out what made her tick."

Was that right? Becca had never heard this before.

"Hudson made her tick," The Third said with a dirty chuckle. Jarrett laughed and Scott grinned.

Renee, on her own track, went on doggedly, "She lived in a bunch of different places before ending up here. She was adopted by the Brentwoods and they moved around a lot."

"Chasing after her, probably," Mitch snorted.

"But she always returned until she attended St. Elizabeth's. She's missing for a reason. If those are her bones, something happened to her."

Scott's expression darkened. "'Something?' You mean, like murder? That's where you're going with this, aren't you? Just like McNally. He acted like we were all in on some kind of conspiracy." Scott half laughed, almost nervously. "What an idiot. He had a hard-on for Jessie and he never even met her."

"He probably killed her." Evangeline was serious. "The cop that gets all obsessed about a girl. It happens. You hear about it. Read about it. See it in the movies, like, all the time!"

"Oh, sure." Jarrett regarded her disparagingly.

"I thought you didn't believe she was dead," Scott pointed out.

"McNally didn't know about Jessie until after she disappeared," Hudson reminded Vangie.

"Well, I don't know. Maybe he did and we just don't know it," she sniffed.

"Stick with your theory that she's still alive," The Third suggested. "It's not as kookoo as 'the sex-crazed cop killed her.'"

This was getting crazier by the minute, Becca thought, the conversation nearly drowning out the background music still straining to offer a calm, relaxed atmosphere while everyone in the room seemed on the verge of freaking out.

Tamara shook her head and twisted up one palm, her bracelets musically jingling. "Well, I don't think the bones are Jessie's, either. Sorry," she said to Renee. "Jessie was just too much of a force, y'know? She's not dead. She's out there. She was . . . different. Don't you remember? She *knew* things."

"Here we go with the mumbo-jumbo stuff." The Third sat back in his chair and Jarrett followed suit. The perfect lieutenant, Becca thought, liking him less and less and feeling the need to run away. She'd never fit into their crowd in high school, and things hadn't changed. If anything, she was more of a misfit than ever.

"The last time I had my Tarot read, I swear it was all about Jessie. Remember?" Tamara looked to Renee for verification. "You saw it, too."

"You believe in that junk?" The Third looked around at the rest of them for support, as if to say, "What a bunch of idiots."

"Oh, learn to have some fun," Tamara snapped at him.

"You did that Tarot crap, too?" Jarrett demanded of Renee.

Hudson's twin waved off his attack. "I've done a lot of things. We all have. It's been twenty years, for God's sake. And sometimes everything isn't black and white, you know, not cut and dried. We did the Tarot thing and Tamara asked questions about Jessie."

"So did you," Tamara reminded her tartly.

Renee nodded. "It's kind of what got me going on the Jessie story."

"So you're not a true believer?" Scott lifted a brow.

"Oh, shut up," Tamara said to him with a faint smile. "Tell them what you learned, Renee."

Renee hesitated, then said, "It was something about how I was about to embark on a quest for knowledge. That someone from my past was reaching out to me. And that I should be warned not to let it take over my life."

Becca eyed Hudson's twin with a wary eye. This, from Renee? The journalist? The girl who always had her facts so straight? What was going on here? What was Renee's real angle?

"And so you decided to chase Jessie's ghost?" The Third looked from her to his friends as if he thought Renee had gone around the bend.

"Yeah, I guess so," Renee stated coolly, her dark gaze hard.

Hudson asked her curiously, "How long have you been on this story?"

"A while. It's just weird the bones have turned up now."

"A sign?" The Third asked with exaggerated interest.

Renee said, "Maybe one of us should call that cop. McNally. Mac."

"What?" The Third demanded.

"He knows more about the Jessie case than anyone."

"That's just begging for trouble," Jarrett snarled as a chorus of denials rose up. Becca had to agree with them, though she said nothing. She noticed Hudson remained quiet, too. McNally wasn't the enemy, no matter what Evangeline theorized.

But something had happened to Jessie. Something bad. Something Becca felt she should know. With a chill she vividly recalled every aspect of her vision at the mall: how Jessie had appeared to her, how the ocean had crashed so loudly she couldn't hear Jessie's warning, how Jessie's toes had touched the edge of the cliff above the raging water. She remembered her own heart quivering fear, and the calm, clear way Jessie had stared at her, called to her . . .

"Becca?"

She jumped back to awareness and turned to Renee. "Yeah?"

"I asked you what you thought." She regarded her with narrowed eyes. "Do you think the body is Jessie's?"

Did she?

"Of course it's Jessie," Glenn answered, reentering the room carrying a tray with four bottles of wine, two red and two white. A waiter followed after him with glasses and began placing them around the table. A waitress carried a tray filled with platters of bite-sized seafood, everything from fried calamari to crab and artichoke dip to crostini topped with smoked salmon, heirloom tomatoes, and sliced mozzarella cheese. Samples of fried razor clams, steamed mussels, and barbecued oysters followed.

While the waiters placed small plates, glasses, and napkins around the table, Glenn added, "She didn't run away. Maybe she was planning to, but something stopped her."

Tamara eyed the heaping trays of food. "I'm on a tight budget."

"It's on me," The Third said in a bored tone that suggested he always picked up the check and found it tedious.

Glenn shook his head as he took his seat. "Compliments of Blue Note."

Tamara smiled gratefully.

"Everything's free at Blue Note," Scott murmured, then waved away the remark as if he were just kidding.

"I'd love to know if those bones belong to Jessie," Evangeline said, once the waiters had disappeared back through the doors and she was helping herself to the calamari.

"So the cop didn't kill her?" Jarrett asked, pretending wide-eyed shock.

"I don't know," Evangeline said with an edge. "None of us do."

"She's alive." Tamara was sure.

"Oh, yeah, you would know. Communing with Tarot and the stars and the charts and tea leaves . . ." Zeke didn't exactly sneer, but the thought was there. He, too, was loading his small plate, and some of the others were serving themselves.

"You haven't changed a bit, either, St. John," Tamara said, running a hand through her fiery curls, bracelets dancing and singing. "And yes, I communicate any way I can, with the spirits and the dead . . . " She lowered her voice to a whisper and waved her hands over the table in a circle, pretending to make her eyes roll upward.

Becca smiled at Tamara's charade while Scott, Jarrett, and The Third glowered. The whole event seemed bizarre and surreal, enjoying wine and seafood while talking about the gruesome discovery at the school, bones that might be the last remains of Jessie Brentwood. The trays were passed to her, but Becca declined, her appetite nonexistent.

Renee held up a hand to restore order. "What do you think, Mitch?"

Mitch, plucking an oyster from the tray, straightened as if he'd been pulled on a string. "About Jessie? I always thought Jessie just left. She'd done it before. Everybody knew it. Maybe she just ran away again." He plopped the oyster into his mouth.

"People usually run for a reason," Hudson said.

"Like a big-ass fight?" The Third shot back. "What was that fight you two had about again? Jessie got pissed because you were making it with some other girl?"

"Nice," Tamara said.

"Not even close," Hudson said. The Third's slings and arrows had never been able to pierce his emotional armor, and Becca was glad to see that still held true.

Evangeline's lips tightened. "I wouldn't put it past her. Running away to make a point. Jessie was sneaky. And mean."

Becca couldn't believe her ears. Evangeline had been one

of Jessie's closest friends. "Jessie was a little secretive, maybe—"

"You didn't really know her," Evangeline cut in. "She had a . . . a cruel streak, a really dark side."

"Oh, yeah, she was Satan," The Third said in a bored tone.

"I'm not kidding, okay! There were things about her that were just plain . . ." Evangeline swallowed hard and looked out the window where rain was still running down the panes.

"Plain what?" Zeke demanded.

"Scary. Dark. I don't know. Vicious or evil or whatever you want to call it." She glanced around at the table and shrugged. "We all know it. We're afraid to say it because she went missing and something horrible might have happened to her, but we all know deep inside that there was something very, very wrong with Jessie Brentwood."

Becca couldn't stand it a second longer. Her vision hovered and she needed air. She scraped her chair back, startling Jarrett. "Excuse me." Quickly, she shoved open the frosted doors and headed through the maze of curtained rooms. It was all too close. Too confining. Too . . . malicious. She walked toward the restrooms, then changed her mind and headed for the front doors, where she stepped out into the cool of the night. The rain had slowed to a thin drizzle and the wind had died, but the air was thick, mist rising off the parking lot. She glanced to a line of parked cars where fir and oak trees defined the edge of the lot. Rain beaded on the hoods, and windshields reflected light from the security lamps blazing overhead. Traffic hummed past and the sound of jazz, muted though it was, filtered into the night.

Becca walked along the front of the building, letting the cold February air clear her head, telling herself that she couldn't admit to anyone that she'd seen Jessie in a vision; they'd all think she'd gone around the bend. But the vibes she'd picked up in that room had all but stifled her. And the body, found at St. Elizabeth's. Had Jessie really been killed and buried, right there? Laid to rest in a shallow, horrid grave at the base of the statue? But who would kill her? And why? She rubbed her arms and glanced around the parking lot again. A woman in a long raincoat was walking quickly through the sparse cars, skirting puddles. A slim woman with light brown hair falling from her face, just the way Jessie's had in the vision.

Becca's breath stopped in her lungs. Her pulse quickened. It couldn't be. And yet . . .

Jessie?

At that moment, the woman turned to face her, and even in the poorly lit lot, it was evident she was not the girl Becca had witnessed in her vision. There was some resemblance, yes, but this woman, now clicking the remote to unlock her car, definitely was *not* Jezebel Brentwood.

You're cracking up, Becca.

Seeing ghosts.

If Jessie's really dead, if the body in the maze is, in fact, Jessie's . . .

The door behind her opened and she turned, half expecting Hudson to step outside, but she was disappointed when Mitch Bellotti, unlit cigarette crammed into the corner of his mouth, lighter in hand, walked up to her. "Freaky in there, isn't it?" he said, flicking his lighter and bending into the flame. He drew deeply on his filter tip.

"Yep." The door swung shut.

He shot a stream of smoke out of the side of his mouth and reached into the inner pocket of his jacket to withdraw a slightly crumpled pack of Marlboros. "Want one?"

"No, thanks." She shook her head and the pack disappeared. "I just needed a break."

"You and me both." He hitched his chin toward one wing of the restaurant. "I gotta say, all this talk about Jessie and if she's alive or dead. Buried up at the school, rotting . . . oh, hell . . . It's kinda sick." He took another long drag and shook his head as he looked at the road where traffic, now thinning, was moving slowly. "I don't need this."

Becca made a sound of agreement.

The door opened again, conversation and music flowing into the night. Becca glanced over her shoulder and this time it was Hudson, his expression grim, walking outside. "You okay?" he asked her.

"Yeah. Well . . . sort of." She shook her head. "This whole thing is so bizarre. It just kind of got to me."

Mitch was nodding as he squinted through the smoke curling from his cigarette. On the arterial, an impatient driver of a sports car honked at a minivan still idling at the intersection though the light had turned green. "So, Renee's bent on getting her story, huh."

Hudson nodded. "I'd like to know if those bones are Jessie's."

"Yeah. Well. I guess." Mitch shrugged.

Hudson's gaze found Becca's. "Coming?"

She nodded and walked through the door he held open.

"I'll be there in a sec," Mitch said, but was cut off by the door closing with a soft thud.

And then Becca and Hudson were alone in the foyer. No customers were crowded, waiting in line, and even the hostess had left the podium. From behind the curtains there were a few whispers of conversation underscored by the ever-present canned music wafting through the darkened restaurant.

"Helluva way to meet again," he offered and his smile had an edge to it, a sarcasm deeper than she remembered. "You want to leave?"

"Now?"

"Mmm."

"With you?"

He lifted a shoulder.

It sounded interesting, but she knew better. Had been

burned before. Hudson Walker was one man she couldn't trust. And then there was the matter of Jessie. "I thought you said we should get through this."

He grinned faintly, some of the darkness fading from his expression. "Maybe I was just trying to ditch Mitch."

"Yeah?" *Do not be charmed by him. Do* NOT*! Remember how he left you. Remember that he never quit loving Jessie. Remember that even now, Jessie exists. Will always be there.*

"I think I should stay and hear Renee out," she said, refusing to be tempted by Hudson. "It is weird . . . those bones . . ."

Hudson inclined his head and she started walking toward the doors to the private dining room. Time to step back into the fray. As she reached the door, she called over her shoulder, "Come on, Walker. Let's just get this over with."

But he was already on her heels and grabbed the door handle, his big hand covering hers, strong fingers curling around the lever. "Let's hope Renee isn't going to be as long-winded as I think she is," he said, opening the door for them both.

First Becca, Renee thought.
Then Mitch.
And finally, so predictably, Hudson.

Three people had left the room. Didn't want to hear anything about Jessie.

Renee had been watching. Making mental notes. Something was up with Becca, and in Renee's opinion, the girl had always been odd, just a little out of step. Even twenty years ago, Rebecca Ryan had hung out with their crowd when she'd been a year younger, the only freshman allowed to run with the sophomores. There hadn't been any rules, of course, just an unwritten code. Renee had thought it was because the goose had been hopelessly in love with Hudson and had manipulated her way into the group, a prediction that had panned out a year out of high school when Hudson had returned from college and Jessie Brentwood was long gone.

Becca and Hudson had hooked up, been joined at the hip for a while. Renee had seen them from her bedroom window, rolling around naked and groping, flashes of their love-making visible through the long, shifting branches of the willow tree.

It had been strange, even desperate, Renee had thought, because her brother, whether he admitted it or not, had never gotten over Jessie Brentwood.

Jessie. Renee glanced over her shoulder uncomfortably. She couldn't help herself. The secrets she'd learned recently had made her realize she was onto a hell of a story, but she was also plagued by bad feelings that had no substance.

Now Renee wasn't as sure as she'd once been that Jessie Brentwood had just run away. Maybe she had met with tragedy. Wasn't that what the strange old lady at the coast had suggested? That Jessie had been marked for death, and that just following her trail marked Renee as well?

Renee had thought the woman was just another nutcase until the bones at St. Lizzie's had suddenly surfaced. Now she wasn't sure what was going on. And though it was weird to say, she wanted the help of her friends, those closest to Jessie, to keep her on track and resistant to these strange feelings of . . . well . . . fear. A part of her even wanted to give up the story entirely, which was ridiculous. She wasn't going to let anything scare her off.

But . . . she was spooked. No question about it. And if she was "marked for death" by God, she was going to find out who and why and wherefore. And her friends were going to help her.

Chapter Five

Renee was about to go after the missing trio herself when Hudson and Becca came in together. Figured. And then Mitch flew in behind them, smelling of cigarettes. She opened her mouth to continue but Tamara spoke first.

"Maybe we should go around the table, tell something we remember about Jessie," Tamara suggested. Zeke groaned, but she ignored him. "Renee can write her piece and we can all put in a little something. Renee's right. We've all been carrying this around way too long. I'm all about closure. Becca, you go first."

Becca, taking her chair next to Jarrett, half choked. "I didn't even know her that well."

"Didn't you?" Renee asked.

Evangeline cut her off. "I'll start. Since you all think Jessie was supposed to be my best friend."

"Your evil best friend," The Third reminded her.

"Jessie had a lot of problems," she said tartly.

The Third snorted. "Aside from the dark-side thing, what kind of problems?"

"Enough," Zeke said, catching The Third's eyes. "Let her talk."

Evangeline linked her fingers more tightly through Zeke's. "There were problems at home. Big problems that she wouldn't really talk about, and she . . . she lived a weird fantasy life, too."

"It wasn't that weird," Renee disagreed.

"She thought all the guys wanted to screw her, okay?" Evangeline's gaze skated to each of the men at the table. "She was obsessed with it. Flirting and playing up to the guys, teasing them. You all know."

"That was a long time ago," Mitch said somewhat uncomfortably.

Evangeline glared at Mitch. "It was all a long time ago, but that's why we're here, isn't it? Anyway, that's what I remember about Jessie. You can make it all hearts and flowers and gee, poor Jessie if you want to, but the truth of the matter was, Jessie wasn't very nice."

Becca gazed thoughtfully at Vangie. She remembered a whisper of a rumor that Zeke had been fascinated with Jessie and had been seeing her behind his best friend Hudson's back. Becca had dismissed the rumor then, as she did now, as the product of Evangeline's own obsession with Zeke.

"What do you think, Walker?" The Third needled. "Your girlfriend want all of us?"

"Shut up," Hudson said, irritated.

"She was Walker's girl, we all know that." Zeke was positive.

Tamara twisted one of her bracelets. "High school was so long ago. A lifetime, but I remember thinking that you, Hudson . . ." She looked into Hudson's eyes. "You and Jessie were the perfect couple. I'd see you hanging out at the lockers, so into each other."

"Well . . . no . . . we were high school kids, like you said. What did we know about anything?"

She flashed a bit of a smile, touched with nostalgia, and Becca realized that Tamara had gone through the pains of a high school crush on Hudson. Well, join the club. Half the girls in the class had admitted to a "thing" for him, and hadn't he been voted the boy with whom most girls would want to be stranded on a deserted isle? The same had been true of Jessie. All the boys had wanted her, and she'd played right into it. Only Evangeline had been true to Zeke; the rest of the girls had been hot for Hudson. Renee knew it, too. She'd been at the top of the class academically and a lot of her friends were girls who'd wanted to be close to her, to Hudson's twin, just so they could get close to him. Renee had been onto them, though, and had never really played along.

"You know what I remember?" Mitch said suddenly. "How Jessie was always saying those things. Those little quotes, or something. Remember? Always had a piece of a song, or something."

"She always pointed out your faults, one way or another," Evangeline agreed.

"Glad you weren't my best friend," Glenn muttered with a grimace.

"Yeah, what did she do to you?" Mitch asked.

Evangeline tossed her blond bob. "None of you really knew her, so don't judge me. Jessie was popular. And she kind of liked to make me feel bad, just to make herself feel better. High school, you know . . . you get older and you realize how godawful it was."

"They weren't quotes. They were nursery rhymes," Glenn said with a nod, as the tumblers clicked.

Mitch nodded eagerly. "That's right! She was always kind of singing them. Singsonging. She said 'em to us guys. Her little joke or something. One of her favorites was about boys."

"Oh, God . . ." Evangeline rolled her eyes.

"I forgot about that," The Third said with a frown.

"Nursery rhymes?" Renee repeated, clearly skeptical. "I don't remember that about her."

"Me neither," Becca said.

"It was all flirty Jessie bullshit, anyway." Jarrett looked impatient. "That naughty boy stuff. We just said she came on to every guy at this table."

Evangeline's jaw set and her fingers clasped Zeke's in a death grip.

Hudson exhaled and looked as if he'd rather be anywhere than in this room with his so-called friends. "The way I remember it, a lot of you guys came on to her. Perception. Hard to know who's scamming who sometimes."

"Oh, come on, Walker." The Third was pissed, his face flushed, his eyes bright with challenge. "It had to be killing you, the way she acted. That the reason you had that fight? Because of us?"

"Yeah," Hudson said with a cynical smile. "It's all about you, Delacroix."

"What the fuck was it about, then?"

Hudson grimaced. "I don't know. She picked the fight with me. I told the cops—McNally—the same thing then. Jessie was edgy and distracted, and she wanted to fight. You all heard most of it. When we went to my place, it was more of the same."

"She thought there was another girl in your life," Tamara guessed.

"She was sixteen," Hudson said. "She thought a lot of things."

"Maybe there was someone else?" Evangeline suggested.

"McNally thought you might have killed her," Scott reminded Hudson. He grabbed a bottle of red wine and Becca watched the liquid fill his glass, glinting bloodlike under the hanging lights. "Wasn't his theory that you killed her after you found out she was sleeping with . . . someone else?"

"McNally was obsessed, grasping at straws, trying to make a homicide out of a missing persons case, trying to pin it on one of us," Hudson said, sounding sick to the back teeth of the whole thing. "God knows. Maybe it was a homicide."

"And you think one of us did it?" Scott gazed at him belligerently.

"No."

"But he thought you *murdered* her?" Renee asked her brother. "Now that I really don't remember."

"It wasn't ruled a homicide," Becca interjected. "They had no body."

"But McNally had a hard-on about it," Glenn interjected. "Hell, that guy was a head case."

"And they've got a body now. Whether it's Jessie's or not, we're going back through it again . . ." The Third said on a sigh.

"Well, I don't think that's Jessie. I think she just ran away. She said she was unhappy," Evangeline reminded them. "And that she had to leave."

"She said she had to leave?" Becca asked.

"Yeah, like she knew something." Vangie swept back blond strands from her face. "She was like that, y'know? Like Tamara said. She knew things. She had some kind of ESP or whatever you want to call it. But it was weird. Creepy. When she said she had to leave, I believed her."

"What exactly did she say?" Renee asked.

"She said 'I've got to get out of here before something bad happens,' or something like that."

"You never told us that," The Third said with mild reproof. "When we were all being grilled."

"Well, it was something like that," Evangeline declared, flushing. "She and Hudson weren't getting along. Maybe that was it."

All eyes turned to Hudson and he agreed, "Jessie had things on her mind."

"Like what?" Scott asked.

"I don't know. There was definitely something driving her."

Renee looked at her brother and Becca got the sense she was calculating something, like whether to reveal some kind of information or keep it to herself. In the end, she said, "I've got some leads to follow. I'm heading to the beach. Maybe we should meet up again in a couple of weeks . . ."

"Let's wait on that for a while," The Third said. He was about to say something more but hesitated as a waiter slid through the door and picked up some of the dirty dishes, then slipped out again. Then he said, "You know McNally's going to be back, hounding us."

"No way. He's gotta be retired by now." Scott shook his head. "It'll be someone else."

"Guys like him never retire. And he can't be that old. But the point is: so what? He can't do anything to us now. We just need to all keep cool. McNally, or somebody like him, is going to start asking questions again. Any inconsistency— any—will just make it worse. But, hey . . . here we are again." He lifted his glass in a toast and everyone followed suit, albeit slowly, as no one knew where this was going. "We're friends. We need to see more of each other and put this Jessie Brentwood thing to bed. There's nothing to worry about."

"So much for all of us saying something about Jessie," Tamara said, disgusted.

That much was true. The meeting and Renee's idea that they should all disclose something personal about Jessie was falling apart. Becca tasted some of the hors d'oeuvres and sipped at a glass of white wine while listening to several different conversations buzzing around her. Scott was bragging up Blue Ocean, his new restaurant at the beach, though, it seemed, Glenn wasn't as excited about the venture as his partner. Glenn groused that the restaurant in Lincoln City was still a work in progress while Scott waved off his concerns, stating only that the menu had to be adjusted; it was too "sophisticated" for the beach crowd. Mitch complained that he was overworked and Jarrett, a commercial real estate salesman, wasn't happy with the economy. Underneath all the idle chitchat there was something more, a restless uneasiness, and Becca knew it was Jessie—her memories, her ghost—haunting each of them.

The Third kept up his mantra that they should all keep seeing each other, though they all knew that it wouldn't happen. Without a class reunion or a funeral, or the discovery of bones in the maze at St. Elizabeth's, members of their high school clique wouldn't search each other out.

Tamara worked at keeping up a conversation with a more and more taciturn Hudson. Becca felt Renee's eyes on her once or twice and wondered if and when she would tell everyone about her brief affair with Hudson after high school. Maybe they already knew, though they sure didn't act like it.

Zeke moved toward Hudson for some conversation as they all got up from the table, but Becca couldn't overhear as Mitch engaged her while they walked toward the door.

"Kind of a weird way for all of us to finally get together again," he said, holding open the door of the private room.

"I guess we'll know more after the bones are tested."

"How long have you been a widow?"

"Oh . . . a while . . . not that long . . ." She didn't want to go into *that* right now. The last thing she wanted to think about was Ben.

"My divorce from Sherri was finalized two years ago."

The Third and Jarrett caught up to them and Becca saw the amusement in their eyes at Mitch's less than sophisticated attempts to get to know her. She was bugged at all of them—and herself, too.

She didn't want to talk to any of them, well, except for Hudson, but she wasn't going to linger around and try to catch his attention. If he'd wanted to see her in the past sixteen years, he damned well could have picked up the phone. Which he hadn't. She made her way through the foyer and pushed her way outside where the air was heavy and moist, the parking lot dim, with even fewer cars than before. As she stepped off the curb, she sank a shoe into a mud puddle.

Perfect.

"Becca!" Renee's voice caught up with her as she reached her Jetta. She glanced behind her where Renee had disengaged herself from the group and Hudson's tall, unmistakable form was backlit by one of the large windows of the restaurant.

"I'd like to talk sometime," Renee said, her briefcase swinging from one hand as she approached.

This was unusual. "About Jessie?" Using her remote, Becca unlocked the car.

"Yeah."

"I didn't really know her." The vision seemed to shimmer in her brain, daring her to tell Renee about it, but Becca kept her mouth firmly shut.

"You knew her as well as most of us. Probably more than her parents did."

Becca saw Evangeline sliding into the front seat of Zeke's vintage Mustang. "Fine. You want to meet this weekend?"

"I'm going to the beach tomorrow, for a couple of days," Renee said, glancing nervously back at the front of the building where Jarrett, The Third, and Mitch had gathered. The Third was already on his cell phone, Mitch was lighting up, and Jarrett looked across the lot, his gaze zeroing in on Becca and Renee. There was something in his intent look that brought goose bumps to her skin, a hardness that she hadn't remembered from St. Elizabeth's. "Listen," Renee was saying, "I didn't bring it up with all of them, but my husband Tim and I are having some problems . . ."

"I'm sorry."

"Don't be. And I'm lying. It's not just problems. We're separated, and I've been spending quite a bit of time at the coast. Alone. You know, trying to put things in perspective." She looked away from the men gathered under the portico. "Maybe that's why I started thinking about Jessie again. Unresolved issues. Anyway, I wanted to talk to you about some ideas I had."

"Just me, or all of us?"

"Everyone, I guess. I just thought we could kick this off."

There was something more going on that Becca didn't understand, but it hardly mattered since she'd already agreed to meet with Renee.

"Why don't I call you after the weekend?" Renee suggested. "Maybe we can get together. I've just got . . . some theories . . . kind of odd information . . ."

"Odd? How?"

Renee glanced back toward the group. Mitch, keys in hand, was walking toward an SUV parked not far from Becca's Jetta. "I'll call you," Renee whispered, then hurried to a black Toyota as Mitch tossed his cigarette into the parking lot and climbed into his Tahoe.

Becca opened her car door and started to slide inside as Hudson, head bent against the rain, headed her way. Hesitating, warring with herself, Becca told herself to let it go. Whatever had happened between them, why he'd never called her again, didn't matter. It was over. Ancient history.

Screw that, she thought and stepped out of the Jetta again as Mitch tore out of the lot. *I want to talk to him.*

She realized belatedly that Hudson wasn't making his way to her, but rather toward a dilapidated truck. Too bad. She stepped over an island of scraggly shrubs separating one part of the parking lot from the other and reached him just as he opened the door to the old pickup. His gaze caught and held hers and he moved her way, whether out of politeness or interest, she couldn't tell.

Renee drove by, the tires of her Camry spraying water. She barely hesitated at the street, then gunned the accelerator and zipped through the intersection as an amber light turned red.

"She's gonna kill herself someday," Hudson said, his gaze following the path Renee's Toyota had taken. "Sometimes I think she has a death wish." He glanced back at Becca and she suddenly felt like an idiot, chasing him down and getting soaked in the process.

"So what did you think about that?" Becca asked.

"Felt a little like high school, all over again."

"Something I could do without," Becca said.

He made a sound of agreement.

"I guess it was interesting to see everyone again."

"Interesting . . . yeah." Hudson glanced back. Jarrett and The Third were giving each other a "high sign" good-bye before angling off to their cars. "Not all that different, though."

"No," she agreed, watching as The Third slid behind the wheel of a BMW with vanity plates that read: III. "Some things never change."

"Oh, maybe some do."

She shot him a sideways glance.

"Sometimes we change for the better. At least a little bit."

"What are you getting at?" she asked.

He seemed to think over his words a long time, then said suddenly, "I was an idiot twenty years ago. I should have called you. I know it. Just wanted you to know it."

"Oh." She couldn't hide her surprise. "Well. Actually, it was sixteen years ago. But who's counting."

He smiled. "I was an ass. All caught up in myself and what life had in store for me." He ran a hand around his neck as the rain started in earnest again, the drizzle giving way to big, thick drops. "If nothing else, at least this whole resurrected mess has given me the chance to tell you that."

Becca thought about the baby she'd lost and couldn't find her breath.

Hudson looked down at her, as if trying to discern her thoughts. The tension suddenly tightened between them and for a wild moment Becca thought he was actually going to kiss her.

"Hudson! Wait up!"

Spell broken, they both looked around to see Tamara dodging raindrops and fighting with an umbrella as she made her way toward them.

"I'd better go," Becca murmured.

"We shouldn't let so much time go by." He lifted a hand in good-bye as Tamara arrived and Becca bowed out.

Call me, she thought but couldn't say the words. She turned away and hurried toward her car, parked now by itself. The parking lot was nearly deserted with only Hudson's truck, her Jetta, and a couple of other sedans parked near the front doors.

Business at the Blue Note was definitely not booming.

Once inside her Volkswagen, she started the engine. Through the blurry windshield, she watched as Tamara, still fighting with her umbrella, was grinning up at Hudson and shaking her head at her own clumsiness, obviously flirting.

So what?

Hudson took the umbrella from Tamara's hands and held the door of his truck open for her.

An unwanted and uncalled-for spurt of jealousy sizzled through Becca's blood.

"Don't go there," she warned herself, but couldn't help but observe Tamara climbing into the cab, her red hair dark and drooping with rain, her smile as wide as a tropical sunrise.

Becca, hating herself for noticing, threw the Jetta into reverse and backed out of her parking slot. Hudson was firing up his old Ford as she drove past. She tried not to glance out of the corner of her eye, tamping down the foolish notion that he was still somehow special. The stark reality was that whatever she'd had with Hudson was over—and most of it had been in Becca's mind anyway.

The light turned green but Becca didn't notice, not until a car pulled up behind her and honked. She jumped and stepped hard on the accelerator, putting Blue Note, thoughts of Jessie and Hudson behind her.

Hudson's night went from bad to worse.

As if the debacle at Blue Note hadn't been bad enough,

he'd had to drive Tamara home and make small talk while she tried to flirt with him. After dropping her off at her apartment, he'd returned home to find his foreman at his back door.

And Grandy Dougherty wasn't bearing good news.

"Something wrong?" Hudson asked.

"Yeah."

"Been here long?"

"Nah, just about fifteen minutes or so, enough to check the stock." The older man stood on Hudson's back porch, dripping rain from the brim of his baseball cap and looking as forlorn as his dismal tone of voice. It was pitch-black outside and the wind whooshed rain at them sideways, reaching harshly beneath the porch's protection. Grandy ducked his head against its onslaught. "I'm sorry about this, but I'm gonna haft leave for a while. I got a grandkid in some big trouble, and I gotta take care of her and my son. I just wanted to talk to you in person rather than call, seein' how this is so sudden and all."

"It's all right," Hudson said, knowing that he would miss the handyman who had a way with livestock. "Why don't you come in, get out of the rain?" Hudson waved the older man toward the door, but Grandy shook his head.

"Don't really have time. The wife, she's waitin'." He glanced up at Hudson, then looked away. "Ah, hell! My Lissa, she's the first grandchild, and she's got herself in some trouble."

He ran a tired hand over his forehead, adjusting his cap. "She lives up near Bellingham, in Washington, near the border with her dad and younger brother. My wife and I are going up there."

Hudson nodded. "Okay."

"You could call Emile Rodriguez, you know. Guy's got ranchin' in his blood and Emile, he's always looking for a little extra work. He could help out if I don't get back before Boston foals."

"I've helped a mare foal a time or two before," Hudson said, thinking of his Appaloosa mare. "So has Boston."

"Yeah, well, then . . . I'll get you Emile's number. Just in case you need a hand or two." Grandy headed down the two stairs from the back porch and into the inky, miserable night before Hudson could offer any further resistance. Hearing the older man's truck's engine cough and catch, Hudson closed the enclosed porch door against the storm, then leaned against its painted frame. The wind rattled the window casings on the old farmhouse. Hudson had made repair after repair to the place over the past ten years that he'd owned the ranch, but there was no escaping the fact that the building was old and full of cracks and its upkeep was a constant battle. He probably should raze the place and start over, but he didn't have the time or inclination. A part of him loved this old house with its ancient beams, chipped paint, and years of hard work and toil etched into the woodwork.

The ranch had been his parents' and after their deaths—his father to heart disease, his mother to cancer—the place had come to him and Renee. Renee hadn't wanted any part of it. To Hudson, who'd spent his years after college buying and selling commercial real estate, the chance to drop out of the rat race for a while and settle into small-town farming and ranching had seemed like a golden opportunity. He'd bought out Renee's share and he'd been settling into his new life for the last four years. It still felt like the right thing to do. The sometimes back-breaking work was welcome relief from the stress of "deal making" and "contract negotiations."

As he walked back into the kitchen, he automatically looked around for his Lab mix, but Booker T. was long gone. He'd died the previous autumn and Hudson supposed it was a blessing. The poor animal had been half blind, all but lame, his death expected and, for Booker T., probably long welcomed.

But the old dog's passing had left a hole in Hudson's life.

Maybe the hole had always been there even in his youth but had grown wider with time, not smaller. Losing the dog hadn't helped, and losing Jessie . . . well, that still bothered him. He wondered about the body found up at St. Elizabeth's. Was it Jessie's? Did she die at the feet of the Madonna in that overgrown maze? If so, she'd certainly been killed.

"Christ," he whispered and pushed his hair out of his eyes. Toeing off one shoe with the other, he decided to pour himself a drink, a stiff shot of scotch. Listening to all the talk about Jessie, then coming face-to-face with Becca again had unnerved him. He'd thought he was long over her, but obviously he'd been wrong. He'd thought about her over the years, of course, but had steadfastly pushed her from his mind. Becca, Jessie, and St. Elizabeth's were memories he'd tried to repress, and he'd generally succeeded.

Then came Renee's call about the discovery at St. Lizzie's and it all came rushing back. He'd dropped his high school friends from his life. He didn't want to know them. He didn't want to think about them. He didn't want to think about Jessie. But as Renee related the discovery of the bones he felt a soul-deep dread—never fully buried—rise again. His sister had never fully gotten over what had happened, either, and she'd spent years writing in a journal about the events, making up stories about what could have happened to the missing Jessie Brentwood. Now it was all real.

"A bunch of kids found bones at the base of the Madonna statue inside the maze at St. Elizabeth's," she said. "Human bones. A human hand popped up and reached from the grave at them, or so they thought. It's Jessie, Hudson. Now we know. Now we finally know."

Hudson held the phone so tightly he saw his own knuckles bleach white as Renee went on to say that she was spearheading a get-together at Scott and Glenn's restaurant to talk things over with some of the "old gang." Hudson heard her as if from a distance as images of Jessie Brentwood, the same ones that he'd carried inside his mind for twenty years, flashed across the screen of his memory.

"I'm going to write about this," Renee had told him. "I've already been on it, actually. This is a hell of a story."

"Is it?" he'd asked.

"You'll be there, right?" Renee responded.

"To talk about whether or not the bones are Jessie's?" He'd had trouble processing.

"And some other stuff. I've got a lot invested in this. It's . . . a kind of personal quest."

Hudson had squinted at the phone, but before he could ask her what she meant, she swept on. "Damn it, Hudson, I'm tired of writing drivel for the *Star*. I think if I have to write one more insipid article about whose house is for sale, who got a traffic ticket, or who's upset with his neighbor for cutting down a tree, I might puke. This, the story of the body at St. Lizzie's, is big, and I'm part of it. We all are. I think we've finally found Jessie."

He'd tried to listen more to his sister, but his emotions had gotten the better of him and he thought about Jessie. Sixteen years old. The first woman he'd ever slept with.

"Catch me, Hudson, if you can," Jessie had sung out as she'd run through the maze of thick laurel. Her footsteps had been light, her breathing shallow, but he'd tracked her down easily as she'd tried to lose him in the intricate pathways. She'd failed, of course, maybe even let him catch up with her. To Jessie, everything, even lying in the thick grass under the stars in the shadow of the church spire and tearing off Hudson's clothes, had been a game.

Jessie, are you dead? Are those your remains? Did you die beneath the Madonna?

"The bones they found, they're female? Young?" he asked Renee.

"Nobody's saying, yet. But who else?"

"It could be anyone—"

"No, Hudson, it couldn't. It's Jessie, trust me. And it makes sense, right?"

"Nothing makes sense."

"I'm just about at the ranch. See you in a minute." And Renee had come in moments later, saying, "I've got a few more calls to make, maybe you can help me . . . ?"

"I'll call Becca. She knew Jessie. But that's it. The rest of this is your show."

That caught her up. "Becca," she said, but didn't say what was really on her mind, though it was probably along the same lines she'd spewed when he'd gotten involved with Becca a year or so after high school. "Rebecca Ryan? Are you nuts? Oh, God, Hudson, get *real*. Are you a sadist or what? Becca's only one step further away from the loony bin than Jessie was. What is it with you and beautiful, out-of-touch women?"

"Enough," he'd said, but Renee wasn't to be stopped.

"You know, brother dear, if you tried, you could do better. Lots better."

Hudson hadn't thought so twenty—no, sixteen years ago— and he didn't think so now. After Renee left he called Tamara for Becca's number, then Becca herself, inviting her to his sister's gathering. He'd wanted to see her again. Face her. Face his own feelings . . .

And the hell of it was, she was just as intriguing and beautiful as before. Maybe more so. Renee was probably right, he thought as he searched inside a cupboard and pulled out a half-full bottle of scotch. He twisted off the cap, found a short glass, and poured in a splash.

No one—not even himself—could separate Becca from what had happened to Jessie. They would just be forever linked. The only two girls from St. Elizabeth's whom he'd dated and, eventually, slept with.

One had run from him, perhaps met her death.

The other he'd pushed away.

"Oh, hell," he muttered under his breath as he lifted his

glass and took a sip. He caught the pale image of his reflection in the window over the sink and noticed the tense lines evident on his face. He'd hoped his inadequate apology tonight was enough to at least explain his behavior; he didn't expect it to make up for anything.

Because the truth of the matter was he'd treated Becca thoughtlessly. Worse than that, he'd treated her *purposely* thoughtlessly. How was that for an oxymoron? He'd wanted her to dislike him. He'd been so attracted to her, even when he was with Jessie, that when he and Becca had actually gotten together, he'd never been able to feel right about it. A part of him had believed Jessie was still alive and watching him. Jessie had accused him of being attracted to Becca. It had been the basis of their last fight, the last time he'd seen her before she disappeared.

Leaning a hip against the counter, twisting off the faucet that seemed to forever drip, he remembered how it had been twenty years earlier in the big room downstairs. Carrying his drink, he walked to the staircase and took the worn steps down to the basement with its low-hanging ceiling and monster of a furnace, then ducked through the doorway to the big rec room where the pool table hidden by its old burgundy faux-leather cover still stood.

In his mind's eye, he saw Jessie as she had been. Seated atop the table, staring straight at him, she'd slowly and deliberately unbuttoned her shirt, then slid it off her shoulders.

He'd lifted a hand in protest, their anger at each other still simmering. "Wait . . ."

"Shh!" she warned, a finger to her lips before she leaned forward just a bit, offering him an intimate view of her cleavage, then unhooked her bra, her gorgeous breasts free as she wiggled out of it, her hazel eyes cool with calculation and hot with fury.

"Jess—"

"You've got a hard-on for Becca," she said in that low, sultry voice that turned him on. It was the same accusation that had instigated their fight earlier in the day. A fight that everyone at school knew about, he'd subsequently learned, when the cops later sought him out and asked about its cause.

For a moment it was as if she were in the room with him now. Still sixteen. Still angry. And he hadn't been able to resist her. She'd pouted and toyed with him, then grabbed him by the shirt and dragged him down on the table with her. Her lips had been hot and moist, her tongue rimming his lips, her fingers eager as they pulled his shirt over his head, then ran feather-light over his muscles.

It had been fast after that. Both of them stripping away each other's pants and underwear. He'd wrapped his arms around her, kissed her breasts and then, despite all his promises to himself, he'd made love to her with all of the heat of his youth, lost in the warm, the mystery, the sheer feminine thrall of her like he'd been since the first time they'd come together, his knees pushing hard against the felt-covered slate.

Afterward, sweating, gasping, while he lay naked on the hard surface, she'd pulled herself away and dressed quickly.

"You don't have to go," he said, levering up on an elbow.

"Yeah . . . yeah, I do."

"Jessie—"

"Don't say it, okay?" she insisted, knowing that he was going to promise that he loved her and for the moment, he did, but that was it . . . only for the moment. They both knew it. She yanked on her clothes and regarded him with sober eyes while he lay on the burgundy felt table, staring up at the ceiling, lost in his own teen angst.

"I'm going," she said, pulling her hair through the neck of her shirt and shaking out the long strands.

"You could stay."

"I don't think so." She started across the room.

"I'll see you tomorrow."

"Maybe." Her tone was fatalistic.

"Oh, for the love of God, stop that," he said in a flash of

anger. He hated the way she sometimes acted like they were only living for the day, that there would be no tomorrow. "Why do you always do that?"

"Because you don't care!"

Hudson swore under his breath.

"Don't lie to yourself," she said as she reached the bottom of the stairs. "And quit trying to make yourself the good guy. You want out of this . . . whatever it is we've got going."

Before he could stop himself, Hudson bit out, "You're the one who wants out."

She laughed. "Oh, right."

He was already reaching for his pants.

"What about Becca?" she demanded.

"What about her?"

"You think I don't know?" she charged, one foot on the stairs, her head twisted to watch him as he struggled with his zipper. "I see things, y'know. I do. And I see the way you look at her."

"I'm sick of fighting," he muttered, angry at her. At himself. At the fact that there was more than a grain of truth in her charges.

"Me, too. But . . . there's something I need to tell you."

"Can't wait."

"Stop being a bastard. I think I might be . . . in serious trouble . . ."

Jessie was silhouetted by the light from the staircase and there was something in her expression that gave him pause. Something darker than their petty argument, something that made her bite her lower lip, as if she were afraid of the next words she might utter. She gazed down at the bottom step, the one his father had replaced, but he knew she wasn't seeing the new boards or nails holding the stair in place. She was somewhere else. Lost in her own thoughts.

"What?" he asked.

"Trouble. Serious trouble." She wouldn't look at him.

Swallowing hard, he prepared himself for the fact that she

might be admitting she was pregnant. *No matter what she tells you, you have to be a man, Walker. Tough up.*

She looked up at him, worry and more—terror?—shadowing her eyes. "Trouble's coming to find me," she said almost inaudibly over the rumble of the furnace and the frantic beating of his own heart.

"What kind of trouble?"

"Bad trouble." She ran a hand nervously through her hair, pushing the golden brown strands from her face. Her fingers trembled slightly. "I don't know what I was thinking . . . I . . . I should have stopped. But I just couldn't."

"Stopped what?"

"Searching."

"Searching for *what*?" he asked, totally confounded. She *wasn't* pregnant? Relief washed over him, but still he was confused. He crossed to her and reached for her hand resting on the banister.

Instead of explaining further, she changed her mood in her quicksilver way. As if by sheer willpower, she straightened up, then winked at him slyly and said, "You're not over me, no matter what you think. You're hooked."

Hudson stared down at her. She was like that. One way one moment, completely changed the next.

"I'm in your blood," she said.

And then she was gone.

She'd run up the stairs and out the back door, and as he'd followed and reached the porch, he heard the engine of her car turn over. From the porch he watched the glow of her taillights disappear in the rising fog.

Now he trudged back up the stairs, hearing the ancient boards creak under his weight.

He'd never seen her again.

And what had he done after Jessie disappeared that night twenty years ago? Mourned? Grieved? Longed for her return?

Well, maybe he had a little, in the beginning. Then there

had been the questions from the cops and the wondering, always the wondering what had happened to the girl he was supposed to have loved.

But in the end he'd sought solace, comfort, and a chance to forget in sex with Becca. Yes, it had been a few years later, but it hadn't felt right. He'd wanted to drown himself in her, but Jessie's face, her voice, her ways . . . had never gone away, not completely.

Had it been his own guilt eating at him? Undoubtedly. But that feeling had been real and raw enough that it had forced him to give up on Becca. Forced him to discover a new life. Forced him to move on.

I see things . . . That's what she'd said, what Tamara had echoed tonight at the restaurant. It was as if they, the friends who'd known her, understood that she was different, a bit ethereal.

He drained his glass, left it in the sink, then walked into his living room and threw himself down on the sofa. The blank screen of the television stared at him but his mind was viewing a film of its own making.

Were those Jessie's bones found in the maze? The only news released through the media was that they belonged to a young female victim. Nobody was saying whether they'd been lying there twenty years or if they were newly deposited. The police were mum, and the story had been eclipsed by more recent local news: a murder apparently from a burglary gone wrong; flooding along lower elevations from a rapidly melting snowpack; a defendant in a criminal trial suddenly hauling off and smacking his own lawyer in the face.

Hudson sighed. He'd been running for years from thoughts of Jessie . . . and Becca. He'd been running for years from his own feelings. Regardless of what was decided about the bones found at the base of the Madonna statue, maybe it was time to remember, think, even conjecture. Figure out what happened, if anyone could.

It was time to stop running.

Chapter Six

"Hey, Mac!"

McNally pretended not to hear Detective Gretchen Sandler's demanding nasal tone. For the love of God, that woman's voice was like the scrape of nails on a chalkboard. Truth to tell, she bugged the shit out of him.

He was bent over his computer screen, though he wasn't near as adept at researching on the 'net as he acted. Sure, he could get what he needed from the electronic equipment that had grown and expanded and reached over the whole department like some alien plant life, invading every aspect of law enforcement, even here in Laurelton. But he still liked to examine real evidence, preferred tromping across crime scenes, and he got off on mentally putting pieces together like a jigsaw puzzle in his brain until he reached that "Aha!" moment.

"Mac!"

"What?" He didn't look up.

"Don't act like you can't hear me," she said from her desk, which was less than three feet behind him. "I'm zippo on fifteen- to twenty-four-year-old missing females through 1993.

Either nobody cares that she's gone, or we've got to go back further."

"Go back further," he said, trying not to snap.

He sensed something behind him, something quiet and building. Glancing around, he saw that Gretchen was barely holding in suppressed amusement, as were some of the younger men and women in the department, who, upon seeing his dark expression, moved back to their stations. Gretchen, however, was Mac's latest partner, a woman who'd earned her job as a homicide detective because she was damn good at her job. Damn good. Just ask her. And she resented being saddled with a has-been, obsessed nut job like Mac who'd earned his promotion to homicide detective out of virtue of simply hanging around long enough. This, of course, was Gretchen's opinion, not Mac's.

But it might be a lot of the rest of the department's as well.

"Maybe I should go back to 1989," she suggested. "Isn't there a vic named . . . oh, let's see if I can remember . . ." She snapped her fingers. "Jezebel Brentwood?"

His temper spiked and he bit out, "Maybe you should have started there."

"And keep you from your obsession? No way. I'll let you begin at that end and meet you in the middle."

"If I had DNA on Jessie Brentwood, it would only be a matter of waiting for the results from the bones." He swivelled in his chair and gave her what he hoped was a cool look, but he felt a muscle working in his jaw.

Gretchen was in her early thirties with creamy, mocha-colored skin and straight black hair, a product of her Brazilian mother, and a pair of icy blue eyes, colder than Mac's own, a product of her father, apparently, one Gretchen had never known. Or so she'd claimed. "You're that sure."

"You got any other missing girls from St. Elizabeth's?"

"I got a few from the surrounding area."

"You sure like making it hard on yourself to prove a

point." Mac turned back to his computer as Wes Pelligree, a tall African American detective everyone referred to as Weasel, nudged an unwilling, rain-sodden suspect in damp sweat-shirt, dirty jeans, and cuffs toward his desk. Hands chained behind his back, the perp had dirty bare feet, lank, greasy hair, a pimply face, eyes at half mast, and a sneer showing bad teeth, and he reeked of his own puke. An obvious drug bust. But then Weasel had a knack for nailing scumbags who sold meth and crack. Rumor had it his older brother, the one who had dubbed him with the nickname in the first place while Wes was still in grade school, before he'd grown to six-three, had died of an overdose before Wes was out of the Academy. Ever since then, Wes Pelligree had been on a mission.

Which was bad news for the drenched white guy protesting his innocence.

Gretchen, standing too close to his desk, watched them pass and wrinkled her nose as the suspect dropped loudly into a side chair at Weasel's desk. Phones rang, conversation buzzed, and police personnel in uniform or plain clothes weaved through the maze of desks and cubicles that were crowded into a central area with little privacy and few win-dows. A heating system that had been "upgraded" sometime in the mid eighties was rumbling and blowing air that was five degrees too warm.

"When are we getting some data we can use?" Gretchen demanded. "The lab techs on vacation, or what?"

"Gotta be patient." Mac was growing tired of always ex-plaining everything to her. She knew it anyway, but liked to hear herself talk.

"Twenty years patient? I don't think so."

She walked off and Mac slid a look after her. She was easy on the eyes. Great figure, nice butt, slim waist, and de-cent enough breasts, he supposed, but she worked really hard on being unlikeable. He watched a couple of other detectives throw her a glance as she passed. None seemed particularly warm and fuzzy. Mac might be the butt of a few jokes because of his obsession with Jessie Brentwood, but Gretchen was the coworker to avoid. No sense of humor. No big-picture thinking. No fun. She dotted all her i's and crossed her t's and fell all over herself in her eagerness to catch the high-profile cases—the few that came along here.

Gretchen Sandler was loaded with ambition, and she didn't care who got trampled in her climb to the top.

"Humph," Mac grunted at the computer screen. Though he didn't give a rat's ass what others thought of him, if those bones proved to be Jessie Brentwood, he'd go from being the goat to the hero of the department.

The same couldn't be said of Gretchen Sandler.

The afternoon was dark gray and the wind was shrieking around and under the eaves of Becca's condo. She'd finished up some work on the computer for Bennett, Bretherton, and Pfeiffer, and had luckily not lost any of the documents when the lights had flickered. Climbing out of her desk chair, she worked the knots out of her neck while Ringo, who'd been sleeping curled under her desk, climbed to his feet and stretched. Becca grabbed her now-tepid cup of tea and tossed it down the sink. She was cold inside and out and the storm wasn't helping.

Deciding to take a bath to warm up, she ran the taps. The lights flickered again. Grabbing her battery-powered radio, she lit the three candles she had arranged in a pewter holder on the tile countertop, just in case. Ringo watched her machinations with interest, his head cocked this way and that.

She'd turned off the lights, opened the shades high over the window of the tub for a view of the sky, and was just climbing into the steaming water when the lights quit altogether, plunging the condo into total darkness aside from her flickering tapers.

Great.

Through the window she saw the limbs of shivering birch trees as they scratched the glass. She gazed past them up at the threatening clouds, then looked over to the fir trees across the way, the same trees that Ringo had barked at on Valentine's Day as if he'd sensed a mass murderer lurking in the shadows. That had been the same day she'd had her vision, the same day she'd learned of the bones discovered at St. Lizzie's.

Shuddering, she switched on the radio and caught sight of bottles of bath oils displayed on the counter. She'd bought them primarily for their colors, glowing aqua and deep gold, but now she picked one up, opened it, and poured the liquid underneath the faucet. She was just sinking down into the water again when she felt a shiver that had nothing to do with the cool air on the wetness of her skin. Glancing out the window, she focused on the fir trees.

Was someone there?

Watching her?

Seeing the candlelight on her skin?

Instantly she yanked down the blind, her pulse rocketing. Was her imagination running away with her? She seemed to feel eyes watching her at every turn.

"At least you're not going nuts," she murmured to the dog.

Turning off the taps, Becca sat quietly, almost suspended, in the hot water. The bath oil was scented, and a light, airy aroma filled her nostrils. It was soothing and after a couple of minutes she relaxed again, listening to the muted classic rock music filtering through the room.

Ringo tiptoed over to the bath mat and curled himself down into a ball. She was glad for the company, because there was no more vulnerable feeling than to be in a bathtub, naked and wet. But was there a more glorious feeling than to practically feel each tightly wound muscle individually loosen?

Becca closed her eyes and let her mind wander. It went to its most natural place: Hudson Walker with his chiseled features and slow-spreading smile, irreverence showing in his expression. Before she could fantasize about him for the most fleeting of seconds, Jessie's visage appeared, clouding her image of Hudson, coming between them now as she had so long ago. Absently Becca picked up a washcloth and ran it over her neck.

Twenty years earlier Becca had been asked by McNally about the last time she'd seen Jessie Brentwood, had been quizzed like all the others about any and all details they could remember about Jessie the week before she ran away. "Ran away," Becca repeated to herself now. She'd believed that's what had happened to Jessie. Even with all the speculation, she'd truly believed Jessie had just run away. It was the most logical explanation. She'd done it before; everyone knew it. Jessie made no secret of the fact.

But if the bones in the maze were Jessie's then she hadn't run away. She'd been at St. Lizzie's all along. Just under the ground. At the feet of the Madonna. Something had happened there that had ended her life.

Becca's brows furrowed. She didn't like this new perspective. What *did* she know about Jessie? She clearly remembered the last time they'd spoken. It had been at school. And it had been about Hudson. Jessie had been standing on the front steps of the school as Becca headed outside, juggling her backpack as she'd shouldered open the glass doors to the gray day beyond.

"Hey, Becca," Jessie said, kind of quietly, thoughtfully.

Becca had looked at her askance. She and Jessie weren't exactly close friends, though they ran in the same crowd. And because Jessie was Hudson's, Becca always felt a bit awkward around her. They hadn't ever taken their friendship to any meaningful level. In fact, they rarely spoke directly to one another. She waved a hand in the general direction she was heading. "I'm . . . late . . ."

"I know something," Jessie said. "Something I shouldn't, maybe." She was eyeing Becca closely, as if waiting for something to happen. A gust of wind blew up, teasing Becca's hair, making her aware that no one else was around. The walkways and lawns leading up to the front doors were empty, not a soul visible.

"What do you mean?" she'd asked and tried not to notice how eerie the late afternoon sky was—steel gray clouds with burgeoning purple bellies hanging low in the sky.

"Sometimes you have enemies you never even knew existed. Sometimes they're right in front of you."

"I'm not sure . . . what you mean . . ." Becca felt a jolt, slightly alarmed. It was as if Jessie were reading into her mind about her feelings for Hudson.

"And sometimes they're not," she said abruptly, looking away, across the parking lot, her gaze off to a middle distance that probably had nothing to do with the dented Chrysler parked too close to a fire hydrant. "I just have this feeling, you know. Like a storm's coming. Do you ever think that way? That you get feelings and they come true?"

"A storm is coming," Becca said, glancing up at the dark heavens and playing dumb. Didn't Jessie know about Becca's visions? Hadn't someone told her?

Jessie skewered her with a disbelieving look. "Not *that* kind of storm, Becca. You know what I mean."

Oh, God. Fear curled through Becca's blood. "I, uh, I've gotta go. Really."

Jessie didn't look away, though her hair blew over her face. "Don't be too trusting, Becca," she warned. "Watch your back."

Becca had practically run down the steps away from Jessie.

And then Jessie had disappeared. Mysteriously. The runaway back on the road. Or so everyone had thought, including Becca. But Becca's parents had become overly frightened and even more protective of their daughter. They'd never really known Jessie; Becca and she hadn't been that close of friends. But they knew Jessie was a runaway and they seemed to think Becca might have picked up some of Jessie's ways because they constantly checked to make sure Becca was happy after Jessie's disappearance.

Happy . . .

Now Becca thought back to her latest vision. How Jessie had mouthed something to her, something Becca couldn't hear. How she'd been at the edge of a cliff, her toes over the rim, how she'd been frozen in time, the same age as when she'd disappeared. Was that because that's how Becca remembered her? Or because that's the age she'd been when she died . . .

The wind threw the birch branches at her window, clattering and tapping. The radio switched songs and Rick Springfield started singing about how he wished that he had Jesse's girl. Becca's mouth twisted at the irony. How she'd wished that she had Jessie's boy.

And how she wished that she still had Jessie's boy's *baby*.

She pushed that thought aside with an almost physical effort. No good would come from her wishing and hoping for the past to realign itself. It just wasn't going to happen.

The electricity switched on, bedroom lamps showing through the open door to the bathroom. Climbing out of the tub, Becca had to nudge Ringo off the mat with a wet toe to make some room. She toweled herself off and grabbed up her underclothes, jeans, and a blue sweater. Padding into the bedroom, she pulled on socks and a pair of sturdy hiking boots. Without really knowing what she intended to do, she grabbed her raincoat and keys and purse and headed to her car, throwing a look toward the stand of firs on her way out.

There was nothing there. No malevolent force. Just branches wavering in the brisk wind, emitting a sad soughing filled with regret.

Becca climbed in the Jetta and headed away from the condo into a heavy sky that was growing blacker by the minute. She glanced at her watch. Four o'clock. Dark as sin already.

Becca told herself she was going out to grab a coffee or a soda as she headed west from her Portland condo. But she passed every coffee shop and fast-food restaurant as night crept up on her. Her hands tightened upon the wheel, her gaze glued to the wet pavement, shimmering in the beams from her headlights. She passed cars and trucks driving in the opposite direction, turned off the main road as if pulled by an unseen force, because not once, consciously, did she admit to herself where she was headed, where she was drawn.

She drove almost unerringly to St. Elizabeth's campus. It was surrounded by chain-link construction fencing, and yellow signs warned interlopers to stay off the premises. But there was a gap in the fencing where vehicles came and went. An opening no one seemed to feel the need to repair. She drove through as if she owned the place and parked at the far side of the lot, closest to the maze. Behind the front building she could see where demolition was in progress. Several large machines with scoops and claws sat idle while rubble lay in untidy piles, one such pile as tall as the cab of a small crane.

Yellow crime scene tape flapped angrily at the entrance to the maze. It had been long enough that Becca suspected the tape had just been left, that it served no purpose any longer. And even if it were still in play, she didn't much care. She wanted to see the site where the human remains had been found.

Jessie's remains . . .

She'd scarcely taken two steps into the maze when she was slapped in the face by a wet branch. She cried out in surprise, then cringed to hear her voice hang in the air. So much for quietly going about her business. Even with the intermittent whistle of the wind, her half scream had seemed loud.

As if in answer to her, the clouds opened up and poured rain that quickly turned to hail, slamming down in a violent rush. Becca stumbled forward, yanking her parka hood over her head, her boots squishing into the water-saturated earth. Late February and miserable. She reached a fork in the maze and turned left, hurrying, wind gleefully tossing precipitation at her face, the ground white with hail beneath her feet.

Three turns later and she was lost. Becca stopped cold, shivering, surprised by her mistake. In high school she would've known the way blindfolded. Now she was uncertain which direction to take. The weather and darkness hadn't helped, but she'd been sure she would find the Madonna.

Mentally she retraced her route and realized she might have erred on the second turn. Holding on to her coat from the snatching fingers of the branches and skeletal berry vines, she reversed her route at the second turn and headed back inside just as the hail stopped, turning to a thick, pelting rain.

Jessie had been a master at the maze. Flirtatious and dangerous, in her way, she would crook her finger and invite the guys in their group to come after her. They ran like dogs with their tongues hanging out. But it had all been for Hudson's benefit, her need to make him jealous, though it hadn't really worked. Hudson was cool. Tolerant. Maybe disinterested. Jessie's machinations hadn't provoked him in the least and Becca had admired him for it. Loving him had been so easy.

Love, she questioned now, holding back a long branch. A fifteen-year-old's love that lingered year after year. Could you even call it that? Love? Maybe it was more like obsession. Or habit. Or . . .

She heard a twig snap behind her. Like in the movies. The signal for danger. But there was no one in the maze but her. She was sure of it.

Are you? *Are you?*

She was frozen on the balls of her feet, listening. Was there someone there? Some*thing* there?

After a few moments of listening to the wind soughing through the branches and her own rapid-fire heartbeat, Becca relaxed a bit, forging onward, ears attuned.

Wet shoes slipping slightly, she rounded a final corner and was suddenly in the center of the maze with its ghostly white statue of the Madonna. The ground was torn up and

Becca shivered at sight of the large, wet hole at Mary's feet and the statue tipped on its side, pressed into the dirt and covered with white pellets of hail. Were the bones that had been buried here really Jessie's?

She gazed through a curtain of rain at the remains of the grave and shuddered inwardly to think that Jessie had been buried in this dark hole all these years. Or had she? Sometimes Becca felt sure the body discovered was that of her sometime friend; other times she wondered if she was just looking for a logical explanation to a mysterious disappearance.

Nothing was for certain.

"Help me," the wind seemed to sigh.

She froze.

Surely she was imagining things . . .

Then she felt it; that slight change in the atmosphere.

The hair on the back of her arms lifted. She blinked against the icy rain.

Her head pounded, as if she were about to have another vision, yet she remained awake and alert. Too alert. Anxious. As if she were about to jump out of her skin.

A shadow fell over her and she sensed another presence, something else in the maze with her. Throat tight, she whipped around, bracing herself for another ghostly image. "Jessie?" she whispered.

Wet laurel leaves shivered, moving.

Not ten feet from her.

Becca's mouth opened on a silent scream.

Her heart thundered.

She felt faint and slightly sick.

She expected Jessie to materialize in front of her.

Readied herself for it.

Waited for the ghost to appear.

Moments passed and she counted her heartbeats.

Nothing happened.

The wind dissipated, dying.

The slapping rain seemed to dissolve into mist.

No one was there. Not Jessie . . . no one.

And yet . . .

Becca felt an undeniable presence. Something with a malevolent purpose. Crouching in the thick umbra. Something that wanted to do her harm.

"Who's there?" she demanded, her voice a whisper.

A frigid drop of rain slid onto her collar and down her neck. Shaking as if from a fugue, Becca tried to concentrate on Jessie, but it was impossible. Something was breathing down her neck. Something dangerous. Something threatening.

And then, from the corner of her eye, she saw a looming shadow. Huge. Dark. Threatening. Oh, God. She turned quickly and the beast shrank back. But she felt its eyes on her.

With a cry stuck in her throat, Becca bolted from the maze, racing unheedingly through the shrubbery, feeling tiny branches claw and scratch her face. Feet slipping as she rounded several corners, she ran as if the devil were on her heels, her breath fogging in the air, fear spurring her on.

Who had followed her into the maze?

Not who: What? What had stalked her through the overgrown hedges and berry vines?

Fumbling for her keys in her pocket, she ran on, tearing out of the maze and across the overgrown lawn and potholes of the parking lot to her little Jetta.

She dropped the keys at the door, then scraped her fingers over the broken asphalt as she dived for them. Quaking, dripping rain, she managed to unlock the car. Only when she was inside, throwing the locks with trembling fingers, staring through the partially fogged windows toward the black maze did she feel almost safe.

"Who are you?" she asked the shifting branches dancing and waving in front of her. "Who the hell are you?" She flicked on her headlights and there was nothing there. With shaking arms, she turned the car around and pointed toward the exit. In her rearview mirror a figure emerged from the maze.

Becca hit the accelerator, blinking hard. In that second the image was gone.

But someone was there! Someone had followed her!

Someone who *hated* her.

A sob edged across her lips and she drove down the long, bumpy lane of the campus. A rabbit caught in the headlight's glare hopped quickly through the brambles. Becca sped by. Barely hitting her brakes, she charged into the traffic of the main road, determined to get as far away from St. Lizzie's as possible.

Sometimes it's easy to find them. Sometimes it's child's play.

I watch the taillights of her car disappear into a blanket of rain.

Rebecca, wicked girl, you are predictable. Of course you would come to the maze. Of course you would follow her footsteps.

Frightened, aren't you? You know you're different. That you're one of Them. You sense it, like I sense you.

Have you guessed it yet?

I see you shiver and quake and tremble. I hear you cry out. Do you know I'm here? Watching. Waiting.

Do you know your fate, devil's spawn?

And now you run . . . RUN . . .

Go ahead . . . run as fast as you can, Rebecca.

I watch the taillights of your car disappear as you flee and I can't help but smile through the rain. Your escape is futile and you know it.

I will catch you.

When it is time.

Chapter Seven

"Detective . . ."

Mac, who'd had a telephone pressed to his ear waiting for the county prosecutor to answer, looked up to see Lieutenant Aubrey D'Annibal give him the high sign from his office, a glass-walled cubicle at the end of the squad room. Dropping the phone, Mac headed into the lieutenant's office without a word, and D'Annibal closed the door behind him.

D'Annibal had smooth, silvery white hair, piercing blue eyes, and a love for Armani suits that was paid for by his wealthy wife's substantial trust fund. He was also damn good at his job, and he expected excellence from all members of his staff. Mac watched as he hooked a leg over the corner of his desk and folded his hands together.

Lecture time. Not a good sign.

"Just got off the phone from the lab," he said with only a trace of his West Texas drawl audible. "They're sending PDFs on a couple of pictures of those bones you're so interested in."

"Yeah?" At long last. It had been nearly a week since the body had been located, but the lab had been "backed up."

Which was nothing new. In the meantime, Mac had been forcing himself to be patient.

D'Annibal rubbed his jaw slowly, a gesture that meant he was deliberating on how to deliver his next news. Mac braced himself, and after a moment, the lieutenant said, "You know, I wasn't here when that girl disappeared. I hadn't moved to the great state of Oregon from Texas yet. I was making my way through the ranks, proving myself, following the path, keeping my aim in sight. Meanwhile, you were out here stirring up a heap of trouble for yourself. Claiming murder without a body. Accusing the students at a private school, some of whom were quite well heeled and whose families were well respected, of killing a young girl—a runaway. From what I understand, you were a regular town crier about it all. That about right?"

"There's some truth in there," Mac admitted, though he could feel how rigid the cords in his neck had become.

"You really tore up the turf. Lots of people didn't like your ways. High-handed. Bullish. Misconceived. Obsessive. Lots of words were bandied about. None of them too complimentary."

Mac nodded, wondering how long this was going to take. He, above anyone else, remembered what had come down. And yes, he'd been too gung-ho, too convinced on too little evidence, he thought now, in this glassed-in office that suddenly felt stuffy. "Has the lab nailed down the girl's age from the bones?"

"Give me a moment," D'Annibal said. "I've got to get some things straight. I've got to *hear* a few things from you."

Mac held back his frustration as best he could but was having a helluva time with it. Mentally counting to ten, he asked, "What do you want to hear?"

"I want to hear that you won't go off half-cocked. I want to hear that you won't act like you want to pistol-whip innocent people. I want to *hear* that you'll conduct a proper investigation."

"I've never pistol-whipped anyone, sir." Mac was having difficulty reining in his temper.

"Only with accusations," his boss agreed.

"Oh, hell, what do you want me to say?"

"That if I turn this investigation over to you, Detective, you'll treat it, and everyone you interview, with respect. I don't want some indignant ass-wipe whining to me about police brutality. And I know"—he lifted a palm against Mac's protests—"that you aren't physical. But you're a badger, and I don't want you badgering."

Mac's pulse began a slow pounding and he was vaguely aware of a phone ringing on the other side of the closed door. "You're giving me the investigation?"

The lieutenant hesitated and Mac waited. He couldn't believe it. Could—not—believe—it. After all the sideways looks, hidden sneers, and snickering, the case was coming back his way. Maybe they didn't believe the remains were Jessie's, but Mac felt it in his marrow.

"It's yours if you want it." He didn't wait for a response. "I think we both know your answer."

Jesus! About time. "Is that all?" Mac asked, anxious to get to work. Anxious to pick up where he'd been forced to leave off, so many years ago.

"Not quite. I've been reminding you about all this for a reason. There was some . . . resistance to putting you on the case again, and information was deliberately withheld until a decision was made."

It wasn't like D'Annibal to tiptoe, but then Mac could imagine what kind of meetings went on behind closed doors concerning putting him in charge of this case. He decided to push the issue a bit.

"How old was the deceased when she died? Do we know that yet?" he asked.

"About sixteen."

"Those remains are Jezebel Brentwood's," Mac said. *I'll eat a kangaroo if they're not.*

"No corroborating evidence." But D'Annibal didn't sound like he disagreed. This was the first time the lieutenant had acknowledged that Mac might be right. Since he'd come to the Laurelton PD, like everyone else in the department, D'Annibal had been interested first in keeping Mac's hopes in line, second in entertaining the myth that sixteen-year-old Jezebel Brentwood had simply run away. But these remains had revealed another, more obvious answer—the same one Mac had expounded for years: Jessie Brentwood had been killed.

"How long have those bones been in the ground?" Mac asked.

"More than ten years, probably closer to twenty."

"Then they're Jessie's until I hear differently," Mac told him flatly.

"All you have to do is prove it."

"Piece of cake." He expected another lecture about running on assumptions rather than facts, but the lieutenant surprised him by keeping his own counsel. But D'Annibal had more to say, apparently, because his chin rubbing had turned into a vigorous buff and polish.

"There's something else . . ." More rubbing. Mac wondered if the man was going to wear off his top epidermal layer. He waited, watching D'Annibal go through his own mental decision-making, weighing the pros and cons of telling Mac whatever piece of news this was. Must be a doozy, Mac decided, just as the lieutenant drew a deep breath and said, "Nobody wanted to tell you as you were so convinced this was your old case, so we kept it under wraps till we could determine if these bones really belonged to the missing Brentwood girl. We still don't know, but with the dates and the location of the remains . . . well . . ."

"You think my obsession might have some credence now," Mac hurried him along. Enough with the disclaimers. "What is it?"

"There was a second, smaller skeleton mixed with the bones of the first."

"Smaller . . ." Mac grew sober. "A baby?"

The lieutenant nodded. "She was pregnant when she was killed. If it's your girl, Jessie, she probably knew. ME says she was about four months along."

Becca didn't sleep for nearly a week.

Her dreams were peppered with visions of Jessie and Hudson and some dark shape that loomed above them all.

"Nuts," she told her dog one afternoon. "That's what's happening, you know. I'm going damned nuts." It was after five by the time she finished working on new contracts for the law firm, making the changes where indicated and sending them via e-mail to the administrator at Bennett, Bretherton, and Pfeiffer, checking her e-mail one last time before glancing outside where a few slanting rays of sunshine were actually permeating the clouds. "A good sign," she said to Ringo as she made her way to the kitchen and checked his water bowl.

She punched Renee's number into her cell phone and listened to the series of rings, then Renee's voice saying to leave a number and she'd get back to her. "Renee, hi, it's Becca. You said you were going to call me, after you got back from your weekend at the beach? Since I haven't heard from you, I thought maybe I should call you instead. Anyway, give me a call when you can. Bye."

She clicked off and tossed her phone onto the table. "Dumb message," she said to Ringo. "I sound like I'm desperate for friendship. And now I'm explaining myself to you. I *really* have to get a life."

It wasn't like she really wanted to connect with Renee, especially as she was Hudson's sister, but Becca didn't like this sense of being in limbo, either.

She clipped Ringo's leash onto his collar and took him outside for a walk. For once the rain and wind were on hold and the pavement was dry. They walked to the park, only a few blocks away. The oak and maple trees were still bare, only a few other pedestrians on the cement pathways intersecting the thick grass and shrubs. A bicycle passed by, the rider balancing a cup of coffee from the local Starbucks, wires running from his ears to the iPod located in his jacket pocket. Ringo took care of business, tangled leashes with two pugs being walked by a teenaged girl, then barked at squirrels who had the audacity to run in front of him.

But they didn't encounter any dark figures in trench coats, no looming, indistinct embodiments of evil as they returned to the condo.

It was dark and threatening rain again by the time Becca unlocked the door to the condo and stepped inside. Ringo danced wildly to be fed while Becca checked all her doors, windows, and locks before measuring out a half cup of dog food. Then she double-checked the front door and slider to her small patio area. She was not only desperate, she was becoming obsessive/compulsive, she thought. Ever since the discovery of the bones, and the meeting with the old gang, and seeing Hudson again, then later feeling spooked at St. Elizabeth's, she seemed trapped in this loop that kept circling back to high school and whatever had happened to Jessie Brentwood.

Her cell phone buzzed on the table, moving itself across the hard surface. Becca snatched it up and saw that it was Renee's number. "Hello?"

"Oh, hey, Becca. I got your message. I've just been so busy since I got back from the beach. Swamped at work and . . . well, dealing with some personal stuff. Sorry I didn't call."

"Not a problem. You just gave me the feeling there was something you wanted to talk about."

"Yeah . . ." Renee hesitated and Becca sensed she was in

a serious debate with herself. She braced herself for something about Hudson, but when Renee let the silence grow to an uncomfortable level, Becca finally had to speak first, "I went to St. Elizabeth's, to the maze the other night."

"Really?" Renee sounded flabbergasted. "Why?"

"Good question. I can't really explain it." *So why try? And why to Renee?*

"So . . . was it still taped off?"

Becca nodded, flipped on the switch to the fireplace. Within seconds flames began licking the ceramic logs. "Yeah, I went around the tape. There was no one there, not at the maze or anywhere near the old school. It was almost dark. Well, it was dark by the time I got there."

"You wanted to see the . . . grave?" Renee asked.

"I guess I went up there to check things out, see for myself . . . maybe even to, I don't know, commune with Jessie." The minute the words were out, she regretted them.

"And did you? Commune with her?" There was less sarcasm in Renee's tone than she expected.

Becca thought of the malevolent presence she'd encountered and seen. Had it been real? Or a product of her visions? "I don't know."

"You want to meet for coffee?" Renee asked suddenly. "Or a glass of wine? I'd really like to talk to you, in person, and I'm heading back to the beach this evening."

Becca considered. "I could meet you."

"Say in about an hour? At Java Man?"

"I'll be there."

Java Man was a coffee shop–cum–wine bar not far from Blue Note. Becca changed into jeans, boots, and a heavy jacket with a hood and was on her way to the meeting spot within the half hour. She beat Renee by a good fifteen minutes, checking in her rearview mirror often, just in case.

Just in case, what? Some unknown demon predator is stalking you? Some evil person or beast, the presence you felt in the maze? Get real, Rebecca. Pull yourself together. Just because you had a damned vision . . .

"Stop it," she warned herself aloud. She could not fall apart; not now. Not when she was meeting Hudson's sister, a woman she wasn't even sure she liked. Snapping on the radio, she listened to songs from the eighties, which was a bad idea. High school. Jessie. Hudson. Old emotions came flooding back in a rush. Angrily, she switched to NPR and some talk radio about the environment.

Safe.

Becca ordered a glass of merlot and a small plate of fruit, cheese, and crackers, then seated herself at a table with a view of the hand-painted dishware, candles, and assorted knickknacks. She wasn't a person who collected things. Her place was remarkably bare as, without fully realizing it, she'd systematically removed almost all traces of Ben. There were a few items still around: a photograph he'd taken of her on a weekend jaunt, the needlepoint footstool from his grandmother he'd forgotten to grab when he left, a gray parka hung in the laundry room she sometimes threw on to battle the elements.

She glanced around to find the barista cleaning the countertop of the bar. Several couples sat over coffee, and a group of three women in their thirties huddled around a small table sipping wine. Jazz floated from speakers mounted over the wine rack, and a few glasses clinked.

Renee came bustling inside under the protection of an umbrella that the wind seemed determined to snatch away. But her grip was hard and she snapped the umbrella shut and looked around, briefly running a hand through her wind-tossed hair. When her eyes met Becca's she lifted her chin in acknowledgment, then went to the counter and ordered herself a cup of black coffee.

"Back to the beach, huh?" Becca greeted her as Renee brought her cup to her table.

She gave Becca a look as she scooted in her chair. "Tim

and I keep telling ourselves that we want to work things out, but I don't know. I've been staying at a beach house almost every weekend, trying to put things into perspective. Jessie's not the only story I've been working on. I started on this small-town story—you know about the largest Sitka spruce tree in the world? The one outside of Seaside that recently broke apart in a storm?"

Becca nodded. Sipped her wine. "I remember seeing it on the news."

"People have been sending me pictures from their lives, their parents' lives, their grandparents . . . all of them around the tree. Really great photos. Anyway, it's a piece for the local paper but it could get picked up as a human interest piece in national papers. You never know." She twirled her coffee cup slowly, spinning it by its handle with one finger. Becca sensed that Renee was prattling on as a means to build up some courage to talk about what she really wanted to discuss, so she just let her go on.

Eventually, Renee wound down with, "The whole area has a kind of small-town mentality, which has been great. It's hell staying at the house with Tim now, so I do it as little as possible. I wish he'd just move out." She rubbed her temple with two fingers as if just talking about her husband gave her a headache.

"This isn't why you wanted to talk to me," Becca said into the sudden silence. She pushed her cheese and fruit plate toward Renee. "Have some."

She waved off the offering. "Got a weird stomach thing going on. I know, I know, coffee's not good, either, but I want to stay awake; I've been having a little trouble sleeping at night. All this stuff with Tim. I have to be sharp to drive to the coast. There's been snow in the pass and I don't do chains. Period."

"Uh-huh."

Renee took a breath, held it a moment, then released it slowly. "You know . . . it's . . . kind of surprising . . . what you can stumble across. Like fate's intervened. I'm not trying to sound like Tamara," she added quickly. "It's just, working on Jessie's story and then having that skeleton appear at St. Lizzie's." She hesitated. "It would be nice to have a source in the police department to find out, y'know?"

Becca nodded.

Renee made a face. "Sometimes . . . well, this is going to sound strange because I really do want to write that story, but sometimes I wonder if we should really open Pandora's box. Maybe we should let bad things lie. Go with the Sitka spruce nostalgia and leave digging into graves alone."

"You were the one who called the meeting at Blue Note," Becca reminded her in surprise.

"I know. I'm not giving up." She ran her hands through her short, dark hair. "I don't know why I'm going back and forth on this." She switched gears and, frowning at herself, picked up a small wedge of Edam cheese. "I guess I can try this." She took an experimental bite. "So tell me more about your trip to the maze."

In for a penny, in for a pound.

Becca dutifully described her trip to St. Elizabeth's, including the moment when she felt there was something there, something . . . if not evil, certainly not good. Renee listened attentively and Becca finished with, "I don't want to sound crazy or anything. It was raining and hailing and windy, and I was probably more susceptible than usual. But it was more than that. I really felt like I wasn't alone."

"Did you think Jessie was there?"

Becca shot her a look to determine whether she was patronizing her, but Renee appeared totally serious as she blew across her cup, then took a swallow of coffee. "No. Not Jessie."

"Who, then?"

"No one, I guess. No one I saw, anyway. It was just a feeling, and maybe I was just too susceptible. The atmosphere: the dark, the maze, the Madonna. It spooked me."

"You don't have to make excuses," Renee said. "I believe

you. I've had some experiences that weren't . . . explainable."
She glanced to her side, to make certain the trio of women
on their second glasses of wine weren't eavesdropping. They
were too caught up in their own conversation to give a second glance Becca and Renee's way.

"Like what?" Becca asked, prodding.

Renee hesitated. "I know we've never been the closest of
friends. Maybe that's more my fault than yours, but . . . this
should be all in the past now." She narrowed her gaze,
seemed to want to say something again, then thought better
of it. Finally, she added, "Sometimes I have a feeling of persecution. Like someone's after me. But then, I've written a
few articles that have really pissed some people off, so
maybe they are!"

She laughed and Becca saw the resemblance between
Renee and Hudson's humor for the first time. "Do you think,
like Tamara, that Jessie might still be alive?" Becca asked.

"Oh, no. Those are Jessie's bones," she stated positively,
her demeanor instantly sobering as she polished off the
cheese. "I'm sure she's dead. Long dead." She peered at
Becca. "I was told she was."

"By who?"

"A crazy old woman who believes she can read the future." She smiled faintly.

"Oh." Becca watched her slowly spin her cup again. "You
think it could have been just an accident?"

As if suddenly remembering what her cup was for, Renee
brought it to her lips and took a long swallow. "Maybe Evangeline was right. Maybe Jessie was planning to run away.
She said bad things were coming her way. Trouble. She wasn't
kidding around, you know, like she sometimes did. Well, like
she did a lot, actually. But this time I don't think she was joking. She meant it. She said, 'Trouble's going to find me.'"

"She said that to you?"

Renee nodded and Becca realized she was revealing one

of her last, if not her very last, conversations with Jessie. "You told that cop what she said?"

"McNally? Are you kidding? I wasn't going to tell him anything." Renee shook her head at the memory. "I was too freaked. I did say she probably ran away again, because that's what I really thought. I wasn't going to tell them what our last conversation was. I kind of thought it was sacred, at the time. I was sixteen," she reminded Becca with faint irony. "Jessie was my friend and I wanted to protect her, I guess. Her parents were kind of weird. Do you remember?"

Becca shook her head. "Jessie and I were more like acquaintances."

Renee cocked an eyebrow. "You were connected to Tamara the most, right? You were in the class below us . . . ?" She left it as a question because at St. Elizabeth's, like high schools everywhere, students tended to stick with their own classmates as if there were invisible fences between the grades.

"Tamara and I had a class together," Becca said. "We worked on a couple of projects as a team and got to know each other." This was practically a lie, but Becca didn't know whether she could admit that she'd worked hard on that friendship. All so she could be part of their group, so she could be nearer to Hudson. It was all so juvenile and downright embarrassing now! She could even feel her face heating and she took a swig of her water, hoping to hide her reaction.

"Did you like my brother even then?"

Becca opened her mouth to respond, thought better of it, then gave Renee a sideways look. All she saw on Hudson's sister's face was mild interest, so Becca gave her a jerky nod. "Yeah. High school crush." She picked up a small orange slice and bit into it.

"I thought so. Jessie certainly thought so, too, and she believed Hudson returned your feelings. Maybe he did."

"Nothing ever happened between us."

"Not until after high school," Renee agreed. "What about now?"

"What?"

"You still interested?"

"In Hudson?"

"Oh, come on. Don't play dumb."

"I'm really not looking to get involved with anyone right now," she answered carefully. "My experience with men has been . . . less than stellar."

"Kind of a nonanswer," Renee observed, then waved the air as if dismissing the entire subject. "All I'm saying is that I'm not sure Jessie believed that you and Hudson didn't have a thing going in high school. I think she might have retaliated. She certainly tried to stir up Hudson's jealousy, but he doesn't work that way."

"We definitely *didn't* have 'a thing' going. Hudson never even looked at me."

Renee lifted a disbelieving eyebrow, but let the subject go. "You know, Jessie's parents acted . . . really worried . . . I mean, before she disappeared. I'd just been to their house the week before and had dinner and Jessie was acting oddly then, too. More oddly than normal, that is. She must have known she was getting ready to run again, and I think it bothered her, how much it hurt her parents. But she just couldn't help herself. If I have a feeling of persecution now, she *really* had it then. Like something was at her heels and she was trying to keep one step ahead of it."

Becca thought about the feeling that someone was after her at the maze and about the vision of Jessie on the cliff trying to warn her of . . . of what? "Have any idea what it was that was chasing her?"

"God knows. Jessie sure didn't. And her parents didn't. They were in a state over her disappearance, almost as if they knew this time was different. Like they were scared. I saw them when Mac, the detective, was talking to them, and yeah, they were worried sick, but more than that, they were terrified." She shook her head. "And the only thing Jessie said to me—I mean before she disappeared, when she was talking all weird—was that it was about justice, like maybe it was payback for something? I wished I'd quizzed her on it more, but what did I know? She kept saying she had to keep on the move and I thought it was a ruse, like it had been before, a play for attention. That's what Jessie was all about, being the center of the universe. More than most teenagers. Anyway, that's what I've concluded, after thinking about it all these years."

"You think whatever she was running from caught up to her, before she could leave?"

Renee half laughed. "I don't really know what I'm talking about. But I do think those are Jessie's remains. It just makes sense, doesn't it?"

"I guess we'll know soon enough."

"Will we? So maybe they get some DNA. Can they match it to Jessie's?"

"Well, or dental impressions, I suppose. Those are bound to be on record, aren't they?" Becca asked.

Renee shrugged. "And when the police learn, are they going to tell us? Or are we all suspects again? I hate to agree with The Third, but if the case opens up we're all going to be under scrutiny, especially Hudson."

Becca didn't like thinking about that.

Renee drained the rest of her coffee, then shot an assessing look at Becca, as if she were debating on something.

"What?" Becca asked.

"I've been remembering a lot of little things lately. Forcing myself, I guess, at first because of the story, and now, I don't know . . ." She drew a deep breath and expelled it slowly. "I really want that story, but . . . I've gotten these warnings."

"Warnings?"

"From the old woman I mentioned earlier."

"A Tarot reader?"

"Sort of." She seemed about to add something else, then hesitated. "This wasn't Tamara's friend."

"I got that."

"I went to the beach and I was asking about Jessie around Deception Bay. Do you know it?" When Becca shook her head, she said, "It's this little town. Quaint. Kind of . . . tired feeling."

"Why did you go there?"

"The Brentwoods have a house there. I thought maybe that's where Jessie was from? Originally? I was staying around the area anyway, so I started asking questions and I got connected to this psychic lady. But when I met with her, all she did was make me feel like I was angering the gods or something. Seeing her was a mistake. She just played on my fears—fears I didn't know I had."

Becca nodded, waiting for her to go on.

Renee didn't seem to quite know how to proceed, then said, "I know you and Jessie weren't the closest of friends. Maybe because of Hudson, maybe something else, but how well do you remember her? I mean really remember her?"

I saw her in a vision. "She had blond-brown hair—long—and was pretty." Becca finished her wine. "I remember that she dated Hudson and that she was kinda hard to pin down."

"Like you."

"Not like me," Becca said quickly.

"Maybe not exactly. But sort of, don't you think?"

Where is this coming from? "Jessie was secretive and remote. I hope I'm not like that. Do you think I'm like that?"

"No . . . I can't quite put my finger on it." Shrugging, she said, "Jessie always had a blithe remark. A throwaway comment. You couldn't get close to her. Yeah, she was full of secrets, but then she could be so blunt, too. And Vangie was right that Jessie just knew things. She was precognitive. She had feelings about things and they came true. A number of times."

"Like a feeling of persecution?"

"Well, maybe . . . and you had those visions, didn't you?" Renee reminded her and Becca felt her face grow hot.

"I'd hoped people had forgotten."

"Maybe they have. But at the time it was the kind of thing that ran like wildfire through the school. A rumor with a life of its own. I never knew just how much was fact or fiction."

"I used to have them," Becca answered slowly. The vision of Jessie practically burned behind her eyeballs, but she couldn't bring it up. Not now. Not yet. Not until she understood Renee's interest.

"Not anymore?"

"No."

She inclined her head. "Well, anyway, sound like a nut job, don't I? I hear myself talking like there's some—evil out to get me, and can't believe I just said that. Forget it. This whole thing with finding Jessie's bones is making me jump at shadows and find meaning in things that aren't there. Dumb. Oh, screw this. I need a glass of wine." Scooting out her chair, she looked disgusted with herself, then walked to the counter and paid for a glass of Chardonnay. Taking a sip as she returned, Renee said, "That's more like it."

"Was this the 'odd' something you wanted to talk about?"

"Yeah." She drank half her glass and shook her head. "I can't tell you how all of this . . . whatever the hell it is has taken its toll. I'm jumping at shadows, second-guessing everything. And looking over my shoulder, like someone's following me."

"That's how I felt in the maze," Becca said.

"Oh, right." She paused. "Maybe we're both just letting atmosphere take over reason."

Becca thought about that and was about to confess that she'd had a vision of Jessie on the very day that she'd learned about the grisly discovery at St. Elizabeth's, but she didn't get the chance. Renee tossed back another gulp of wine, glanced at her watch, and scowled. "Oh, God, it'll be almost ten when I get there if I don't leave now." She swept up her purse and got to her feet in one swift motion. "Keep in touch," she said brightly, but there was something about the way she hurried through the door that made Becca think Renee had no intention of following her own words.

What the hell was it about Rebecca Ryan Sutcliff? Renee asked herself as she punched the accelerator of her Camry and slid through an amber light just before it turned red. She was headed west, ever west, merging onto Sunset Highway, a section of Highway 26.

You're running away, her mind insisted over the pain of a headache that was pounding at the base of her skull. "No," she answered herself aloud as she flipped on her blinker and passed a yokel in an ancient truck that refused to go over forty, a truck not too many years newer than the pickup her father used to drive. She wasn't running *away* from anything, she was running *to* what promised to be a new life; one that didn't include her husband Tim and the *Valley Star.*

What a two-bit rag. It kinda matched with her two-bit husband and her two-bit life. Well, it wasn't good enough. None of it. Not now, not when she knew the brass ring was finally within her reach.

She'd always been looking for a story, no, make that *the* story that would propel her to the big time, and thanks to Jessie Brentwood, Renee was about to make that leap. No one was going to stop her. Not a whining husband who had lost most of her inheritance in the stock market, nor an editor who couldn't see her talents.

And she wasn't going to let strange mumbo-jumbo predictions and a feeling of persecution stop her, either. And what had she been thinking when, outside Blue Note, she asked Becca if they could get together sometime and talk things over? What had she expected from Hudson's ex-girlfriend? Just because she kind of reminded Renee of Jessie—probably because of Hudson—didn't mean she had any answers. Worse,

Becca seemed to have her own problems dealing with Jessie's disappearance.

She slowed to sixty because of the drizzle and the fact that she really couldn't afford another speeding ticket. That was the trouble, Renee thought, the rest of the world was cruising along at fifty-five and she was revved up to ninety. Sometimes it seemed that she was dragging everyone through life with her and they were all limp, dead weight.

The rain poured down in earnest and she cranked up the speed of her squeaking wipers. They slapped away the drops and Renee wondered again about Becca. Hudson, it seemed, was taken with her all over again. Oh, yeah. Renee had witnessed it the other night at Blue Note. No big surprise that they were hooking up again, though Renee didn't understand it.

Becca was pretty enough. Streaked hair, light brown with pale highlights, large hazel eyes that hovered between green and gray, and a smile that showed off teeth that weren't quite straight, probably even a little sexy. Her cheekbones were prominent, her eyebrows arched, and she had one of those long Audrey Hepburn necks. She was definitely his type. He always went for the blondish, mysterious-looking chicks.

A flaw, in Renee's opinion. But then her twin had many.

The needle of her speedometer hit seventy-five, her tires hydroplaning on the slick asphalt before she noticed and slowed again. It was as if she couldn't get to the damned beach fast enough. She checked her rearview mirror, afraid she might have blown past a cop and sure enough, another car was bearing down on her, one with bright headlights.

Great.

She slowed, not by braking, but by taking her foot off the gas until she was going a lawful fifty-three miles an hour and the car behind her slowed. Probably to run her plates.

This was just getting better and better, as the Camry belonged to Tim. She steeled herself, practiced her smile and "Oh, dear me, Officer" routine, had her excuses all in a row, but no red and blue lights began to streak the night, no siren screamed at her to pull over. If anything, the vehicle behind her just hung back. Maybe he hadn't clocked her and was waiting for her to speed up.

Screw that!

She pulled into the right-hand lane and sure enough, the guy following her did, too, tucking in behind a compact.

Not a cop, then.

Or at least not a cop interested in her.

No lights. No siren.

Maybe just her imagination, her sense of persecution. She plugged an old Springsteen CD in and watched as the compact swung off the highway at Hillsboro. Another few miles, past North Plains and Laurelton, and the car behind her just kept coming. She sped up, he sped up, she slowed, he slowed.

Goose bumps raised along the back of her arms and she told herself she was being paranoid. No one was following her. No one knew what she was up to. No one could. She hadn't told a soul.

And yet, she was almost certain she was being followed. She glanced to her purse. Pulled her cell phone out of the zipper pocket. If she was going to call someone, it had to be now, before her service cut out as it did in several spots along this stretch of road.

Call who? Say what? That you suspect someone is following you? Why? Because you're digging into the Jezebel Brentwood mystery?

She snorted in disgust and tossed her cell into her purse.

The headache was getting to her. The impending divorce was getting to her. All the talk about Jessie was getting to her. And that strange prediction from the old lady at Deception Bay—that was *really* getting to her. The thought that someone was out to do her harm was her constant and worrisome companion.

"It's bunk," she told herself as the CD played and the wipers slapped away the rain. "Bullshit. Nothing more."

But she knew better.

Her teeth sank into her lip and she swallowed hard.

Payback?

Justice?

For what?

What have I done?

"Mother Mary, help me." Renee sketched the sign of the cross over her chest, a movement she hadn't practiced since her senior year at St. Elizabeth's, but the comfort she once had found in murmuring a quick prayer now eluded her, reminding her only of the bones that had been found at the base of the statue of the Madonna.

She glanced in her mirror again and the trailing vehicle's headlights seemed brighter than before, more intense.

"It's no one," she muttered under her breath as another obscure Springsteen song drifted through the speakers. Renee barely noticed. Her gaze was split between the rain-spattered windshield and the rearview mirror that burned bright headlights back into her eyes. "Bastard," she muttered.

She'd lose whoever it was in the mountains. Didn't want anyone knowing where she was going, that she had screwed up her courage and planned to visit the old hag of a fortune teller again. That she intended to learn more about her fate and what the woman knew, if anything, about Jessie.

For the love of God, she was starting to think like Tamara, and that was scary. Damned scary.

She glanced at the headlights in the mirror again and set her jaw. She wasn't going to spend the next two hours worrying about him. Or her. If they were following her, they were in for a race.

Renee stepped on it.

Her Camry shot forward to the foothills of the Coast Range, where anyone, even a reporter for a half-rate newspaper, could disappear in the twisting canyons, inky tunnels, and rising mist.

Chapter Eight

Motive, Mac thought with dark satisfaction. *Motive.*

It was late. There was no one in this part of the building but the janitor, who was down the hall singing a medley of Elvis hits off-key and with replacement words when he forgot the lyrics, which was every third line. Mac listened to a butchered version of "Can't Help Falling in Love" while he sifted through the evidence found buried near the Madonna statue.

He knew it all by memory, practically by Braille, he'd passed the pieces between his fingers so often, but he kept feeling he'd learn something new if he just kept at it.

. . . Wise men say, only fools rush in . . . but I keep keeping myself away from you . . .

"But I can't help falling in love with you," Mac muttered, his satisfaction still in place. Jessie Brentwood had been pregnant. Okay, correction: the remains in the grave revealed the victim had been pregnant, and Mac fervently believed those remains belonged to Jessie Brentwood. If all that was true, then Mac finally had a motive for Jessie's disappearance and murder: one of the Preppy Pricks didn't want to be a daddy.

That's what had been hard to come up with at the time of the girl's disappearance. Motive. Mac had sensed so much more than what those young bastards were telling him, but he had no proof . . . and no motive. An argument with her teen boyfriend—the Walker kid—hadn't been enough. Now, thinking back, he wondered why he'd been so sure, why he'd always been, when the evidence had been so slim.

He'd just known something had happened. Known it in the marrow of his bones. Felt it. Lived it. But couldn't prove it.

Maybe now . . . maybe . . . now . . .

And the case was his.

Finally.

The small pile in front of him contained bits of leaves, several cigarette butts, disintegrating candy wrappers, an indistinguishable piece of white plastic, and a small jackknife. The knife appeared to be the murder weapon, as there was a nick along one of the vic's ribs, indicating she was stabbed at least once. They were not able to lift prints from the knife; it had been in the ground too long. The lab was working on DNA from the bone marrow, but unless they got a match from someone in their database, there was no way of identifying the remains by that method. If these bones were adoptee Jezebel Brentwood's, that would mean they were looking for her biological parents, who could be anywhere, or a sibling or other relative, and that they would also have to be in the system. Mac had made contact with the Brentwoods, who had assured him they knew nothing about Jessie's biological parents. They'd been less than thrilled to talk to him after his bullish investigative tactics years earlier, and so for now, he was leaving them alone.

But the baby's bones—if they weren't too degraded—now, that was another matter. If DNA could be extracted, or even a blood type discovered and one of those damned Preppy Pricks turned out to be the father . . . He smiled to himself. What was it they said? Something about revenge being best when served up cold. Hell, this case was twenty years cold. Damned well freezing. And yes, revenge was already tasting sweet.

Twenty fucking years of taking crap.

And now, he was about to be vindicated.

Eat that, Sandler, he thought, still hearing his latest partner's taunts. He couldn't wait to prove to her that he'd been right all along.

But there was something else that bothered him.

Mac picked up the note from the technician that stated there was an anomaly with the bone structure of both the adult and infant's skeletons. A bone burr. "Anomaly," he muttered for about the hundredth time. He'd called the tech, who'd been rushed and hard to pin down.

"Her bottom rib is extra, more like a partial rib, and it's fused to the one above it. I've never seen anything quite like it," the tech with a slight Mideastern accent had told him.

"Well, that might help us identify her if there's an X-ray somewhere . . . ?" Mac said somewhat hurriedly, sensing the tech was about to hang up. "Is it from an injury?"

"The baby's, too?" The tech practically sneered. "More like the bottom rib is an extra. A spare."

"So it's genetic."

"You're a genius, you know that?"

Mac ignored the jibe. "Don't women have extra ribs anyway? One more on either side than men?"

"Yes," the tech said with extreme patience. "Call this an extra extra rib, then, and it's only on one side. Some kind of birth defect." *Click!*

Looking at the picture now, it was hard to tell. The dental impressions hadn't helped, either, because Mac had learned from Jessie's adoptive parents that Jessie was one of those lucky people who never had any problem with her teeth. The parents admitted they never took her to the dentist. Mac thought that could be considered child abuse, in some circles, but the lab techs said the victim's teeth were "cavity-less." Which, in a roundabout route, gave more weight to the fact that the remains could be Jessie's.

There were no personal items left at the scene. No purse. No wallet. But then a lot of years had transpired in between, and this, too, was actually consistent with proving the bones belonged to Jessie. At the time of her disappearance, her parents said that she hadn't taken her purse from the house, which she had every other time she'd run away. This had fueled Mac's belief that she'd been harmed or killed, that she hadn't left of her own volition.

Something had happened to Jezebel Brentwood, and he was even more certain now than ever that that something was murder.

"One of the Preppy Pricks stabbed her to death," Mac said. "That's what happened."

. . . we're caught in a trap . . . I can't walk out . . . because I'm all about you maybe . . .

"Because I love you too much, baby. Jesus." Mac scowled down the hallway. Was it too much to ask to get the words right? *Was it?*

Maybe he should just go home. There was nothing further to come up with tonight. He was tired and losing patience. The only reason he was staying was because there was nothing at home. His ex-wife had custody of their only son, Levi, and though Mac got the kid most weekends, now that he was at the preteen stage, he'd started making some of his own plans and even the weekends were iffy. In some ways that was fine, as Mac's hours could be pretty unpredictable. But lately it had just left him with empty time he couldn't fill outside of work. And the niggling feeling that he wasn't doing as much as he could as a dad, that Levi might be headed down a wrong path, though none of his attempts at father-son talks had gotten anywhere. It was as if the kid were stonewalling him. Not a good sign. He'd brought it up to his ex, and Connie's exact words had been: "So what d'ya expect, Super-Dad? It's not as if you've been such a constant influence on him." When Mac had started to argue, she'd cut him off with, "And don't, I mean do *not* give me any BS about your job and long hours. Other cops have time for their kids and wives."

This weekend already looked bad. Levi was waffling and had already mumbled about a sleepover at Zeno's—was that a made-up name? Mac had never heard of the kid. But Connie had.

Lucky for him, he had a whole list of interviewees coming up. The Preppy Pricks and their girls.

Gathering up his things, he heard . . . *come on let's rock . . . everybody let's rock . . . everybody in the whole cell block, was dancin' to the jailhouse rock . . .*

As he pushed through the door Mac tried to find fault with the lyrics, but they seemed all right. Maybe because the guy was cleaning out a police station, a jailhouse of his own. Maybe that was the key.

. . . *Jimmy Jannie Jerry and the slide trombone, da da da da da da on the xylophone . . .*

"Good God." Mac headed into another rain-soaked night.

The day after she'd chased ghosts at St. Elizabeth's and had a drink with Renee, Becca quit work in the early afternoon. She'd gotten a call from Elton Pfeiffer, one of the senior partners at the law firm and a very real reason Becca was glad to be working from home. Elton, in his late sixties, still considered himself a ladies' man. Thrice divorced with a red Porsche, condo on the coast, and unlimited supply of Viagra if his secretary could be believed, he'd asked Becca out several times and even tried to kiss her once outside when she'd brought some papers into his office to sign.

It had been late, the glassed-in office on the twenty-second floor offering a panoramic view of the city lights and dark Willamette River rolling slowly under the Morrison Bridge when Pfeiffer, smelling of scotch, had come up behind her, wrapped his arms around her torso, and dragged her to him, his lips grazing the back of her neck. She'd promptly turned around, pushed hard, and threatened to knee him if he didn't back off. He had, and rather than attempt to sue him for sexual harassment, Becca had turned in her resignation. It had just been so demeaning and damned predictable.

Pfeiffer, rebuffed, had offered to allow her to work from home and she'd leapt at the chance, telling herself it was temporary and a way to have a little freedom, create her own work schedule. The only time she'd been to the office in the past few weeks was to drop off the mermaid baby gift for her pregnant coworker.

Today, Elton Pfeiffer, all business, had needed a real estate contract for a strip mall retyped with some changes. "I've already e-mailed it. Check with Colleen," she said, then hung up.

Though she'd never been great at picking men, Becca had known from the get-go that "El," as he liked to be called, was a person to avoid. She'd never been looking for a father figure and didn't want to start now. In some ways her job was perfect.

But apart from work, she felt stressed and tense, and thought about Hudson. Considered calling him.

Again.

Despite what she'd told Renee.

"Liar," she muttered to herself. Ever since seeing Hudson a week earlier at Blue Note, she'd had trouble keeping her mind off him.

So why not call him? Why not take the initiative? Don't be an insecure schoolgirl. You were friends once. Lovers. You nearly had a child together.

Becca picked up the receiver and put it down three times before, exasperated with herself, she dialed Hudson's number with such speed, it was as if the touch-tone pads were on fire. She was putting way too much energy and emphasis on this one phone call. So she was calling him. So what? She wanted to see him. She was a widow. There was nothing wrong with it.

It rang six times before his answering machine picked up and then the sound of his recorded voice made her breath catch in her lungs. Which was just damned stupid! As soon as the recorder buzzed, she said, "Hi, Hudson. It's Becca Sutcliff. I was thinking . . . (*about you*) . . . about things . . . and I feel a bit unsettled, I guess . . . about the bones found at St. Elizabeth's. I keep thinking . . . (*about you*) . . . about Jessie. If you have some time, maybe we could get together and talk? My number is . . ." She rattled it off quickly, almost breathlessly, then replaced the receiver with a hammering heart. Then she literally banged her forehead against the kitchen wall several times, feeling like an idiot.

"This can't be healthy," she muttered to Ringo, who cocked his head with interest.

Becca changed into her running shoes and threw on a lightweight jacket, then grabbed Ringo's leash and bustled him outside, running her words through her mind again and again as she started jogging. Ringo wanted to stop and sniff every twig, leaf, and blade of grass, but Becca was having none of it. After stopping to allow him to relieve himself, she took off toward the park, the dog at her heels, running hard. Her feet slapped the pavement, water in standing puddles splashed, but she kept at it, feeling her heart begin to pump faster as she passed an apartment building and a few cottages on large lots, original houses built in the twenties or thirties that hadn't yet fallen to the subdivider's axe. She thought about the fact that she'd felt someone watching her, in her apartment, from the bushes, at the maze, someone evil, but she set her jaw. She wouldn't be controlled by fear. Would *not*.

Ringo, sometimes nervous, wasn't on edge. He was enjoying the exercise as much as she.

The air was cool, the afternoon clouds high and wispy as

she rounded the far end of the park and cut through a copse of oaks, nearly running into a kid on a scooter. He swore at her with invectives she'd heard a million times before and she barely broke stride. Up the short hill and down the other side, across a footbridge spanning the creek, then back toward the condo. By now she could feel her muscles working, her rhythm established, the dog running effortlessly with her.

All in all, she ran nearly three miles, and by the time she walked through the front door, her face was flushed and sweat had broken out on her scalp and down her back despite the cool weather.

The first thing she did was check her messages. Zero.

What did you expect? That he'd hear your voice and hit his speed dial to connect with you? Idiot.

Muttering to herself, she showered, then, at a loss, headed for her computer again. She was glad to find that Colleen at Bennett, Bretherton, and Pfeiffer had sent another pile of paperwork. Good. She wanted to lose herself in busywork *forever.*

It was early evening before she lifted her head and wondered when the last time she'd deigned to eat was. Climbing from her chair, she stretched her back, heard it make a disturbing pop, and tried to ignore the words that ran in a circle inside her head: *he hasn't called . . . he hasn't called . . . he hasn't called . . .*

When the phone rang, Becca jumped as if someone had goosed her. She snatched up her desk phone and said, "Hello?"

"Hey, Becca, it's Tamara," her friend greeted her cheerily.

Becca's heart sank.

"Are you busy? I'm going to grab some dinner and wanted to know if you could join."

"Sure," Becca said, hoping she sounded more enthusiastic than she felt. She hadn't forgotten the last time she'd seen Tamara climbing into Hudson's truck. *Big deal. So what? It's nothing.* She might as well get out of the house. Waiting for a phone to ring was too much like being thirteen all over again.

She agreed to meet Tamara at a Mexican restaurant only a couple of miles away, then changed her clothes, fed Ringo, and was heading for the door when the phone rang again.

She recognized the number and her stupid heart started to pound as she picked up.

"Becca?" Hudson's voice greeted her, and a flood of warmth rushed into her veins.

"Hi, there," Becca responded, pretending that her nerves weren't vibrating like electrical wires—there it was again, that back to thirteen thing. Disgusting.

"I saw you called. Heard your message. I've been thinking about things, too, and yeah, I think we should get together, talk things through. It might not be such a bad idea."

Her stupid heart was slamming against her ribs. "Great."

"How about later tonight?"

"Sure, after dinner," she said, frustrated that she'd just made plans with Tamara. "I've got plans earlier, but we could meet somewhere . . . ?"

"How about my place, you remember where it is? The old ranch?"

Like it was yesterday.

"Sure do. I'll be there, sometime after eight," she said and found that her damned hands were shaking as she hung up. "Maybe thirteen's too mature," she confided to the dog as she dashed to the bedroom to change.

She met Tamara at the small restaurant with its faux stucco walls painted as if they were in a Mexican villa, complete with views of an azure ocean and fishing boats. As if here, on the top of Capital in the south hills of Portland, they had a view of the Sea of Cortez. She tried not to keep looking at her watch or rush the meal, but found it hard to enjoy the platter of fajitas they shared or the piped-in peppy, upbeat, almost frantic music.

Not long after the sizzling platter of shrimp and vegetables was served, of course, the subject turned to Jessie.

"Do you think she's dead?" Tamara asked. She was on her second margarita while Becca sipped through the ring of salt on her first.

Becca shrugged. She was tired of the question. Tired of not knowing.

"I think she's just messing with us, like she always did." Tamara spooned shrimp, onions, and peppers into a warm flour tortilla. "Just because Jessie went missing and just because she attended St. Elizabeth's doesn't mean she's dead."

"Then who is?"

"God knows." She licked her fingers. "What did you think of Vangie and Zeke?"

"Déjà vu all over again."

Tamara snorted. Her red hair caught in the lights high overhead as a waiter called out orders in Spanish to a line cook, visible through an open window to the kitchen. "She was sure flashing that ring. Think it's real?"

"She acted like she and Zeke were engaged."

"Wonder if she's gotten over her jealousy?" Tamara lifted a brow. "She sure as hell kept him on a short leash in high school."

Becca remembered Evangeline pining after Zeke in high school, attending every game or wrestling match in which he competed, and there were a lot, as Zeke had been a star, all-league athlete in something . . . baseball?

"Weird, huh, to wait all these years—almost twenty—and still be hung up on the same guy? She should have her head examined, or maybe her palm read, see what's up with her love line."

Becca smiled faintly. "Think it'll show in her palm?"

"Laugh if you will. There's a reason that astrology and alternative religions or beliefs are still around after centuries and centuries. There's something to them."

"You've got Renee believing."

Tamara shook her head. "Renee . . . I don't really know what it is with her, she's the last person I would have thought would look into alternative spirituality. She saw somebody else who spooked her."

"A woman at the beach."

"I don't know what she said that got Renee going, but she's got a lot to deal with. Her job and Tim—the guy's practically a stalker, or so she says. She caught him with someone else and basically told him to take a hike, and now he acts like they have to stay together."

"Through good times and bad."

"She told you?" Tamara gave her a look.

"We had coffee and wine at Java Man."

"Thank God I've never been married. Engaged twice and once I nearly ran off to Reno with a guy, but I managed to regain my senses first."

The people at the next table began arguing about their kid's inability to quit texting messages from her cell phone throughout what the dad insisted was "a family meal. Quality time."

Glancing at their table, Tamara leaned a little closer over the table toward Becca, whispering, "My point is—it's got to be worse when you really go through with it. When you walk down the aisle, exchange I dos and plan for your future and family."

"Been there, done that," Becca murmured.

"Oh, sorry. I'm an idiot."

"It's all right. It never would've worked with Ben."

Tamara raised her margarita to Becca, then took a long swallow. Setting the glass back down, she eyed it critically. "I have to lay off these, they are no good for you, I mean *no good*. I only drink alcohol when I'm really stressed, like I am about all this Jessie stuff. Much as I believe in ghosts, it's a little eerie for everyone to think she might be one of the souls who can't pass over."

"What are you talking about? You still think she's alive."

The waiter returned with the check. They paid the bill and were out the door, walking toward their cars, fighting gusts of late-February wind, the Mexican music following them outside when Tamara said, "Okay, I confess, I had an ulterior motive for meeting tonight. And it's not completely about Jessie or whoever's bones were found in the maze."

"Thank God."

"Well, maybe. Maybe not." Tamara fished in her over-sized bag for a set of keys. "It's Hudson. I picked up the vibe between the two of you at Blue Note. Something's still there, isn't it?"

Becca couldn't lie, but she couldn't admit she'd never gotten over him. "What do you mean?"

"Didn't you guys ever get together? I always thought you did. I mean a few years after Jessie disappeared, not in high school or anything. I think Vangie said something once."

Evangeline had always been a gossip.

"I ran into Hudson and Zeke a time or two after high school," Becca admitted as they reached her Jetta. "And Hudson and I hung out some. Renee knew. Vangie, too, I guess."

"Just hung out?" Tamara arched a brow.

Becca shrugged. "It was a long time ago."

"But you still have feelings for him? I mean, come on. I pick up this stuff as a matter of course. You and he were sending out shock waves the other night, so I just want to know, is it on again? Are you seeing him? I don't want to get in the way, if that's the case."

"I'm . . . not . . . well . . . we're . . ." She didn't know how to admit that she was on her way to meet him, that she was thrilled about the chance to be alone with him again, but that she also knew it might be emotional suicide. She'd loved him so much, with that schoolgirl fanaticism that could be fatal.

"What?" Tamara demanded as the wind, icy with winter, kicked up.

"I'm on my way to his place now," Becca finally admitted, lifting her hands in surrender. A hank of her own hair blew across her face as the wind chased wet leaves across the parking lot.

"Ahh . . ." Tamara nodded and let out a long sigh as she opened the door of her Mazda. "I was hoping my radar was wrong, but it rarely is. Say hi for me. And if it doesn't work out, let me know. He's the best of the bunch. By a looonnnnggg shot. We were all kind of jealous of Jessie back in high school, weren't we?"

"Yeah, a little."

"So . . . if you're involved with Hudson—"

"We're not involved."

"Not yet," Tamara said. "Then maybe I should set my sights on The Third."

Becca groaned.

"Or Mitch. They're both single."

"So is Jarrett, I think."

"I'm not a masochist," Tamara said, swallowing a smile, "but please, please, don't ask me about sadism."

She sketched a wave and slid behind the wheel of her car.

Becca, parked two spots over, did the same, nosing her Jetta out of the lot, heading west toward Hudson's and wondering if she was about to make the biggest mistake of her life.

Chapter Nine

Hudson shoved the bottle of white wine he'd just purchased into the refrigerator. It was Chardonnay. Medium-priced. Should be right, but there was no way in hell he would know because if he drank, it was beer. Maybe scotch. Wine was outside his interest level, and his knowledge of the subject could be summed up in two words: red and white.

But he'd watched Becca sip white wine at Blue Note, and he'd figured that was what she'd like to drink.

He ran a hand through his hair. "Good God," he berated himself. He'd fought the urge to call her for over a week and had just about given in when he'd heard her voice on the answering machine. He'd told himself to back off, keep his distance, that now that Jessie's body might have been discovered, this was the worst time, the absolute worst, to start trying to rekindle old flames—flames that just didn't seem to die despite all the years that had passed.

Becca . . . Lord, she was beautiful.

As had been Jessie.

Sometimes, in his dreams, those kind of sexy, almost kinky dreams when he woke with a hard-on, he'd be making love to one of them, usually Jessie. Always her long brown-blond hair spilled around her, her hazel eyes were wide with excitement, pupils dilated as he touched her between her legs. "More," she whispered in his ear, and as he rolled atop her, spreading her legs with his knees, she grinned devilishly, as if she knew something he didn't before she faded, her image bleeding into Becca's. The scene would shift suddenly. Instead of lying atop the pool table or in his bed, more likely than not, he and Becca were entwined beneath the old timbers of the barn or under the swaying branches of the willow tree. In the distance, where the long branches and vibrant leaves shifted, he would catch a glimpse, an ashen, ethereal image of Jessie watching them. A ghost. Dead, yet existing.

And smiling.

Knowing.

Accusing him silently, sarcastically, of his betrayal.

As if she'd known that even in high school he'd been attracted to Rebecca.

Jesus, it was chilling. He'd wake up in a sweat, his cock shriveling, his head pounding with a lust that was forever split between two women.

No wonder he'd never had a wet dream; Jessie's wide-eyed voyeurism took care of that.

Grabbing himself a beer, he snapped off the cap and took several long swallows. His thoughts turned to Becca. She'd run hot and cold with him. Wanting him, then backing off, just as he had with her.

With Rebecca Ryan, no, Becca Sutcliff, he didn't know what to expect.

But he was about to find out, he thought, opening the window a bit to let in a little of the cool night air. The kitchen tended to get stuffy with the wood stove burning, the scent of charred oak sometimes overpowering. He had to check the pipe, clean it out or rip the damned thing out altogether. It was part of the plan, but tonight he'd settle for a bit of cold winter air. He noticed a spiderweb, swatted it down, then thought to hell with it. If Becca didn't like the way he lived, she could bloody well lump it.

He heard the sound of an engine and, through the window, caught the splash of headlight beams against the old garage as he drained the rest of his beer.

"Showtime," he said to himself, leaving the emptied longneck on the chipped counter.

Hands damp on the wheel, Becca turned her Jetta off the two-lane road that wound through shaggy fields of brush and headed toward the gravel drive that led first through a copse of trees, then split a tended field, and ended at the gray two-story farmhouse with various and sundry outbuildings behind it.

Lights were on and the front porch was lit from inside lamps. Becca parked her car to one side, took a deep breath, and stripping the keys from the ignition, told herself it was now or never. Out of the Jetta, she walked across a patch of gravel and up three wide wooden steps to the porch. Memories assailed her, though she found the old swing where she'd sat with Hudson was missing. She glanced toward the fields and the solitary willow tree with its drooping branches.

She felt an ache in her heart, a shifting deep inside. How many times had they made love there? Ten? Twenty? More? She remembered kissing Hudson, his lips hot, his hands, pressed against her spine, strong and large.

"Oh, Lord," she whispered, shaking the image.

The front door was inset with a rectangle of beveled glass, and she could see right down the hall. She rang the bell, which tolled somberly inside the house.

Hudson came into view, striding toward the door, his long legs eating up the length of oak planks that led from the rear. In a moment he was opening the door to her.

"You made it."

"Like riding a bike."

"Doesn't seem that long, does it?"

"Nope," she admitted as he stepped out of the way, and she crossed the old threshold, looking around. Some changes she noticed right away: the aroma of Hudson's father's beloved cigars was gone. But his mother's furniture remained in all its floral glory.

Becca found herself smiling.

"What?" he asked.

"Just remembering," she said with a gesture around the room as she shrugged out of her coat.

He hung it over a curved arm of the hall tree that stood at the base of the stairs, then glanced around, seeing the room through her eyes before leading her to the kitchen where the wood stove and television shouted that this was clearly the heart of the home. "One of these days I'll change things," he said.

"Why?"

He laughed. "Oh, I dunno. Maybe it's time to jettison out of the seventies. Would you like some wine?" he asked, heading toward the kitchen while Becca cruised slowly behind him, taking in the house.

"How about one of those," she said, hitching her chin toward the empty bottle resting near the sink.

"Huh." A girl after his own heart. Always . . .

He reached into the refrigerator, popped open a longneck for each of them, then returned to the table, turning the chair around to straddle it backward. Becca smiled to herself. Just like he had in his teens. It was as if sixteen years slipped away as their conversation drifted into small talk. He asked her about her job and she told him a bit about the kind of work she did, then inquired about the ranch. He mentioned that he'd just hired a new foreman and that he'd given up what sounded like a successful real estate career to enjoy the fruits of his labor on these sprawling acres located near the foothills of the Coast Range.

When there was a lull, Hudson rolled his nearly empty bottle between his palms, then looked up and said, "Okay, now that that's out of the way, tell me what you're really thinking."

"About?" Becca asked cautiously.

"Jessie. The bones. The meeting with our longtime . . . friends . . ."

"Do I have to?"

He shot her an indulgent look, then she watched the amusement fall from his face. "I think she died right there. In the maze. And I think someone killed her. It's not like whoever it was had a heart attack, happened to fall into a hole at St. Lizzie's, then was somehow inexplicably buried."

"But it doesn't have to be Jessie."

"Seems the most likely answer."

"I don't know . . ."

"You think she's alive."

Becca took a swallow from her Budweiser. "No. I guess I'm assuming she's dead like everyone else, except Tamara, though she might be waffling a bit. I guess I just don't really want it to be, though I can't think of another explanation why Jessie would leave her parents wondering what happened to her, worrying about her, if she were still alive. Twenty years is a long time to be missing. Renee definitely believes those are Jessie's bones."

Hudson's eyebrows slammed together. "You talked to Renee?"

"We had a drink together."

"Really?" Obviously this was out of left field for him. "Because you're such good buds?"

"Because of Jessie and this mess."

"She tell you about Tim? The separation."

"A little. Mostly we talked about Jessie and our feelings about her."

"Huh." Hudson finished his beer and set it down on the table. "She didn't try to convert you to the Tarot?" he asked dryly.

"She tried. I resisted."

Hudson gazed into Becca's eyes and a smile teased his lips. "I've . . . missed you," he said slowly.

Becca felt the backs of her eyes burn and she had to look down at her beer. She was not going to embarrass herself. Not. "So, you think Jessie was murdered and left in that grave?"

"I think she ran into—trouble—and she died because of it. She's never contacted me," he added. "Maybe I'm giving myself too much credit, but I always thought she would, if she were alive."

"You never thought she ran away?"

"Oh, sure. At first. I didn't want to believe she was totally gone, and I sure as hell didn't want to believe any of Mc-Nally's theories. And I didn't want any of us to be involved," he added as an afterthought.

"But now . . . ?" she asked, a sense of dread crawling up her spine. "Do you think one of the kids who went to St. Lizzie's is involved?"

"I hope not."

But he sounded like he were trying to convince himself. "So, what if it's not Jessie?" Becca asked. "I mean . . . what if it really is someone else?"

"Then who is it? And where the hell is Jessie? What's she been doing? What kind of life did she make for herself? Can you see her married? Having children? Living a *normal* life?"

"That would be a leap."

"Was she as different as I remember?" Hudson suddenly asked, as if the question were wrung from him. He got to his feet and paced around the kitchen, stopping by her chair. She had to turn her neck to look up at him. "We keep talking about her and she's taken on mythological proportions, but she was just a girl with a history of running away. All we know for certain is that bones were discovered in the maze. If they aren't Jessie's, then whose are they?"

Becca lifted her palms.

"I don't want to think about it anymore," Hudson said. "I'd rather talk about—anything else. Got a subject you want to discuss? The economy? Global warming? Whether Zeke and Vangie will actually ever get married?"

"I pick number three."

"No."

"No?"

"No."

Uncomfortable, Becca got up from her chair, but she was too close to him so she moved toward the counter, leaning her hips against it. "Okay, what's going on there? There was a ring on her finger . . . ?"

"Zeke's never been in love with her."

"But he gave her an engagement ring."

"He'll find some reason not to go through with it. He won't follow through. It's not his way."

"Ahh . . ."

"We were both bad about follow-through once. I like to think I've gotten better about it." He came to lean beside her at the counter. A long pause ensued. Becca was fully aware of his slim hips so close to hers. "I'm sorry I never called."

"You already apologized. Sort of. I could have called you, too."

"No, I should have called," Hudson said tautly. "I wanted to. I wish I had."

"I thought you were still in love with Jessie," Becca admitted with difficulty. "I'm not sure you aren't still."

"Like Zeke, I'm not sure I ever was," he admitted. "We were sixteen."

"Some people fall in love at sixteen."

"I wanted to—be with you."

Becca glanced sideways at him in surprise. "When Jessie was still here?"

"She knew I had feelings for you, though I never said anything. She always knew."

"I didn't know," Becca said a trifle breathlessly. Her heart was starting a giddy galloping. She couldn't believe what she was hearing!

"I couldn't act on my feelings, and I didn't know how to break up with her. I was thinking about it and then she was gone. I kept thinking she'd come back and I'd make this clean break. When I saw you that summer I didn't care anymore. Zeke thought I was trying to bring Jessie back, but that wasn't even close. I let him think it, though."

"He talked you out of seeing me," Becca realized.

Hudson grimaced. "Zeke didn't want me with anybody, but his words made me rethink things. I wasn't really ready to be with anyone seriously. I was a dumb college kid. And Jessie's disappearance was still like this entity."

"It's not anymore?"

"No." They stared at each other for long moments. She saw his blue eyes darken with a simmering emotion, one she understood well.

Feeling slightly light-headed, Becca murmured, "I think I'd better leave before I do something I'll regret."

He seemed about to argue with her, then inclined his head in agreement.

"You're not going to try harder than that?" she asked, her words sounding far away to her own ears.

With a sensual smile curving his lips, he slowly reached for her, turning her into him, his hands sliding up her back. She ran her arms around his chest and for a moment their lips were a hairsbreadth apart.

He said, "I think I'd like to kiss you."

"I think . . . you should . . ."

She felt his lips press against hers. Felt the promise of something about to ignite. Her insides seemed to melt. She wanted nothing more than for him to sweep her into his arms and carry her up the creaking old stairs to his bedroom.

"Hudson . . ." she whispered against his mouth.

"Hmmm?"

"I've missed you, too."

In the next split second her fantasy became reality: he picked her off her feet and carried her up the ancient stairs to a room that faced the mountains—his parents' bedroom all those years ago. Without another word, he fell with her onto a mattress that sagged and groaned, and kissed her as if he thought he might never again get the chance.

Becca let go.

Of her guilt.

Of her reservations.

Of her sanity.

Her mouth opened of its own accord, the taste of him familiar and erotic, the scent of him bringing back memory after memory of pleasure. His hands scaled down her ribs as if he knew her, and as he peeled off her clothes, she returned the favor, kissing his exposed skin, feeling the strength of taut, male muscles. Exploring his hard, strong shoulders and the sinewy arms that held her tight.

His mouth touched all those places he'd found years before. Behind her ear, the slope of her neck, the cleft between her breasts. She felt his heat, as white hot as the blood running through her veins.

She reminded herself that she would feel regrets, that nothing so incredible came without pain, but she didn't care. Her need was too fierce, and she reveled in the pure, potent passion that streamed from his body to hers. His tongue ran rough against her breasts, circling her areolae, teasing and toying with her nipples, then delving lower while her hands threaded in his hair and the scent of him filled her nostrils.

Be careful, Becca . . . you haven't told him about the baby. His baby . . .

Refusing to listen to the voice in her head, she gave in to the pleasure, felt his hot breath against her skin, his hands molding her flesh, his tongue and lips causing quicksilver pulses to run through her blood.

The back of her throat went dry as sand, but inside she was melting, hotter and hotter, her body beginning to writhe, the throb of desire pounding through her brain. She closed her eyes as the first spasm hit, rocking her, and when the second quake followed, she cried out, her fingers curling in the sheets, her body convulsing.

He came to her then, body and soul. His lips found hers and she kissed him with the need of all those years of wanting him, hating herself for her desire, dreaming of him. Hudson . . . it had always been Hudson, even when she'd married another man and now . . . now . . .

She let out a low moan as he entered her, her legs wrapping instinctively over his, his lips and mouth hot and wet. He thrust once, then again, and she cried out as he shifted, lifting her so that she was sitting, facing him, his legs beneath hers as he forced her buttocks tight against him.

"Oh . . . Oh . . . God," she whispered as he moved, faster and faster, and the heat consumed her, perspiration covering her body, need consuming her. She met his rhythm, faster and faster, the room spinning, her arms wrapped around him, her hands on the fluid muscle of his back. She was gasping for breath, her heart pounding so hard she thought it might explode when he stiffened and cried out. Her own body responded, tightening around him, the world shattering in a billion pieces of light.

Only when it was over and they'd collapsed together on the wrinkled sheets, still drawing in ragged, sated breaths, did Hudson say, "Was it good for you?" Then they both laughed.

"Worst sex I've ever had in my life. Couldn't you tell?" she said through shattered breaths.

"Maybe if you weren't so damned frigid." Her mouth curved as her head rested in the hollow of his shoulder and his fingers twined in her hair. "Remind me why we waited so long?"

She closed her eyes and inhaled his scent. "Too long . . ." She felt the grin that spread across his lips and asked, "What?"

"We're not waiting that long ever again," he said, sliding his body atop hers, blue eyes slow and sensual.

"Good," she breathed, pushing all thoughts aside except for him.

Chapter Ten

Renee's eyes narrowed as she pulled into the small coastal town of Deception Bay the following evening. The night before the drive had been stalled by a phone call from Tim, an excruciatingly nasty fight, then a stop to pick up a few groceries at a twenty-four-hour Safeway store, and finally the slow drive through mixed rain and snow on twisting mountain roads. She'd stayed in the cabin all day today just unwinding.

The sensation that she was being followed had hung with her all the way through the Coast Range and south along this winding stretch of Highway 101 that cut into the steep hillsides overlooking the Pacific. She'd had to creep to keep the damned car on the road. All the while she'd kept checking her rearview for the glowing headlights that had loomed behind her like the eyes of some great, feral beast.

"Puh-leeze," she told herself now as the few streetlights of the small town emerged from the fog. She was still thinking about her fight with Tim. Jesus, he was a piece of work. He somehow thought that he could have an affair with a coworker and expect Renee to (a) understand, and (b) forgive him. Now, he insisted, he didn't want a divorce, that he'd thought things over and decided it was better for "everyone" if they stayed married.

Like it was that easy.

Renee didn't figure adultery was something she could get over very quickly though she herself had been tempted to step over that invisible marital line a time or two. But she hadn't. She'd come close but had stopped short. Not that it mattered now. Tim could rant and rave, remind her that she was "his" until kingdom come. It was over. O-V-E-R, and she'd told him so tonight in no uncertain terms.

He'd been in a rage, and for the first time she'd seen the extent of his temper and had been glad there hadn't been a gun in the house. Not that she thought he would ever really physically harm her . . .

Still, he'd lost it. Really lost it. His face, once boyishly handsome, had turned tomato red, and his big hands had clenched into hammy fists. He'd even gone so far as to punch through the entry hall wall. That's when she'd left. In a hurry. Only pausing to pick up a few essentials in Hillsboro.

Had he followed her?

Decided to have it out again?

He wouldn't, would he?

She returned to the gravel drive of the small cottage she used on her weekend getaways. Three blocks off the beach and within walking distance of town, the cabin was owned by a friend of her father's, a man who, since his wife had died, rarely spent any time here. His kids were flung to the winds, one son in Miami, another in Denver, his daughter trying to make it as an actress in LA. No one spent any time at the cabin he'd renovated with his own hands sometime in the early eighties.

Renee nosed her Camry beneath the carport. She hurried through the fog to the porch where the exterior light, always illuminated, had burned out. "Damn it all," she muttered, fumbling with her keys and the old, rusted lock.

She heard the sound of footsteps and turned quickly, her heart in her throat, to see someone appear through the mist. She nearly screamed until she spied the large dog ambling beside a man, out for their evening constitutional.

Get a grip, she told herself just as the lock sprang and she let herself inside. She dropped her things on a futon with a faded print cover that served as a couch, then returned outside for her two bags of groceries.

She was back in the cabin within seconds. After locking the door behind her, she flipped on the lights, lit the gas fire, and told her heart to stop its ridiculous knocking as she tossed her suitcase into the single bedroom on the main floor, then flipped open her laptop computer and waited for it to boot up.

She was lucky enough to jump onto a neighboring family's wireless Internet as this little cottage was barely equipped with electricity, let alone anything as technologically advanced as a router; there wasn't even a phone line. The owner refused to take any money from Renee and only asked that she "spruce the place up a bit" when she came, so she didn't argue with him and accepted the tiny abode as her retreat away from Tim and her disintegrating marriage.

It was also here where she had first decided to do her story on the missing Jezebel Brentwood.

And Jessie Brentwood was the reason she felt such overwhelming persecution. As if she were being watched and followed. And it was all because she'd taken that first trip to Deception Bay.

Jessie's adoptive parents, the Brentwoods, had been reluctant to talk to Renee when she'd first posed the idea to them for a story about their missing daughter. They knew Renee and liked her. She'd been a tenuous link to Jessie, the one friend who'd kept in contact with them off and on over the years, but they'd balked at the idea that Renee would drag it all up again. They still believed Jessie might walk through their door. Stranger things had happened.

Renee had been quietly persistent and when she asked

about Jessie's birth parents, they both clamped their jaws shut as if afraid of revealing government secrets. Renee had asked them point-blank why they seemed so—scared—to talk about the adoption, but neither would open up to her. The one piece of information she gleaned was that the adoption—a private one—had taken place in the small coastal town of Deception Bay. The Brentwoods had a cabin there, although it appeared they hadn't returned there in a long time. Renee asked if Jessie knew about the cabin. Had she been there before, on previous occasions? Could that be where she went as a runaway? The Brentwoods assured her that no, Jessie never went to the cabin. It was one of the first places they always looked for her, but she was never there and certainly hadn't been since the last time she disappeared.

That information was what had sent Renee initially to the beach and Deception Bay. She'd asked some questions of the town residents about the area, what it had been like, who were some of the notable families, whatever she could think of to get the conversation rolling. Then she would insert that she knew a family who'd adopted a daughter from somewhere around Deception Bay, that daughter being a friend of hers from high school. No one seemed to know anything, but an old salt who spent his time on a lookout bench above the ocean and fed the seagulls, much to the annoyance of the townies who found them scavenging pests, told her she should go see Mad Maddie.

"Mad Maddie?" Renee asked dubiously.

"Lives up there . . ." He waved in the direction of a rocky tor. "Coupla nice motels there once. Run down now. Maddie owns one of 'em, I guess. Leastwise she stays there. Someday some big resort company'll buy it up and build somethin' hee-uge. Cost a fortune to stay there, but ain't happened yet."

"You think Mad Maddie could help my friend locate her biological parents?"

"She's as fruity as a punchbowl. Lost her marbles. She reads the future." He snorted out a few chuckles. "She'll tell ya a whole buncha drivel."

"She's a psychic reader?"

He snorted. "Call it what you want. Her and her crazy family."

Renee had driven up a winding road to the crest of the tor and had to agree with the old salt about the beauty of the area. Someday maybe a resort company would build "somethin' hee-uge" here and it would have an amazing view of the Pacific. But for now there wasn't much left of the motel but a gray, weathered, beaten-down, one-story set of buildings with sagging carports and weed-choked gravel parking. There were a couple of equally sad cars parked outside, vacation renters, who could stay by the day, week, or month, according to the handwritten sign propped against the wall.

Renee guessed the unit at the end was Mad Maddie's residence, as there were items stacked outside the front door: used furniture, old plastic toys, a propane stove that had seen better days, various and sundry kitchen and bathroom items, and a couple of lawn chairs set out to view the approach of visitors, not the commanding view on the back, western side. A hoarder's dream.

She'd knocked on the door that sported a cockeyed sign that read: Office. It took a while, but Mad Maddie opened the door to reveal a woman with iron-gray hair pulled into a severe bun and a stony, oddly blank expression. She appeared to be somewhere in her late sixties, but Renee figured she could be off a decade either way.

"Are you . . . Maddie?" Renee asked.

"You wantin' a room?"

"Actually I—was told you do—readings?"

Something shifted in her gray eyes. "You want to see Madame Madeline." She stepped aside and Renee hurried across the threshold.

"Yes."

And so Mad Maddie aka Madame Madeline had sat Renee down on a faux-leather couch with springs that felt as if they were going to break through the worn surface at any moment, and then she'd pulled out an equally worn set of Tarot cards. Renee had been fascinated. A frisson had actually crawled up her spine. There was something eerie and authentic about this old woman that the almost antiseptic, staged Tarot reader she'd visited with Tamara couldn't compete with. Here, the ambience was rich, and instead of the heady scent of incense, she smelled rotting wood and the salt of the sea.

Premonition had feathered along her arms and Renee automatically rubbed her elbows. Mad Maddie regarded her in a blank way that caused Renee's heart to beat a little faster. She didn't look down at the cards. She stared straight at Renee.

"What do you want?" she asked.

So Renee had rambled on about her friend, searching for her biological parents, her friend from high school, St. Elizabeth's, who'd been missing for years and who Renee was searching for. She told more than she expected to, a little unnerved by Maddie's great silences. Only once did Maddie move during the recitation, and that was to look a bit wildly over one shoulder toward the back of the motel. Renee automatically looked as well, but there was nothing there. A gust of wind had rattled the panes and Renee had started.

"She's dead," Maddie told Renee.

"Jessie? Jezebel?" Renee had been stunned at her bald announcement.

"Jezebel . . ." That's when Maddie threw the fearful look over her shoulder.

"You see that?"

But then Maddie had moved on to the cards, making banal predictions that seemed to peter out as if she forgot them before the end of her thought. Renee's attention had wandered around the room and she thought she saw a shadow creep inside the partially opened door to the back.

And then Maddie had said she was marked for death. Just like that. She, or one of her friends from that school.

And that had been the end of the reading.

Now Renee wasn't sure what she'd learned. She'd come to believe the "she's dead" line was just something Maddie threw out to jolt her. A tactic. A pretty damn impressive one, actually, as it had followed Renee ever since. And then when the skeleton was discovered inside the maze, Renee got a total, all-over sense of the heebie-jeebies.

She's dead?

How was that for coincidence?

Even now another shiver slid down her spine, and Renee shook it off with an effort. She vowed to herself that she would not be so susceptible, and purposely headed toward the galley kitchen. She sliced cheese and apples, placed them on a plate with some crackers, then found the coffee she'd left in the cupboard from her last stay, brewed up a pot of decaf, and sat at the old desk tucked into the corner on which she'd propped her laptop. Sipping the coffee and picking at the fruit and cheese, she began working on her story.

Instead of going on impressions and feelings, she turned to her usual methods of preparing for a story. She began by deciphering her notes from the meeting at Blue Note, what she thought of the girls who had supposedly been Jessie's best friends and who had known her intimately, and the boys who had lusted after her and ended up being suspects, at least for Detective Sam McNally, now a homicide cop. When Jessie had gone missing, McNally had been with missing persons, but he'd been particularly rabid about finding the where-abouts of a girl who'd been known for running away. It was almost as if he'd had a thing for her. Renee made a note to herself to check and see if McNally had some other connec-tion to Jessie, especially something romantic or sexual. Now *that* angle would turn the story on its ear. Though Jessie had been Hudson's girl, Renee guessed—by virtue of her sexy behavior—that Jessie had been involved with other boys and men. How many or how much, she didn't know, but maybe she should concentrate on McNally.

She frowned, her coffee forgotten. The thing of it was, no one really had known Jessie. Not her parents, not the boy who had supposedly loved her, not her friends. She'd been a mystery in life and was even more so now, in death.

Renee glanced over the names of the guys and her eyes settled thoughtfully on her brother's: Hudson Walker. He had always been pretty mum on the subject of Jessie. Renee had once thought it was a matter of not kissing and telling, Hudson's personal code of honor, but maybe Hudson hadn't really been as involved emotionally as everyone had thought.

She scribbled a note to herself and wrote down Becca's name with a question mark. Her brother had sure been hot for her several years after Jessie went missing; and now, it seemed that fire was still burning.

From the corner of her eye, she caught a glimpse of a shadow in the windowpane at the side of the house.

Oh, God! She froze as the dark figure shifted and her heart began to race. A face appeared, shadowed as if by a hood or a cowl, and eyes as dead as she'd ever seen seemed to look through the glass.

Jesus!

Her heart squeezed.

She bit back a scream and pushed her chair back so quickly the legs screeched against the floor.

Searching wildly around the room for a weapon, any kind of weapon, expecting at any second for the glass to shatter, she nearly fell off the chair, then ran, half-stumbled into the hallway and the darkness beyond.

You're imagining things, you're imagining things, you're goddamned imagining things! She slipped into the darkened kitchen where the palest of light shone through the windows and back door . . . Oh, hell, was it locked? She crossed the room, tested the dead bolt, then, with every hair standing straight up on her arms, she grabbed a butcher knife from the block on the kitchen counter and fled to the windowless hall again.

Cold sweat collected over her spine and the sound of the wind whistled through the rafters.

The cell phone! Use the damned phone!

"Oh, God," she whispered, realizing her phone was in her purse, at her desk.

Moving silently, her heartbeat echoing in her eardrums, she inched down the hall. Her fingers, gripping the handle of the knife, were sweating and she was certain at any second someone or some*thing* would leap at her from the back bedroom or broom closet.

Carefully, heartbeat roaring in her ears, she eased back to the archway to the living area. She barely dared breathe as she poked her head around to view the room and beyond the window.

No figure.

No dark shadow.

Nor was there anything but pure darkness at the other window near the door.

Had it gone?

Or had her fertile mind played a horrid trick on her?

She snapped out the lights, and the interior, aside from a soft glow from the computer screen, was as dark as the night outside. Waiting for her eyes to adjust to the darkness, she eased to the window and peered out.

No face.

No dead eyes.

No one looming, ready to pounce.

Just the shivering shadows from the fir tree standing near the porch.

A raving, paranoid freak, that's what you are!

She returned the knife to its spot, then quickly she closed

all the shades, double-checked the windows and latches, then went back to her computer, one eye ever vigilant. On the Internet she searched for anything she could learn about Jezebel Brentwood, St. Elizabeth's High School, girls who'd gone missing around the same time as Jessie, and Detective Samuel McNally of the Laurelton Police Department.

She didn't go to bed until after two, only after rechecking all the locks. Keeping the butcher knife on the bedside table, she fell into a restless sleep where dreams of high school kept her tossing and turning.

The next morning, suffering from sleeplessness, she saw the big-bladed knife she'd left on the nightstand and mentally chastised herself. "Fool," she muttered. She was still letting herself be affected by the odd elements of the story.

Determined to shake it off, she showered, threw on beach clothes, and spent nearly two hours walking along the foggy beach, feeling the salt spray against her nose and cheeks. Then she hiked back to the cabin and reviewed her notes again, hoping something would leap out at her. She had an address for the Brentwoods' cabin. One of the reasons she'd come to the beach was to find it, so she climbed into her Camry and tried to follow a local map of the area, wishing she owned a GPS system. It took a while, and she drove down a number of dead-end streets, but she finally found the place. The house was weatherbeaten and slightly tired, like many others along this stretch of coastline. She eyed it carefully, a low-slung ranch with a picture window and, when the sun was out, an incredible view of the ocean. Today, though, it was still gray and close, with mist clinging to the surrounding hills and obscuring the horizon. The sea itself, the color of steel, was hard to discern in the fog, the abandoned lighthouse on that craggy rock off the shore, invisible.

Had Jessie ever been here during one of her runaway adventures? Renee was half inclined to wander around the place and check, but changed her mind when a maid-cleaning crew arrived in a van and parked in the drive. They glanced toward Renee, who turned back to her car. The house was obviously a rental now. No place for Jessie to hide.

Renee returned to Deception Bay and parked near a local coffee shop and bakery where a few patrons were sipping their morning jolts of java and munching on cinnamon rolls, croissants, and scones. The interior of the Sands of Thyme was warm and smelled of coffee and spices. Newspapers were left open on a few tables and the walls were lined with coffee, tea, utensils, and cups, all for sale.

"Do you know Madame Madeline?" Renee asked the girl at the cashier stand.

She made a disparaging sound. "She's more than a few rolls short of a dozen, if you ask me. Makes those cultees at Siren Song look normal."

"Hey!" a man in the back yelled, shooting the girl a don't-gossip-with-the-customers look as he bagged the sliced loaf and the espresso machine screamed as it spewed white foam into huge cups.

"Siren Song?"

"That big house up on the cliff." She pointed away from the ocean toward the other side of the highway where the land broke upward sharply into the Coast Range. "They all wear weird stuff and act strange. I expect their heads to turn around if you look at 'em too long."

"*They* mind their own business," the man from the back said loudly.

The cashier mouthed, "Sorry," to Renee, who took her cappuccino to a table, picked up the newspaper, scanned the headlines, and decided the *Coastal Clarion* made a rag like the *Star* look sophisticated. Thinking it might be better to approach Maddie a little later in the day, Renee passed the time working on a word puzzle, realizing that an elderly man and woman at a nearby table must have overheard her conversation with the cashier because she heard Siren Song mentioned several times. The elderly woman unfolded a plastic rain hat from her purse and said tartly, ". . . nothing but trouble up there, if you ask me. Like those ones in Waco or . . . Arizona. Got all kinds of strange ways of behavin'. Been that way for over a hundred years."

The man with her, in thick glasses, plaid jacket, and driving cap, nodded as he stood and folded his paper under his arm. "Bad news, that. Good thing they keep to themselves."

They walked—he with a cane, she with her arm linked through his—out of the bakery and into light, sprinkling rain, leaving Renee to eavesdrop on a trio of women obviously on a weekend getaway together but laughing and outtalking each other about the hilarious antics of their small children.

Renee packed it in, making tracks from the bakery and taking a turn through town, her breath fogging in the chilly air, the smell of the sea ever present, and peek-a-boo views of the sea visible along the streets running east and west. A few cars ambled along the narrow roads, though few pedestrians braved the winter elements as a thin drizzle leaked from the sky. She wasted some time at a cozy antique shop whose proprietor, a middle-aged woman with a silvery gray bob, watched her closely. Renee struck up a conversation with her by asking about the lodge called Siren Song, but the woman responded quickly, "It's a cult. Mostly women. Been there longer than Deception Bay. You could look it up. I heard a couple of the girls worked in town for a while, but they were yanked back real quick-like."

"You have some colorful characters here," Renee observed. "I ran into Madame Madeline earlier."

"Madame Madeline?" She snorted. "If she's a psychic, I'm the Queen of Sheba."

Renee didn't know whether that made her feel better or worse. But when her watch read ten, she walked back to her Camry and headed in the direction of Maddie's old motel. Her tires scrunched on the weedy gravel, and as she pulled to a stop a dark cloud blocked out the faint rays of a watery sun. She climbed from the car and then hesitated again. Why was she here, really? What could this old woman tell her that she didn't already know? What kind of answers could there be?

Annoyed with herself, Renee got back in her car and drove back toward the cabin, taking a last-minute detour to drive in the direction of Siren Song. It took her a while to find the large house shaded by fir trees from the road. All she could see were snatches of windows and cedar shakes and stone chimneys, and she was reminded of an old northwest lodge much like the one built at Crater Lake or Timberline, although not nearly as large.

At the cabin, she headed for her laptop, wondering whether she should stay and work some more or head back to Portland and the myriad of problems that awaited her with Tim. Stuffing the laptop into its case, she headed for the bedroom, grabbing up a T-shirt she used as a nightgown and tossing it into her bag. She packed up some toiletries from the bathroom, then shot a last look around the bedroom, intending to close her bag.

Her gaze skated over the nightstand, then snapped back.

No knife.

She looked more closely. Not on the nightstand, nor was it on the floor beside the bed.

She inhaled and exhaled a long breath, then headed to the kitchen where the knife block was filled—except for the single slot wherein the butcher knife had rested.

Renee bit back a sound of disbelief.

Where the hell was it?

Dear God . . . how? Who?

Oh, shit.

Listening to the sound of the wind pushing against the old cabin, the creak of ancient timbers, the light patter of rain on the roof, the thunder of her heart, she strained to hear any foreign noise. Was someone in the cabin with her even now? She thought of the loft, the second bedroom where she never ventured, and her blood became ice water.

She had to go up and check it out. The prospect filled Renee with dread. She was on the bottom step when she thought better of it and turned, grabbed her bag, laptop, and purse, and headed swiftly out the door, locking it behind her.

She had seen a face in the window. She *had*. A dark figure with soulless eyes.

She had . . . hadn't she?

Sliding behind the wheel of her Camry, Renee spun backward out of the driveway, nearly hitting a post before slamming the car into Drive and glancing at the cabin again. The curtains in the loft window moved slightly and she was damned sure there was something dark and ominous behind them.

Only when her car was miles away, heading north on 101, and she was pushing the speed limit on the winding road high above the sea, the lighthouse barely visible on its tiny island, did she breathe again.

From the upstairs window, I watch her leave.
Frightened.
Trembling.
Scrabbling around like a frantic chicken running from a fox. Throwing her bags into the backseat. Too late. I've seen what's on her computer screen, know where she's been, what she's doing. She's getting close—stopping by the old woman's shop, asking questions. That damned old hag. Never to be trusted. I should have known, should have dealt with the crone.

I think of it—the killing of the old one, the traitor. I've thought of it often enough, suspected she knows more than she pretends, but here, in this tiny gossipy town, it might prove difficult.

And now there are others, one of whom is fleeing even now.

But she can't run far.
And I know where she'll go.

Back to the others.

She'll lead me to them.

Standing behind the gossamer curtains, I finger the long-bladed knife in my hands and wait until the tail-lights of her car disappear around the corner, heading east, away from the sea, to the highway that runs parallel to the ocean, wandering in twisting turns north until it reaches the intersection where it splits and she'll head inland.

To the others.

As she vanishes I rub my thumb over the razor-sharp blade, imagining what the thin steel edge can do. Quick and clean, a neat slice across the jugular and carotid.

But the time isn't right. I need this one to lead me to the others.

Even though she has no scent, no odor.

She's not one of them.

But she must be followed.

And she must be stopped.

Once I have no further use for her.

Chapter Eleven

Glenn Stafford raced down the stairs of his house, a gargantuan Georgian building of nearly four thousand square feet that Gia had insisted upon. He hoped his wife wouldn't catch him on his way out. He was late getting to the restaurant. Late getting tasks done. Late, always late.

And that asshole cop McNally had called, wanting to meet with him. Wanting to meet with all of them, he'd said. But was he telling the truth? Or had he singled Glenn out? Not that there was any reason. Lord, no. He'd barely known Jessie Brentwood. She'd been Hudson's girl, flirt that she was. But she'd had no serious interest in him, or any of them, well . . . maybe Zeke? . . . but that was short-lived. Nope, the girl had been interested in Hudson Walker, then, now, and probably forever.

Glenn headed toward the back of the house. He'd put McNally off. God, he didn't need more damn stress. The restaurant was enough. Hadn't he heard over and over again how difficult it was to make a go of a restaurant? Hadn't he? But he'd believed in himself, believed in Scott. But Jesus . . . things were running in the red. How, how to get more interest in the place, more exposure? Did they need more Internet advertising? What the hell did it take to make a spot "in" or "hip" or whatever they called it these days? Not enough people knew about Blue Note, and that goddamned venture in Lincoln City wasn't even hardly off the ground and Glenn felt it already might be doomed. Bleeding money. Scott had more faith in the place; he was the one taking off for the coast, trying "to get 'er going." But Glenn was in charge of Blue Note, and it was bad business. Bad, slow business.

And . . . something was off financially. Things just weren't adding up, literally. Did they have a sneaky employee who had found a way to siphon off funds and juggle the books or inventory? The books just didn't seem right, but Glenn hadn't found where the discrepancy was—yet. It was only a matter of time.

Passing through the kitchen, his hand on the door to the garage, he saw the pile of yesterday's mail. Damn Gia. She hadn't even looked through it. Probably a mountain of bills that he couldn't pay. And that damn lease on the restaurant. Highway robbery. It was drowning them in a sea of red ink. Drowning them.

Glenn felt a burning in his throat. Acid reflux. His stomach was probably riddled with ulcers. He didn't even want to jump Gia's bones anymore, but then ever since her last miscarriage she'd been a crying, chocolate-devouring, weepy-eyed rag doll. Hell, she'd sworn she never wanted children when they got married, but now she came after him with lacy, baby-doll lingerie and a panting avid mouth, the only spark of energy she could ever muster—all in the name of pregnancy with a capital "P."

Lucky for him, Mr. Ready spent most of his time curled up and flaccid these days.

Which wasn't helping their marriage much, but Glenn had bigger fish to fry.

He almost ignored the mail, irritated at Gia's apathy. If sex wasn't on the agenda, she was useless. Like a queen bee.

Only good for mating and laying eggs. Tended to by minions. One of those repulsive insects—maybe termites—had a queen that was a white, quivering blob—couldn't move unless it was pushed and prodded by the workers. Well, that was Gia these days. A blob.

"Glenn?"

He looked over. Well, there the blob was. Risen from her bed. Red-eyed and scraggly haired. She'd been pretty once, not so long ago, but now she didn't care. Simply didn't care.

"Where're you going?" she asked.

"To work."

"I thought you had tonight off." A whine entered her voice.

"I never have a night off. Never. I work all the time. It's called owning your own business, y'know?" *And what do you do?*

"Why can't you divide your time with Scott?"

"Because Scott's at Blue Ocean, trying to get the menu in line with the clientele. And we have problems at Blue Note."

"We have no life, Glenn. No life!" She threw up her hands in despair. "What are we going to do?"

"I don't know what you're going to do. I'm going to work."

"When's Scott coming back?"

"I don't know," Glenn mumbled. A lie. Scott usually returned on Sundays, after the weekend, and then he sure as hell put his time in at Blue Note. The man was everywhere, looking over Glenn's shoulder, criticizing, pointing out when things weren't done to his satisfaction. Glenn couldn't fault him, though he'd like to. Right now he wanted to fault someone. *Any*one. And he really didn't want to face Scott tonight, though his partner had said he'd be in later. Well, good. They needed to talk. Seriously talk. Something had to be done or the business would fail. Since he'd personally guaranteed loans against Blue Note and Blue Ocean, everything, including this monster of a house, would be stripped away. How would Gia feel then? "Why didn't you go through this mail?" he asked.

"What? Oh." She rubbed her forehead with both hands. The useless piece of dead weight seemed to sleep all day and all night. Glenn couldn't imagine what she ever thought she'd do with a kid. From what he'd heard, they never let you sleep at all. "I—I don't know." She lifted her fleshy shoulders in a shrug.

God, she was useless.

Glenn swept up the pile and sifted through it, making a big production about it, just so she'd know he was the one doing all the work, he was the one supporting them, he was *the one*.

"What time'll you be back?" Her chin was bent down and she looked at him from the tops of her eyes. If she thought that was sexy, she had a rude awakening coming her way. She was about as sexy as cold meatloaf.

"I'll call you," he muttered.

Bills, bills, bills.

An advertisement for some new cell phone deal that would probably cost him a fortune in hidden charges. Several notices to "occupant," which really was a pisser, when you thought about it. Couldn't be bothered to find out who lived in the place. Those went straight to the trash.

And a card addressed to him with no return address: Glenn Stafford.

No Gia listed at all.

Huh?

Gia was smoothing back some of her bleached-blond hair. "I could wait up for you."

Fat chance. She'd be out cold in an hour if she got into the wine, which she did almost every night now.

Yep. A marriage made in heaven.

"I'll be late." Glenn stuffed the envelope in his pocket and banged out the back door to his car. A Honda. He'd traded in his Porsche last year. Traded down. It had hurt like a hole in his heart, but he hadn't been able to afford the payments along with two mortgages. He kept thinking the damn restaurant would turn around, but it was a hungry alligator and its teeth were planted firmly in Glenn's backside. His ass was getting chewed off bit by bloody bit, month by month.

He drove to Blue Note, a dark cloud over his head, and he checked his rearview mirror more than usual. All the talk and speculation about Jessie Brentwood was kinda making him crazy and paranoid—as if living with Gia didn't do a good enough job of that as it was. No one appeared to be following him, at least not tonight, but lately he'd had the feeling that someone was watching him.

Gia. It's Gia, you idiot. She wants to know where you are every second.

Parking the Civic in a spot at the rear of the building, he cut the engine and spent several moments listening to the tick of the motor as it cooled.

What was he going to do?

What the hell was he going to do?

He was trapped.

No way out.

Angry at the world, he slammed out of the car and swore he saw someone skulking around the bushes flanking the parking lot, but on second glance, he saw only a raccoon lumbering off after raiding the Dumpster.

"Damned pests," he muttered, circling around and entering through the front door. He liked catching the staff unawares, seeing who was standing where, who was actually working versus who was yakking. Pete was sure a waste of space. The guy schmoozed and glided around, wooing the customers, and he didn't help out in the least with the grunt work. Why people liked him was a complete mystery to Glenn. He'd already banged two of the waitresses in the back, one up against the wall, according to Luis, who could barely speak English. But Luis had communicated the incident well enough so Glenn had had to confront the oily Pete, who simply smirked and said it was beyond his control. Glenn would have fired him on the spot, but Scott had stepped in. Pointed out that Pete brought in good business, which, damn it all, was the truth.

Glenn felt Mr. Ready twitch at the thought. His sleeping penis could rise from the dead with the right incentive. Like a lusty waitress or two. Glenn wouldn't mind slamming one up against the wall and screwing her brains out, but he couldn't afford to. That was just crying for a lawsuit. Sexual harassment, and then Gia would divorce him and take everything that the lawsuit didn't eat up.

He was stuck with Gia, the wallowing termite queen, he thought for the thousandth time. No matter which way you cut it. He thought about the meeting they had here. Becca, Tamara, and Renee had all looked hot. Trim. Fit. Beautiful. And *interesting.* Jesus, any of them would be better than Gia.

Inside, the dark rooms buzzed with conversation and the clink of glassware. People were laughing, eating . . . drinking. He passed by several curtained alcoves where diners were deep into their meals. Blue Note was surprisingly busy, and everyone seemed to be in their right places as Glenn took in the place with practiced ease. Except for the people by the far window. They looked as if they hadn't been served in a while, and their entrees and their appetizers were long over. Glenn was about to rectify the situation himself when he saw the footsie they were playing beneath the table and realized the staff was simply giving them a little extra time as they really weren't interested in food.

Probably having an affair, Glenn thought with a hint of jealousy. But he was proud of his wait staff. Discernment. That's what Blue Note needed. The ability to read the customers and discern their needs, whether those needs be drink, food, or something else.

He strolled through the kitchen. Luis and crew were getting out the meals like a well-oiled machine. They'd lost their top chef a month earlier, but then Patrick had been more of a head case than a head chef. Luis, with little experience, was pinch-hitting. He was a quick learner, but Blue Note had no signature dishes, no standouts, nothing to make it rise above the hundreds of other restaurants in and around the city.

And if they didn't find that special uniqueness that would make Blue Note the name on everyone's lips, it would be in serious trouble. It already was.

Glenn grabbed a short glass at the bar, filled it with ice, and poured in a couple of ounces of bourbon. He took a sip, felt instantly better, then headed to the back office where he sat on a worn leather chair. His domain. Old pictures lined the wall. Photos of him. Scott. Even a few from about a million years ago—the friends from St. Elizabeth's. He saw one, the color faded, of the smiling faces of Zeke, Garrett, Hudson, The Third, Scott, and himself . . . no girls. No Jessie.

He wondered about her and really hoped it wasn't her body that had been located at the old school. Glenn liked to think that she'd escaped, gotten away from whatever demons had been chasing her. Hudson's girl.

Yeah, right.

A chick like Jessie . . . so mysterious and damned sexy, she didn't belong to anyone. Shit, she'd been hot. *Hot!*

So what had happened to her? Glenn thought again about missed opportunities as he clicked on his computer to pore over the books. Man, they owed a lot of accounts payable.

His stomach nose-dived as he glanced at the total.

It was shocking, how many places had offered them supplies on credit, but then Scott could be a silver-tongued devil when he needed to. Pascal was a closer. He could charm, cajole, and squeeze vendors like a virtuoso. Sometimes Glenn wondered where and how it was all going to end. If things didn't improve, not only the lease wouldn't be paid, but payroll was going to be a problem. And shouldn't there be more funds available? Sure, the restaurant had off days, but when they were on, they were *on*, man.

Look at tonight.

Determined to get to the bottom of their cash-flow problems, Glenn examined the accounts as best as he could. He'd had no formal training in business and finance, but he knew when something was owed and whether the restaurant had enough money to pay it.

A couple of hours later after juggling figures and making minimal payments on overdue bills, Glenn remembered the card. He pulled it from his pocket and examined the light blue envelope with the typed address. It was postmarked Portland. Almost looked like an invitation of some kind.

He sliced it open with a letter opener, and pulled out a piece of plain white card stock:

What are little boys made of?
Frogs and snails and puppy dogs' tails.
That's what little boys are made of.

Glenn dropped the note as if it had scorched him. His heart pounded hard and painful in his chest. The spit dried in his mouth.

Jessie!

What the hell?

Panicked, Glenn could hear Jessie's singsonging voice. Could see her saying those very words. "What are little boys made of . . ."

He tried to calm down, but once the image was loose in his mind, there was no holding it back. As if high school were yesterday, he could remember how much his fingers had wanted to caress her curves. He'd wanted Jessie with a fiery desire that had plagued him like a curse. Sure, she'd only wanted Hudson. Sure, she'd never looked his way. But she'd teased. How she'd teased. With that sexy lilt and twitch of her hips and a knowing look and something about the way she talked that was way more adult than the rest of them. She knew things. Hadn't Vangie said it the other night? That Jessie knew things?

A shudder ripped through him as her image came to mind.

God in heaven, he'd wanted to wrap her legs around his waist and pound himself inside her. Just stick it to her, man, for all he was worth. He could imagine her head thrown back, her mouth open and slack, her hazel eyes like glittering agates.

Mr. Ready jumped to flagpole attention and Glenn reached a hand to take care of things, but then the import of the card wilted his desire like a bucket of cold water never could.

Was Jessie *alive*?

She had to be!

"Mr. Stafford?" A light knock on the office door. Glenn instantly adjusted himself, stuffed the card back in his pocket, then pulled open the door. Amy, one of the newest employees who wasn't yet eighteen, regarded him with her usual deer in the headlights look. "Mr. Pascal's here but he's talking to a policeman? He told me to come get you."

"I'll be right there," Glenn told her. Policeman . . . ? McNally! Had to be. Damn the man. Did he *have* to come to their place of work?

Glenn checked his appearance in the mirror by the door, sucked in his gut, promised himself he would cut down on the pasta intake. He headed out the door, walking steadily and with confidence toward the front of the restaurant even though he felt a quivering worry growing inside his gut.

Sure enough, there was that cop. Older now. But Jesus, really better looking than before, the bastard. How was that possible? He'd been in his mid-twenties before, now he was in his mid-forties, and it looked like he hadn't lost one goddamned hair off his head. And the hair was still dark brown, the temples only faintly silver. McNally gazed at Glenn through light hazel eyes that pierced like steel. He looked fit and hard and just as mean as he had twenty years earlier.

Scott was smoothing his bald pate with one hand in a gesture that could mean anything between nervousness and amusement. He lifted an eyebrow at Glenn. In a gently mocking tone, he said, "Detective Sam McNally's paying us a call."

"Probably not a social one," Glenn said shortly, trying to temper his tension with a smile. He hoped he wasn't gritting his teeth. "Let's all go back to my office."

Amy and some of the other employees watched them head down the hall, wide-eyed. Glenn wanted to smack each of their avid little faces.

Repositioning himself behind the desk, Glenn noticed his hands were shaking ever so slightly. Damn it all. He placed one over the other on his desk as Scott propped himself against the wall and McNally accepted one of the club chairs, sinking into it as if he were there for a very long stay.

"I called you," he said, looking at Glenn.

"Yeah—I—I've kinda been buried." Crap, what was the guy asking? "I couldn't find time to meet with you."

Scott broke in, "We've both been busy. I just got back in town not half an hour ago. Glenn and I have another restaurant just outside of Lincoln City—Blue Ocean—which we're just getting going."

"I'm not planning to waste your time," McNally said. "You know about the remains found at St. Elizabeth's, I'm sure. I believe they're Jezebel Brentwood's, and I want to run over your statements at the time of her disappearance once more."

"But you're not sure they're Jessie's," Scott stressed gently.

"No corroborating DNA evidence yet."

Glenn felt his anxiety notch up. *No corroborating DNA evidence yet.* The card in his pocket felt as if it were on fire, burning up. Should he mention it? Let them know Jessie could very well be alive? And what did it mean? What did she want from him?

True to his word, McNally didn't waste time. He went over the sequence of events prior to Jessie's disappearance, and Glenn was kind of surprised at how detailed his notes were. But then, McNally had put them through the wringer twenty years ago. The man knew more about what had happened than Glenn could ever remember.

"I knew Jessie, we all did because of St. Elizabeth's, but I was really into sports, didn't much pay attention if it wasn't anything to do with jocks," Scott said when McNally finished and looked from one to the other of them, waiting for someone to speak up. "Jessie, she was good-lookin', yeah, but really, she was just a girl who dated one of my friends. I didn't really know her, and neither did Glenn. We said the same thing then, and nothing's changed."

"That's right," Glenn said, suddenly glad for Pascal's glib tongue.

"Have you seen any of your group since?" McNally asked.

Glenn's heart clutched and he looked to Scott for guidance. There was no crime in it, for God's sake, but he didn't want to fall into some kind of trap by shooting off his mouth when he shouldn't.

"Mitch is a good friend," Glenn blurted out.

Scott threw him a dark look. He'd always objected to Glenn's friendship with Mitch and sometimes, just because he could get a reaction, Glenn liked to remind Scott that he wasn't the end-all be-all of good friends. Sometimes Scott Pascal wasn't a friend at all.

"We all met here at the restaurant a couple weeks ago," Scott told the detective, and Glenn relaxed slightly. Of course. No reason to worry. Just tell the truth. Let his partner do the talking. But leave out the nursery rhyme . . . "We heard about the bones being discovered, so we got together." Scott glossed over the meeting—just a bunch of concerned friends worried that tragedy had befallen one of their own.

Glenn ignored his drink, the ice cubes melting, the aroma of bourbon in the air of the closed room.

McNally was noncommittal. Did he buy it? Glenn couldn't tell and it made him nervous. He eyed his drink, caught the slight shake of Scott's head from the corner of his eye, and let the bourbon sit.

McNally ran over a few more questions about Jessie and her relationship to all their friends. From Glenn's point of view, it was all very banal and he had the suspicion that Mac was simply getting a feel of them. He couldn't wait for the detective to leave so he could talk to Scott.

Eventually Mac did just that. He'd written down some notes, chicken scratchings from what Glenn could tell, then flipped the small notebook shut and placed it in a pocket of his black leather jacket. Seeing that, Glenn wondered if the card in his own pocket was visible, outlined like some kind of scarlet letter. It was all he could do not to reach up and touch it.

As Mac got up to leave Scott said, "You've mellowed out over the years."

McNally paused, giving Scott a long look. "Have I?"

Scott met his gaze. "Maybe not."

A moment passed between them. Glenn's pulse began a slow, hard beat through his veins. He managed to walk with Scott to show the detective out, but as soon as they were alone, they headed back to the office and Scott closed the door behind him.

"What is it?" Scott asked tautly.

"What do you mean?"

"You're white as a ghost. McNally scared you. What the hell's going on?"

"He didn't scare me."

"If I saw it, he saw it," Scott assured him. "Come on. Give." He beckoned his fingers in an impatient c'mere gesture.

"We've got goddamned problems, okay? The money's just pouring out of this place. I don't know where it's going. Maybe someone's stealing from us? One of the wait staff? Or they're embezzling somehow?"

"You keep everything locked up, don't you?"

"Of course. I'm not an idiot." Glenn's teeth ground together. Scott had a way of pissing him off and the cop . . . Oh, shit, he'd never been comfortable around cops, always thought they were after him.

"Then we're just short," Scott was saying. "Income isn't what it should be, and expenses are out of control."

"I've got 'em under control," Glenn snapped, miffed. Scott was always so quick to blame him.

"Yeah?"

"Yeah."

The two partners stared hard at each other. Scott seemed to be thinking very, very hard, and Glenn realized reluctantly that he wasn't as immune as he would have liked the detective to believe. He was tense, too, and kind of spooked. So Glenn decided to come clean. "All right, look. Something happened," he said.

He could see Scott brace himself.

"Nothing about the restaurant," Glenn assured him. "It was this." He pulled out the card and handed it to Scott, who seemed reluctant to accept it. Reading it over, Scott drew his brows together and seemed lost in a world of his own.

"How'd you get this? Where'd it come from?" he asked after a long moment where Glenn's nerves were stretched tight as guy wires.

"It came in the mail, to my house, addressed to me."

"What the hell does it mean?"

"I don't know, but I sure as hell wasn't going to tell McNally."

"Christ, we have to call The Third. What kind of game is that bitch playing?" Scott said, shaking his head. "She's alive. God. She's alive . . . *so who's in the grave*?"

Glenn lifted his hands to ward off that thought. "I don't know. I don't know."

Whipping out his cell phone, Scott suddenly stopped himself in the middle of punching out a number. "What if it's not Jessie who sent this? What if it's someone trying to freak us out?"

"Who the fuck would do that?"

"I don't know, but . . . oh, shit. Someone who's just messin' with us."

Glenn nodded rapidly. He liked that idea better. "But why?"

Scott drew a breath. "Hell if I know." He flopped into the chair so recently vacated by the detective. "It's dumb. It's a dumb joke."

"It's no joke," Glenn assured him. "God, I could use a drink." He picked up his watery bourbon and drank it down.

Scott was still tossing things over in his mind. "Why would she contact you? Jessie? If she were alive?" His face was a knot of confusion. "She wouldn't, so it's a joke."

Glenn ground his teeth together. In the back of his mind he'd been asking himself the same question. Jessie had scarcely noticed him. That singsong nursery rhyme had been something she'd teased The Third with, or Zeke, maybe even Jarrett. It wasn't something she'd used on him. He'd been wallpaper to her, nothing more.

Scott snorted, following Glenn's thoughts. "Stop thinking about it," he said dismissively. "That damn detective rattled me, too, but it's all just routine stuff. Whoever sent this thing?" He tossed the card across the desk. "I wouldn't be surprised if it's Jarrett or The Third, actually. Would be just like them. Trying to get your goat. We got more important things to worry about."

"Like the business," Glenn said, his eyes on the white square of paper.

"Like this fucking business," Scott agreed. "I'll bring you and me both a drink. Throw that thing in the trash."

Glenn could have told him he had a bottle of Bushmills stashed in his desk drawer, could have offered him a drink, but he didn't.

As Scott stalked out of the room, Glenn picked up the card. After a moment he grabbed a pair of scissors and shredded it and the blue envelope into slivers of paper, dusting them off his hands into the trash can. He closed his eyes then, consciously trying to put it behind him.

For a moment he thought he heard a girl's giggling. Someone laughing at him. His eyes flew open and he glanced sharply around the room.

But he was alone.

* * *

Becca was working at her computer when the phone shrilled. She jumped like she'd been goosed, scrabbling to pick up the receiver of her land line.

Hudson, she thought, a smile crossing her lips. She instantly had a mental picture of him lying in the darkness of his bedroom, his arms reaching out as she tried to slide from the bed. "You're not leaving."

"I have to. I have a dog at home." His hand had grabbed hers and he'd pulled her back atop him. It had taken her another hour before she'd disentangled and made her way home.

"Hello," she said now as she answered the phone, not recognizing the number from Caller ID. She glanced at the clock. Late afternoon and almost dark as pitch outside already. As if aware she'd noticed, the heavens suddenly opened up and spewed rain, then hail, a storm of precipitation blasting outside her window. It was awesome in its power but it just meant that the dog wasn't going to want to go for a walk.

"Becca? It's Renee."

"Oh, hey." She sat up straighter. Did Renee know about her night with Hudson? It had been just a few days since they'd tumbled together in his bed. Since that time they'd been on the phone several times a day. It was thrilling. Unbelievable.

"I've just been feeling so weird about all of this, I guess," Renee was saying, echoing Becca's own thoughts. "About Jessie and those bones and all. I just wish we'd find out once and for all if the body belonged to Jessie."

"I know." She thought about the presence she'd felt in the maze and wondered if she should tell Renee. At the time the pure, unfiltered evil had seemed all too real. Even now, goose bumps raised on her arms and she looked hurriedly over her shoulder.

"Have you heard that McNally—the cop that was so into Jessie's disappearance years ago—has been interviewing the guys?" Renee asked, her voice sounding edgier than usual. "He stopped by Blue Note to talk to Glenn and Scott, then called The Third at his office downtown. McNally already left a message on my phone. I called back but missed him."

Becca's fingers tightened over her cell. "Then they know it's Jessie," she said. "DNA must've come back or some other proof that the body is hers."

"That's what I think, too. God . . . it's hard to believe." She paused for a second, then said, "I thought maybe we should get together again."

"All of us?"

"The girls. Actually, I'm already meeting Vangie and Tamara at Java Man after work. Around seven."

Another meeting? For what? Because the police were sniffing around? So what? It almost sounded as if Renee wanted them all to get their stories straight, which was ridiculous. No one had anything to hide.

Right?

"What about Hudson . . . and Zeke?" Becca asked. "Did they get a call from the police?"

"Not that I've heard, but I haven't talked to Hudson in a few days and Vangie didn't say anything about Zeke when I called her. I think she would have. Anyway, it doesn't matter if they have or not. They've got to be on the list. I'm sure we all are."

"List? As in suspects?"

"Or persons of interest, whatever you want to call it. So, about tonight . . . can you make it?"

"I'll be there."

Becca hung up, then clicked off her computer. She double-checked all the doors and windows, then changed into a red cowl-necked sweater and added some lip gloss. Glancing at her watch, she turned on the news, wasting another half hour before she headed out. There was talk about discovery of an unidentified woman's body, and Becca zeroed in on the newscaster. But it appeared to be that this particular body had been thrown from her car following an accident. Nothing to do with Jessie Brentwood.

"Of course not," she said aloud, annoyed with herself. She grabbed her raincoat and bundled herself inside. There were other accidents and crimes out there. The world was huge. Just because her group of friends was affected by the remains found in the maze didn't mean the discovery wasn't already yesterday's news. Maybe they would never know the identity of the bones for sure. Maybe this limbo they'd been living would continue just as it was.

With a sigh, she sent up a silent prayer for resolution.

Chapter Twelve

Becca drove to Java Man with one eye on the rearview mirror, but none of the cars behind her seemed to have any interest in following her. Once parked, she flipped up the hood of her jacket, and hurrying through the rain, she caught sight of her friends through the window. Tamara's red curls burned under Java Man's lights. Evangeline's blond paleness was even more ashen; she looked washed out to the point of illness. And Renee's face was pinched, her dark hair untidy, as if she'd been running her hands through her brunette strands over and over again.

"Sorry I'm late," Becca greeted them all, shaking excess water onto a mat by the door. "I was all set, wasting time actually, then suddenly I'm behind."

"We ordered you a decaf latte. That all right?" Renee asked, indicating a steaming, foaming cup.

"Works for me."

"Coffee first, then wine," Tamara said.

Becca slid into the empty seat next to Renee, which left her across from Evangeline and catty-corner from Tamara. Everyone was more sober now, more careful than they had been at Blue Note, as if a current of tension was making them cautious. And Renee looked as if she'd dropped five pounds in less than a week.

"So, what's up?" Becca asked, sipping her latte.

The corners of Renee's mouth turned downward as she twirled her cup around and around again. "I think something's going on. Something more than what we're seeing." She was picking her words carefully, as if afraid to panic them. "And I think we're all in danger at some level."

"Danger?" Evangeline drew back as if repelled.

"What kind of danger?" Tamara asked.

"Yeah, what kind of danger?" Evangeline tried to play it off like she thought Renee was overreacting, but her shoulders were hunched and her eyes practically swallowed her whole face.

"The same danger that killed Jessie." Renee's gaze swung to Evangeline. "She was damn near precognitive sometimes. Twenty years ago she knew she was in trouble and she tried to run, but she didn't get away. She *died* in the maze. Someone killed her."

"We don't know it's her," Evangeline stated.

"It's her." Renee was positive. "Jessie had a sense of danger coming. 'Trouble,' she said. And I guess I feel it, too. Trouble."

"So you're precognitive as well." Again, Evangeline tried to sneer at Renee's worries, but she just succeeded in sounding more frightened.

"Is this from the Tarot reading?" Tamara asked Renee. Her brows were knit in concern. "Because you have to look at the cards as a guide. You can't take them so specifically."

Renee made a disparaging sound. "No. This isn't about my Tarot reading, although I was at the beach and met this old woman—a psychic who gave me a creepy feeling."

"Why? What did she say?" Tamara asked.

"She said we were . . . I was . . . I don't know . . ."

"What?" Tamara insisted.

"Marked for death. You like that? She was nuts. The whole town knows it, but I wanted to ask about Jessie." She shook her head. "It's so silly I can't believe it now. She spooked me."

"Jessie?" Tamara questioned carefully.

"No. Look, I know you think she's still alive, Tamara, but she's gone. Even Madame Madeline said she was dead. It just feels like . . . whatever she was afraid of might still be a threat. I don't know. I was doing some research, going through some of Jessie's last days, thinking about all the things she said. Something happened to her, or she learned something, that made her decide to run. You know it, Vangie. You were her best friend. She must have told you."

"Why do you keep saying that?" Evangeline demanded. "I was not her best friend."

"You can't rewrite history," Renee snapped. "You and Jessie *were* best friends. I was in there, too. Tamara and Becca were good friends, and Tamara brought Becca into the group. That's the way it was. Those are the dynamics. Sorry. It's just fact."

Evangeline's mouth trembled slightly. "We weren't best friends," she insisted. "We were pretty good friends. But I don't remember her being 'precognitive.' Maybe she said something that scared us once or twice when it came true, but that was it."

"Fine." Renee sighed. "Have it your way. But you do remember Jessie telling us she was in danger."

"I . . . don't think so." Vangie lifted a shoulder.

"Why don't you want to go back there? What scares you so badly?"

"Back where?" Evangeline asked.

"To the past." Renee didn't bother hiding her exasperation. "To the fact that *something* was after Jessie. She tried to make light of it, but she said things that now . . . when I think of them with the benefit of hindsight, they make more sense." Renee raked her hands through her hair and tugged on the ends.

Becca thought of her vision of Jessie with one finger over her lips.

"She said she wasn't safe," Renee said.

Tamara shook her head. "What's gotten into you?"

"Okay, forget it. I'm trying to explain something I can't explain. I feel . . . like I'm in danger, sometimes. That's all. And it really started when I began looking into Jessie's past."

"I've had a weird feeling. Like I was being followed," Becca confessed.

"You, too?" Tamara gazed from Becca to Renee and back again.

"Maybe it's the cops," Evangeline ventured.

Renee assured her tautly, "It's *not* the police."

"I never thought you'd be the kind to take a warning from the Tarot so literally," Tamara said.

"I told you, it's not the Tarot," Renee said with extreme patience, her voice lowering. "You know I've been investigating, trying to dig up an angle for my story on Jessie, but . . ." She heaved a deep sigh that seemed to come from her gut, then pressed her palms to her cheeks. "You're not listening. None of you are listening. And I don't know how to get you to."

"We don't know what the hell you're saying," Evangeline said tartly but her face was gaunt, her eyes wide. She hadn't missed the emotion, regardless of what she said.

"Okay, so I'm warning you. Me. *Us.* If anything weird happens, let the rest of us know right away," Renee went on doggedly. "Maybe we can—avoid it—if we work together. If we watch each other's backs."

Watch your back, Becca . . . Jessie's last words to her reverberated through her mind.

Tamara snorted, but Renee forged on, again rotating her nearly full cup on the table. "It's like stirring up Jessie's bones has awakened it."

"Okay . . . *It?*" This time Evangeline's tone had a hefty amount of disparagement, as if Renee were out of her mind. "Now you sound melodramatic."

"God, Renee," Tamara murmured. "Whatever you're feeling, it's . . . just what you're feeling. Real to you, yeah, but come on. Whatever you're going through . . . with Tim or with your work, it's affecting your judgment. This isn't like you. There are no demonic forces coming after us."

"I didn't say demonic."

"You said stirring up Jessie's bones awakened it," Tamara reminded her, picking up her purse and grabbing her coat. "Close enough."

"I hope Jessie's dead," Evangeline said suddenly.

Renee frowned at her, then turned to Becca. "She is dead. You think so, too, right?"

Tamara hesitated, her shoulder bag over her arm, but she was half turned toward their table, waiting for Becca's answer. In fact, they were all staring at her. Becca said, "It all gets back to, if those bones aren't Jessie's, then whose are they?"

"That's a good question," Renee said.

"It's been twenty fucking years," Tamara snapped. "I don't know what you expect us to say to you, Renee. You're, like . . . falling apart. And you're the smart one! You're really starting to scare me." She shot Becca another look. "You look scared, too."

"It's . . . disturbing," Becca said. "I don't know what happened to Jessie, but the police'll figure it out."

"What if something happens to us before they do?" Renee asked.

"Nothing's going to happen to us," Evangeline said, her voice an unconvincing whisper.

"I have to run." Tamara, with a wave of her hand, headed out the door, leaving a swoosh of cold air in her wake that sent a little shudder up Becca's spine.

Renee stared at Evangeline, who gazed back almost defiantly. "Nothing's going to happen to us," Vangie repeated as the door slammed shut.

Renee turned to Becca. "Be careful," she said, then picked up her purse and coat as well.

"I'm a part of this investigation," Gretchen Sandler stated flatly, her palms spread on Mac's desk as she stood in front of him. "Your latest after-hours attempt to get me out of the picture is . . . at the very least, amateurish."

It was dark, but then it felt like it was always dark this time of year. Mac knew his partner was pissed at him and didn't much care. She, like many before her, would hang around for a couple of months, maybe even years, but soon enough she would get one foot on his back and another on the next rung to success and catapult herself forward. He was more interested in when the autopsy report and DNA would land on his desk, and if an artist could do facial reconstruction on her skull if there was no DNA match. Twenty years ago, DNA was in its infancy as far as law enforcement went, but it was available, and there were hair samples from a brush of Jessie's follicles intact, that were being tested.

He knew in his gut the girl found in the maze was Jessie, and her parents suspected it, too. They might not want to talk to him, but he'd heard the weary acceptance in their voices nevertheless.

Mac still felt his partner's presence at his desk. "D'Annibal ask you to keep an eye on me?" Mac didn't glance up as he reread his notes on Jarrett Erikson. The guy was the slipperiest eel in the barrel and the least forthcoming. What a bastard.

"I—am—your—partner."

"Could you say that a little slower? I'm not quite catching it."

"You can be as big an asshole as you want. I'm still part of this investigation."

Mac gazed into her sharp blue eyes, then leaned back in

his chair. No point in a stare-down. "Okay, so I've talked to most of the guys of the group."

"I need to be with you when you interview anyone else. You need another perspective."

"You have been talking to D'Annibal. Perspective. That's one of his favorites."

She moved sharply and Mac automatically flinched. He'd been around enough perps to sense a threat in a hairs-breadth. But Gretchen just twisted like a robot, then stormed away to her own desk, which was behind his and halfway across the room. She'd been seated closer to him once, but it had left her away from the rise and fall of gossip that other detectives and cops engaged in. She might be universally disliked, but she was going to be in the center of the action, by God. Hanging out with a has-been like Mac wasn't going to cut it.

He gazed down at his list. There were checkmarks and notations beside the names of the Preppy Pricks he'd already re-interviewed. Nothing much had come from those meetings other than a feeling that they all universally disliked him and that they were reluctant to give anything away. He probably deserved that. He'd pretty much squeezed them through the wringer back in the day.

The only ones he hadn't met with yet were Hudson Walker and Zeke St. John. He hadn't started on the girls—women—of the group yet. He hadn't learned much from them twenty years earlier and he didn't expect to learn much now, but you never knew. He paused over each of their names.

Tamara . . . Renee . . . Evangeline . . . Rebecca.

He circled Rebecca's name, feeling something stir in his memory about that one. She was different. A bit of an odd duck. But there was just something about her, something he couldn't quite remember. She wasn't Jessie's closest friend, but she seemed the most like her in ways he couldn't quite analyze. "What is it you know?" he said aloud, staring at the old picture.

"What?" Gretchen called from the other side of the room, as if he were addressing her.

"Nothing."

"Damn you, McNally. Don't leave me out."

As usual, Mac didn't respond.

Becca had driven about two miles from Java Man when her cell phone jangled and she saw Hudson's number on the screen.

"Hey, there," she greeted him warmly. "I heard the police have started calling."

Hudson made a sound of annoyance. "Bound to happen. McNally called me and we talked on the phone, but he still wants to interview me in person. That's probably in the cards."

Becca thought of Renee and the investigation that had led her to the coast. "I suppose we'll all have to talk to him."

"When can I see you?" he asked.

"I just happen to be free right now," she said and smiled as she turned on her blinker and slid into the slower lane.

"Can I talk you into pizza at my place?"

"You just did. I'll be there in twenty minutes."

She clicked off, a grin on her face, and turned west onto the Sunset Highway to Laurelton. Traffic was thick through Beaverton and out to Hillsboro, but by the time she cruised into the area known as Laurelton, it had thinned to nearly nothing. She headed toward Hudson's and when she turned down the gravel drive she was met by welcoming lights. She hurried up the steps and rang the bell.

Hudson called, "It's open," and Becca pushed the front door handle and entered. Leaving her coat on the hall tree, she walked toward the kitchen where the smell of tomato sauce, garlic, and onions beckoned.

"Hi," he said, a slow grin stretching into place. Hudson was also in jeans, and he had on a chocolate corduroy shirt, the sleeves rolled up his forearms. They stared at each other a moment, then were in each other's arms. She started laughing and couldn't stop and he grinned at her.

Then he suddenly bent her over his arm so that her hair was almost sweeping the floor and he pressed his lips hard and hot against hers. She clung to him for fear she might fall backward, but opened her mouth when his tongue slipped between her teeth and the deepest part of her started to tingle.

She let out a low moan and he lifted his head. "Missed you," he said.

"Missed you, right back."

"Pizza can wait," he said, blue eyes intense.

"Yes . . ." Becca murmured as he swept her off her feet and carried her up the stairs to his bedroom, kicking the door shut behind them as they fell together on the bed.

There wasn't much more conversation after that. They yanked at buttons, flies, and zippers, and once the clothes were tossed aside, came together hot and fast. Hudson kissed her in all the places that made her go crazy, touching her intimately, sometimes gently, other times a little more rough, and she returned the favor, surprising him by exploring his body with her fingers and lips.

"God, Becca," he finally muttered as he could stand the torment no more. Flipping her onto her stomach and holding her bare breasts in both hands, he slid into her and made love as if he'd never stop. She closed her eyes as she clenched around him, her spasms echoing his as he collapsed, sweating and breathing hard.

"Sweet Jesus," he whispered against her ear.

She could barely breathe, couldn't think, as she held him close, enveloped in a warm shawl of afterglow, lost in sensation.

It seemed like eons later when he lifted up on one elbow and the low rumble of his voice asked, "Is it pizza time?"

She turned to him and guided his head so that he kissed her, sucked at her breast and began rubbing his hands over the small of her back and the slope of her rump. "Not yet," she murmured.

They made love again, more slowly this time, and Becca was slightly amazed at how much she wanted him, how languid and lovely she felt in his embrace, how wild and sensuous she could become without a whit of reserve. When finally they both stirred, dressed, and headed downstairs, it was hours later.

"I believe that pizza might be cold," Becca said.

"That's what microwaves are for."

"Just so you know, that wasn't a complaint."

He shot her a warm look as he placed several pieces of pepperoni pizza in the microwave. Becca's gaze fell on a dog bowl shoved by the back porch, something she'd missed earlier. He must have guessed what she was thinking because he said, "My lab, Booker T., died last year."

"Oh, I'm sorry," Becca said, heartfelt.

"He was old."

"I have a dog. A mutt. Ringo. He's kind of . . . my sanity meter. As long as Ringo's around, everything else can be a problem and it'll still be okay."

Hudson glanced at the empty bowls. "I suppose I should put them away."

"When you're ready, you will."

When the pizza was hot, they took their plates and sat down at the banquette in the corner, a scarred version that was surprisingly comfortable with gold cushions.

"I've always liked this place," she said, looking out the window toward the barn, visible beneath the security lights. How many times had she and Hudson made love in the hay loft?

"Yeah . . ." He sounded pensive, as if his thoughts had traveled down the same path. "I told you I have a new foreman? My old one, Grandy, was with my parents for years. He was so much a part of this place, it's a whole new world without him."

"Did he retire?"

"He's got personal stuff going on, so he suggested some-one else to help me." Hudson shrugged. "Hasn't quite been the same. I'm hoping he'll be back soon."

"Personal stuff encompasses a lot of things," Becca ob-served, thinking about her own issues as she bit into a pizza.

"His son is raising kids alone, broke his leg or something, and Grandy's granddaughter's pregnant. The whole family thinks the father's a loser. She might be moving in with him. It sounded messy."

"A baby?" Becca asked, trying to keep her voice neutral.

"Grandy's stepping in to help. Not the ideal way to bring a new life into the world, without any kind of stability."

"She's keeping it?"

"I think that's the plan, but there doesn't seem to be any solid decision-making going on."

She swallowed and looked away, wondering if she'd ever be able to tell him about the baby they'd almost had, wonder-ing what kind of effect it would have, if any, at this late date, wondering if he would be glad the decision had been taken from them.

The conversation turned away from the tricky subject and Hudson gave her an oversized jacket and they walked through the rain and darkness to the barn where Hudson switched on the light and Becca was greeted by the smells of dry hay and old leather mingled with the warm scents of horses. She was introduced to three mares, Christmas, Tallulah, and Boston, an Appaloosa who seemed heavy with foal. "This is really more of a hobby than anything else, I guess," Hudson admit-ted. She knew, though he didn't say so, that he'd made his money elsewhere. That this farm was a dream he'd turned into a reality.

"You've never been married, have you?" Becca said as the horses snuffled in their mangers and she petted Boston's soft nose. Tallulah, the bay, nickered softly for attention and Hudson scratched her between her dark ears.

"Nope." He shot her a look. "Would you do it again?"

"Maybe." She shrugged. "I don't know. Ben and I, we . . . just weren't suited to each other."

"What was wrong?"

"What wasn't."

"Mmmm . . ."

"I don't know why I married him," she said, not wanting to sound completely bitter. "I wanted the dream, I guess. A husband. A family. Children. After we were married he would always tell everyone we didn't want children, when he knew good and well that I did. I never knew what to say in front of people. I couldn't really respond by saying, 'No, my husband's wrong. I do want kids. He's lying. *He* just doesn't want kids.' I couldn't figure out how to put that in words without starting a huge argument, so I said nothing. And then he got involved with someone else and he died in her arms. And she was pregnant when he died. So she has a baby now." Becca stuffed her hands in the deep pockets of his jacket. She could feel him looking at her, but she couldn't meet his gaze.

"You still want the dream?" he asked.

"Well, yes, but I don't really expect it to happen."

He seemed to want to ask her more questions, but in the end he let the conversation shift back to safer topics and entertained her with a story about how Tallulah had scraped him off her back using tree boughs and how he'd had to trudge home on a sore ankle only to find the mare waiting expectantly at her stall for her next meal, completely unrepentant.

Hudson snapped off the lights. As they returned to the house, skimming puddles and ducking against the rain, he said, "It's strange, but all this stuff about Jessie seems to have brought us together again."

"Yeah." She half laughed. "Fairly ironic," she said over the patter of the rain hitting the roof of the porch as they walked up the steps.

The phone was ringing as they walked back inside and Hudson let the answering machine pick up.

"This is Detective McNally," a deep male voice said. "I'd still like that face-to-face meeting with you, Walker. Call me back." He finished by leaving his number.

"Guess there's no way out of it," Hudson said, frowning as he stared at the phone.

"Maybe he has more information."

"More likely he wants some." But Hudson returned the call, catching McNally and agreeing to meet the detective the next day at a diner a couple of miles from the police station.

"An informal meeting, whatever the hell that means," he said, reaching into the fridge for another beer. "Want to come with me?"

"Hell, no. But I'm sure my name's on that list somewhere, too, so . . ."

"Then it's a date," he said.

She laughed as she exchanged his jacket for her coat in the front hallway. "You, me, and Detective McNally."

"I'm sure it'll be a blast."

Chapter Thirteen

"How long does it take to draw a picture?" Gretchen kvetched as she and Mac drove to the Dandelion Diner, where they were to meet Hudson Walker. McNally was behind the wheel, squinting against sunlight that bounced off the wet pavement. "Facial reconstruction on a computer can't be that hard. It's just a matter of dimension, measurement of the bones, right? I mean, if that's your area of expertise, why the hell does it take so long? Who are these techs anyway?"

Mac grunted, passing an RV that was edging into his lane. He halfway agreed with his partner but hated being subjected to her monologue. It was as if the woman couldn't keep an idea inside her head. Once formed, it ran right past her lips and there was no stopping it. She had no governor. She just spewed.

And it was a pain in the ass.

"If we knew those bones were your little girlfriend, then we could take this investigation to the next level. And waiting for the damn DNA results is Chinese water torture. Unless you're sleeping with one of the lab techs, nobody gives a shit about a rush order. Even then it's fifty-fifty."

"You know from experience?" Mac asked mildly as he stopped for a red light and the RV, driven by an older woman in a trucker's cap, pulled alongside.

"If I did, I wouldn't tell. Your complacency scares me, McNally. When did that happen?"

Twenty years ago, he thought. And it wasn't complacency. It was cautiousness and diligence and awareness. But there was no way he was going to convince Gretchen she might not be employing her best investigative skills. She had all the answers already. No use in him wasting his breath.

As the light turned green and some idiot in a Ford Focus ran the light, crossing in front of him, he hit the brakes. Gretchen swore. "For the love of Christ, we oughtta pull that moron over!"

"The traffic guys'll get him," he said, gunning it to get in front of the RV, then whipping the cruiser into the gravel lot of the diner.

Inside, the Dandelion was painted bright yellow and the booths were covered in green plastic. Mac slid into one and Gretchen sat down opposite him as a waitress offered coffee, turned over the cups already on the table, and filled them each with a stream of steaming liquid. "I'll give ya a minute," she said around a wad of gum. "Specials are written on the board." She indicated a chalkboard hung near the counter, then wandered off to a table of four men in their sixties.

Mac stared through the window to the outside lot.

"What do you ask them—these 'friends' of Jessie Brentwood's?" she queried sarcastically as she picked up a plastic-encased menu and scanned it. "What kind of investigation is this? I should probably know."

He felt irritation flare and tamped it back down. "Don't piss me off."

"What? I can't ask questions?"

"You know the drill. Don't act like you're an idiot."

"You're a piece of shit, McNally. You act like the Lone

Ranger. No, worse, you wouldn't even trust Tonto. You seem to think that this case is yours and no one else's."

It has been. For twenty years.

He didn't have time for this. It was annoying as hell to be saddled with her. But it won't be for long, he reminded himself. His partner would get restless and move on. With that thought in mind, he decided to be more conciliatory. "We just talk. About what was up twenty years ago. Cover the same ground. See if anything else pops up, something they might have forgotten they're supposed to keep secret."

"Like they're part of a conspiracy? All in it together."

"Not quite."

"And this guy is one of the ones you call the 'Preppy Pricks.'"

Mac nodded. As men they didn't seem as privileged or entitled as they'd been as teenagers, but he wasn't able to completely forget their behavior when they were younger.

"Do you write off this meal?" Gretchen asked, flipping the menu over. "The department doesn't pay for it." She gave him a look and he realized she was asking. As if anyone would give him special treatment.

"The department doesn't pay for much."

It was her turn to grunt an assent.

Mac watched a blue Jetta pull in and park. Seconds later a woman climbed from the driver's side. Mac felt his gut tighten, but he showed no emotion. Rebecca Ryan, now Sutcliff. He recognized her instantly and remembered his last conversation with her as if it were that morning.

"I didn't talk to her before she left," Becca had said to him, seated on the front steps of the high school. She'd been nervous talking to a cop, her hands clasped in front of her, almost as if she'd been praying, her book bag on the step beside her, and she'd glanced into the parking lot. Her hair had been long and a light enough brown to appear almost blond, her eyes hazel and wide. It was her profile that reminded him of Jessie Brentwood, whom he'd only seen pictures of, though full on, Becca's face was rounder, appearing more innocent whereas Jessie appeared to have secrets filling her head, a wicked little smile teasing her lips, her eyes a shade of green and gold that reminded him of a restless ocean.

He'd quizzed her up and down, backward and forward about Jessie, but Becca Ryan had known little, basically nothing. She'd run with Jessie's crowd and that was it.

"I didn't ask her to come here," he said now, his gaze following Becca's entrance into the diner.

"She's one of 'em?" Gretchen asked, her head swiveling with interest.

"Yeah. Rebecca Sutcliff. She must be meeting Hudson Walker." *Has Sutcliff, now a widow, somehow hooked up with Jessie Brentwood's ex?*

At that moment a large, beat-up pickup wheeled into the lot and parked next to the Jetta. Mac tore his gaze away from the approaching Becca to witness Hudson slam the door to his truck and stride toward the diner's front entrance.

How long had they been an item? he wondered.

Becca waited for Hudson, but they didn't so much as touch as they entered the diner. Mac was shifting his thoughts on how he planned this interview to go when Gretchen took the bull by the horns and gestured toward a nearby table. "Let's move over here." She grabbed her cup of coffee, slid from the booth, and shifted to a chair. Mac would have agreed that the table was a better choice than the intimacy of a booth, but her ever-constant decision-making—never so much as waggling an eyebrow at him for direction or corroboration—really bugged the hell out of him.

It was evident Walker and Becca Sutcliff were together and, Mac guessed from the looks they passed between them, definitely a couple. He made quick introductions all around, then they sat and the waitress poured a couple more cups of coffee while a busboy swabbed at their recently vacated table.

Becca's hair was scraped into a ponytail. She wore a

black-and-white plaid scarf around the neck of her leather
coat, and the way she pulled the scarf from her neck was
nothing short of sinuous, at least in Mac's opinion. He remembered very clearly how she'd been as a teenager: wide-
eyed, skinny, skittish, and smart enough to keep her thoughts
to herself. He hadn't put together that Hudson Walker might
be more interested in her than his own girlfriend, Jessie
Brentwood, but then maybe that was just conjecture on his
part now.

Hudson Walker had filled out over the years and had earned
a few more lines around the corners of his eyes, as if he
squinted in the sun a lot. He was dressed down, jeans and shirt,
lightweight jacket—a far cry from Christopher Delacroix III's
tailor-made wool suit. The man's tie had probably cost more
than Mac took home in a week.

Hudson took a seat across from Mac's. He gazed across at
Gretchen, who was sizing him up but good. "You're Hudson
Walker," she said. "The vic's boyfriend from twenty years
ago?"

"The 'vic' being Jessie Brentwood? You're saying you
identified her body?" Hudson asked, turning to Mac.

"Still unconfirmed," Mac said. "We're waiting for DNA."

Hudson swivelled his gaze to Gretchen. "I dated Jessie,
yeah."

Walker was weightier since high school, more in demeanor than actual pounds. And Mac understood before the
man said a word that Hudson Walker had no intention of
helping him any more now than he had when he was younger.

"You wanted to see me," he said in a tone that let Mac
know just how he felt about that.

Mac opened his mouth, but Gretchen jumped in again.
"Everybody said Jessie Brentwood ran away, but then those
bones showed up."

"But you're still not certain they belong to Jessie, so
maybe this is a little premature."

Mac said, "I think it's just an exercise—confirmation.

We've gone through all the missing persons files. We'll find those remains belong to Jezebel Brentwood."

Becca drew in a quick breath. Her skin was pale. In fact, she looked out-and-out sick.

"You all right?" Mac asked.

Hudson turned to her. "Becca?"

"I'm fine."

"Was it something I said?" Gretchen asked wryly.

Mac cringed. His partner had no class. "Are you sure you're—"

"Excuse me." Becca suddenly scraped back her chair and headed toward the women's room, which was clearly marked at the end of the row of booths.

Hudson half rose from his chair but let her go.

"She always scare so easily?" Gretchen asked in mild surprise.

Hudson's gaze shifted to Mac's partner, and Mac had to fight to keep his lips from twitching with amusement. Gretchen was pissing Hudson off but good. One of her favorite tactics, though what good it would do in this case, he had no idea. Before Hudson and Gretchen could go to the next level, Mac said, "I'd like to just run over the sequence of events before Jessie Brentwood disappeared."

"You just said you don't know if the remains are even Jessie."

"Slow days at the department," Gretchen said. "We're up to our asses in cold cases instead of current events." She took a sip from her cup, scowled, and added cream. "Crime's on a downswing. What can I say?"

"It's no secret I thought something happened to her twenty years ago," Mac cut in. "You were one of the last people to see her."

Hudson hesitated a moment. Mac could almost see when he made the decision to tamp down his annoyance and just get on with it. "We had a fight," he stated rotely. "She didn't think I was being honest with her. I didn't think she was being honest with me. We were both right."

"And what were you lying about?" Gretchen asked.

"More like omissions of the truth. We were in a high school romance that had run its course."

"You liked someone else," Mac said, his eyes following the path Becca had taken.

"It was over. That's all."

"You didn't follow her into that maze and stab her to death?" Gretchen asked conversationally.

"She was stabbed?" Hudson asked. He turned to Mac for corroboration.

Mac nodded curtly. "That's the ME's opinion."

Walker seemed to think that over while Mac, with a warning look at Gretchen to keep her big trap shut, asked more questions about the timeline of the last night Hudson saw Jessie. It was more of the same from his notes from twenty years ago, less really, as Hudson's memory wasn't as clear as it had been then.

"She said she was in trouble," Hudson said. "Something was out there."

"In trouble? What do you mean? Trouble with her parents? At school? Maybe pregnant?" Gretchen leaned a little forward in her seat.

Mac wanted to smash his foot down on hers. She seemed determined to blab all aspects of the case before he was ready. Some of the information had to be held back from the press, the populace in general, so that only the police and Jezebel Brentwood's killer knew the truth.

Walker lifted a hand and dropped it again in weary exasperation. "It wasn't as defined as that. More a case of something unclear—like trouble was going to find her. I think she said something like that. 'Trouble's coming' or something. I don't remember her exact words, but she was on edge. She couldn't sit still."

His story was the same as it had been for twenty years.

"Did you suspect she wanted to run away?" Gretchen asked.

"I just thought we were having a fight. We'd had a bunch of 'em. The only time she said she wanted to get away was when she asked me to take off for a weekend with her." He snorted and picked up his cup. "Like either of our parents were going to go for that."

Something niggled at Mac's brain, something he couldn't quite catch. So Jessie had wanted to run off for a weekend, so what? And yet . . . He reminded himself to look at his notes.

Walker glanced in the direction Rebecca had gone again, and Mac could tell he was starting to get antsy over her prolonged absence. But then the door to the restroom opened and Rebecca came back to their table. Her skin was no longer pale, it was flushed, and Mac deduced that she'd been damn near scrubbing her cheeks raw.

"You okay?" Walker asked, obviously concerned. Yep, they were involved.

"Yeah. I've been fighting a bug. Guess it's trying to get the upper hand." She smiled wanly. Mac didn't buy it.

"Can you handle some questions?" Mac asked her. "Or we can check in later."

"No, go ahead." She clearly wanted to get the interview over with. "I heard you wanted to talk to all of us, and since Hudson was coming anyway . . ."

"So you two are a couple now?" He wagged his finger between them.

"We've known each other since high school," Becca said. Her gaze was steady now. "We hang out sometimes."

He let it go. For the moment. Then he asked her about her own timeline of what had happened in the days before Jessie Brentwood disappeared.

Rebecca was even fuzzier than Hudson; she wasn't a close friend of Jessie's and only kind of remembered what they'd said to each other in their last meeting. Mac ran through the events of those last few days—what had been happening at their school—but Rebecca could add nothing noteworthy.

Luckily Gretchen kept her tongue in her head.

In the end, Mac knew about as much as he had to start with, and that the sexual tension between Hudson Walker and Rebecca Sutcliff was almost palpable.

Did it have anything to do with Jessie? Was it something entirely new?

"If those two haven't hit the sheets already, it's only a matter of time," Gretchen observed as they left the diner. Becca and Hudson were climbing into their respective cars as Mac and Gretchen got into the cruiser. "They act like they're just friends, but something's going on."

"Maybe."

Mac pulled out of the lot and, in his rearview mirror, noted that Becca and Hudson's vehicles drove off in different directions.

"And what did you say that sent Rebecca to the bathroom for a dash of cold water to the face?"

Mac looked at Gretchen, then gunned the cruiser into traffic heading toward the station. "Who, me? I didn't have a chance to say anything."

"What then?"

Mac shook his head, but admitted, "She did look like she was about to pass out."

"Something scared her."

Mac reviewed what had been said and remarked slowly, "She was already scared when she got here. Why did she come?"

" 'Cause she knew you were going to be calling her and she wanted it over with the support of Loverboy. Who, by the way, is just a friend."

"They say that attraction in high school is the easiest to rekindle. What attracted once can really heat up in the now."

"Look at you—Mr. Love Life."

"Yeah, that's me."

"But you might have something there. I went to my last class reunion about three years ago and I witnessed a couple of hook-ups. A few of 'em divorced their spouses and ended up together. I couldn't believe it. My high school boyfriend was a jerk then and a major loser now. It wouldn't have happened. No way."

He eased down the road, barely noticing the other vehicles.

"I bet she's the reason Brentwood and Walker had their little spat. You know, the whole 'Hell hath no fury like a woman scorned' theory?"

He mentally chewed on that. Maybe there was something to it. "Rebecca Ryan wasn't a big part of the investigation twenty years ago, so I didn't expect her to be now." Mac cut the cruiser through a back alley, avoiding a Dumpster and a double-parked delivery truck.

"I think *we'd* better add her to the suspect list."

"Or elevate Walker a bit."

"He's close to *numero uno* anyway, isn't he? Being the boyfriend and all? With her pregnant?"

"He's up there."

"Maybe Rebecca Ryan should be, too," Gretchen said.

Mac didn't respond. The more he learned about the Jessie Brentwood case, the stronger he felt he was growing closer to some dark and unexpected truth.

Becca watched her fingers shake as she threaded her key into the lock of her front door and let herself inside. Ringo jumped off the couch and trotted over to her happily and she bent at the knees and scratched his ears and held him close for long minutes. Then she checked that she'd locked the door behind her and walked into the kitchen, grabbed a glass, filled it with water, and drank it down completely, her eyes closed, her heart still racing.

She'd seen Jessie at the diner.

Outside the window. Clear as day. Her hair blowing in the sharp wind. She'd pressed a finger to her lips, asking for Becca's silence. Another vision. Similar to the one at the mall. She'd glanced ahead into the eyes of Detective Mc-Nally, who'd been watching her so intently it made her short of breath.

I can't faint, she'd told herself sternly, feeling that familiar headache take over. Then she'd made an excuse and quickly headed to the bathroom, filling the basin with cold water and pressing her face into it, counting slowly to ten. She did it twice more, turning her skin red but bringing her ringing ears into line and her woozy head back to sharpness without actually passing out.

Jessie had dematerialized in those few moments. When Becca had returned to her seat in the diner and risked a glance at the window, all that was outside had been their respective vehicles and a stretch of parking lot gravel.

What did it mean? What did Jessie not want her to tell?

"Am I crazy?" she asked, bending down to the dog, who licked her chin line and woofed softly.

Becca headed for the living room couch and sat down heavily. Ringo jumped up beside her and curled in a ball, watching her with dark, sharp eyes.

What's going to happen next? she thought worriedly.

Renee felt they were in danger. Believed Jessie had said they were in danger. Twenty-year-old danger . . .

Becca ran her hands through her hair. She hoped she didn't have to see McNally again. She hoped that this interview was it. She hoped he wouldn't want to talk to her "alone" without Hudson. "Get real," she muttered to herself. If the police thought that either she or Hudson were involved in Jessie's disappearance, her *murder,* McNally would be back and it wouldn't matter what she wanted.

She hoped this feeling of impending doom that seemed to be weighing on her was just an aftereffect of her vision.

But she knew better. Deep in her heart, she knew better.

* * *

With the ever-present notes of jazz surrounding him, Glenn looked down at the invoices on his desk, invoices that carpeted the entire cherry expanse, and wondered what the hell was going on. Blue Note shouldn't be in the red, at least not this far in the red. They had customers. Not as many as before, but according to the receipts, Blue Note wasn't doing that badly, and actually, they'd been doing great for a while. It was just that ever since that incident with the college kid who'd died after being served at Blue Note, things had gone bad. It wasn't their fault that the kid had tried some kind of recreational drug and had a bad reaction to it before he'd come to their restaurant, but Blue Note kept getting lumped in with the event, so . . .

But that still didn't explain the flood of red ink in which he was drowning, both here and at home, where the spending just kept happening.

His mind jumped to thoughts of Gia. Damn the woman. She'd tried to haul him into bed just before he'd bolted for the restaurant. He'd thought about telling her about the nursery rhyme, but all she wanted to do was get laid and conceive. He needed a baby like he needed a hole in his head.

"Glenn," she'd called from the stairway. "Bring your big, luscious self over here!"

He'd been in the kitchen and he'd walked toward the front of the house. The blob had been bare-ass naked and hanging onto a newel post, jiggling her goods in a way that had made him feel slightly nauseous.

He'd run for his life. But now he was here, the clock on his desk reminding him it was after seven, the minutes of his miserable life ticking by, the dinner hour, what there was of it tonight, in full swing. Make that half swing. Or maybe no swing at all, he thought sourly as he sat in the midst of all this financial misery and wondered if it might not be a good idea to take a long walk off a short pier. Who would miss him? Gia? She'd find someone else. Scott? Like he cared about him beyond what he could get in sweat equity. His good friends from high school . . . ?

If they'd been so good, where had they been in the last twenty years?

After the cop had come to the restaurant, he and Scott had told everyone about how Detective McNally had paid a visit. But Glenn had kept the nursery rhyme note to himself. Scott hadn't mentioned it, either. Most of the guys had spoken with the detective and it had put everyone on edge. The Third had warned them to keep their cool. None of them had wanted to speculate about Jessie, at least not too much. They all wanted the investigation—and maybe Jessie herself—to just go away forever.

Glenn rubbed his temples.

Jessie . . .

He felt almost physically ill, thinking about her. Yanking open one of his desk drawers, he pulled out his bottle of Bushmills and poured himself a half glassful. Drinking sounded like a good idea. A damn good idea.

He was deep into his second glass when there was a knock on his office door. "Come in," he called garrulously. He didn't want to be disturbed by anyone.

"Glenn?" a female voice asked.

A shiver ran through him. Premonition. His lips parted and he half expected Jessie to enter the room, but it was Renee whose cap of dark hair and brown eyes peeked into the room. His heart rate had skyrocketed and now, with the rush of adrenaline dissipating, he felt goddamn good and mad. Hudson Walker's sister—excuse me, *twin* sister—had always bugged him. Even in high school she'd been nosy and high-handed, as if she were better than everyone else.

"What the hell?" he muttered.

"Sorry. I know you're busy. I tried to call, but my cell phone's dead—forgot to recharge, so." She shrugged, clutching her purse in a death grip as she walked into the office. Despite her apologies, she seemed tense, even worried. "Look,

I heard from Hudson that you talked to McNally, and I'm sure my name's coming up on his list. I just wanted some feedback. What did you tell him?"

So that's what the visit is all about. Weird. He wondered if Renee was working on her "story" about Jessie, or was this something else? Glenn selfishly didn't offer her a drink. He hoped she wasn't going to sit down, but she did just that, perching on the edge of one of the club chairs, her elbows now on her purse in her lap, her fingers pushing through her hair.

"I haven't said anything," Glenn told her. "There's nothing to say. You sure look like hell."

"Thanks." Her voice was dry but oddly unsure.

He squinted at her, wondering if he was just feeling the effects of the Bushmills or if Renee was hiding something, holding something in. "Talk to Scott. He was here when McNally showed up."

"Is he around?"

"Yeah. He's going back to the beach tomorrow."

Was it his imagination or did she stiffen slightly? "Where's your restaurant again? What part of the coast?"

"Lincoln City."

"Oh. South."

"South of what?"

She hesitated. "Deception Bay. I go there sometimes."

"Really? Why? It's like . . . nowhere. We checked out all the towns before we opened Blue Ocean, well, Scott, he did the searching, and Deception Bay didn't make the top ten, or even the top fifty."

"It's . . . a good place to get away. Writers, we need peace and quiet. But anyway, back to the cops."

"Yeah?"

"If you thought you knew something. Nothing concrete, but . . . something that might actually have bearing on the investigation . . . would you tell the detective?"

"I wouldn't tell him anything. Nada." He thought about

the nursery rhyme and wondered if he should mention it to Renee, but saw no reason. "You've been working this story. What do you think? Did you learn something?"

"No," she said quickly.

"That sounds like a lie."

"It wasn't," she assured him and seemed about to unload. God, he hoped it wasn't about her divorce. Women *loved* to talk about relationships, good or bad, but he just wasn't interested. He had his own domestic problems.

"What then?"

"I was at the coast a couple of days ago. I ran into some people . . . that I think knew Jessie." Renee looked away from him, to the pictures on the wall, snapshots of Scott and Glenn when they opened the restaurant.

"At Deception Bay, right?" Glenn was having trouble following and sitting up straight. The booze was hitting hard.

"Jessie's family used to have a house there and there was talk of a cult nearby and—"

"Does this have a point?" Glenn asked just as the door opened and Scott stepped into the room.

"Renee," he said in surprise.

Doesn't anybody goddamned knock anymore?

Renee got to her feet. "I'm glad you're here. I came by because I heard that you two met with McNally."

"More like he met with us." Frowning slightly, Scott threw a look Glenn's way. "Are you drunk?"

"Workin' on it," Glenn said, wishing they'd both just go away so he could continue his drinking in peace.

It wasn't about to be.

Renee and Scott discussed McNally for what felt like eons before they headed out together.

As soon as the door closed behind them, Glenn drew out the bottle and sloshed his glass a hefty refill.

He just wanted to stop thinking.

Chapter Fourteen

Mac rubbed his face as he sat at his desk, poring over all the details from twenty years ago, trying to mesh the past with what the Preppy Pricks recalled now. He'd been at it all day and should hang it up. But the station was quiet now and he had time to himself, time to concentrate. Not that being alone was helping. There was nothing new. Nothing he could grasp on to. It was all just as it had been. Maybes. Possibles. Tiny mysteries. Nothing concrete and credible.

He'd listened to the cassette tapes he'd taken of their interviews twenty years ago and thought how young their voices sounded, how young his own voice sounded. He wasn't taking audio notes now, though he supposed he should. Instead, he wrote copious notes on the interviews from today, comparing them to the tapes and chicken scratchings he'd jotted down at the time of Jessie's disappearance.

Now he glanced at the more detailed report from the lab that had been tossed on his desk earlier that day. No DNA results. Just more about the bits of detritus found at the scene. The little bit of white plastic turned out to be a teensy bit of oyster shell—no prints on it.

Mac thought about that hard. Oyster shell . . . from the beach? Was it significant? Was it even related to the victim in the shallow grave?

And then the thought he'd tried to come up with when he'd been interviewing Hudson surfaced. It had been prompted by Hudson's mentioning a weekend getaway. Mac's mind had touched on a trip to the beach. And that reminded him of something about a guy—a caller who, twenty years earlier, after seeing mention of Jezebel Brentwood's disappearance on the news, claimed to have picked her up hitchhiking several weeks before. It had seemed superfluous to the girl's disappearance and Mac had pushed the incident aside, deeming it not that important. Her parents had a cabin in some little burg on the coast, and he'd assumed she'd been coming back from there.

Now Mac meticulously combed through his notes till he found the small information he'd written on the stranger. He remembered how impatient he'd been. How little he'd cared for any information that took him away from the Preppy Pricks. He'd been so hotheaded, with his head stuck up his ass in those days. A young buck determined to nail one of those kids.

Hell.

He reread the passage. The stranger was a man named Calvin Gilbert who lived outside of Seaside and made a living selling firewood from an old pickup. He traversed Highway 26 from Astoria, Seaside, Cannon Beach, and a string of smaller coastal cities through the Coast Range and nearly to North Plains and Laurelton. He happened to catch a news report about Jessie on his television and he called the Laurelton police and was connected to Mac.

Re-examining his notes, Mac could almost hear the guy's voice again. "I picked 'er up outside of the cutoff to Jewell and Mist, y'know? It was black as hell's furnace and rain sheetin' somethin' fierce. This little girl is just trompin' along, so I rolls down the window and says, 'I could be one of them psychos, or I could be a guy just offerin' you a lift,' and she says back, 'You're not a psycho—probably a nicer guy than people think,' and she jumps in and asks me to take her to this school. Saint Teresa's, I guess." Mac had interjected at that point, "St. Elizabeth's," and the fellow had said, "Could be. So I drives her there, and it's still black as hell's furnace, so I try to talk her outta gettin' outta the truck, but she gets a little stubborn and says it's where she wants to go. To change the subject, she asks if I cut my firewood off Highway 53. And I says, 'Yeah, missy. How'd you know?' And she gives me this sexy little smile and says, 'I know things,' as she gets out of the truck. Kinda eerie, like out of one of them damned Stephen King movies. Anyways, she slams the door and doesn't look back. Not once. Which was okay with me, cuz I'm thinkin' she might have snake eyes or somethin', you know—that she wasn't quite human. I watch her go, till she was out of the glare from the headlights, you know, and she kinda disappears into the darkness. Then I leave, though I didn't want to, fire up the truck again and take off. Then I saw 'er face on the news, so I called you."

"I appreciate it," Mac had told him, though it didn't mean much.

"You know what's weird, son? My pickup was empty that trip. I'd dropped my load and swept the truck bed. How'd she know about the firewood?"

Mac hadn't offered any explanation, expecting there was more evidence of Calvin Gilbert's pursuits in his vehicle than he'd believed—sawdust, a chainsaw, bits of bark. Now he thought about that odd bit of information and wondered what Jessie Brentwood had been doing hitchhiking in the dead of night and why she'd asked to be taken to St. Elizabeth's.

Not home.

Not to a friend's house.

To the campus.

Where she probably died.

Shit.

The guy, Calvin Gilbert, it had turned out, spent a lot of time at a local watering hole and he'd been drunk more often than not, picked up for a DUI twice since that report. He hadn't been specific about the date he'd found Jessie in the mountains with her thumb out. Had it been the day of her disappearance? Three days prior? Mac had tried to piece together the last days of Jessie's known existence at the time, but Gilbert's call had been almost considered a crank. A guy getting his jollies by acting as if he knew something.

But maybe he'd been straight with them.

Maybe Calvin Gilbert had been the last person known to see her alive.

Rolling the small bit of oyster shell between his thumb and forefinger, Mac considered Jessie Brentwood. She was secretive, had run away from home several times before her final disappearance, was somewhat psychic, by all accounts, and there was something about the beach that seemed to run like a thread through the fabric of her life. Why he thought that, he couldn't quite say. It was more than just this bit of oyster shell, more than the fact that she was found halfway from the coast to Laurelton. But if she was hitchhiking— well, more accurately, just walking, apparently—along the highway that led straight west to the coast, where had she been? What or who had she seen? What was she looking for?

Hudson had said she felt trouble was after her. What kind of trouble? Did it have anything to do with her pregnancy? Hudson didn't seem to know about that, or else he was a consummate actor worthy of an Oscar as he hadn't even lifted a hair when Gretchen asked if he thought she was pregnant.

And Rebecca . . . Mac wished he could have talked to her more. She struck him as another person with secrets, though he couldn't begin to guess what they were at this point.

He sat at his desk and thought, stretching minutes to hours. The department went into night mode, with only a skeleton crew at the station. He sat and thought, and thought and sat, and when he finally surfaced it was after midnight and all he'd learned from his ruminations was that this cold case—which had warmed right up with the discovery of the remains at St. Elizabeth's—was cooling off again. Even when he got the DNA evidence, what did he have to compare it with? Just twenty-year-old hair with, he hoped, enough of the root attached to pull the DNA. But if not, how would he prove the body was Jessie's?

"And it might not be," he said aloud, accepting that fact for the first time, listening to his own voice finally entertain the possibility. As he left the station he heard the janitor warming up on "Blue Hawaii."

Glenn Stafford was dead drunk. Drunken. Drunked . . .

He eyed the liquid at the bottom of the bottle and could not believe—simply—could—not—believe—that it was gone except for a swallow or two. He'd done that? Drank down the whole dang thing?

Vaguely he remembered the cooks going home and the wait staff closing up. Several people had stuck their heads inside his office and given him updates on the ending of the evening, but they were gone now, the restaurant closed. Scott had cruised through again and given Glenn the old evil eye.

Screw you, buddy. I'll get goddamn good and wasted if I want. It's my booze, too!

Now he staggered to the door, steadying himself on the jamb. The place was quiet. Unearthly quiet, he thought. Unearthly. Kind of like he felt. He could see his feet moving one in front of the other as he navigated his way toward the front entrance. Outside, the parking lot lights made little bluish moons on the pavement. Inside, the ambient lighting around the floor sent a diffused yellow glow to sections of carpet.

Glenn turned back toward the kitchen and bar area. What the hell? He deserved another bottle. He thought of Gia. Man, would she be pissed. Probably lying naked on the bed waiting, hoping he'd come in and screw her just to make a damned baby. Talk about taking the fun out of things. She'd called twice—or had it been three times?—but he'd told the hostess to tell his wife he was busy, and he'd let his cell phone go straight to voicemail.

Now he squinted at the rows of bottles of booze and caught sight of himself in the mirrored wall behind the hedge of liqueurs and spirits. Damn, Stafford. You're . . . too . . . stocky.

"Stocky," he said aloud, then grinned at his reflection like an idiot. Fuck 'em. It was time for another drink.

He rooted around and found an unopened bottle of Bushmills.

Clink.

He cocked his head toward the sound, his hand hovering over a bottle. He was alone, right? Hadn't Luis said, "Good night, I'll lock up, Mr. Stafford," a little while ago?

The noise had come from the kitchen.

Or had it?

Maybe he'd tipped one bottle into another himself as he was checking labels. He was a little wasted. He could have thought he'd heard something from the kitchen. Yeah, that was probably it. He strained to listen, but could hear nothing but that irritating smooth jazz that Luis hadn't turned off. Still . . .

"Hey," he called, swaying on his feet, his fingers around the neck of his next bottle. Geez, maybe he didn't need another drink.

He sniffed and froze. Wait a minute. Was that smoke? Was someone in the kitchen smoking?

"Goddammit," he muttered. Holding the bottle by its neck, he weaved his way into the kitchen. Under-cabinet fluorescents showed him the gleaming stainless steel surfaces and he felt a moment of pure pride. Why wasn't the restaurant making it? Why . . .

Glenn's nostrils flared. The smell of smoke was much stronger here. "Who's there?" he yelled.

Bang!

Something hit the floor. Hard.

"Jesus!" His heart began to thud. "Hey," he said, more cautiously, stepping forward, a sense of panic overtaking him.

Whoosh!

The sound was as loud as wind through a tunnel.

"What the fuck?"

SLAM!

The back door?

The skin on Glenn's nape crinkled. Fear congealed his blood. Something was wrong here, but he was too drunk to figure it out.

He blinked as he realized smoke was billowing from a back closet, the one behind the stove. He tried to step back, but slipped and smacked on his ass just as molten gold flames suddenly shot upward. Glass broke, the Irish whiskey splashing over the floor. The stainless steel changed to a blinding mirror of flame.

"Oh, God!" He tried to backpedal, crawl away, but it was too late.

Glenn's eyes popped open as a wall of fire rushed at him. He opened his mouth to scream.

Ka-BOOM!

An explosion rocked the restaurant. Glenn was tossed against the wall.

Trapped.

Crackling, wild flames shot outward. Heat seared his skin. His lungs burned hot as hellfire.

"Gia!" he shrieked, knowing he was about to die.

His mouth was an "O" of horror as he cowered and coughed, black smoke filling his lungs, his skin curdling.

He was screaming and screaming and the last thing he remembered was the roar of the inferno burning through his ears.

Burn. Burn in hell, you bastard.

I stand in the shadows, watching as the flames climb through the roof and burst against the night sky. Golden. Glorious. Rich. Like shimmering hands reaching for the heavens, as if in supplication, consuming everything in sight, black smoke clogging the air.

The fire is perfect.

And protection.

Far in the distance sirens scream and a few cars even now are slowing, people shouting. Panic ensuing.

I want to stay but I can't be this close. Perhaps I can slip into the crowd, watch the spectacle unnoticed.

I must melt back into the shadows.

For now.

The phone rang loudly on Becca's nightstand and she shot into a sitting position, her pulse leaping. She fumbled for the receiver and glanced at the clock as Ringo growled from the foot of the bed. *One thirty-six? Who would be calling? Oh, God . . .*

"Becca, it's Hudson," she heard as she pressed the phone to her ear. "Sorry to wake you. I thought you should hear it from me. Scott and Glenn's restaurant is on fire."

"What?"

"Scott just called. He thinks Glenn was still inside."

"What? What?" Becca snapped on a light, panic running through her. Ringo was now on all fours on the bed, the fur at his neck standing on end. "No . . . we were just there a couple of weeks ago." An image of Glenn with his short brown hair and thick build came to her. "There must be some mistake."

"Something exploded in the kitchen, apparently. Or that's what they think. Neighbors heard the explosion, saw a tower of fire shoot through the roof. It happened less than a half hour ago."

"And Scott called you?" Becca felt sick inside.

"He's panicked. Hoped that Glenn might have been at my house. I'm on my way."

"I'll meet you there," she said, climbing from the bed, her senses returning.

"No, you don't have to come. I just wanted to keep you informed."

"Thanks, but I'm going to come. See you soon."

"Be careful," he said, then hung up.

Be careful . . .

The same warning Renee had issued at Java Man, as if she'd known something terrible might happen.

The words followed her around as she stumbled into her clothes, brushed her hair into a quick ponytail, then ran out the door. She was in her car and driving to the scene of the fire before she'd really thought through what might have happened. The kitchen exploded? How did that happen? Faulty gas line, or a stove left on unattended, unwittingly? Or arson?

Becca shook that thought aside. Certainly until the ashes had cooled and the fire investigators had done their job, no one would know. And maybe Scott was wrong. Maybe Glenn wasn't inside. She sent up a silent prayer as she pushed the speed limit down the dark, deserted streets.

Only when she was nearing Blue Note did the traffic snarl. She arrived to a blast of red and white flashing strobes from several fire trucks, their hoses arcing cascades of water on a brilliant orange and yellow fire that lit up the black night and sent choking smoke and heat at ever-growing clusters of bystanders, forcing them to wrap more fully in their jackets and robes and turn protective shoulders to the scene. The police force had barricades erected and the crowd was forced back several blocks.

Becca parked in the empty lot of a bank nearly five blocks away, then walked quickly toward the inferno. Television crews had arrived, vans parked near the barricade, helicopters circling overhead, reporters with microphones and cameramen in tow.

The noise was deafening. Over the roar of fire and hiss from the water spouting over the flames, firemen shouted and people stood talking. She found Hudson with one of the firemen who stood near a ladder truck, his eyes on the scene.

Narrowing her own eyes against the dense smoke, she headed their way, only to be stopped by a policeman and told to wait. Hudson, too, was pushed behind the barricade and he found Becca waiting. His jaw was set, his eyes dark, and Becca knew as he approached that the worst had happened, their fear for Glenn was realized.

She felt ill. "It's true, isn't it?"

Hudson nodded and ran a protective arm around Becca's shoulders, tucking her to his side, which made her want to bury her face into his chest. The warmth of him brought memories circling just beneath her conscious thought, memories of making love to him. It felt ghoulish to be so intent upon her own internal thoughts with such a spectacle around them. A wall of heat burned over her right shoulder.

"What about Glenn?" she asked.

"They found someone inside. It was too late. No ID yet, but . . ."

"Dear God," she whispered.

He told her he'd gotten the information from one of the firemen—Dave. They knew each other slightly, she learned later, so Hudson was offered up some information that he might not have otherwise gleaned.

Dave remained at the fire truck staring at the still-raging flames.

Hudson pulled Becca away from the barrier, deeper into the crowd, and she could feel the relief from the searing heat almost instantly, her hot cheeks cooling in the frigid night air.

"How could this have happened?" she asked, her throat dry and tasting of the soot that filled the air.

Through the crowd she saw Scott, who had spotted Hudson. He walked briskly toward them, his bald head shining in the fire's hot light. He looked haggard and wild-eyed. Shocked.

"The whole place," he said. "The whole place. Jesus, all gone . . . and . . . Glenn . . . he was drunk."

"You saw him?" Hudson asked.

"Earlier. Drinking in his office. He must have gone home . . . he must have . . ." He looked around himself. "But Gia . . . she's hysterical."

"Is she here?" Becca asked.

He put a hand to his head. "Oh, my God."

They followed his look. Gia Stafford was being held up by a fireman who'd just caught her as she started to fall. She was crying, pulling at her hair, a down jacket covering her shoulders and torso while the hem of her nightgown dragged in the water from the fire hoses.

"They found a body, Scott," Hudson said. "Dead."

"No . . ." He shook his head, unable to take it in.

The crowd had edged closer, and one of the other firemen barked at them to get back. Hudson and Becca stood near a neighboring building and watched in silence for a while as Scott staggered away. They stayed long minutes, immobilized, mesmerized. Becca's eyes strayed often to Gia, who softly blubbered and clung to anyone who came within reach of her arms.

It seemed to take forever before the flames came under control and the building became a smoking, stinking hulk with areas that glowed inside like yellow eyes in a twisted, blackened mess.

"You people need to leave," one of the firemen stated grimly to the group as a whole. "Right now."

Hudson suddenly inhaled a sharp breath.

"What?" Becca looked up at him.

"I think they're bringing a body out. That's why they want the crowd to disperse."

Becca glanced past him to a stretcher being carried by two grimy firemen. A black tarp covered the contents but a charred appendage slipped out. A blackened arm.

She turned away in horror as the odor of seared human flesh made her gag.

"Come on," Hudson said, "I'll take you home."

"No—I've got my car—"

Gia's cries became shrieking wails and two of the firemen hustled her away from the scene though she clawed at them, desperately trying to stay.

"Mr. Walker?"

They both turned to see Detective McNally approaching them, his face grim. *Not now. For God's sake, not now!* Couldn't the damned cop just leave them alone? Becca looked away, aching inside. She wanted to make love to Hudson. She wanted to fuse her body with his and push all this away. She felt like shrieking and crying but she had no energy. Instead emotions churned inside her stomach and chest, and she squeezed her eyes shut.

Beyond her cocoon she could hear Hudson talking to Mac about the fire, could feel his voice in his chest as her face was pressed close to his torso. It was an exchange of information between the two men. The body was still unidentified but from the wristwatch on its arm, recognized by Scott, it appeared to be Glenn's. No one moved to tell Gia, who was being kept away from the grisly view. Becca felt her stomach heave and she kept its contents intact by pure force of will.

And then a wave came over her. That same inundating sensation that preceded a vision. She clung to Hudson for all she was worth.

"Becca?" he asked, glancing down at her.

"I'm . . ."

Falling, she meant to say, but it wasn't possible. She crumpled limply in his arms and only his strength kept her from hitting the wet pavement in a heap. Inside her head Becca could see a room. An office of some sort. She reached out one of her own hands and saw she was holding pieces of paper. A white card of some sort and a blue envelope. Words swam into her view, blurry and indistinct. Watery. Squiggles that weren't words, but maybe were if she could only read them. She saw that it was someone's name, written in an uneven hand: Glenn.

When she turned the card over she squinted as if she needed glasses and slowly the squiggles turned into words, the words into sentences.

What are little boys made of? Frogs and snails and puppy dogs' tails.

That's what little boys are made of.

Her heart clutched.

Jessie's rhyme! Jessie's taunt. As Becca gazed at the note, the edges began to blacken and curl and suddenly the words burst into flame. She let go of the fiery note, her fingers singed, smoke filling her nostrils, choking her.

"Jessie!" she cried out. "Jessie!"

Holding her, Hudson froze.

Jessie?

What the hell was Becca saying? Hudson nearly missed the fact that her legs had given way, but he caught her as she collapsed. A dead weight that he had to grab hard or she would fall to the ground.

What the hell? Why had she cried out Jessie's name? He held her tightly, half dragging, half carrying her away from the smothering smoke and the ear-deadening rush of water and engines.

"Becca," he whispered, tamping down his alarm as she had turned pale as death. He should have never let her come to the scene. He should have stopped her somehow. Forced her to stay home. Never called her.

But he'd wanted to see her again. From the first second he'd spied her in Blue Note two weeks earlier, he was right back to those days in high school when thoughts of her had consumed him, when he'd felt the guilt of wanting her company more than his own girlfriend's, when he'd wanted to hold her to him, press himself into her, make love until they were both senseless and sated with passion. He wanted to be with Becca. Wanted to breathe in her scent and bury himself inside her. He'd always wanted to.

"She okay?" Scott asked from thirty feet away, but his face was turned toward the disaster of the fire.

Hudson didn't answer. Becca was breathing. Breathing hard, actually, as if she were running. He could feel the rapid pounding of her heart against his own. It was like she was in some kind of trance, but it was an active one. She was no passive participant in whatever was going on.

"Becca?"

He was holding her close, but he'd tilted her head back so it was resting in his hand. Her lips quivered and she tried to speak. There was rapid eye movement behind her lids. He was both scared and energized. Vaguely he remembered something from the past—some distant rumor about Becca Ryan fainting and speaking gibberish. He could recall tight knots of high school girls looking at her and snickering. Not Jessie, who, though she'd been jealous of Becca, had not treated her like an outsider. But then Jessie had felt like one, too, sometimes. And not Tamara, who was Becca's friend, and he didn't think Renee was part of it. But Evangeline . . . ? Maybe it was just his own feelings about her, but he felt certain she'd been an instigator, one of the finger-pointers eager to slur someone else because her own self-image was so fragile and weak.

"Jessie . . ." Becca murmured again, and the hairs on the back of Hudson's neck rose.

Slowly her eyes blinked open and she gazed at him dully for several seconds. Then she jerked in his arms as if pulled by a string.

"I've got you," he said. "It's all right. It's okay."

"I . . . I went out . . ." She wrapped her fingers in the lapels of his coat, clinging to him. Her eyes squeezed shut as if she were in pain.

"Are you all right?"

"Yes." She swallowed hard, several times. "This . . . happens to me."

"I know."

She squinted an eye at him, her breath catching. "You know . . . that I had . . . a vision?"

"Vision, dream . . . loss of consciousness," he said, relieved that she was coherent, her color returning. "You sure you're okay?"

"Yes. But I saw something."

"Jessie?"

She ripped herself from his grasp and stared at him. Then she looked around as if slowly remembering where she was and what was going on. "Jessie? No. I—why did you think so?"

"You said her name."

"I spoke aloud?" That seemed to startle her and she suddenly looked pale enough to faint again.

"Let me drive you home."

He thought she was going to argue with him, but she jerkily nodded, then lifted her hand to her forehead. "I get headaches," she said.

"Where's your car?"

"Uh—in a lot. Willamette Bank and Trust or something like that," she said, trying to focus.

"I know where it is."

He helped her to her car and then ensconced her in the passenger seat. She gave him her keys and he, after adjusting the seat away from the steering wheel, pulled out of the parking lot. "What about your truck?" she asked, her head resting on the passenger window. She still looked wan.

"It'll still be here tomorrow."

"I'm okay," she said. "Truly."

"Uh-huh."

"This hasn't happened in a long time, but now it's . . . back.

They're back." She let out a long sigh, then yanked out the rubber band holding her hair away from her face.

"The visions?"

He hadn't meant to sound dubious but he heard it in his own voice. She turned slowly to stare at him and her eyes seemed huge in the dim glow of the dashboard lights. He asked her for directions to her condo though he knew the general direction from the list of addresses and phone numbers they'd given each other at their meeting at Blue Note. Becca pointed out the way, lost in her own thoughts.

When he pulled into her parking spot and hurried around to help her from the car, she tried to wave him off. "I'm really okay. I can get by on my own power."

"Humor me," he said, clasping her hand because she looked like she would refuse any other support.

At the rear door of the condo he handed her back her keys and she slid one into the lock. As soon as the door pushed inward he heard the half growl, half bark of a dog. The black and white scruffy beast glared at him and stood stiffly. Becca bent down to him, grabbing him though he wanted to be the watchdog, cooing to him and massaging his ears while he glared at Hudson and kept growling.

"Hush, crazy puppy," she said fondly.

"You've got a good watchdog there. He's just being protective."

Becca smiled. "Don't make excuses for him until you know him better. He's known to prejudge people."

She headed straight to a cupboard and pulled out a bottle of white pills. "Aspirin," she said. And then, as if anticipating what he would say next, she looked his way, her hazel eyes full of an anxiety she was trying hard to hide. "Sorry you had to see that. I'm—not a freak."

"Nope."

"Not a total one anyway." She swallowed the pills, chasing them with water. Hudson wanted to fold her into his arms again and was about to reach for her when she placed the glass back firmly on the counter, drew a breath, turned to him.

"I used to have these visions when I was a kid. Into my teens. The visions. I hadn't had one in years and then just recently—bam—they were back."

"You don't have to explain."

"Sure I do." She waved a hand dismissively, as if she wanted to brush away any and all of his lame protests. "My first one was of Jessie. A few weeks ago. I passed out at the mall. Right there near the food court! Fell down in front of a group of kids and really freaked them out. One of them took pictures of me on his cell phone."

Hudson made a strangled sound of anger that encouraged Becca.

"Yeah, I know. The kids were reacting."

"They were jerks. Uneducated morons."

"I think I scared them half to death, but anyway it was Jessie. She said something to me and put her finger to her lips. She was standing at the edge of a cliff."

He leaned a jean-clad hip against the kitchen counter while Ringo, in the doorway, still regarded the intruder with wary eyes. "These are different from the ones from your past?"

"Well, yeah. In content. They used to be just about people I knew. Like what they were thinking. Sort of a scenario would play out in my head about my parents, maybe. When they were fighting about something—usually me. They were always arguing about what was best for me, and sometimes I would see their fights in my mind and I think my visions were fairly close to the truth. Then when I got to high school the episodes got more intense and were mostly about boys I liked . . . or maybe girls who were mean to me . . ." She drew a breath. "They've never really made sense. More like dreams that hit me hard. One second I'd be normal, the next I'd wake up on the floor of the gym or hall or playground or science lab. It was more than a little embarrassing. You didn't know?"

"I remember rumors about them," Hudson admitted. "I think Evangeline helped spread them."

"Did she?" Becca's mouth turned down.

"She's never been the nicest person around," Hudson observed.

"She doesn't want Jessie to reappear."

"Maybe she thinks she'll steal Zeke from her."

Becca smiled faintly at his insight. "She was always thinking that. Anyway, fast-forward to today. I can't explain what they're about, but I had my first one recently *before* I'd heard about the body being found at the maze."

"And that was of Jessie."

"Yes."

"And you haven't had any other visions between high school and now."

"None. Not one the whole time I was married." Becca sounded sort of surprised. "I've always associated the visions with stress, but I had some really stressful times when I was married and I never had one."

"So maybe they're not stress induced."

"Maybe. Although tonight and the fire . . ." Her hands were trembling slightly and she flexed her fingers.

"Let's go into the living room."

He stayed close behind her but she was stronger than she appeared, he decided, as she made it to the couch with no problem, her dog jumping up beside her and curling into a tight ball, his eyes intense as they glued on Hudson, who took a chair opposite them.

"These visions," she said softly. "They're kind of a curse."

"Maybe it's your subconscious trying to warn you of something. The way you work out problems." Hudson shrugged. "It's no big deal."

"No big deal," Becca repeated through a hot throat. "I don't know whether to laugh or cry. I've spent so much time making myself crazy over them. So afraid to make a fool of myself. Be the object of ridicule."

"Don't worry about it," he said quietly.

"Easier said than done."

"What about the vision at the fire? It was about Jessie, too?"

"Not exactly."

Becca wondered how much to tell him. Sure, Hudson was being nothing but supportive, but she couldn't trust that he would remain that way if she revealed the extent of her idiosyncracy.

But still, her vision was strange.

"I saw the nursery rhyme," she admitted slowly. "In a note. Jessie's nursery rhyme. The one she used to taunt the boys with? I think . . . I think she may have sent it to Glenn. His name was on it."

Hudson went completely still. She watched his expression turn inward and felt her heart stop. Maybe he was reviewing his own feelings, deciding whether to keep championing her or dismiss her as a total nutcase. For a moment she'd felt unburdened, but now she braced herself, certain that was what was coming. Despite what he'd said, she knew his support might be weaker than he believed.

"What nursery rhyme?" he asked.

She rubbed her arms briskly. "Jessie's taunt. You remember it: *'What are little boys made of? Frogs and snails and puppy dogs' tails. That's what little boys are made of.'* "

Hudson closed his eyes a moment, touched his hand to his forehead as if making a monumental decision.

Becca's heart jolted. "Hudson?" She wanted to take back the words. She'd gone too far. She wanted him to think she was normal, but if he got up and walked out she wouldn't blame him.

"I'm the one who got the note," he said slowly, his gaze holding hers.

"No . . . it said Glenn. I'm . . . I'm sure . . ."

For a response he reached into an inner pocket of his coat and pulled out a white card identical to the one in her vision.

He turned it over so she could read the front.

HUDSON was scrawled across the paper in an uneven hand.

Chapter Fifteen

I watch as the fire begins to dim and the crowd starts to disperse. It's late and I should rest, there is so much to do, but the licking flames and billowing smoke have energized me.

No one has recognized me, though I've seen some who are familiar to me.

Rebecca . . .

Ah, yes . . .

Did you feel me here? Did you know that I observed you?

But she left, taken away by one of the others.

I followed their trail, caught a glimpse of her sliding into the passenger side of a little blue car . . . her vehicle, though he *drove it.*

Now the night closes in around me and I start back to my own vehicle when I sense it, that special scent, the one that propels me. It's faint, barely discernible over the odors of charred wood, burned plaster, and smoke, but it hangs briefly on the air. Luring me. Making me nauseous.

I close my eyes, concentrate.
Inside I quiver . . . anxious.
It's been so long . . .
But as surely as the tide changes with the moon, the time is near.
My mission is at hand.
Soon . . . soon . . .

Mac stood by his car, doused by dull, sprinkling rain, and stared at the rubble that had so recently been a restaurant and bar. Puddles had formed from the water from fire hoses and the ever-falling precipitation. The drama was all but over; the fire no more than foul-smelling steam. Standing water gleaming beneath the parking lot sodium vapor lights as drifting smoke hovered thick in the air.

The place had an almost vacant feel to it, even though the firefighters were still wrapping up their hoses and the trucks stood by, engines thrumming. Any looky-loos had left and Gia Stafford had been driven home by someone, thank God. The only person Mac still recognized was Scott Pascal, who sat on a wet curb and stared through red-rimmed eyes to the black, sodden hulk of Blue Note. Mac, who was rarely known for flights of fancy, had a sudden, sharp vision of a trumpet player squealing out some impossibly high note that ended in an echo of sadness. Blue note, indeed.

Pascal half turned. "Did you talk to Gia?"

He gazed at Pascal's profile, noting the deep weariness etched in his face. One thing Mac had discovered from his years of interviewing people was that you never knew what they might say in times of deep stress. He'd found it beneficial to keep his mouth shut. Ask a few tight questions, but just wait for it, something Gretchen had yet to learn, if she ever would.

"Accident or arson?" Mac posed.

Pascal went quite still. "Who's saying arson?"

"Maybe no one. It's always a question, though, in a case like this."

"A case like what? They're not telling me anything." He shot a vituperative glare at the departing firemen. Belligerence uglied his face.

"Come on, Pascal. You were bleeding money."

"You went through my financials?" He half rose from the curb.

"More like a guess. Your employees weren't exactly shy about saying how long they felt the restaurant would hang on."

He thought about that and sat back down. "Nice," he said sourly, then lifted an eyebrow. "How much time did they give us?" he asked with a touch of irony.

"A week or two. Maybe a month."

"You know Blue Ocean is taking off. Everyone said we'd never make it at the beach, but you'd be surprised."

"At the coast?" Mac reiterated, thinking of the oyster shell, the fact that Jessie Brentwood had been hitchhiking along the road leading from the coast soon before she disappeared.

"Yeah, Lincoln City."

Quite a bit south from where the Brentwoods had once owned a cabin.

Pascal said, "It's been a problem getting it going, sure, but it's a great location, and we lucked out with this chef who doesn't know how damn good he is, which is absolutely unheard of. Glenn, damn him . . ." He swallowed hard. "He never really knew what we had. He just used it as a place to escape from his wife." He barked out a bitter laugh. "Guess he finally achieved his goal."

"Their marriage in trouble?"

"Everything was trouble for Glenn."

"Yeah."

Pascal ran his hands through what was left of his hair and sighed. "Man, he was a pain in the ass."

Mac smiled faintly. This was as honest as Scott Pascal had

ever been with him. All the barriers were down. He almost hated to send them flying upward again, but that was his job.

But Pascal beat him to the punch. Throwing a look at Mac, he said, "You probably think this has something to do with Jessie. That's kind of your M.O. Everything that involves my friends has to do with Jessie."

Mac lifted his palms.

"Go ahead. Ask me all kinds of questions about Jessie. Here I am . . . I've damn near lost everything . . . maybe the insurance company'll pull me through, but Glenn's gone and God knows what's next . . . but you . . . You want to know about Jessie. So ask, Detective McNally. Ask away."

"I don't really see how this fire, and Stafford's apparent death, have anything to do with Jessie," Mac admitted.

"Well, he got a note from her."

"Glenn got a note from Jessie?" Mac's pulse leapt but he frowned at Pascal, not wanting to give too much away. "When?"

"Don't know, a couple of days ago, I guess. It was that nursery rhyme Jessie used to say." Scott singsonged the message to Mac in a high, girlish voice that sent icy fingers sliding down his spine. That was the second imaginative thought he'd had this evening and he wondered if he was losing it, just a little.

"Where is this note?"

"Maybe his office. Maybe it's burned up with him."

"Don't suppose it had a return address on it? Postmark?"

"Portland. I caught a glimpse of it. The zip code was somewhere near Sellwood—yeah, I checked."

This was making no sense whatsoever and Sellwood was across the Willamette River, in southeast Portland.

"Why did Glenn get it?"

"You tell me. He always kind of lusted after Jessie, but he was kinda like that anyway. His tongue hanging out over every pretty girl. It never changed over the years. Jessie had nothing to do with him, though. She wanted Hudson. She'd use a guy to get to Hudson, but that was all it was."

"You're talking from experience?"

Scott sighed and looked toward the sky. The rain had ceased completely but the wind was picking up, shaking water from the soot-laden leaves of a nearby tree. "She liked the dark, mysterious ones."

"Like Jarrett Erikson or maybe Zeke St. John?"

"Zeke was Hudson's best friend," he said, as if the thought had just come to him again. "That might have appealed to her. Jessie was"—he looked away, as if searching for the right word—"a little twisted, I guess."

"Why Glenn, then?" Mac repeated. *And how would a dead girl send a note?* He was damned near certain Jessie had been dead for twenty years, and no way could she have sent anyone a note.

"She was a tease. It's what she did."

"Who else did she sing the rhyme to?"

"Every one of us." He got to his feet and dusted off the seat of his pants, which were wet and looked cold. As if reading his mind, Pascal shuddered and turned away, toward his vehicle.

"You know, the body we found. We're pretty sure it's Jessie Brentwood, so unless she's a ghost with her own stationery, I don't think she's sending anyone any mail, not from Sellwood or anywhere else."

"I'm just saying Glenn got a note, anonymously, okay? And inside were Jessie's words." His gaze was steady. "Maybe someone played a sick prank on him."

"Someone who knew about the nursery rhyme."

"We all knew."

"You think anyone else got notes?" Mac asked, wondering if the jerk was bullshitting him. It wouldn't be the first time.

"Ask 'em," Scott said, then jogged away through the trees

to a parking lot in a strip mall. Once there, he climbed into a dark gray truck and drove off.

"I will," he said to himself. "I'll ask every damned one of you."

"Let's start over," Hudson said to Becca. "You saw an image of this note burning and you think it was sent to Glenn." He was still holding the damning piece of paper in his fist and he was confused as all get-out. So far, it had been one helluva night. First the fire, then Glenn's death, and now Becca's visions or whatever you want to call them about a note he'd received just today.

"No, Hudson," she said, her voice taking on an edge. "I don't think it. I *know* it."

"Fine. Then there were two of them."

"At least."

"Yeah, at least." He wanted to know what this meant. Needed to know.

She'd examined the message and then placed it on her coffee table, shrinking away from it as if it were poisonous. He felt a little repelled himself. Who had sent the note? Jessie? He couldn't believe that. Wouldn't.

"Why?" he asked.

She shook her head and walked into the kitchen.

He followed her as she heated some water for decaf herbal tea or something equally innocuous in her microwave. Her dog had decided Hudson wasn't worth the fuss and had settled into a round little bed in the living room. Ringo was now snoring softly.

"There has to be a reason I got one and . . . Glenn got one."

"Maybe Jessie wants some of us to know she's alive," Becca said.

"You don't believe that any more than I do."

"I know, but—" The microwave dinged and she retrieved her cup, then dunked the bag of aromatic non-tea into it. "There has to be a reason. This isn't just happening all of a sudden, after twenty years. Everything has to hinge on Jessie and those bones at St. Elizabeth's."

"So, why me? Why Glenn?"

"Maybe there are more," she said and stared at him.

He felt it, too. That they were being manipulated. "Someone's got a sick sense of humor."

She tossed her tea bag into the trash. "Who?"

He thought of everyone connected even vaguely to Jessie and couldn't think of a soul. "And why? I'm just not buying that someone's getting his rocks off by trying to freak us out."

"Maybe we should go to the police," she said, testing the hot brew in her cup.

"And tell them what? I got a note and you 'saw' one that was meant for Glenn? If the police get involved, they're not going to accept that you just 'saw it.' "

"They'll think I wrote the note," Becca concluded. She walked back to the couch and sank into the cushions.

Hudson shook his head. "I don't know what they'll conclude, but calling McNally now might create more problems than it's worth. Becca . . ." He trailed off, sounding uncomfortable.

She glanced up at him.

"Could you have seen that note to Glenn? Somehow. And then just recalled it?"

There it was. His disbelief. She felt a flicker of anger and frustration even though she knew he would feel this way. What did he know of her really? How could he just go on trust? "No."

"Then you need to make up a story before we go to the police, if we decide to go to the police. Say you saw it on his desk or something."

"Great. Lie to the police. Like I've got something to

hide." Becca clasped her hands together so hard her knuckles hurt. Why had she said anything to Hudson? Trusted him? "Maybe Scott knows about it."

"You think Glenn showed it to him? Wait. Maybe Scott got one, too. Why should Glenn and I be the only ones?" Hudson was instantly in motion, yanking his cell phone from his pocket and scrolling through numbers. "What about The Third, or Zeke?"

"It's three in the morning, Hudson."

He snapped his cell shut, almost in anticipation of her words. "You're right. I'll check with them tomorrow." He gave her a studied look. "Maybe we should go to bed."

She nodded her head and couldn't help but grin. "That's the first good idea you've had all night."

"All morning," he corrected. "Come on."

The first thing Becca noticed when she awoke was the smell of smoke. She sat bolt upright but it was only the lingering aroma from the night before. Though she'd changed out of her hastily donned clothes and made love to Hudson until nearly four in the morning, the scent was in her hair and clung to her skin. Ringo had given up his vigil enough to lay his head on his paws, but as soon as Becca stirred he was on his feet. Hudson snorted and rolled over, never even opening his eyes.

She glanced at him, his face unlined and relaxed in sleep, dark lashes lying on his cheeks. God, she loved him. She wondered if she'd ever stopped.

"Quit staring at me."

"What?" she said, startled. "You're awake?"

A smile stretched across his stubbled jaw. "I am now." He reached for her and before she could protest, he'd drawn her close again and began kissing her as if they hadn't made love all night already.

But she didn't protest.

Couldn't.

She was too caught up in the thrill of it all.

Later, once she'd caught her breath again, Becca rolled off the bed, hurried through her shower, and blew her hair dry in record time. She touched on makeup and yanked on her jeans and a long-sleeved black shirt and, in less than twenty minutes, was hurrying down the stairs, trying not to trip over the dog in his haste to be first. "It's not a race, you know," she scolded gently, but Ringo was already at the door, waiting to be walked.

"Okay, okay, a short one." She snapped on his leash, slipped into mules, and tossed on a jacket, taking him for his morning constitutional as the gray light of dawn cut through the streets and alleys and cars whipped by, tossing up water from standing puddles. High clouds blocked the sun, and it was cold enough that Becca's breath fogged, but at least, thank the weather gods, it wasn't raining.

They returned, opened the door to the warm scent of coffee and Hudson walking out of the downstairs bath. His hair was wet from the shower, his jaw still dark with beard shadow, jeans from the night before hanging low on his hips. He was tossing on his shirt as Becca closed the door and hung up Ringo's leash. "Mornin', sunshine," he drawled as she slid out of her jacket.

"Good morning . . . I guess." She shuddered. "I'm still sick about Glenn."

"Me, too. I've already got a couple of calls in to the rest of the guys."

"And?"

"You were right. The Third downplayed it, but he got a note."

"He *did*?" Becca stood still.

"Zeke didn't. Not yet, anyway. And I haven't got a hold of Jarrett or Mitch. Or Scott, for that matter. I was going to see them this morning."

"I want to go with you," she said and poured two cups of

coffee from the pot on the counter. "I want to see the other notes."

Hudson hesitated as she handed him one of the mugs. "I'd like to know more before we take this to the police."

"If Glenn got a note, do you think it might be at his house?"

"I thought you said it burned."

"It did . . . at least in my vision."

He nodded but she sensed he was having some trouble with the whole vision thing. "Do you want to ask his wife? Gia?" he asked.

Becca grimaced as she tried to imagine what Gia Stafford must be feeling this morning. Last night at the fire, Gia had been sobbing wildly and clinging to everyone within range. She wouldn't want people descending on her with their own agendas. Then again, she might be interested in anything connected with her husband's death. "It's hard to say how she'll react. If it were me, I'd want to know every scrap of information that might help explain how the person I loved was suddenly taken from me." There was a pause and Becca asked, "Why Glenn? Was it an accident? Arson? How do these notes fit in?"

"What if the fire was set on purpose?" Hudson suggested, staring into his coffee mug. "Maybe to get rid of Glenn? He was drinking himself into a stupor and no one was around. It was a perfect opportunity."

"Well, they were really lucky to just happen to have their firestarter arsenal with them—the night Glenn decides to tie one on?"

"Maybe he tied one on a lot."

Ringo was dancing at her feet, whining and trying to catch her attention. "Oh, buddy. Sorry." Opening the pantry door, she found the bag of dog food and measured a ration into his bowl. The dog was on it in an instant.

"Maybe it was planned in advance," Hudson said as she

closed the pantry door. "By someone who knew Glenn's habits and waited for the right moment. And last night was it."

"Who are you thinking of? Gia?" Becca asked.

"I can't picture her planning anything so detailed," he admitted.

"And the notes?"

"We don't know for certain that Glenn got one," Hudson said carefully.

Becca knew he was right, but she was inclined to believe in her vision. "Maybe we should ask Gia."

He reached for his cell phone without hesitation. "She might not be up to a visit."

"Let's go see."

"Where are you going?" Gretchen demanded as Mac grabbed his coat from the back of his chair and made for the nearest exit of the police station.

Her hair was pulled back severely, causing pressure at her temples and straining her eyes so she had a Siamese cat appearance. It looked uncomfortable and he figured it wasn't going to help her temperament. He'd tried to be absent when she arrived at the station this morning, but he'd gotten caught up in the case and suddenly it was eight-thirty and Gretchen was there with a box of doughnuts.

"Home to bed," he told her. "Pulled an all-nighter."

"Doing what?"

"There was a fire. Glenn Stafford and Scott Pascal's restaurant. Looks like Stafford's dead."

"Are you for real?"

He nodded, slid his sidearm into his shoulder holster, and grabbed his jacket.

"Why wasn't I called?"

"Because the fire investigators haven't labeled it arson, so there's no homicide. And it's outside of our jurisdiction."

"Bullshit. It involves our case." The wheels were turning in her mind, the box of doughnuts dropped unceremoniously onto the corner of his desk.

Mac headed toward the door, his head full of images from the night before. He intended to do just as he'd told Scott Pascal the night before: he was going to ask the Preppy Pricks about the notes. He'd made a couple of calls already and was on a mission.

Gretchen was hot on his heels, her footfalls short and angry as she followed him outside. "Your attitude sucks, McNally. I'm this close to reporting you." She held her hand out, so he could see the index finger and thumb separated by only a hairsbreadth.

"To who?" Mac asked at his own personal Jeep. He'd parked the prowler around the back since he was going off duty—at least officially.

"D'Annibal, for starters. The chief if I have to."

He'd had it with her. "I don't know what your gripe is, Sandler. You've been to a number of interviews. You think the Jessie Brentwood investigation's a waste of time, my personal white whale. You hate everything about being my partner. Do whatever the hell you want."

"You should have called me when you decided to go to the fire."

"Wake you up at two in the morning for something that might not be a crime?"

"It was Pascal and Stafford's restaurant! That's critical to our investigation!"

"What investigation?" Mac finally snapped back. "You don't give a damn. All you want is a fresh body, not a twenty-year-old corpse."

"Fuck you."

"Back atcha." He slammed into his Jeep and drove away, wishing the pavement was gravel so he could peel out and choke her with the dust. He slipped a pair of nearly forgotten sunglasses onto his nose as shafts of rare winter sunbeams slipped through the clouds and bounced off the wet pavement.

Christ, she was a pain. And he didn't need the headache. Between his obsession with this case, the other cases he was investigating, and his home life, which was centered around his kid, he didn't have time for Gretchen Sandler's histrionics. Not for the first time he wondered who she'd slept with to make detective. Worse yet, she had a way of making him lower himself to her level. The fact that he'd just baldly and gleefully lied to her pleased him in a way that defied explanation. Maturity was highly overrated, he concluded as he turned the Jeep away from the direction of his home and toward the garage where Mitch Bellotti spent his days.

Hudson had checked on Glenn's address and found the house without difficulty. It was a white-pillared colonial with an excruciatingly steep driveway and little ceramic gnome-like creatures hiding in an expansive yard. There was a brown older model Chevrolet sedan parked precariously on that slope. Hudson parked Becca's Jetta on the street below and they walked up a set of steps that switchbacked through sliding mud and bark dust, courtesy of the nearly incessant precipitation.

An older woman with coiffed gray-white hair answered their knock and looked at them with suspicion. "Yes?"

"We're high school friends of Glenn's," Becca said. "We wondered if we could see Gia."

"Well, Gia's sleeping right now. This isn't a good time. She's been medicated." She was brusque and determined.

"I understand. Would you tell her Becca Sutcliff and Hudson Walker came to see her?" Becca added.

"Oh. I think Glenn mentioned you." She glanced past them to Becca's car. "I'm Gia's mother. I don't think it's worth your while to stay. She could be out a while and when she's awake, oh, dear, the medication makes her a little . . . unclear."

Becca half expected Mama Bear to slam the door on them when Gia herself appeared on the stairs beyond. Tousled and red-eyed, clutching a bathrobe closed with one hand, she walked barefoot to the entry. "Who's here?"

Mama Bear kept trying to close the door but Hudson put a palm on the panels and pushed it back open. He received a glittered glare for his troubles but Gia gazed at him with shadowed eyes, full of misery.

"You were there last night . . . ?" she asked, her voice drifting off.

"I'm Hudson Walker. Glenn and I knew each other in high school."

"Oh! Yes! Hudson." Tears filled her eyes and she came flying forward, throwing herself into his arms, bawling like a baby calf. Mama Bear seemed startled by this turn of events, stepped backward, and Becca used the moment to squeeze in behind Hudson. She felt Gia's pain like a live wire between them, though they weren't touching. Her grief filled the room and it made Becca feel like a charlatan, given her reasons for being here.

"I can't believe he's dead," Gia was saying over and over as they stood beneath a huge chandelier in the foyer. She was petite and soft, her round body giving her a cherubic look. "We wanted to have a baby. We were planning on it. Now what am I going to do? What am I going to do!" She pulled away from Hudson to the waiting arms of her mother.

Becca heard the word "baby" and her heart lurched. She hadn't known the circumstances of the Stafford marriage, but this window into their now-unfulfilled hopes and dreams burrowed deeply into her own heartache.

Gia's mom gave her daughter a hard hug, and Gia's already red eyes puddled up all over again.

Hudson said gently, "I'm sorry to bother you right now."

"It's not a bother. You were friends. Glenn talked about you . . . all of you." She swept a hand toward Becca. "I know you were all worried about the dead girl, Jessie."

"Glenn believed Jessie was dead?" Hudson asked.

"No . . . I don't know. I guess I just assumed." She swallowed once, seemed to think about it some more, then her eyes flooded again. "And now Glenn's dead, too. Oh, God, oh, God. I'm . . . sorry . . . this is all so new . . . so unexpected. He was my soul mate. We were going to be married forever." Her voice cracked, but she huddled into the safety of her mother's arms.

"We hate to bother you, but we wondered if you could answer a question for us."

"Not now." Gia's mother bristled but Gia gazed up at him blankly.

"What?" she asked.

"Did Glenn receive any note recently?"

"What kind of note?" Gia asked emotionlessly.

"A nursery rhyme," Becca said.

Gia turned to her. "Is that a joke, because it's not funny." She slowly released her grip on her mother.

"I think this has gone on long enough," Mama said.

"I received one," Hudson said, "so we wondered if Glenn had, too."

"A nursery rhyme. Let me see it." Gia stuck out her hand and Hudson, after a brief hesitation, reached into his pocket and handed over the note and the blue envelope.

"It came through the mail."

Gia shook her head. "Who sent it?"

"We don't know."

"You think it was the dead girl," she said with sudden understanding, and her mother drew in a hiss of breath and looked around as if evil spirits were about to materialize. "Glenn said something about nursery rhymes and that girl. She was a tease."

"We don't even know if Glenn's note exists," Hudson said. "Another friend, Christopher Delacroix, received one."

"The Third. I know him. The same as this?" She glanced at the card, her nose wrinkling.

"That's what I understand. I haven't seen it yet."

"And you think Glenn may have got one. Why?"

"It's a mystery," Becca said. "We're trying to figure out who received them, who sent them, and why."

"Well, if he got one, I never saw it." After a moment, she said, "Have you told the police? Like maybe that's why Glenn's dead . . . something to do with that Jessie?"

"We haven't talked to anyone but you," Hudson said.

"It's like she killed him," Gia said suddenly, and her mother shook her head. "That's what she did, that bitch! She reached right out of the grave and burned him up!" Gia started crying in earnest again, and after a few awkward moments where Becca and Hudson could only stand by while Gia's mother rocked her daughter in her arms, they expressed their condolences again and took their leave.

"Are we going to see The Third?" Becca asked.

"Next on the list."

Mitch Bellotti was in overalls that tightened around his bulging middle. He was wiping his hands on a gray rag as Mac slammed the door of his Jeep and crossed the asphalt apron that led to Mike's Garage, a surprisingly clean establishment where tools hung on the wall in precise rows. An older-model blue Triumph was on a lift and Mitch was conversing with a skinny, sixtyish man whose craggy face practically fell in on itself, it was so lined.

Hearing Mac's door slam, Mitch looked his way. There was a moment or two of blankness, then recognition dawned. He didn't offer to shake hands, just kept wiping his own on the rag as his expression grew grimmer. Mac introduced himself but it wasn't necessary as Mitch responded with, "I knew you'd come. You've talked to everybody else. But God, man, on this day? You know about Glenn, don't you?"

"I went to the scene last night."

"I don't want to talk to you. Especially now." The smell of oil and grease permeated the air and an old greyhound was lying on a rug near the back door.

Mac realized Mitch was fighting back tears and felt a twinge of pity. He'd never really thought Mitch had anything to do with Jessie's disappearance, then or now, but he felt he might know something—maybe something he didn't know he knew. "I'm sorry about Glenn," Mac said, meaning it.

"You think it has something to do with—Jessie? Is that why you're here, man?"

"Do you?" Mac asked curiously.

"I guess it could just be a coincidence." He sounded as doubtful as Mac felt.

"We'll know more after the fire investigator's report."

"Has to be arson, doesn't it?"

"Why do you say that?"

Mitch gazed at him guilelessly. "Well, things like that don't just happen. The restaurant just goes up. How? A gas leak? Or a burner on the stove left on near something flammable? Grease fire? Doesn't sound like it from what I've heard."

"What have you heard? Who called you?"

"Scott. He was freaking, man. Glenn and I were friends, but Scott was his best friend. They were kind of mad at each other, but it was like they were brothers."

"Scott thinks it's arson?"

"I don't know for sure. He just said Glenn was inside and it shouldn't have happened. He said she cursed us."

"Jessie?"

"Yeah, Jessie." His face flushed as if he heard the idiocy of his statement. "Who else?"

"What happened all those years ago, Mitch?" Mac asked

quietly. He felt his pulse rush a bit, wondering if this was the moment someone finally opened up to him.

Mitch's eyes watered as the tears he'd been fighting got the better of him and spilled down his cheeks. "Not a damn thing," he said wearily. "That's the problem, man. Nothing happened to her. She just left, but now she's back even more than she was in high school. Sending notes. Burning down the restaurant. Killing Glenn. If she isn't alive, then she's making it happen from the grave. I don't know how, but she's behind all of this. She is. Back then some people thought she was weird, y'know. Like she had ESP or somethin'. I thought it was all just crap, but now . . . who the hell knows?" He reached a hand toward an upper, nonexistent shirt pocket, then dropped it. "I need a smoke," he said and headed toward the office where he grabbed a pack of cigarettes from a jacket hung on a peg. He shook one out, then pushed through a back door to the rear of the building. Mac followed. The greyhound, long snout grizzled with age, didn't move.

"What notes?" Mac asked quietly as Mitch cupped his hand over the lighted end of the cigarette and sucked hard on the other. Both of his hands were shaking, and as if noticing Mac's stare, he clenched one and pulled out the cigarette from his mouth with the other, moving it to hide his tremor.

" 'What are little boys made of? Frogs and snails and puppy dogs' tails.' " He puffed harder on the cigarette, as if the carcinogenic smoke were giving life, not taking it. Mitch made a half-choked sound. "She used to say it, now she's writing it down."

"What do you mean?"

"That's the same damned nursery rhyme she used to taunt us with. She'd say it and she had a way of making it sound dirty. Sexy. And now she's goddamned sending them to us!"

"You got a nursery rhyme note?" Mac asked carefully.

"*That* fuckin' nursery rhyme. The one she used to sing. Yes. I got it. From her." He was nodding rapidly and took another drag.

"From Jessie."

"That's what I said, man." He was coming visibly undone.

"It came in the mail? Had a return address?"

"Fuck, yeah . . . I mean, it came in the mail. No return address." Abruptly he went back inside and yanked a card from another pocket of the same jacket that had held his cigarettes. He handed it to Mac and took a step back, staring at it as if it were poisonous. "You take it. Maybe it'll help you find her, but when you do, make sure she stays the hell away from me!"

Chapter Sixteen

The offices of Salchow, Wendt, and Delacroix were in Portland's Pearl District in the Grassle Building, a gray granite and glass monolith that knifed upward thirty stories. Today, a black and gray sky hovered outside and Christopher Delacroix III gazed at it with a grim expression as he dropped the receiver to his office phone into its cradle.

Detective Samuel "Mac" McNally had called. He'd wanted to know if The Third had received a nursery rhyme note in the mail.

Now The Third opened a desk drawer and pulled out the blue envelope. Initially, he'd been more perplexed than alarmed. It was childish. The work of some amateur who was trying to goad them. He'd talked to Jarrett and learned he'd received one, too, so he'd assumed the rest of the guys had gotten one.

But he'd kind of hoped the notes would escape McNally's notice. They would just add fuel to the Jessie fire, and he was getting really sick and tired of even thinking about her. She'd been a high school tease, for crying out loud. None of them had gotten lucky with her. Jarrett sure as hell hadn't and neither of those losers, Mitch and Glenn, ever got close.

He closed his eyes, feeling a jolt of regret. The fire and discovery of a body at Blue Note was all over the news. It was clear that the body was Glenn's, though that piece of information hadn't been officially released as yet. Glenn. Dull, unhappy Glenn. He and Jarrett had used both Glenn and Mitch as their personal whipping boys over the years. He knew it. Usually didn't care all that much. But today . . .

"Damn you, Jezebel," The Third said quietly to the boiling dark gray clouds beyond his windows.

His intercom beeped gently, a soft tone that befitted the moneyed appearance of his office. "Yes," he said, depressing the switch.

"A Mr. Walker and Ms. Sutcliff would like to see you. They don't have an appointment."

The notes . . . and Glenn's death . . .

"Send 'em up," The Third said.

Becca and Hudson rode in the Grassle Building's glass elevator in one of two cubicles that shot upward and offered a dizzying view of downtown Portland and the Willamette River. It gave Becca a disembodied feeling that she could have done without, and she was glad to step onto the dark gray carpeting of the twenty-fourth floor.

The Third had a corner office, and his desk faced away from windows that gazed toward another building farther west whose windows stared back like a row of unblinking eyes. The whole room was made of glass and chrome and black leather, a far cry from the wood-paneled offices of the firm Becca worked for. It wasn't a surprise that The Third's law firm was as slick as he was.

The Third himself was dressed in a navy blue suit and crimson tie, and as they entered he waved them toward a set of black and chrome director's chairs on the other side of his desk. Neither Becca nor Hudson took a seat, preferring to stand.

"I'm guessing you want to see the note," The Third said. He slid open a drawer, pulled out a card, and handed it to Hudson, who held it for Becca to see. *Christopher* was written in an uneven hand on one side of the white card and the same nursery rhyme was on the other.

"Just like mine," Hudson said.

Becca felt a chill slide down her spine. "Did Jessie call you Christopher instead of The Third?"

"Beats me." He shrugged. "I can't remember."

"I got one. You got one. And you said Jarrett got one?" Hudson turned the card over and examined Christopher's name more closely.

"Yep. And Glenn. And Mitch."

"You sound certain," Hudson said.

"Well, that's what McNally told me."

"McNally? You talked to him?"

"Just got off the phone with him." He pointed to both of them. "Expect calls. He'll probably want to talk to everyone. He said Mitch got a note, and Scott told him Glenn got one."

Hudson took a moment to absorb that news. "How about Scott?"

"I didn't ask. I just assumed."

"Zeke hasn't gotten one yet," Hudson said.

"Maybe today." The Third sounded almost bored, but then they realized it was more grief than apathy when he said softly, "Damn, I just can't believe Stafford's gone." He drew a long breath and eased himself farther into his desk chair, which made protesting noises. "God, what a weird world."

"Got any idea who would send these notes?" Hudson asked him.

"God knows. Not Jessie, though." When neither Hudson nor Becca responded, he skewered them with a look. "You can't think she's still alive."

"No." Hudson was positive.

"She was a tease, though," The Third said. "She loved this kind of stuff."

"Maybe someone knows that."

The Third gave him a hard look. "And is pulling this shit for their own reasons."

"Maybe."

"Why?" Becca asked. "Who?"

"To make us think she's alive?" The Third proposed. "To send the hounds in another direction?"

Hudson nodded thoughtfully.

"Yeah, well. Jessie's a ghost and now Glenn's a corpse." He grabbed the arms of his chair and levered himself to his feet. "What's with you two? Are you together now?" He waved a hand to encompass Becca and Hudson. "Your own little team?"

"Something like that," Hudson said.

"Great. Amateur investigators. Just let this damn thing blow over so we can all get back to real life instead of looking for dead girls who don't exist." He opened and slammed shut one drawer, then another, yanking out his keys and a wallet. "What time is it, eleven? I've got a lunch meeting at twelve, and I want to get there early so I can have a few drinks first. Sorry to rush you out, but there's nothing much more to talk about. Anything else, take it up with McNally."

With that he shoved his chair back, then strode out of the room, leaving Hudson and Becca to look at each other and follow suit.

On Saturday Becca drove herself to the site of Glenn's memorial service, a small nondenominational white clapboard church with a steeple cutting upward to a sky thick with gunmetal gray clouds. As she pulled into the gravel parking lot, she saw Hudson standing outside with Renee, Zeke, and Evangeline, the wind blowing the women's skirts around their knees and playing havoc with their hair. Evangeline wore a wide-brimmed black hat that she anchored firmly to her head with one hand. Renee seemed oblivious to the weather, her face turned away from the church, her short dark hair whipping around her cheekbones, her eyes fastened on some remote point that Becca was pretty sure she wasn't even seeing.

Zeke's hands were in his pockets, his head bent, his expression stony though Becca got the impression he was desperately holding his emotions inside. "Why didn't I get a note?" she heard him ask Hudson as she approached.

"You haven't got one *yet*," Hudson pointed out.

"Oh, who cares?" Evangeline's nose and eyes were red and she was sniffling. "Be glad Jessie didn't send one to you."

"Jessie didn't send the notes," Renee said woodenly, as if she'd repeated the same words a thousand times. Her cheeks were as hollow as someone dedicated to a starvation diet. "She's dead. Remember?"

Hudson frowned at his sister. "You okay?"

"I'm more than okay," she snapped right back. "I keep telling you."

"Think we should go in?" Evangeline asked, looking around. People were climbing the steps and entering the front doors.

"You just seem like you've got something you're dealing with," Hudson said to Renee. "Is it the Jessie story?"

"Among other things. I am going through a divorce, you know." She frowned, her features pinching into a knot. "You don't see Tim anywhere, do you?"

"I thought that's the way you wanted it."

"Who knows what I want."

"Come on," Evangeline said, grabbing Zeke's hand and dragging him toward the church steps.

Renee pressed her lips together, looked at her brother as if she had something to say, then threw a glance at Becca and clammed up. After a taut moment, she said, "Sometimes a story's just a story, and sometimes it's a hell of a lot more. Jessie was running from something, and I don't know what. I've got some answers, but I've got a lot more questions, too." She glanced over her shoulder as if expecting to be overheard.

Becca observed, "You still feel like you're being followed."

She shrugged.

Hudson said, "Who's following you?"

"No one. Someone. The bogeyman. A damned ghost. I don't know."

"What the hell's wrong with you?"

"Nothing."

"Maybe you should come and stay with me," he said as they walked up the steps to the front doors.

"I don't think so. I can take care of myself."

"Can you?"

"Been doing it for years," she said as they walked through the open doors and into the vestibule. Absently Becca picked up a small program with Glenn's picture on the front page, then slid into one of the rear pews. Organ music swelled and Gia began crying softly somewhere in the front row. Becca turned her eyes to the ceiling of the church with its curved wooden beams and wished she felt comforted. She closed her eyes and swallowed hard, but when she opened them again she found herself looking at Detective Sam McNally, who had unobtrusively entered and taken a seat in the pew across the aisle, opposite theirs.

She felt Hudson stiffen, though he stared straight ahead. It seemed weird to have the cop at the service, a man who had been dogging Glenn as well as his friends since high school.

As a preacher began to talk about Glenn's life, Becca spotted the other members of their group. So far Mitch, seated three rows in front of McNally, was still unaware the detective had joined them. She could see the way he was jiggling his leg, as if he were made of nerves. The tension in his shoulders was obvious as well. Jarrett, two rows almost directly in front of Becca and Hudson, turned his head at that moment, gazing coldly toward McNally, his heavy eyebrows and grim mouth menacing. Somewhere toward the front The Third was seated next to Tamara.

After the reverend had said a little about Glenn, Scott Pascal rose from a front pew and moved stiffly toward the podium. He made a short speech about his friend, describing how they'd decided to become partners in the restaurant. It was clear Scott felt the emotion of the moment, for he stumbled over his words and had to hesitate several times before continuing.

Then Mitch jerked to his feet and took a turn at the podium. He glanced over their numbers, his round cheeks red and glistening with sweat under the lights. He looked hot and uncomfortable in his dark suit, and Becca wondered briefly if he was going to have a heart attack or something. He didn't look well.

"Glenn and I were friends a long time. He was a good guy." Mitch looked to Gia, whose gaze was riveted on him. She held herself stiffly, as if her connection to Mitch were held by a tight, invisible rope. "We shared stuff. Good and bad. Now that he's gone I don't know who I'll talk to." As if of their own volition, his eyes searched through the crowd, fastening on McNally. He blinked several times, then said on a rasp, "We're gonna miss you, buddy." His hands were clenched as he walked back to his seat.

A young woman approached the podium next, and she filled the small church with a beautiful alto version of "Amazing Grace." By the time the back doors were opened, Becca felt heavy with unshed tears and sorrow and practically gulped air as she headed down the front steps to the graveled lot.

Hudson was right behind her. One hand dropped lightly on one shoulder. "Hey," he said softly.

"I know. I'm okay, really. No vision to worry about this time." She shot him a smile meant to lighten the mood, but his blue eyes were sober.

"Let's get out of here," he said.

His hand clasped hers and she squeezed hard, feeling

emotion sweep over her. As if they'd choreographed the event, they headed to their cars and Becca followed him to his farm.

Once inside the old clapboard farmhouse, they didn't waste any time. She was in his arms in an instant and he was taking off her clothes, peeling off her blouse as she kicked off her shoes and worked at the buttons of his shirt. Hudson's cell rang and he ignored it, turning the damned thing off and leaving it in the kitchen as they hurried upstairs, dropping clothing on the floor, kissing and touching and not getting enough of each other. They made love hungrily, as if in the act of joining they could redefine living, could push away the taint of death, the fear of the unknown.

Several hours later Hudson lazily reached for his cell phone and reluctantly switched it back on. He kissed Becca's bare shoulder and she curled toward him as he listened to the messages. Her eyes swept over the trail of clothing their urgent coupling had left in their wake: his pants in a heap by the bedroom door; her bra clinging to the corner of the bed; one of his socks sitting atop the TV at the end of the bed.

She gazed at him through slitted eyes, afraid if she opened them wide he'd see her love reflected in their depths. She couldn't be that transparent. Not yet, and she was certain she would be. She'd never stopped caring. All these years. Pathetic. Yes. But true, and if he knew—

Suddenly every muscle in Hudson's body stiffened. He lifted half up, the cell phone pressed to his ear.

"What?" Becca asked, alarmed.

He clicked off the phone and made himself lie down beside her once more, staring at the ceiling.

"Who was it?"

"The Third. McNally talked to the group after the memorial service and told everyone he wants us all to give him DNA samples. All of us. Guys and girls."

"What?" she said, sitting up. "Why?"

"He's working on Jessie's case, and he wants to rule out some things. Said the strangest things pop up from DNA testing sometimes. The Third asked him if the bones are really Jessie's, but he said they still don't know for sure."

"Now wait a minute . . . why would they ask for that? I'm not a CSI authority, but the only reason they would take DNA is if they had something to compare it to."

"Maybe they found more than they're saying. A weapon, blood or skin samples under her fingernails. They want female DNA as well, so that must mean that there was something buried with Jessie, a clue. Maybe she fought off her attacker and blood or flesh was left. I don't know. The Third didn't say."

"Did everyone agree to the testing?"

"The Third's heading to the station now and having them swab the inside of his cheek. Says he's got nothing to hide and doesn't want to wait."

All the warmth, the feeling of well-being she'd felt in Hudson's arms had dissipated. "Were there two calls? What was the other one?"

Hudson shook his head. "It was Renee. Said she was going to the station this afternoon, then heading to the beach. She sounded . . . better . . . stronger, like she'd made a decision."

"Good."

"I suppose we should give up some DNA."

Becca made a face. "I suppose."

"But later," he said, pulling her into his arms.

"Later," she breathed into his mouth as it captured hers.

It was dark by the time they took Hudson's truck to the Laurelton police station where a tech swabbed both their cheeks, labeling each vial carefully. Becca couldn't see how giving her DNA could help. There was no way there could be any trace of DNA from whoever had killed the girl, be it Jessie or someone else, after all these years, but hey, if that's what McNally wanted, fine.

When Becca and Hudson stepped out of the room together, they encountered McNally himself standing by the station's front doors and looking toward someone who was just heading out to the parking lot: Renee.

"Hey!" Hudson yelled, hurrying after his sister. Becca would have followed but McNally said softly, "Have you got a minute, Ms. Sutcliff?"

No, Becca thought, but she hesitated, watching Hudson approach his sister. Renee's body language said she was in a hurry and didn't want to wait. Reluctantly, Becca turned her attention back to the cop and followed him down to a cubicle in a large open room where other detectives were seated at desks, talking on phones, typing reports.

She sat carefully in the chair next to his cluttered desk and noted a picture of a blond boy of about six, his big smile showing a spot where he was missing a baby tooth—a school picture. So McNally had a kid. Somehow that surprised her.

The detective gazed at her for a long moment, enough to make Becca feel uncomfortable. She wondered if this was one of those police tactics meant to intimidate criminals into spilling all. She felt like blabbing her fool head off, and he hadn't yet asked her a single question.

"Was Jessie pregnant when she disappeared?" he finally inquired.

"Pregnant?" Becca could feel her eyes widen in surprise, her lips part.

"The bones of a fetus were found with the dead girl's remains."

Becca felt blood rush to her head, roaring through her ears. Pregnant? Jessie? "I . . . don't know," she heard herself say. Was that what Jessie had been trying to tell her? Was that the secret she wasn't supposed to speak of?

She felt faint and she gazed past him to Hudson who, as if called by her urgent need, had appeared in the door to the large room. He strode purposely in her direction, and she swallowed hard as she thought that the baby McNally had told her about was undoubtedly his.

What the hell was this? Hudson wondered, seeing Becca's white face and the shoulder she'd turned toward the detective, as if she were trying to block him out.

"I'll let you know when I'm coming back from the beach," Renee had called after him.

Hudson had hesitated. He'd asked her to postpone her trip. With the strange nursery rhyme notes, Glenn's sudden death, and her sense of persecution, Hudson wanted his sister to stay within reach. But she was on a mission of her own, apparently, and wasn't listening either to him or the feeling that something was very, very wrong.

More people were leaving the station, a group of them, and Hudson had felt like he was swimming upstream as he pushed his way to reach Becca and McNally. But he found them, Becca seated at the cop's desk in the Homicide Department.

"Can I help you?" A tall, African American cop with a name tag that read Detective Pelligree stepped in his way.

"Lookin' for McNally. Found him."

Pelligree watched as Hudson made his way to McNally's desk where Becca sat, white as a sheet, her eyes wide. Oh, hell, was she about to have one of her spells again. "You okay?"

"No," she was saying to the detective, shaking her head, and Hudson saw that her hands were curled into trembling fists.

"What's going on?" He looked to Mac for an explanation.

"He asked if Jessie was pregnant," Becca said. "There was a baby . . . The bones of an unborn child . . . were there, in the maze, too."

Hudson stared at Mac. "You think *Jessie* was pregnant?"

"The girl in the maze was."

"So that's why you're doing the DNA swabs," he said slowly, thinking. "If I'm the baby's father, then it's a pretty sure bet the mother is Jessie."

McNally nodded.

"Jesus H. Christ." He couldn't believe it. This had to be wrong. Had to be. "Then . . . then the remains aren't Jessie's." But even as he said the words, he knew he could be mistaken.

"Was that the trouble she was talking about?" Becca asked softly.

"She would have told me."

"Would she, Mr. Walker?" McNally asked and Hudson had no answer.

Gretchen stalked toward Mac like an angry jungle cat, meeting him at the station's front doors as he came back inside after watching Hudson Walker and Rebecca Sutcliff leave. They were a couple, no doubt about it, and they'd both offered up their DNA. Actually, he'd had no resistence for the request even from that bastard of a lawyer Delacroix.

Which was interesting.

But he didn't have time to think about it as now he was facing the she-cat, all ruffled, claws extended, fangs showing. God, she was wearying.

She met him at the door and walked with him back to his desk. "You leave me with the tech while you do the interviewing?" Her blue eyes shimmered with annoyance.

"You could have come to the memorial service."

"You remember Johnny Ray, the meth cooker? And the dead body found at his lab?"

"It wasn't homicide. It was an accidental explosion. Johnny Ray at his baking worst. I didn't think I needed to be there."

"You *did* need to be there, rather than running after those rich boys you wanna bring down so badly. The Preppy Pricks," she harrumphed. "You'd better hope the press never gets wind of that or they'll crucify you."

Not that he cared.

"As for our meth boy, the sheriff's department is trying to take over this one, but Johnny Ray's place is in Laurelton's lovely city limits."

Gretchen's mockery was because their resident meth problem, Johnny Ray, had a tract house on the edge of the city, where railroad tracks vied with Scotch broom and scraggly volunteer pine trees, all making a hardscrabble living out of rocky dirt. Perfect place for a meth kitchen, successful until Johnny Ray tried to start making pounds of crystal meth rather than mere ounces for his own use. Then he got on the PD's radar when the neighbors grew alarmed at the smells emanating from the place. With Johnny Ray's lack of focus, it was only a matter of time before someone stopped paying attention and the place exploded.

Mac just wasn't interested. Drug use and abuse amounted to a large percentage of the homicides he investigated, but there was no mystery to the method, means, or motive. It was more an exercise for the legal system: were they guilty of murder, manslaughter, or simple stupidity, and the only question that remained after they were apprehended was for how long they should be put away.

"Did you ask them about the notes?" Gretchen asked, looking out the window toward the station lot, seeing Hudson Walker's beat-up truck rumble away.

"I called everyone. The only one who didn't get one was Zeke St. John, but it might still be coming because Scott Pascal got his a day late."

"And they've all given DNA samples."

"Yep."

"They were all mailed from the same post office, right? In Sellwood. Maybe they were sent at different times," Gretchen said, though she was looking past him, her tone distracted. She

couldn't care less about the notes, though Mac was fascinated by the mind that would put them together.

"What are they for?" he asked aloud, thinking about
Mitch Bellotti's reaction. The guy was certain they were from
Jessie, and he was all nerves. It had been about all he could
do to have his DNA swab taken before he bolted outside for
a cigarette—make that two, back to back, or more accurately, end to end. Did he know something? Something he
wasn't telling? Or was there something else at work outside
of this investigation?

"Maybe your little ghost girlfriend just forgot about St. John,"
Gretchen suggested, once again trying to bait him into an argument.

"Maybe," Mac said. This time he wasn't going to bite.

Six days later, Hudson lay on his back, staring up at the
dark ceiling in his bedroom, one arm draped possessively
around Becca's hip as the curve of her spine nestled next to
him, skin to skin. He'd spent the time almost exclusively
with Becca. Sometimes they were at her condo, most of the
time they were at his ranch. Last night she'd even brought
her dog over so that she wouldn't have to leave at the crack
of dawn to let him out. Ringo was downstairs in his bed and,
after hours of whining, had apparently decided to accept his
fate that he wasn't sleeping in the bedroom with Becca.

All the feelings from high school that Hudson had done
his damnedest to deny seemed to be back full force. He
could scarcely stand to be away from her and, lucky for him,
she seemed to feel exactly the same way.

They hadn't talked about Jessie. Or much about Glenn
and/or the fire and his death. They hadn't pursued further
discussion of the nursery rhymes—like The Third said, let
McNally figure out who sent them and why. Hudson really
didn't give a damn. He didn't want to think about Jessie or

Glenn or any part of their group dynamics—the secrets, the lies, the undercurrents. If Renee wanted to dig around and come up with a story, she could have at it. All he wanted to do was breathe in Becca's scent, feel the silkiness of her skin, listen to her musical laughter.

And make love.

Over and over again.

Now his hand caressed her smooth skin. They'd come together twice last night and it hadn't felt like enough. He hadn't been celibate the intervening years since his first relationship with Becca, but he hadn't been actively looking for sex, romance, and female companionship, either.

It was as if he'd been waiting.

Maybe he had.

The sun was just starting to rise, and for the first morning in God knew how long its rays, though coolly blue in the early dawn, were not slanting through a gray haze of rain. Hudson could see the dark outlines of clouds through the window, just beginning to be visible in the first light, but it appeared, at least for the moment, that precipitation had been suspended.

Carefully, he climbed out of bed, pausing to take a look at the woman lying in the rumpled blankets. Her eyes were closed, lashes fanning her cheeks, her breathing even and restful. He felt like he knew everything about her, yet she was still full of mystery and complexities. It was intoxicating and vaguely dangerous. There was too much going on, too many unanswered questions to start a relationship. But he didn't care.

And Jessie Brentwood might have been pregnant at the time of her death, at the time she'd been killed.

You might have been a father if something horrible hadn't happened to her in that maze, in front of the Madonna statue.

How his life would have changed. He wouldn't be here at the ranch with Becca, that much was for sure. He probably would never have known how it felt to be touched by her or kissed by her. He would have been tangled with Jessie— wild, mysterious, and dangerous Jessie.

But a kid—a kid who would now be nineteen. Hard to damned believe.

Pulling on a pair of boxers and jeans, Hudson headed downstairs only to encounter Ringo, whose low growl indicated he wasn't quite sure of both the new surroundings and the intentions of this stranger. Hudson half smiled as he made a pot of coffee. The sun was lifting higher, widening the arc of its rays, burnishing the outbuildings beyond the kitchen window. He knew Rodriguez would show up soon. Grandy's replacement had been as reliable as promised, though Hudson would rather have his family's longtime ranch foreman back.

It was really too early to make phone calls, but Hudson unplugged his cell phone from his charger and pushed the speed button that accessed his sister's number. Renee didn't pick up and he decided not to leave a third message telling her to call him. She'd sounded better. He was being over-protective. And the phone call to her soon-to-be ex, Tim Trudeau, earlier in the week, hadn't been a wise choice, either.

Tim had acted as if he couldn't be less interested in any-thing to do with Renee, saying only, "When you talk to her, tell her I'm putting the house on the market. Real estate agent's coming by today and we're coming up with a price. All I need is her signature."

Oh, yeah, pal. I'll pass that along.

Renee and Tim owned a house on the east side of the Willamette River, in an area known as Westmoreland. Hud-son had steered clear of all the marital infighting that had broken out between them the last few years, but with Renee's strange change of attitude lately, he'd felt the need for more information.

His phone buzzed in his hand and to his complete sur-prise he saw the call was from Renee. He clicked on. "Finally," he greeted her, stepping onto the outside porch in order not to wake Becca. "Where have you been?"

"I told you I was going to the beach."

"Well, what the hell are you doing there? I've left messages."

"I've been really buried in my story." Her voice came and went, as cell phone reception was spotty along the coast. But he could hear an element of excitement in her voice. Or was it fear?

"The Jessie story?"

"Do you ever think this is the end of the . . ." She disappeared for a sentence or two.

"Renee? Can you hear me?"

". . . and people formed colonies along the cliffs that became towns, mostly. It's like a history lesson. But very weird. I've been interviewing . . ."

"Interviewing?" Hudson listened hard, but he heard only fuzz on the line. "Renee? Renee?"

". . . you there?"

"Yes, yes, I'm here."

"Remember? Jessie . . . all about justice? . . . Now I know . . ."

"Know what?"

". . . Jessie . . . I'll talk to you when I . . . Be there soon, okay? On my way back. If you can hear me, good-bye! Love you!"

"Renee!" Hudson heard the distinct sound of his phone disconnecting. He ended his call and made a sound of frustration. Well, at least she was coming back. He was determined to get to the bottom of what was driving her, be it a story or some inner worry or fear that she'd been reluctant to name so far.

On bare feet he climbed back up the stairs to check on Becca. He peeked into the room and saw her eyes were open. A soft, sexy smile caressed her lips and she lifted her arms to him. Thoughts of Renee drifted away and he quickly stripped naked and came to bed once more.

Renee tossed her cell phone into her purse as she drove north. The damned thing would be useless for a few more miles. There were stretches on the coast where there was poor service and then a place in the mountains where there was no connection at all. But she'd be home in a couple of hours.

Good! She'd had it with the beach. Even the tidy little hotel where she'd rented a room in Pacific Beach, ten miles north of Deception Bay, had become tiresome. She hadn't gone back to the cabin where she'd thought she'd seen a man with dead eyes outside the window, a place where she'd "misplaced" a butcher knife. No way. She wasn't *that* secure. No, she'd rented a room at the hotel ten miles away, a place she could write her story and sleep in peace.

Now she flexed her fingers on the steering wheel of her Camry, a hard smile crossing her face. She'd known something was wrong. Off. But she hadn't known exactly what.

Nor all of the implications.

Now she did. And it was a story and a half. So much more than what she could have ever anticipated. She, and all her friends, had only seen the tip of the iceberg, not the bulk of secrets and deceptions that floated beneath. But she'd followed Jessie's path and she was pretty sure she'd now learned what Jessie had.

"Justice," she said aloud, feeling a familiar frisson slide down her back.

There was danger because she'd learned enough to put the pieces of the puzzle together. She knew the who and, sort of, the why. She was certain that those bones in the maze belonged to Jessie, but she didn't understand what Glenn's death had to do with anything. She was still working that angle, needed to figure out if he'd been murdered or had just been an innocent victim in a tragic accident.

And she needed more information about Siren Song, though it was hard to come by.

Cults, she thought. This one was steeped in mystery and lore. Just the kind of thing readers loved!

But Jessie had died because of what she'd learned. Renee was certain of it.

And Madame Madeline—Mad Maddie—had warned Renee that she, too, was in danger.

She clamped her emotions down hard. She wouldn't think of that as she drove away from Deception Bay. Nor would she think about that stranger with the icy eyes staring at her. It had chilled her soul but good.

But now . . . now she had the story, at least a good part of it.

"My God," she whispered as she followed Highway 101 north along the Pacific coast, the ocean appearing gray and restless, its surface far below the cliffs on her left lit by streaks of sunlight and shrouded by dark clouds. She was glad the southbound lane was a barrier between her and the edge as she headed on her way to the turn-off to Highway 26, which led east to Laurelton and Portland. She felt the need to stay safe. To keep herself from danger of any kind, because she'd prodded the monster with a stick and it had lifted cold eyes and stared her down.

Another quiver swept through her body.

All she had to do was get home. Back. To Hudson and sanity.

Her toe touched the accelerator a bit harder.

Hurry, she told herself.

She glanced at her rearview and saw the vehicle approaching fast from behind. A truck of some kind. Where had it come from? She'd been alone on the road as the sun rose.

Not to worry. It's just another driver.

Still, Renee pressed her toes to the accelerator some more, just a bit, though the road wound around sheer dun-colored cliffs on her right, cliffs that would turn to the rolling foothills of the fir-choked Coast Range when she turned east. To the left, across the opposite lane, was the low metal guardrail, no serious barrier to the edge that dropped to the boiling surf, far below.

The truck, its front end protected by some kind of metal bars, closed the gap, alarming Renee. Maybe she should slow down, let him pass. She wished she'd decided to make this trip later in the day, when more traffic was about.

Ahead were tricky turns. An outcropping of rock on the Pacific side humped upward. A last barrier before the road snaked into two hairpin turns with just the guardrail as a barrier. No turnout to pull into. No shoulder.

Renee lightly touched the brake as the outcropping flashed by and she headed into the first turn. Rays of light shone through the boiling clouds like a message from heaven, sparkling on the surf.

Ram!

Renee's head snapped back and her grip on the wheel loosened. Frantically she tried to regain control. The truck had slammed into her.

And he was coming back. Full speed!

"Stop!" she cried. "Stop!"

She punched the accelerator.

Her car leapt forward.

Too late!

Bam!

The truck shot into her car again, spinning the Toyota from her control. She yanked hard, turning the car toward the cliffs. *Ram!*

With a shriek of metal, the Camry spun around, glancing off the cliffs to her right, careening toward the guardrail. Heart pounding, fear shrieking through her body, Renee yanked on the steering wheel and her compact shimmied around, its rear end facing the guardrail, its front staring into the face of the pale-colored truck.

And then the truck crept forward, its front end bearing against hers, pushing her toward the edge.

"No!" *Oh, God, no!*

Screaming, terror shooting through her, she slammed her foot onto the accelerator, her wheels spinning madly but gaining nothing as the SUV forced her backward. Closer and closer to the edge of the cliff, where the guardrail was but a small strip of steel.

"Please, God, no. Not now."

She looked through her windshield and saw the face of the driver.

It was *him*!

The man she'd seen in the window.

Him!

Oh, God, those dead, flat eyes!

The truck's engine roared, pushing forward, a beast of a machine.

Her Toyota was no match and slid ever backward, smoke coming out from the tires, gravel spitting.

Renee jerked on the wheel.

Too late.

With a shriek of metal, the car's rear end broke through the guardrail and the Camry was forced over the edge.

Renee stared upward in horror as her car slid into space. Her scream tore from her throat and echoed off the sheer cliffs as the Camry then spun end over end into a greedy, reaching sea far below.

Chapter Seventeen

She knows!

As our eyes meet, I see the recognition, the under-standing.

My heart is thundering, pounding, full of excitement, my fingers clutching the steering wheel as I step on the accelerator.

Her face is a mask of horror and I can almost hear her screams.

God has given me her as a gift. She is not Rebecca. She is not Jezebel. She is not one of them. She is just a stupid woman who threatens the mission.

I cannot smell her, only the heady scent of the sea crashing on the rocks far below.

Yet she must die because she knows.

Bam! My truck's grill guard hits the car hard a last time and the Camry slams into the weakened guardrail to plummet over the edge, spinning and toppling as it dives into the sea.

Trembling, I back up quickly, throw the truck into Drive, and make good my escape. Though this is a lonely stretch of road at this hour in this late part of winter, I must be careful.

If anyone were to see, my mission, my life's work, would be destroyed.

There is still so much to do and there is a scent in the air, the hint of an odor that I haven't smelled in a long, long while.

I smile to myself as I drive northward before heading east.

To her.

Hudson swept his cell phone from the kitchen table as he and Becca headed out to his truck, Ringo on his leash zigzagging across the gravel drive. Becca climbed inside, helping the dog onto her lap as Hudson dug his keys from his pocket.

It was early afternoon. They'd spent the morning at his house, waking late, drinking coffee, tending to the livestock, eating a leisurely brunch at a diner in Laurelton before returning to the farm. The day had been clear and the horses had stretched their legs, trotting, tails lifted around the pasture. Boston, the Appaloosa, her belly large with the foal she carried, rubbed her side against the rough bark of an oak tree, snorting in contentment, her breath two cloudy bursts from her nostrils, and Becca stroked her neck and murmured to her.

Now Hudson smiled to himself. Who would have thought that he would feel such a sense of contentment here, a peace he'd never experienced in his days of selling, brokering, and investing in commercial real estate? He'd done well enough, but he'd always been restless.

You're too damned young to retire, he'd told himself often enough, but he'd ended up here anyway, working on the farm, managing the properties he owned at a distance, and satisfied, if not happy with his life.

From the moment he'd seen her at Blue Note he'd known he'd never gotten over her.

And Jessie had brought them together, which made him feel almost guilty about falling in love again.

He caught himself up short—*Love? Jesus, you're an idiot. Love? Ridiculous.* But glancing at Becca as she climbed into his truck made him quiet that nagging little insistence. And the restlessness that had been with him for years was sliding away.

The phone rang as they were bumping down the gravel drive. He examined the Caller ID. "Tillamook County?" he read, then punched the talk button. "Hello?"

Becca gave him a shrug as he said, "Yeah, Tim. What's up?" In an instant his face turned to stone. "Wait a minute . . . Slow down. Where? . . . Yeah, I know Renee went to the beach. *What?*"

Becca's heart froze.

"Wait . . . which hospital?"

Hospital? Becca's fingers tightened over the handle of her purse. Her blood turned to ice. "Hudson?"

All color drained from Hudson's face. He stopped the truck at the end of the drive, his fingers crushing the phone.

"Hudson?" she repeated, her mind racing.

"She's alive?" he said into the phone.

Becca's hand flew to her throat.

"I'm on my way." He clicked off, breathing shallowly. "That was Tim. Renee's been in an accident. The sheriff's department called him, told him she's at Ocean Park Hospital."

"Is she all right?"

"I don't know. Shit!" He threw the truck into gear again.

"But she's alive."

"I think so."

Becca was trembling inside, her blood turning to ice. Another "accident," so soon after Glenn's death. What were the chances of that happening? "I can't believe it," she whispered, but that was a lie. Fleetingly she thought of Renee's sense of persecution—Renee, with her need to return to Deception Bay, her determination to find out what happened to Jessie, her yearning to write her story.

"I'm going straight to the hospital after I drop you off."

"I'm coming with you," she said. No way was he leaving her behind.

"It's at—"

"—the coast. Ocean Park. I heard."

"What about the dog?" Hudson asked.

"He'll come, too. Ringo loves to ride in the car." To the dog, she said, "Lie down, Ringo."

"Are you sure about this?" They were at the end of the lane waiting for a truck towing a fifth wheeler to pass. "It doesn't look good, Becca."

"I want to be with you."

"The hospital is a good two hours away." He glanced through the windshield to the fields beyond, not, she suspected, seeing the stubble of bent yellow grass in the fields.

"Then we'd better not waste any time."

"Okay." He accelerated onto Highway 26, heading west where the sun, sheltered by thin clouds, was already lowering behind the ridge of mountains separating the Willamette Valley from the Pacific Ocean.

Becca sent a prayer toward the gauzy heavens. Renee couldn't die. She just couldn't. They'd lost too many already.

But as she stared ahead, she thought about Jessie and her warning . . .

What was it she'd tried to tell her? Two syllables? Maybe one word?

As Hudson's truck roared upward into the foothills and the towering fir and oak obliterated the sun, Becca felt a cold chill settle in her spine.

Ocean Park Hospital was known for the twisted pine trees that flanked its blacktopped entrance. The pines, their trunks and limbs tortured over the years by blasting gusts of wind, shivered and bent their heads as Hudson's truck barreled between them on his way to the low-rise concrete hospital that had been constructed for function, not beauty.

Hudson had placed a call to the sheriff's department and gotten nowhere. A return call to Tim had found him despondent. Renee's soon-to-be-ex-husband, who too was driving to the hospital, had sounded slow and perplexed, as if he had no idea what his role was in this event.

For her part, Becca just felt still inside. A forced stillness. A way to insulate herself from whatever was coming next. She had burning questions about Renee's accident, but neither she nor Hudson knew much more when they arrived than when they'd started.

Ringo barked at them as they left him in the truck.

"You'll be okay," Becca said to the dog automatically, though her mind was elsewhere and she wasn't sure that any of them would ever be "okay" again. Even the dog.

Hudson, his expression calm but worried, clasped Becca's hand and they entered through the emergency room's automatic sliding doors together.

"Renee Trudeau?" Hudson said to a clerk behind an admitting window. "I was told she was admitted earlier today. Victim of an automobile accident. I'm her brother, Hudson Walker."

"Could you wait a moment," she said, inclining a hand toward the adjacent waiting room with its fake ficus tree and row of tired-looking chairs. Dog-eared, tattered magazines littered an old coffee table and an elderly man sat with his elbows resting on his knees, his gnarled hands tented under his unshaven chin. "I'll let the doctor know you're here."

"I'd like to see my sister." Hudson looked past the clerk to the line of doors beyond.

"I'll let him know." The woman, probably fifty though she sported new braces, smiled patiently, but there was something in her gaze that warned things might not be as bright as her grin suggested.

Becca perched on the edge of her seat but Hudson paced like a caged lion, glancing out the window, then at the rooms behind the glass partition and admitting desk, then Becca, then back again.

It wasn't the doctor who approached them but a man in a crisp tan uniform with badges on his chest and upper arms. Deputy Warren Burghsmith of the Tillamook County Sheriff's Department introduced himself to Hudson, who had been pointed out by the clerk in braces.

Becca steeled herself. This couldn't be good news.

"You're Renee Trudeau's brother?" he asked.

"That's right. How's my sister?"

"Still alive, but barely. Lucky she didn't die on impact." He explained how Renee's car had plunged through a guardrail and into the ocean, how someone had called in the accident, and how the Coast Guard had retrieved Hudson's sister from the wreckage. The deputy was calm, grim, and careful. He asked Hudson a few questions, mostly about where Renee was going and what she'd been doing. It didn't take a rocket scientist to figure out something about the accident had alerted the authorities, though what that could be wasn't apparent until the deputy admitted that Renee's Toyota appeared to have been pushed—*thrust*—over the cliff.

"On purpose?" Hudson demanded.

"We don't know."

"When can I see her?"

"That's up to Dr. Millay, but I'll see what I can do." The deputy walked through a pair of swinging doors marked No Admittance.

Minutes later a doctor in pale green surgical scrubs pushed through those same doors and while the elderly man looked up expectantly, the doctor, who had removed his gloves, headed straight for Hudson and Becca. "I'm Dr. Millay," he introduced himself. He was tall, somewhere in his sixties, with the build of a runner. "I understand you're Renee Trudeau's brother?"

"Hudson Walker. Yes. How is she?" he asked, but the doctor's somber expression said it all.

"I'm sorry. We did everything we could."

Becca's knees nearly buckled. What? What was he *saying*?

The blood drained from Hudson's face as the doctor went on, "Your sister's injuries were extensive. Broken clavicles, ribs, crushed pelvis, perforated lung . . ." In medical terms he described a body crushed from impact, but only a few of the phrases stuck in Becca's brain. ". . . deep trauma to the chest and abdomen . . . heart and liver damage . . . unable to stop the internal bleeding . . . unconscious throughout . . . little or no pain . . . no response . . ." then finished with, "Ms. Trudeau died on the operating table. We called her time of death at 9:23 am."

Hudson continued to stare at him. "Time of death?"

Becca squeezed his hand hard. Her heart started pounding in her ears so loudly she could scarcely hear.

Hudson seemed lost in another world. Becca pulled him unresistingly back to a chair but he sat on its edge, searching Dr. Millay's craggy face for answers. The surgeon, who'd delivered the news quietly and without emotion, touched a hand to Hudson's shoulder and said with a measure of kindness, "You can see her when you're ready."

Hudson rose to his feet like an automaton. Becca stood up as well, but he turned to her and said, "I want to see her alone."

"Are you sure?"

He nodded jerkily and left with the doctor and Becca stared after them, feeling caught in a vortex that was pulling her down. Ever since the discovery of the bones at St. Elizabeth's, death and tragedy had dogged their footsteps. How could this happen? Renee had been so vital. Such a force of nature. And now . . . and now she was *dead*?

In her mind's eye Becca saw Jessie again, standing high on a cliff, near the ocean, the very ocean into which Renee's car had plunged.

The ocean . . .

Through glazed eyes she watched as Deputy Burghsmith waited outside the inner sanctum doors. She realized Renee's body would be moved to the morgue very soon.

A strange sound erupted from her own throat. A cry of anger and disbelief. The deputy came her way. "Are you all right, ma'am?"

"The car went over a cliff," Becca said, as if committing it to memory. "Renee's car."

The deputy frowned. "Yes."

"On Highway 101, and the car went into the ocean?"

"Yes, ma'am. Your friend was life-flighted to the hospital."

"She lost control of the car because . . . someone pushed her over the edge on purpose?"

"We don't know all the circumstances. The accident scene is still being reconstructed." He glanced at his watch. "Well, they've probably about finished up by now."

"But you believe someone ran her off the road," she said again, though whether she was talking to herself or the deputy she wouldn't have been able to say. She was lost in her own memories of another accident, where she'd been forced off the road by a hit-and-run driver and her car had plunged into a deep ditch, smashing into huge rocks that formed one side, crumpling the front of her car like weak cardboard. She'd been trapped inside for hours. Had to be freed by the Jaws of Life, though she remembered none of it. All she recalled was the horrific awareness that her baby was gone. She was empty. And she cried herself to sleep for weeks afterward and relied on medicine to dope her up and help remove the pain.

And now someone had run Renee off the road and she'd lost her life. She wasn't alive anymore. Becca couldn't quite grasp it. Hudson's sister, the only family he had left, was gone. The vibrant dark-haired reporter with the feeling she was being *persecuted* was gone.

She was about to follow after Hudson despite what he'd said when he came back through the doors, his face pale. She wanted to gather him in her arms and hold him tightly, but he seemed somewhat distant, clearly still unable to process all that had happened in such a short time.

"I called Zeke," he said in a strange voice. "He was the only one I could think of to call."

"I'm so sorry." Becca's eyes burned.

"I don't believe she's gone, Becca. I saw her. I saw . . . the body. But I still don't believe it."

Then she wrapped her arms around him and he pressed his forehead to hers. She felt the shudder go through him and squeezed her eyes shut on her own teary emotions. She wanted to be strong for him. She wanted to help.

"I'm going to the crash site," he muttered, pulling away. "I want to see where it happened."

"You're sure?"

"Yes."

Becca followed him out to his truck. "You okay to drive?"

He nodded, got into his cab, pulled back onto Highway 101, and drove south, past the turn to 26 and inland. It was a spot they hadn't passed on the way to Ocean Park Hospital, but it was definitely on the way to Deception Bay, the small town near where Renee had been staying.

It was a surreal trip. Neither Becca nor Hudson said much. The day had been surprisingly nice with the sun gaining control of the clouds, not the other way around, though now the early evening shadows were stretching inland and the sun was descending toward the sea.

And then they were there. A section of guardrail was twisted back, the metal hanging over the edge of a cliff. A gaping hole. Gravel had been stained with differing colors of spray paint, evidence left from the team reconstructing the accident.

Hudson pulled the truck to a stop, and he and Becca sat and stared at the break in the rusted metal rail far above the ocean. Then they climbed from the vehicle and Hudson walked to the edge, but Becca hung back, feeling queasy and strange. She stayed by the truck, one hand on the front fender, while Hudson went to the rim and looked over, his hair ruffled by spurts of wind, the sleeves of his denim shirt pressed against his arms from its force.

Becca couldn't move forward. Logically, all she had to do was put one foot in front of the other but there was a barrier she couldn't see, holding her in place. An oppressive, invisible wall. And then she heard the dull roar that heralded a vision, the sudden blindness, the building headache. "No," she pleaded, although it could have been in her mind.

Ringo whined at her from the car. One of her hands was still on the hood, and she concentrated on it with all her strength, turning toward the vehicle for support before she was completely taken over by the vision.

She expected to see Jessie but instead she was in a vehicle herself, spinning the steering wheel, screaming, desperately trying to gain control. Trees and brush flashed by as her car plunged off the road and down the embankment. Her car. It was her car! Her accident! Instinctively Becca cradled her abdomen, protecting her baby. She could hear the rush of the engine from the car behind her, the one that had forced hers over the edge. In a panic she glanced back. She saw him driving away, heading like a maniac away from the scene of the crime.

And then blackness. Nothing but blackness.

Hudson scanned the accident scene. He was sick with grief and it had driven weariness into the marrow of his bones, but he couldn't stop. Couldn't let this terrible nightmare become a reality.

"Who did this?" he whispered. He didn't believe it was an accident. Someone had purposely run Renee off the road. And the colored paint on the asphalt road and gravel shoulder told him the sheriff's department agreed.

Why?

He tore his gaze from the sheer rocks that led to the gray and white plumes of surf far below. He glanced at the ground, saw the tire tracks. He could see where she had stomped on the brakes but had been unable to gain purchase. The tracks just lost their tread as the wheels locked and the car kept moving straight toward the edge and through the guardrail, propelled over the cliff.

Pushed!

Intentionally forced over the edge to her death.

"Goddamned son of a bitch." His body was freezing. The deputy had alluded to the accident but he'd been holding back information; Hudson had felt it at the hospital but had been too absorbed in his own pain to pick up the signals. Someone had intentionally run Renee off the road.

His chest swelled with misery. He felt incapable of crying and didn't know why. He wished he could. That there was some way to release the weighty buildup of sorrow that was choking him.

Becca made a strangled sound and Hudson looked her way to see her clinging to the front of his truck just before she slid to the gravel. He raced to her side, covering the ground in four large leaps, grabbing her just as she sprawled in a heap.

"Becca!" He heard the tremor in his voice. The quake of real fear.

She was breathing. Her eyes moving. And he was glad that it was one of her "visions" and not some deadly disaster. There had been too many of those.

He cradled her head and rocked her and his eyes burned, unaware of the crash of the sea and the wind blowing through his hair. Cars traveled past, slowing, then speeding forward in this snaking area of roadway, but he clung to Becca, his thoughts jumbled with fear and fury. Something was happening to their group. Something was after them. Wasn't that what Renee had said? Or near enough?

What *was* it?

Several minutes passed while Becca lay in his arms, her body twitching as if she were fighting off an attack. When she slowly opened her eyes, she gazed at him for a moment in bewilderment.

"Jesus, Becca, you scared the hell out of me," he said.

She blinked several times, then inhaled sharply. "Renee," she murmured.

"You had another vision." It wasn't a question.

"Yeah." She slowly sat up, feeling weary.

"What did you see?" he asked tautly. "Anything about Renee?"

She looked into his tortured blue eyes. He believed in her visions at some level, but it was small comfort in the face of such loss. "I saw an accident," she said carefully. "Where a car was run off the road by another driver. But it wasn't Renee."

He gazed at her blankly. "What do you mean?"

"I think it was . . . me. My accident. From my past."

"Was Jessie any part of it?"

"No . . ."

"It was more a memory, then?" He held her close and she could feel the pounding of his heart as he struggled to understand. "Someone deliberately killed Renee," he said tautly. "I don't know why yet. Or who. But I'm sure as hell going to find out!"

Zeke grabbed for the large bottle of water he'd placed on the kitchen table and took several more long gulps. He was going to drink down the whole damn thing to keep himself from reaching for a bottle of bourbon, which was what he really wanted to do. But now was not the time to get ass-stinking drunk.

Renee was dead.

Jessie had killed her.

He was sure of it.

Evangeline was standing in the archway between the kitchen and hall, shrunken, her arms cradling herself, looking ashen and pale, her entire body shaking. "This is a joke. A cruel joke. Hudson's trying to get you to say something, to admit to something."

"Shut up, Vangie!" Zeke grabbed the water bottle, twisted the top, then threw it forcefully against the wall. The plastic bottle hit the ground and water gurgled onto the floor in a spreading pool. "Stop saying that!"

"Renee's not dead. It's not true."

"It is true! Hudson doesn't play sick games like that. It's his sister. His twin. What the fuck's wrong with you?"

"It's just not true. Don't be so mean. You're so hurtful." She folded in on herself even more, her big eyes pleading with him to come and hold her, to love her, to help her.

Zeke slammed out of his chair and grabbed the bottle of water, tossing it into the sink. Then he leaned against the edge of the stainless steel basin and stared at the rivulets of water circling the drain.

"Is Tamara coming over here?" Evangeline asked.

"She went to see The Third, I think. I don't know. She was crying."

"Now they'll think it's true," she sniffled.

"It is true!" Zeke slammed out of the kitchen and through the front door, gazing around wildly for his car. He'd parked it at the curb, hadn't he? Where was it?

Evangeline suddenly had hold of his arm. "Where are you going? Where are you going?"

"The hell away from you! She's dead, Vangie. *Dead.* Renee's dead. Glenn's dead. Jessie's dead. They're all gone!"

"No . . ."

"Goddammit!" He shook her off him and ran down the steps. There was no car anywhere, so he took off at a run and kept running until there was not a drop of energy left in his body and he threw himself onto the grassy berm that bordered the playground of a nearby school.

"Jessie," he murmured brokenly, then broke down and sobbed.

"What was it that Renee said when you met with the other girls?" Hudson asked Becca, holding a cool washrag over her head as she lay on the bed.

They'd checked into a motel near the county sheriff's offices, basic and weatherbeaten, willing to take pets, and surrounded by a small strip mall and a couple of fast-food eateries. Neither of them felt like driving home, and Hudson had decisions to make about the disposition of Renee's body anyway.

So they'd just headed into the musty-smelling room and Hudson had insisted Becca lie down on the bed while he ministered to her. He'd shaken out a couple of aspirin and handed her a glass of water while Ringo paced around the top of the bedspread, occasionally glaring at Hudson as if Becca's condition were his fault.

Becca had tossed back the aspirin, insisting she was fine, though her headache wasn't giving up its grip. Hudson, meanwhile, kept going over everything and anything that could explain what had happened, a circular litany that did not require any input from her. She understood that this was his way of trying to grasp his sister's death, and she lay quietly, petting her dog, as he paced the room, running on restless energy, unable to stop.

"What was it Renee said when you met with the other girls?" Hudson asked.

"She thought something was after her. Us. She was digging up stuff about Jessie and she stirred it up."

"It."

"She couldn't explain her feelings. Tamara thought she'd taken the Tarot too seriously, but it was more than that. But she was determined to get the story, like it was going to save us all, I guess. I don't know. She didn't say that. It just seemed like that."

He squinted his eyes, as if in pain. "Something that killed her."

"Why would anyone kill Renee?"

"Her story about Jessie. God, I don't know." He shook his head in frustration.

Becca sighed, feeling that same frustration. "You said Renee called you. What did she say?"

"I couldn't hear her. It was a bad connection."

"You didn't hear anything?"

"She was excited about the story. About Jessie. Something about getting justice and some history . . . about people living on cliffs. Colonies forming on cliffs," he corrected himself.

Becca shook her head, perplexed.

"Your visions," he said. "You said you've had a series of them since Jessie's remains were found."

She looked into his tense face. He was grasping at straws. Lines of weariness radiated from the corners of his eyes. She suspected she looked much the same.

"Like I said, I had the first one at the mall. Jessie was standing on a cliff above the ocean. She put her fingers to her lips and then she said something to me. I couldn't make it out. And then I saw her outside the Dandelion Diner."

"When we met McNally and his partner?"

She nodded. "That's why I went into the restroom. I was afraid I was going to pass out. And then I saw the nursery rhyme note to Glenn, and then this latest one, my car being pushed off the road."

"Do you think you were reminded of it because of Renee's accident?"

"Possibly." But it had felt far more real than that. A vision, not a memory.

Hudson came back to the bed and lay down beside her, moving a reluctant Ringo aside. "I can't take it all in."

"Me, neither."

He draped an arm around her, pulling her close. Time passed while they were lost in their own thoughts. Becca eventually heard Hudson's breathing grow more even, but her own mind ran through a maze of alleys, seeking answers that were always around the next corner, always just out of reach.

Gretchen was waiting for Mac when he crossed the room to his desk, and she didn't waste time with hellos or even to ask where he'd been all afternoon. "Reports are on your desk. The fire was arson, gas line was purposely damaged. The DNA results are back from the Preppy Pricks. And we've got our artist's mock-up on what she looked like."

"Jesus." Mac snatched up the files and glanced through them. "Good things really do happen in threes."

"That's bad things."

"Hmm. See if Hudson Walker's DNA matches with the baby's."

"Already told 'em. We should get a call soon."

"And the rest of the Preppy Pricks," Mac added as an afterthought.

"They're checking them all," Gretchen said impatiently. "What do you think of this?" She plucked the rendering of the victim's face from the pile and held it in front of Mac's eyes. He gazed at it hard. "This your little girlfriend?"

"I only saw pictures of Jessie."

"Me, too. And?"

"I think this is pretty close," he said slowly, though his heart was beating like a drum as he looked into those sexy, knowing eyes, the perfect mouth that he imagined twitching upward in a teasing, knowing grin. *"What are little boys made of?"* He could almost hear the rhyme slip through those sensuous lips.

"Don't go all careful on me now," Gretchen warned with a snort. "You've been saying it all along and now you've finally made me a believer. This picture's a dead ringer for Jezebel Brentwood. Those bones are hers and her baby's. And DNA's gonna prove it."

The phone on his desk rang and Mac swept it up. "McNally."

Gretchen's brows lifted and Mac nodded that it was indeed the lab tech with the information. "Thanks," Mac said thoughtfully, hanging up a moment later.

"Well?" Gretchen demanded.

"It's Jessie. The baby's DNA matched her father's."

"Walker?"

"Zeke St. John."

Gretchen screwed up her face in disbelief. "Walker's BFF?"

"Mac!" Pelligree called from across the room. "Tillamook County Sheriff's Department reported a fatal accident on Highway 101. Victim's name is Renee Walker Trudeau."

"What?" Mac jumped to his feet.

"Jesus Christ," Gretchen murmured.

Pelligree was sober. "Her brother identified the remains."

"I'm going," Mac said, snatching his coat and heading out the door.

For once Gretchen remained behind, sinking slowly into a chair. She and Pelligree looked at each other in the wake of Mac's departure.

"He was right," she said on a note of admiration. "There's a helluva lot more to this case than any of us thought."

Chapter Eighteen

Soft music . . . some vaguely familiar hymn whispered through the funeral parlor. Becca sat staring vacantly at the closed coffin, a testament to how badly Renee's body had been mangled in the "accident." Sprays of flowers surrounded the glossy wooden casket and candles burned brightly, but the cloudy, gray day seeped through the windows, bringing in the gloom of winter. The gangly nondenominational preacher with a bad comb-over and rimless glasses stood at the dais as the music faded. He led the mourners in prayer, though Becca could barely concentrate.

Seated next to a grim-faced Hudson, a few chairs away from a blubbering Tim Trudeau, Becca kept her own ragged thoughts at bay. The group of mourners was larger than the small room in the funeral home, and the back doors had been opened to a covered area that had been extended with tents and outdoor heaters. Either Renee had made an incredible amount of friends in less than forty years, or a lot of those who'd come to pay their respects were the curious.

Renee Trudeau's death had made every major and local paper, as well as the news. Her connection to St. Elizabeth's, a school that had been previously riddled in scandal and murder, as well as the discovery of the bones and the supposition that they belonged to Jezebel Brentwood, had given her an unwelcome celebrity. The police had yet to make a formal statement, but Becca was certain it would be forthcoming soon. She'd seen the news van parked in the lot and had witnessed Detective Sam McNally arrive and slide into a back row, just inside the doors.

". . . tragic loss . . . trust in the way of the Lord . . . always be remembered as a wife, friend, sister . . ."

Becca's fingers were linked with Hudson's, but he was staring straight ahead, miles away, his gaze upon the preacher but his sight turned inward to thoughts of his twin.

Would Renee still be alive if she hadn't been so fascinated with Jessie's disappearance? Whether her car had been intentionally pushed off the road or sideswiped by a hit-and-run driver—which seemed more and more unlikely—Hudson's sister's death could be directly attributed to her quest for the truth about Jessie.

Becca thought of her visions and felt Hudson's grip tighten over her hand. Fighting tears, she bowed her head when instructed to pray and heard Tim, Renee's soon-to-be ex-husband, sniveling and snorting, as if he'd lost the love of his life.

Maybe he and Renee could have patched things up. Now no one would ever know. Nor would Becca be able to reconnect fully with Hudson's sister, his twin, the only family member he'd had left.

She was gone . . .

Killed. As was Jessie. As was Glenn . . .

All of the group from St. Elizabeth's was in attendance, all mourning and grief-stricken, all not saying what everyone was thinking—*Who's next?* Becca had caught a glimpse of The Third, taciturn as he fingered the small pamphlet about the service, and she'd seen Mitch chain-smoking on the porch right before the service, looking like an absolute wreck. Tamara, toned down in a long black skirt and sweater, was a couple of rows over, not far from Zeke and Evangeline. Zeke was glum and Vangie was a doe in the headlights.

None of them could believe another member of their group, Hudson's vibrant, passionate sister, was actually dead.

Becca's insides twisted and she fought the sting of tears as the preacher recalled some of the most noteworthy times of Renee's life. As he brought up Renee's education and her graduation from St. Elizabeth's she felt Hudson stiffen beside her. From the corner of her eye, she saw Tamara, shaking her head in sadness.

God, this was horrible. Never in a million years would Becca have thought that she would be at Renee's funeral at so early an age. But then, there were lots of things she wouldn't have imagined. She caught a glimpse from Scott Pascal, who sat, hands clasped between his knees, his brown suit jacket pulling at the seams. He looked away and then Becca felt someone staring at her. Hard. Like a knife between her shoulder blades.

She stiffened, half looked behind her, but at that moment the preacher asked them all to pray and Becca bent her head.

But she was being watched. She felt those eyes digging into her. Whoever was staring so intently at her wasn't a friend. Just before the end of the prayer she hazarded a quick glance over her shoulder and saw only a sea of bent heads before she caught McNally's unguarded stare. He'd asked her and Hudson a ton of questions about Renee's accident but they'd had no answers for him. Now his eyes were trained on hers and she looked quickly away, whispering a quick "amen" as the preacher closed the service.

Becca couldn't wait to get outside, away from the coffin, away from the heavy onus of death. But there was a gathering afterward at the grave site, and though there were fewer people in attendance, all of their friends made the trek to the hillside cemetery on the outskirts of Laurelton.

Flanked by old-growth timber dripping in moss and knifing into the low-hanging clouds, the manicured acres of grass dotted by headstones appeared bleak and somber. More prayers were said, more condolences whispered as high heels sank into the rain-sodden loam and Tim tossed a rose onto the coffin before it was lowered into the neatly cut earth. A hundred yards away, a man sat smoking on a big yellow piece of earth-moving equipment. As soon as the crowd disbursed he would make short work of filling the hole where Renee's coffin was resting.

It wasn't just close family friends at the grave site. Seated in his car, parked with a view of the graveside ceremony, Detective Sam McNally, their group's nemesis, was just far enough away not to be part of the service, close enough to observe. Now, gazing at them through his windshield, he seemed to be talking on his cell phone. He just never gave up. Not for twenty damned years. "Obsessed," The Third had once called him. It wasn't far from the truth.

And now he was here at Renee's burial two decades later. The entire ceremony was disturbing.

As the crowd dispersed, Hudson spoke to old friends of his family while Becca huddled with Tamara and The Third, both usually flamboyant and now quiet and reserved.

"This is Jessie's doing," Mitch said as he approached. He was lighting one cigarette off the butt of another.

"This is not the time, man," The Third said.

Mitch blew out a stream of smoke. "You all know it, you just won't admit it."

"Don't talk crazy." Tamara shook her head. "Come on, let's get out of here."

"It's not the end, you know. More of us are gonna get it," Mitch predicted, glancing at the dark trees surrounding the graveyard. "How well do you know your friends?" he yelled to the group as a whole. "Somebody's a killer!"

"Shut up!" Tamara fished in her purse for her keys and Becca noticed that the detective had gotten out of his car and was approaching Hudson. "God, Mitch. What's wrong with you?"

"I know too much," he muttered. "And none of you do."

Tamara retrieved the jingling keys and snapped her purse shut.

"Tamara's right, man, pull your shit together," The Third said as Hudson, hair blowing in the wind, spoke to the policeman.

"You should all watch out," Mitch said.

"Look, I've gotta run." The Third was having none of it as he made his way to his BMW and slid inside.

"You could be next," Mitch called after him. "You got one of those notes, too!" The BMW roared away.

"That's what this is all about? Those damned nursery rhymes?" Tamara demanded. "You look like hell, Mitch. Really. Get some sleep."

"It's more than that," Mitch said. "The cop's still hanging out, isn't he? Mac? And he's talking to Hudson."

"He's investigating," she said tightly. "That's what he does."

He glanced over his shoulder to an area where a solitary tree stood next to the firs in the surrounding woods, then took another long drag, as if the smoke were life-giving rather than stealing. "Oh, hell, just forget it." He left them as he headed for his Tahoe, shoulders tight.

Tamara whispered to Becca, "I think he's using again—mixing his prescription drugs. He had a little problem before." She pulled her coat closer around her slim body as her eyes watched his Tahoe disappear. "He's losing it."

We all are, Becca thought. *Some of us just hide it better than others.* She stared into the forest, her gaze following the same path that Mitch's had only a few minutes before. The trees were shrouded in fog, ferns, and faulty shadows. For a second Becca thought she saw someone hiding in the dark, misty depths, but as the wind shifted, the mist lifting a bit, there was no one standing beside the gnarly old oak tree.

She, like Mitch, was imagining things.

And yet . . .

Hudson walked toward them. "Ready?" he said to Becca.

"Sure." She managed a small smile that she didn't feel.

"You need a ride?" he asked Tamara, but she shook her head.

"Got my car." With a wave, she picked her way through the wet grass to the spot where she'd parked her Mazda.

Becca watched her drive away from the passenger seat of Hudson's truck. He put the pickup into gear and said, "Zeke told me McNally wants to talk to him at the station. What do you think that's about?"

Becca stared out the side window. "He never got a note."

"Must be something more," he said wearily as he slid his truck into the slow file of vehicles driving toward town. "I'm getting to the point that I don't even want to know."

Becca felt that same stabbing sensation of being watched. She glanced back toward the trees, watching their limbs flail in the stiff breeze. "I don't, either," she said firmly.

The scent of betrayal, of unholy lust is in the air, teasing at my nostrils, reminding me that I must not fail.

She looks my way.

Through the haze I see the worry in her eyes; so like Jezebel's.

You can't see me, Demon Bitch. I'm invisible to you, but you feel me, don't you?

You know I'm coming for you.

I sense your fear.

God will make you pay for your pact with Satan, Rebecca. I am His messenger.

And I'm coming for you . . .

"Have a seat," Detective McNally told Zeke, indicating a chair on the opposite side of his desk.

Zeke did as he was told, his body as taut as a bowstring. He cupped his jaw in one hand, his arms tucked in tight, a position of defense.

Mac gave him a moment to relax and drew a long breath himself. He'd spent half the week in Tillamook County, learning all he could about the accident that had taken Renee Trudeau's life, and half the week in Laurelton dealing with a double homicide where the only man left standing—thirty-one-year-old junkie Harold Washington—claimed the deceased man and woman with the fatal gunshot wounds had fired at him first. They were all meth users—a lovely bunch of Johnny Ray's clientele—and it was hard to say just what had happened at the rented three-bedroom ranch at the east side of town. Gretchen was in her element; she loved interrogating low-life scum like Washington. Mac was tired of all that, and as he sat down at his desk across from Zeke St. John, he wondered if he might be becoming the burnout everyone thought he was.

"Know why I asked you here?" Mac asked.

"I'm the father," he blurted out. "That's what you're going to tell me. I'm the baby's father."

Mac had put the paternity issue aside in the wake of Renee Trudeau's death; he'd been too caught up in those events to even think about it. His thoughts had been occupied by Renee, Hudson Walker's sister. Why had someone pushed her car off the cliff? Did it have something to do with Jessie's murder? Whatever the case, the Tillamook County Sheriff's Department was on an all-out hunt for a vehicle with a smashed front end.

So when Zeke jumped in and hit the issue head-on, Mac was slightly surprised. "That's exactly right," he admitted. "You are the baby's father. You slept with Jessie."

He nodded jerkily. "A couple of times. She was trying to get back at Hudson. She teased like mad. She was so wild and scary. I don't think she slept with anyone else, though she acted like it. She chose me."

"Because you were Walker's best friend."

"I thought she wanted me, at the time." He looked faintly ashamed.

"Walker have any idea?"

"I don't think so."

"He's going to have to know now," Mac said.

"Yeah. I see. Yeah . . ."

Mac thought over a few things and the moment stretched out between them. The pause made Zeke antsy. His eyes darted around the room as if now that he'd made his confession, he wanted to escape.

"You think this has something to do with the fact that you never received a nursery rhyme note?" Mac finally asked.

Zeke looked flummoxed. "What do you mean?"

"Does anyone else know about your relationship with Jessie?"

"No . . . uh-uh. I don't get what you're driving at?"

Mac said, "You're Jessie's baby's father, and you're the only one of your buddies who didn't get a note. You see? It's a difference. Something that stands out."

He went quiet, internalizing, and his face seemed to grow more gaunt.

"It's a connection that doesn't make any sense," Mac said. "Unless maybe . . ." Zeke's gaze flew to Mac's. "Someone is trying to direct the attention away from you?" Zeke didn't respond, though it looked like it was taking all he had to keep quiet, so Mac pushed a little harder. "Someone who knows you're the father. Someone who thinks you killed Jessie?"

"No."

"It seems like a woman's idea of terror."

He gulped out a laugh. "Now you're going to tell me Jessie's alive!"

"I don't think it's Jessie."

Zeke's eyes were hollow, like he'd stared into a hellish world. "Vangie did not kill Jessie! She couldn't have done that. She doesn't have the strength." He was breathing rapidly. "And what about Renee? And Glenn? What happened to *them*?"

Gretchen had been at her desk when Zeke came in but she'd moved closer to hear the exchange. Mac felt her presence behind his right shoulder and was glad she had chosen to keep her mouth shut instead of breaking in.

Zeke looked ready to fall into pieces. Mac told him the investigations into Glenn and Renee's deaths were ongoing, but he didn't seem to hear. He was lost in his own thoughts and when the interview concluded he rose from his chair in a daze. Together, Mac and Gretchen watched him walk out of the station.

"He thinks his fiancée wrote the notes," Gretchen observed.

"He's been thinking that for a while," Mac concluded.

"You gonna let him drop that bomb on her?"

Mac shrugged. "Do you see Evangeline Adamson as Jezebel Brentwood's killer? Following her into the maze, stabbing her in the ribs? Murdering her and her baby?"

"Zeke's baby, too."

"I agree with Zeke. I don't think she has the nerve. The note sending is more her style, sneaky and anonymous. She was trying to protect Zeke, when in fact she pointed an arrow right to him."

Gretchen's blue eyes narrowed and she smiled her thin smile.

"What?" Mac asked.

"You better stop this, or I might start thinking you're a decent detective after all."

Mac harrumphed and turned away from her. He didn't want to start liking Gretchen, either. She was a pain in the butt, then, now, and forever.

Hudson drove away from the house Tim and Renee had shared and tried not to hate the guy. All he'd wanted was

Renee's laptop and notes about the story she'd been working on, but Tim didn't have them. Stunned that his wife was gone, Tim was a walking automaton. He acted like he didn't hear Hudson's request, going on and on instead about what a great relationship he and Renee had had, how much he'd loved her, how alone he felt now, how miserable. He seemed to have conveniently pushed away all the contention their relationship had been fraught with at the end. Hudson had wanted to explode at him, but had held his temper in check by sheer will, and finally Tim paid attention enough to say that the laptop hadn't been found when her Toyota was pulled from the sea. It, and whatever luggage Renee had carried with her, had been lost. Not that a computer that had been submerged in the sea would be of much help.

"I'll have to add that to the insurance report," Tim said to Hudson. "Thanks for reminding me."

In a foul mood, Hudson pushed thoughts of Tim aside as he drove home. Ignoring the calls from reporters on his answering machine, he spent the rest of the day caring for the livestock and fixing a broken gate. The physical labor of forking hay into mangers, shoveling manure from the stalls, and replacing hinges and broken boards gave him time to think and sort things out.

He tried to remember more of what she'd said in their last phone conversation, but there didn't seem to be anything there that meant anything. He knew her user ID and password, so he switched on his computer and flipped through her unread and "kept as new" e-mails. There weren't a lot of them. And none of them had to do with the story she was working on. Less than an hour later, he logged off in frustration.

Maybe the only way to learn something was to follow in her footsteps, like she'd followed in Jessie's.

His cell phone chirped at the same moment he heard tires crunching on his gravel driveway. He answered the phone, then glanced up the stairs, where Becca was working on her own laptop, getting some overdue work done for her job. "Hello?"

"Hey, Hudson. It's Zeke. I'm just pulling into your driveway."

"Yeah? What makes you come out here?"

"Just wanted to talk to you."

"Come on in. Door's open." He hung up and yelled, "Zeke's here."

When she didn't answer, he headed upstairs and caught her coming out of the bathroom, wiping her mouth with the back of her hand. "You all right? Zeke's just pulling up. He wants to talk to me."

Becca grimaced. "I ate something that didn't agree with me. I'll be right down."

"Okay."

Hudson clambered back down the stairs and Becca watched from the upper rail. She'd just lost her dinner. Food poisoning, or . . . *pregnancy*?

Too soon to know, she told herself with a flutter of anxiety in her already nervous stomach. She couldn't think of it. Couldn't hope. Yet elation was building, a sudden, blinding certainty that ran down her nerves like electricity.

No. No. Oh, please . . . yes!

It took her a few moments to collect herself, to quash her growing thrill and put it in perspective. This was way too early. If it was true, she was barely a month pregnant. But then, she'd known immediately last time she was pregnant as well.

Oh, God, let it be true!

By the time she joined them, Hudson and Zeke were in the kitchen. Hudson was in a chair, but Zeke was standing. Becca's head was full of swirling thoughts and it was all she could do to even wonder why Zeke had suddenly stopped by.

"I just got back from the police station and McNally. I went home but I couldn't stay there."

"What's wrong?" Hudson asked, frowning.

Zeke hesitated, clutched his fingers around the back of an

empty chair, then rocked back on his heels. "The DNA proved I'm Jessie's baby's father."

"What?" Becca asked softly and Hudson stared at Zeke like he was speaking a foreign language.

"The body has to be Jessie's," Zeke went on raggedly. "It has to be, because I didn't sleep with anyone else . . . except Jessie . . . at that time."

"You slept with Jessie," Hudson repeated. Zeke's gaze implored his friend's, but Hudson was having trouble shifting gears.

"You can hate me, man. I wouldn't blame you if you did! She was just trying to get back at you and I was a fucking idiot. I don't know. I don't have any excuse. She was just hot and I wanted her. I'm sorry. I'm really sorry!"

Becca's pulse shot into the stratosphere. Her mind was a jumble of pieces of information. *Jessie's baby wasn't Hudson's. Zeke slept with Jessie. Hudson's best friend slept with his girlfriend. Jessie's baby* wasn't *Hudson's!*

"Who killed her?" Hudson asked in a strangled voice.

"I don't know, man. Not me."

"Did you know about the baby?" Hudson demanded.

Zeke shook his head. "No way. I just thought she ran off, maybe because we were screwing. She was messed up. So was I. I'm sorry."

"Do you think she knew?"

"About the baby? It was, like, a few months along. That's what McNally said." He turned blindly to Becca. "Girls know that stuff, don't they?"

"Yes," Becca said weakly.

"I don't think she knew I was the father. I mean, you and her . . ." Zeke struggled for words, his gaze on Hudson, who'd gone unnaturally quiet. "You were together during that time?"

There was a long silence. Zeke's anxiety and torture over wondering what Hudson was thinking and feeling filled the room. Becca felt light-headed and sank onto one of the kitchen chairs. The past consumed the present. *You're not pregnant,* she told herself. *You just want it so badly your subconscious is making you think you are.*

But you haven't used birth control, have you? Haven't thought about it!

Hudson's cell phone rang and Zeke and Becca both visibly jumped. He pulled it from his pocket and checked the Caller ID. "It's Mitch," he said.

"Maybe I should go." Zeke looked to Hudson for confirmation, but his friend had turned his attention to his cell. Becca nodded to him. There wasn't much more to say, and Hudson was clearly still processing.

Zeke hesitated, but when he heard Hudson say, "Hey, Mitch, what's up?" he left, shoulders hunched, through the back door.

Becca glanced over and saw Booker T.'s empty water dish. She wondered when Hudson was going to put it away. The dog wasn't coming back.

But maybe there'll be a baby . . .

Hudson listened for a few moments, then said into the phone, "Why don't you just tell me, Mitch? I don't think anything could surprise me now. If you know who killed Glenn, just say it. And don't tell me it's Jessie, because I just learned those bones are definitely hers. Yes. For a fact." His gaze met Becca's and he said into the receiver, "That's right. Jessie did not send the notes because she's dead." He listened a little longer, then half sighed and said, "You're at the garage? How long are you gonna be there?" A pause. "Sure, I'll stop by." He shrugged to Becca as he hung up.

"Mitch is working late at the garage and wants me to stop by so he can talk to me about who killed Glenn."

"All your friends are suddenly into confessions," Becca murmured.

"You still feel sick, or do you want to go with me?"

"I'm okay. I can go. Think it'll be all right with Mitch? Maybe he wants to see you alone."

"To hell with that. I want to be with you." He pulled her into his arms. She hugged him so hard he started laughing.

"Are you all right?" she asked, her face pressed into his chest. "After what Zeke said?"

He exhaled a short breath. "Y'know, I'm almost relieved. Thinking the baby was mine, and I never knew . . . pissed me off. I've been really mad at Jessie—and she's been dead for twenty years! She never told me. I don't know how to explain it, but I was goddamned mad at her."

"I understand." A whisper of fear swept over Becca's skin. She'd kept that same secret herself.

"I'm not mad at Zeke. I would have been at the time, but a lot's happened and I just don't care." He stroked her hair. "And I believe Zeke. He didn't know she was pregnant. I don't know why she was killed—maybe she just ran into the wrong person—but I don't think it has anything to do with the pregnancy."

"Neither do I."

"Are you ready to go see Mitch?" he asked.

She curled her fists into his shirt and said, "Would it be bad of me to say, 'not just yet'?"

"Did you have something else in mind?" She heard the thread of amusement in his voice.

For an answer, she took his hand and led him back upstairs.

The garage was full of the smells of oil, dirt, and stale cigarette smoke, though no one was allowed to smoke inside. Mitch swiped the sweat from his brow with a red cloth stained with grease. He was sweating like a pig and trying like hell not to freak out. The card he'd received had scared the shit out of him, but now he had other worries loading him down. He'd had stomach problems ever since Glenn had died in the fire at Blue Note. He forced a picture of Glenn trapped in that damned inferno from his mind, but hell, he missed him. They'd been good buds. He'd listened when Glenn pissed and moaned about Blue Note or Gia. He'd been there.

And he and Glenn had bonded over getting their asses kicked by The Third and Jarrett time and again. Jesus, those bastards could make life miserable if you had a few extra pounds or some other kind of weakness.

Good old Glenn.

He tasted acid burning up his throat.

"Just the medication," he said, then clapped his trap shut. He didn't want Mike, the owner of the garage, to have any inkling that he was on prescriptions. Mike, an ex-druggie, was death on anything put in a person's bloodstream, even those prescribed by a doc.

So Mitch kept his pills on the down-low. No one but his doctor knew what medications were in his night table drawer or his body. But lately these new antidepressants coupled with his sleep aids had been playing tricks with his mind. He'd been hallucinating.

Or at least he thought he was. Who the fuck knew?

"Hey." Phil, the skinny sixtysomething mechanic whose craggy, collapsed face might scare little kids, lifted a hand as he headed through the bay and out the big garage doors. "You're closin' up, right?"

"After the Grand Am." Mitch checked his watch. He still needed to put in some time on the car, and Hudson had agreed to stop by. Mitch wasn't sure how much he was going to say to him. He hated being a tattletale, especially if his ideas were wrong. And it was kind of a betrayal, too. But Glenn was gone . . . and Renee, too, though he still was blaming that one on Jessie.

"She's dead," he reminded himself aloud. Hudson had confirmed it.

It just sure didn't feel like it.

"You talkin' to me?" Phil asked.

"Hey, change the channel back to country and close the doors, will ya?"

"Look who's the boss."

"You want to work on the damned Pontiac?"

"Fine, fine." Phil adjusted the station from the all talk radio that Mike always insisted upon and soon Randy Travis's voice boomed through the bays. "Tomorrow," Phil called as he pressed the electronic opener button so that the doors began their clattering descent. Before they closed completely Mitch caught a glimpse of Phil as he pulled himself up into the cab of a pickup that was jacked two feet into the air to support its huge tires.

With Phil gone, Mitch was completely alone. Everyone else, including Elsa, the greyhound, Mike's rescue dog and unofficial garage mascot, had already left for the day.

These days, Mitch didn't really like being completely alone.

With an effort, Mitch turned his attention to the Pontiac supported by a hydraulic jack. Something wrong with the front-end U joint. A big job. Shit. He slid beneath the vehicle on the creeper, rolling it into position, then began working. He hooked a lamp over the axle and frowned at the under-carriage. A trick one, this, but he'd always enjoyed working on cars, ever since he'd been a freshman at St. Elizabeth's, years before he could drive legally. He began humming along to Brooks and Dunn, spying what looked like another oil leak—more problems—when he heard something . . . a scrape of a shoe? Or just some static from the radio?

No one was in the place.

Mike had been gone since two.

Phil had left less than twenty minutes ago.

Mitch strained to listen over the sound of country twang and the thrum of guitar chords.

It was the damned medications, making him all paranoid. All the weird shit surrounding those bones, and the damned notes, and the fire and Glenn . . . and then Renee up and dying. Made him crazy, that's what.

Still nervous, he slid out from under the Grand Am bumping his head on one of the rims. He stepped outside for a smoke, and ducked under the awning of the overhang where they'd once pumped gas. Now the old tanks were empty and Mike only did auto repair work. The parking area under the overhangs was used for cars waiting for a part. Rain was starting to fall again, beating on an old tar roof.

He finished his cigarette, lit another, and wondered what was taking Hudson so long. Maybe he shouldn't have called him. Maybe he should've called that cop. But what did he know, really? Not the kind of evidence they were always yammering about on those TV shows. More like suspicions.

And he didn't know anything about Renee. Nothing. Whatever happened to her at the beach was just a weird co-incidence, probably. The work of thrill-seekers who just ran her off the road, maybe. He didn't see how it could tie into Jessie.

Maybe her dick of a husband did her in. What a fucking asshole that guy was.

Then there was Glenn . . . God, he wished Hudson would get here.

Mitch took a last, long drag, then walked around the corner of the building and through the open door, only half aware that it was ajar. Once under the ear again, he went back to work, moving leisurely on the creeper. He knew he could wrap this job up if he could just get the fuckin' universal joint—

Scccrraaaape.

Someone *was* inside.

"Hey!" he yelled.

No answer.

Just the sound of static over the notes of a slide guitar. "Phil? You there?"

Every hair on the back of Mitch's neck rose.

"Listen to me, you cocksucker. If you're fuckin'—"

The lights in the entire garage went out.

All the bays were plunged into darkness.

Holy shit!

Mitch's ticker about exploded.

He started to roll out from under the car, but the Pontiac groaned above him.

He reached an arm out, scrabbling for purchase, desperate to get out from under the car. Before he could shift free, he heard the snap of the release on the jack. "Shit," he whispered, his mouth turning to an "O" of horror just before three thousand pounds of General Motors metal pinned him to the creeper, which somehow didn't fold in on itself. Something punched into his chest. The weight of the car crushed him, cracking his bones. Pain like he'd never felt before screamed through his body. His lungs burned. He gasped for breath. Heard the hiss of his lungs. His heart was pumping furiously and he sensed blood leaking from his broken, aching body.

His eyes rolled back in his head, but he clung to consciousness. And then he saw her . . . as she was twenty years earlier—beautiful, sexy, and teasing.

"What are little boys made of?" she said.

"Jessie," Mitch cried, his voice strangled. "Jessie . . ."

Chapter Nineteen

Hudson's truck rattled down Highway 217 before turning off at Canyon and heading east toward the city. Mike's Garage, Mitch's workplace, was about another mile in.

He looked across at Becca. She'd been awfully quiet since their lovemaking and he wondered if he'd done something wrong. "What is it?" he asked her again, feeling like one of those idiots who keeps asking, "What's wrong?" when the person clearly doesn't want to say.

"Just tired," she said.

They passed auto dealership after auto dealership pressed shoulder to shoulder along the road that cut through this ravine in the west hills surrounding Portland. She glanced at her watch. "It's kinda late. Shouldn't he be off work by now?"

"He said he was working late, and that was a little over an hour ago. If he's not there, we'll check his apartment, and if he's not there, we'll go home." Hudson ran through a yellow light and drove the remaining quarter mile to a cross street where Mike's Garage was located.

The low, flat stucco building that once had been a gas station looked empty. The lights in the building were out, the

Closed sign visible, not a soul in sight. But Mitch's black Tahoe was parked in a spot at the side of the building.

"He must've gone with someone, gotten a ride," Becca said as Hudson pulled up next to the big rig and parked, cutting the engine.

"Maybe."

"The place is closed."

"I know." Hudson opened the glove compartment, retrieved a small flashlight, then stepped out of the pickup, leaving the driver's door open. He punched out a number on his cell phone and walked toward the garage, listening. "It's ringing." He nodded toward the garage. "Inside." Becca heard the faint sound of some downloaded tune.

"Maybe Mitch left it by mistake."

"Left his truck and his cell phone?" Hudson was already walking around to the back of the garage as Becca shoved open the passenger door and hopped to the ground, catching up with Hudson. By the time they reached a slightly ajar back door, the cell phone was still playing a song from the eighties. "Mitch?" he called into the darkened interior, his voice echoing slightly. "Mitch?"

"He's not here," Becca said again, but even as she stepped over the threshold of the garage she felt that something was wrong. No security lights were lit and country music was playing softly from speakers. But there was a strange, eerie quietude to the place that caused the hairs on the back of her arms to lift. Her stomach knotted as she kept up with Hudson. They picked their way through the parked cars in various states of disassembly, the scents of rubber and grease mingling with the odor of dust. The beam of Hudson's flashlight slid over the open hoods and raised carriages.

"Mitch, you here?" Hudson said again and Becca shivered.

This time Becca heard a low, nearly inaudible moan.

Her heart glitched. She stopped dead in her tracks.

"Mitch!" Hudson shone his light in the direction of the sound. The beam tracked over a stained cement floor to a man's legs poking from beneath the weight of a sporty red car crushing his chest, pinning him beneath. "Shit!"

They ran to the mechanic's—Mitch's—side. "He has to be alive. Has to," Becca whispered, trying to convince herself. As she peered beneath the car and caught a glimpse of Mitch's face, a mask of death, his eyes closed, only the raspy sound of his breath indicating there was a bit of life in his body.

Hudson was kneeling by Mitch's side. "Hit the lights!" he ordered Becca, shining the beam of his flashlight onto the far wall where a switch was visible. "And call for help."

Becca was already on her feet, fumbling in her purse, retrieving her cell, dialing 911. She hurried across the concrete, nearly tripping on a drain before she reached the switch and threw it. Immediately, flickering fluorescent overhead lights cast a bluish glow over the garish scene.

"He's still alive," Hudson said as the 911 operator answered.

Becca wasted no time. "I need an ambulance immediately."

"What is your name and the nature of your emergency."

"I'm Rebecca Sutcliff and I'm at Mike's Garage, off Canyon Boulevard. There's been a horrible accident, Mitch Bellotti—he's trapped under a car, he's bleeding and . . . and . . . send someone to . . ." She turned anxiously to Hudson.

"The cross street is Eighty-sixth or seventh!" Hudson had jumped to his feet, heading for the roller jack.

"Did you hear that? Eighty-sixth or seventh and Canyon. Send someone quickly."

"The victim is alive?"

"Barely. Send an ambulance now!"

"There's a squad car in the area, if you'll please stay on the line. Ma'am, please stay on the line and—"

Screw that! Becca hit the speaker option on her phone and left the cell on the hood of a Ford Escape. She couldn't waste time talking.

Hudson's hands grabbed the jack's lever and he rapidly pumped it upward. Slowly the car began to rise off Mitch's broken chest. In tandem they grabbed the creeper and pulled him from harm's way.

Blood covered the front of Mitch's garage jumpsuit where metal had punched through his skin, smearing his name. His entire abdomen looked as if it had fallen in on itself.

The sound of sirens split the air and Becca thought she'd never been so relieved in her life as she and Hudson eased Mitch out from under the car's carriage. Hudson found the button to raise the garage doors and hit it. The doors on all three bays began grinding upward as a squad car—lights flashing, siren screaming—flew into the lot. The driver stood on the brakes and two officers emerged.

"What the hell happened here?" the taller of the two cops asked. Another siren sounded—the ambulance, thank God!

Hudson said grimly, "We found him this way."

"Alive?" the shorter officer, a woman with a blond ponytail, looked at Hudson from beneath the brim of her hat.

"I think so, but he's in bad shape."

While her partner knelt at Mitch's side, she was on the phone, barking orders, talking to the EMTs as the ambulance roared into the parking lot. A crowd had begun to gather, traffic slowing and snarling around Mike's. Within minutes another squad car arrived, and while the first officers interviewed Becca and Hudson and the EMTs worked over Mitch, the newly arrived cops worked to hold back the crowd and keep the traffic moving.

Becca and Hudson were asked to stick around while Mitch was placed on a stretcher, wheeled into the ambulance, and whisked away. The owner of the garage was called and the area roped off with crime scene tape.

Hudson and Becca, standing beneath the overhang, were barraged with more questions but finally allowed to leave. They headed directly to the hospital, and on the way, Becca called as many of their friends as she could. The EMTs hadn't given them a diagnosis, but both Becca and Hudson realized that Mitch was hanging by a thread. Hudson didn't say it, but Becca read it in his eyes. He didn't think Mitch would make it through the night.

"Glenn . . . Renee . . . and now Mitch?" Becca whispered to Hudson.

"It's not a conspiracy," he said, but she sensed he was trying to convince himself as much as her.

"What is it, then?" she asked, but he couldn't come up with a response.

Mac was on the phone when Gretchen, who'd been slipping into her jacket and getting ready to leave, received a call on her cell phone. She was halfway to the door but she stopped in the act of pushing her arms through her sleeves and turned to meet Mac's eyes.

Mac glanced away, needing all his attention for the phone call he was already handling. But Gretchen wouldn't be put off. He heard her say grimly, "Thanks for the heads-up," then marched back to Mac's desk and stood in front of it. He lifted an impatient hand to her. She could just damn well wait for once.

"Mitch Bellotti died tonight," she told him loudly. The other officers still in the station turned to look.

Mac was taken aback. "Something's come up," he said into the phone. "I'll call you back. Mitch Bellotti died?" he demanded as he hung up. "How?"

"At his job. Got crushed by a car that slipped off a jack. It fell on his chest before he could get out. Punched right through his chest and broke his ribs." She went on with other details she'd obtained from a Beaverton police officer she was friends with, and Mac learned he was found about an hour or so after the incident by Hudson Walker and Becca Sutcliff, who had called 911. The EMTs who worked on Bellotti got him to the hospital, but he died within five minutes of arrival, the broken ribs having penetrated other organs. There'd been too much damage and he'd bled out before they could save him. "Unconscious the whole time," Gretchen finished. "Last person to see him alive was a guy who worked with him, Phil Reece. All the stories jibe according to the Beaverton PD."

"It's been ruled an accident?"

"So far." Her tone suggested it was just a matter of time until they learned otherwise.

"Jesus," Mac said. He could hardly take it all in.

Gretchen pointed out, "Someone's killing your suspects."

"Someones, maybe."

She cocked her head. "You know something."

He shook his head, sorry he'd said anything so soon. "You've got friends with Beaverton PD, I have friends with Portland."

"Give," she demanded.

"When there's corroboration."

"You're talking about the arson at Blue Note. Know who set it?"

"Not for sure."

"C'mon, McNally. We were making so much progress." She slipped a hip on his desk and looked at him through her lashes.

Mac yanked out the sheaf of pages trapped by her hip. "Go home, Sandler," he growled.

"You're starting to like me. I can tell. What are you doing?" she demanded as Mac started searching through the thick file labeled *Brentwood*.

He ignored Gretchen. He needed to sort through the information that seemed to be coming at him from all sides, none of which connected. He needed to be alone. He needed quiet.

"You're a glutton for punishment," she observed. "When you feel like talking, I'm only a phone call away." She waved her cell phone at him as she strode toward the door.

Mac slid a look after her, then shook his head. She was actually becoming an active participant rather than departmental dead weight. It wouldn't be long till she moved on.

"Just when I was starting to like her," he said dryly, then turned to his notes. Mitch Bellotti: Ex-jock, football player, average student at St. Elizabeth's, married and divorced, worked at Mike's Garage for nearly ten years. Two traffic tickets in the past decade, no kids. Not the sharpest tool in the shed, but certainly not anyone whom someone would want to kill.

What the hell was going on? He had some pieces but not enough. There was more at play than he knew.

The station was quiet; nearly everyone was gone. He leaned back in his chair and thought about the dead. Disregarding his computer, he drew columns, labeling them: *Jezebel Brentwood*, *Glenn Stafford*, *Renee Walker Trudeau*, and *Mitchell Bellotti*. He made note of their sex, date of death, place of death, marital status, closest friends, beneficiaries of their wills if he had that information, and anything else he could think of.

The most obvious fact that linked them was that they knew each other, had gone to high school together. And somehow, Jessie's disappearance was the start of it all. He circled her name. She was killed twenty years earlier than the others, but what had set off these last three deaths? He had an idea about Glenn Stafford; the Portland PD were closing in on the arsonist. But he didn't know how it related to Renee Trudeau and now Mitch Bellotti.

Mitch and Glenn had been good friends, but Renee . . . ?

And then there was Jessie.

Renee had been working on Jessie's story and she'd found a link to the Oregon coast. Glenn owned a restaurant with Scott in Lincoln City, south of Deception Bay. Jessie's parents had owned a beach house in that small town, but Mitch had no connection with the coast that Mac could discern. Credit card records showed Tim Trudeau had been in Seaside and Deception Bay in the last five months, something he'd been less than forthcoming about. He and Renee had been having troubles, so maybe her death was completely separate from the others?

Mac groaned and rose from his chair, running his hands through his hair. Glancing at the picture of his son, he walked toward the windows on the south side. They overlooked the parking lot but he wasn't seeing anything but the images within his own head.

Renee Trudeau's Camry was still being searched, tested, and gone over for any kind of evidence, but so far there was nothing out of the ordinary and the Tillamook County Sheriff's Department hadn't located any body shop who'd done repair work on a truck or car that might have pushed her car over the cliff.

Renee's cell phone records hadn't helped much either. A couple of calls to her brother and friends, but nothing significant. Mac wondered if another run to the coast might turn up something new.

Mac went back to his desk and sorted through his files till he pulled out his report on the man who'd picked up Jessie Brentwood off Highway 53. She'd been coming back from the beach or somewhere near it. Had she been visiting the Brentwoods' cabin? Why was she hitchhiking? Had something happened there that precipitated her death?

Had Renee learned what that was?

And what about Mitch's death tonight? Could it really be an accident? *Could it?* Could the poor bastard have just gotten unlucky? The Grand Am just slipping off the jack?

"Nah," he told himself. Not with all the other friends of the Preppy Pricks dropping like flies.

He stared down at his jumble of notes. All the pieces were there, a massive jigsaw puzzle that just needed to be put together in the right order.

* * *

Becca felt as if a stone were stuck in her gut, weighing her down. All of her burgeoning joy at the thought of maybe being pregnant was superseded by a horrifying sense of despair. Someone was killing them, one by one. All of them.

She looked around the room. It was late, but she wasn't alone. Most of their friends had collected at her condo after rushing to the hospital upon hearing the news about Mitch. Now they stood in a semicircle in front of her fireplace. Tamara, Scott, and Jarrett stood on one side, Zeke and Evangeline on the other. The Third had slumped into a chair, and Hudson stood next to Becca. They were drinking coffee or wine, but mostly they just stood and stared blankly at each other. Even Ringo was subdued, lying on his bed and observing the group while the gas fire hissed and outside a deep fog settled in.

"I just don't understand," Tamara said, perching on a bar stool near the kitchen counter. "You all think that Mitch was killed, that this wasn't an accident."

"Not just Mitch," Hudson said.

A murmur of agreement swept through the room.

"Been a bunch of murders," Jarrett said.

"Oh, no." Evangeline was shaking her head, her blond hair moving against her shoulders. Her hand reached for Zeke's but his were in his pockets. His head was bent and he was remote enough to be on a different planet. "I don't believe it," she went on shakily. "No one would want to kill Mitch or Glenn . . . or Renee."

"Well, they did," The Third said, all of his cockiness gone. His face was lined, his hair falling over his eyes instead of neatly combed. "Something's up. And it started with those kids finding Jessie's body. Someone's picking us off. And it has to do with Jessie."

"Mitch's death wasn't murder," Scott said, shuddering.

"Someone dropped that jack handle," Hudson said. "It didn't fall on its own."

Scott asked, "You tell the police that?"

"Yep. Wanted everything on the table. No secrets."

Hudson gazed at Zeke hard and Zeke flushed. Unless Zeke had gone straight to the phone and started calling the group, they still didn't know he was the baby's father and therefore the bones belonged to Jessie. Zeke's uncomfortable posture said the secret was still under wraps.

Zeke couldn't hold his gaze.

"Who sent those notes?" Hudson asked him.

Vangie caught the tension between them and said quickly, "You can't think it's Zeke?"

"Was it?" Hudson asked Zeke point-blank.

"No." He was positive.

Hudson said, "Jessie didn't send them. Jessie's dead. Those are her bones. DNA's proved it."

"How?" Scott asked, surprised. "I thought there was nothing to match Jessie's DNA to."

"The baby's DNA was matched to her father's," Hudson said. "And the father is one of us. Stands to reason the bones are Jessie's."

"You're the father?" Jarrett's dark brows slammed together and he looked at Hudson, then slowly followed his gaze to Zeke.

"I am," Zeke stated flatly.

The group collectively absorbed the shock of that news, turning toward Zeke and staring at him.

"Oh, my God," Tamara exhaled.

Evangeline blinked several times, as if her brain couldn't process something so abhorrent. "It's Hudson's baby," she finally said. "She was Hudson's girlfriend."

"I slept with Jessie," Zeke said. "We were seeing each other behind Hudson's back."

Becca shivered, wishing she were in Hudson's arms, but he had taken a half step back, watching the drama play out among his friends.

"No, you weren't." Vangie was positive.

"I'm not proud of it. And Jessie only really wanted Hudson, anyway. I just *wanted* her. I just wanted to have her. You knew I was seeing Jessie," he suddenly accused Evangeline, whose eyes nearly popped out of her head. "Jessie told me she confided in you."

"No! No!"

"What the fuck is wrong with you?" Zeke demanded. "Why are you so afraid of the truth?"

"I didn't believe her," Vangie said. "She was always saying hurtful things. We weren't best friends!"

"Oh, my God," Tamara said again, staring at Evangeline in fascination. "Jessie was confessing the truth, but you couldn't stand to hear it because you've always had this obsession over Zeke!"

"This is all Jessie's doing." Evangeline's whole body was quaking.

"Jessie's dead," Zeke said harshly.

"And so are Glenn and Renee and Mitch," Hudson pointed out.

"I don't believe you would do that to Hudson," Vangie said. "You wouldn't go behind his back."

"I just wanted her." Zeke's jaw was set in anger.

"Fuck, we all did," The Third said, trying to defuse the situation.

"But Zeke was the one who scored, apparently." Jarrett started to see amusement in the situation. "Wouldn't have guessed that one."

"Zeke, come on," Vangie pleaded. She wrapped her arms around his torso but he stiffened in her embrace. "We're getting married."

"Well, who the hell killed her?" The Third demanded. "Zeke? Is that what we're saying?"

"Shut the fuck up," Zeke said angrily.

"If anyone did, it was one of you!" Flushed, Evangeline gazed around the room at the men. "And Jessie sent those nursery rhymes to point the finger at you!"

"How many ways do I have to say it?" Zeke demanded. "Jessie is dead. She's been dead for twenty years!"

"Why didn't Zeke get one of the nursery rhymes?" Scott asked.

"Yeah," Jarrett said, looking thoughtfully at Vangie.

"Because Evangeline sent them," Hudson said quietly. "To point the finger at the rest of us."

"You're all—hateful!" Evangeline's eyes filled with unshed tears.

Becca gazed at the shaking blond woman and realized Hudson was right. "You heard at Blue Note about the nursery rhymes, when Mitch and Glenn brought them up. You're afraid Zeke really did kill Jessie. That's why you've been so adamant that she's alive."

"No . . ." She raised a hand, as if to ward off Becca's words.

"You never really believed it," Becca went on. "You've thought she was dead from the beginning."

"Jessie was some kind of witch! She could see the future, I'm telling you! She knew she was going to die! But it wasn't Zeke!"

"Did you kill her?" Tamara demanded.

A deep wail boiled from inside Vangie's soul. She clung to Zeke for support as the sound reverberated through the room. Becca turned to Hudson and he moved swiftly to take her in his arms.

"You did kill her," Scott said on a note of wonder.

"I didn't! I couldn't! It was someone else. Someone evil. Renee was right. Jessie thought someone was after her. Hunting her down. She'd been to the beach looking up her past. And this . . . *thing* . . . found her!"

"Trouble," Becca said.

"Go ahead and make up stories." The Third got up from his chair and glared at Vangie. "All this mystic crap. You killed her. You hunted her down and killed her because she was pregnant with Zeke's baby."

"Zeke," Evangeline pleaded. "Tell them it's not true." Her cheeks were wet with tears.

"I found the envelopes in the shredder, Vangie. Blue strips where you shredded the evidence. I saved them for the police."

"What?" She backed away from him, her hands slowly letting go, her face a mask of horror.

"McNally guessed. When he told me that my DNA matched the baby's, he also as good as said you sent the notes. He knows, Vangie."

"Then why hasn't he picked her up?" Scott demanded.

"Because I don't think she killed Jessie."

"I didn't." A ray of hope entered her voice.

"She sent the notes. She was afraid I'd killed Jessie. But Jessie's death, I don't know. And Glenn and Renee and Mitch . . ." Zeke closed his eyes and wearily shook his head. When Evangeline tried to embrace him again, he jerked away as if burned. "We're done, Vangie."

"Okay, okay. I believe Jessie's dead. And I sent the notes— but it wasn't because I thought you killed her. I just wanted the investigation to leave us alone. I love you, Zeke," she implored. "So much."

He gazed at her a bit helplessly. "But I don't love you. I never really did."

Chapter Twenty

"She went to a helluva lot of work," Mac observed, turning over the nursery rhyme note with Hudson's name on it that Becca and Hudson had brought in. He pulled out the one he already had in his possession from Mitch and looked at them side by side.

Becca sensed the detective wasn't quite taking them seriously and she sent Hudson a "what gives?" look, but Hudson's gaze was glued to McNally. It had been three days since Mitch's death and the scene at Becca's condo. She and Hudson had wondered when Zeke and Evangeline would contact the police, but when Mac called up and politely asked them if they could meet again, they'd said they would join him at the Laurelton station. McNally had assured them it was just an informal discussion, so Hudson and Becca had decided to preempt Zeke and Evangeline in the interest of keeping the investigation moving forward into Renee's accident.

The woman detective appeared from an inner door carrying four paper cups of coffee. She handed them around, then stood back from the proceedings.

"Thanks," McNally told her.

She shrugged a response.

"Zeke said you probably already knew who sent the notes," Hudson said. "Sounds like you led him to that conclusion."

Mac inclined his head. "I thought it was a woman. And when Zeke's DNA came through, the possibility seemed to be there."

"You obviously don't think Evangeline's a killer or you would have picked her up," Hudson observed.

"We got somebody else in mind," Gretchen couldn't help saying.

Mac felt his temper rise but he held it inside. He'd confided what he'd learned from the Portland PD to Gretchen, but she still had those "jump in too soon" tendencies that drove him nuts.

"Who?" Hudson asked. Both detectives hesitated, which pissed him off. "If you have any information on who killed my sister, I want to know."

"We're looking into the arson/homicide at Blue Note," Mac said. "One of your group has been picked up for questioning in Portland."

"Who?" Hudson asked.

"Scott Pascal."

Becca nearly sloshed her coffee from her cup. "What?"

"Scott was Glenn's business partner," Hudson said.

"Their businesses were running in the red. Portland PD has evidence he was in the area that night. We think he set the fire."

"But he and Glenn were friends!" Becca protested.

"Money does strange things to people," Mac said.

"He ever involved with your sister?" the woman detective asked Hudson.

"No."

"Didn't have a thing for her? Wouldn't want to see her dead?"

Becca gasped.

"No!" A vein throbbed in Walker's throat, his anger palpable.

Mac shot Gretchen a quelling look, then said, "I plan to give the Portland PD any and all information I can on why Scott Pascal would kill Glenn Stafford, Renee Trudeau, and Mitch Bellotti. That's why I asked to meet with you. Can you think of any connection we're missing?"

Becca and Hudson looked at each other, then at Mac.

"Mitch was harmless," Becca said.

"Maybe not, if Stafford told Bellotti he thought Scott Pascal was an embezzler. And then Bellotti put two and two together and figured Pascal had more to gain by burning the place down than trying to keep it afloat."

"He wouldn't have killed Glenn." Becca was certain.

"That could've been a mistake. If Pascal thought he could control Stafford once the place was gone, he may not have meant to kill him."

"What about Renee?" Walker asked, his expression dark.

"That's what I'm trying to find out," Mac said on a sigh.

"She was not involved with Scott."

"They both went to the beach a lot."

"For work," Hudson pointed out.

"And maybe a little afternoon delight," the woman detective said.

McNally's desk phone rang and he hesitated a moment before picking up. Everyone sat tensely as the detective listened, answering in near monosyllables. When he hung up, he said, "Thank you for coming in."

"That's it?" Hudson asked.

"For the moment."

"You're wrong about my sister and Scott," he said as he and Becca shrugged into their coats and headed for the door.

Mac didn't answer as he watched them leave. Gretchen lifted her brows at him after they were gone.

"We've been invited to witness the Pascal interrogation," Mac said. "Maybe we'll get some answers."

* * *

"Renee was not involved with Scott," Hudson stated firmly as he punched the accelerator and his truck leapt away from the police station parking lot.

"No," Becca agreed. Her head was full of too much information, but what kept ringing through her ears was Detective Sandler's last remark.

And maybe a little afternoon delight.

It brought to mind images of all the afternoons and days and nights she'd spent in bed with Hudson, and the fact that she still hadn't had her period.

Hudson was cutting through traffic on his way back to Becca's. The sun was rising over a bank of clouds, the promise of a clear day. He followed two motorcyclists riding side by side. "Renee and Scott really were little more than acquaintances."

"What if she found out something in Deception Bay, or maybe Lincoln City, that tied him to the other murders and he thought he had to get rid of her . . ."

"You believe that?" he demanded.

"Not really. The police always have a way of rattling me."

Hudson grunted. "Renee was after a story. It had nothing to do with Scott."

"But everything to do with Jessie." Becca's stomach suddenly nosedived and she sucked in air in a hurry. "Would you mind pulling into the Safeway? I could use a soda."

"Feeling sick again?"

"Kinda."

As he nosed into a parking spot, she grabbed hold of the door handle, her knuckles showing white. She hesitated a moment, getting her bearings.

"You're not pregnant, are you?" he said, half joking.

Becca's hairsbreadth too long hesitation was answer enough. Hudson stared at her. "Are you? Are you pregnant?"

"Maybe. I don't know yet."

"I thought you were on the pill," he said blankly.

"I wasn't even thinking about it. I haven't used birth control since my marriage. I just . . ." She didn't know how to explain. She could scarcely explain it to herself.

"But you aren't sure yet."

"No. It's just conjecture. I've been meaning to get a pregnancy test, but a lot's been happening. Maybe I'm not. I mean, maybe I'm just feeling nauseous." She looked away. "I'm afraid to find out. Afraid it might not be true," she admitted in a rush.

"You want to be pregnant?"

"Yes." She was emphatic. "Yes, I've wanted a child forever. I didn't plan this. I didn't think about it. I was going on emotion . . . wanting you . . ." She heard the note of excitement and pleading in her voice and had to turn away. If he didn't want this, she would understand. She would. She would make herself.

"Well . . ." he said slowly.

"Well," she repeated.

"I guess we'd better find out, then."

She couldn't read him. "You're okay with this?"

"I'm just—taking it in."

She heard something in his voice then, a note of wonder. "Yeah?" she asked uncertainly.

"Yeah."

"Okay," she said, watching him closely.

A kid, he thought.

He might actually have a kid.

To raise on the farm where he himself had grown up. He hadn't planned on it, hadn't even considered it, but now that the chance for fatherhood was facing him, he felt a surprising buoyancy, a lifting of his spirit. "A kid," he said aloud. "Our kid."

"Well, it's not for sure yet. My periods don't exactly run like clockwork."

"They sell those tests here, don't they?" He indicated the grocery store.

"They have a pharmacy department." She reached for her

door handle and looked back, an anxious smile touching the corners of her mouth. "What if it's true?"

"What if it is," he replied, smiling, and Becca, full of emotion, slid back across the seat and hugged and kissed him for all she was worth until she felt his chest rumble with laughter and his arms squeeze her back hard.

Scott Pascal's interrogation was taking place in a bare narrow room with two rectangular tables surrounded by eight metal chairs. As expected, Pascal had lawyered up. Mac and Gretchen had arrived at the station, half expecting the interview to be over, but Pascal's lawyer had been delayed, so they got to witness the full proceedings from behind the two-way glass window. The invitation had been extended because their case was linked to the arson/homicide at the restaurant. An assistant DA and another officer rounded out their group of four as they watched the interrogation which, of course, was also being recorded.

The guy was sweating, looking nervous and continuously listening to his lawyer before answering. But he was having trouble explaining why his car had been spotted parked in a shopping center lot three blocks away, courtesy of a security camera, during the time of the explosion. Another traffic camera had caught Scott nearly running a red light, and an employee who had left her car at Blue Note to have some drinks with a friend had come forward saying she'd seen Scott enter through the kitchen as she was driving away. The fact that the fire inspector had claimed the fire was caused by arson only added to Pascal's troubles.

The fucker was nailed.

He knew it.

The cops knew it.

And his tight-assed lawyer knew it.

When the evidence was laid in front of him, Scott collapsed and put his head on the table.

"If I could have a minute alone with my client," the lawyer said.

On their side of the glass, the ADA, a sharp-dressed black man with clipped hair and rimless glasses, nodded. "He's gonna want to cop a plea."

"About time," McNally said. Finally a break in the case. "When he does, see what he knows. He set the fire and killed his partner. I want to know about the other dead bodies. I think he killed Mitch Bellotti to keep him from talking."

"We've got it covered," the ADA said, "and we'll find out if he knows anything about the Jezebel Brentwood case."

Mac doubted that Pascal would admit to killing the girl, but it was a start.

Finally, the case was pulling together. Except for Renee Trudeau. Pascal had been in Portland on the day her Camry had been forced through the guardrail and off the cliff into the Pacific Ocean.

But he could have an accomplice. Or, as Mac was coming to suspect, there might be a second killer.

From inside the room, Scott's lawyer said, "I want to talk to the DA. My client is willing to tell you everything he knows, but in consideration for his testimony—"

"—confession," one of the officers corrected.

"—Mr. Pascal would like to know what he can expect."

"He wants a deal," one of the officers said and looked into the glass.

"Okay, showtime." The ADA walked out of the observation room, and in the next few minutes, Scott, assured he'd not get the death penalty, admitted that he'd set the fire at Blue Note and also killed Mitch Bellotti.

"I knew it. That son of a bitch," Mac whispered, watching as Scott, sweating and holding out his hands as if anyone with half a brain would understand his reasoning, explained.

"The restaurant was hemorrhaging money. Blue Note couldn't be saved and Glenn, he wouldn't believe it."

"Because you were cooking the books. And taking some

of that money to the casino in Lincoln City. We found those records, too," the officer said, and the wind seemed to go out of Pascal's sails. "You'd better be straight with us, Pascal, or all deals are off."

"Okay, okay, so I 'borrowed' a little of the company funds. It wasn't a lot. Jesus Christ, I owned the damned thing. I was the brains behind the business. Glenn with all his marital woes was useless." He was red in the face, angry all over again.

"So you decided to off him."

"No . . . not really. I was just going to burn the place down. I didn't know Glenn was inside. That was a pure accident."

"That accident sure worked out for you," the officer said. "No more Glenn Stafford to worry about."

"He shouldn't have been there! That was his fault, not mine!"

"Oh, brother," Mac muttered, staring through the glass.

"And Bellotti?"

Scott rubbed a nervous hand over his forehead. "I feel bad about that. This thing just became an out-of-control roller coaster. First Glenn, and then Mitch started asking questions. I had no beef with him. He wasn't so smart, but an okay guy. But Glenn had told him things and I could tell he was putting it all together. So . . ." To his credit, Pascal actually seemed guilt-riddled. "The body was found in the maze, we got the notes, and at first I thought I shouldn't say I got one . . . but then when everybody did except Zeke it seemed fortuitous, y'know? Stupid Evangeline was trying to save him, and she just made him look guilty."

"But you're the one guilty of killing four people."

"Four? No way!" Scott was rising from his chair, but his lawyer placed a staying hand over his forearm.

"Mr. Pascal is telling you what he knows. About the deaths of Glenn Stafford and Mitchell Bellotti."

"What about Renee Trudeau and Jezebel Brentwood?"

Scott wasn't waiting for his lawyer. "I had nothing to do with that. I wasn't anywhere near the coast when Renee had her accident. Jesus, I have an alibi. I was at a meeting with bankers about refinancing Blue Ocean. The meeting was in Portland at Second Community Bank. Check with Davis Sheen, he's my banker."

"We will."

"And I didn't kill Jessie. I hardly knew her." He was nearly convincing as tears glistened in his eyes. "You have to believe me." He turned his tortured gaze to his bland-faced lawyer. "It's the truth. I didn't kill Renee, and I didn't kill Jessie. And I don't know who did."

Sitting on the edge of the bathtub, Becca gazed at the wand in her hand with its two bright pink lines that indicated, yes, she was indeed pregnant.

"Oh, my God," she breathed, staring at the two lines in wonder.

I'm having a baby. Hudson's baby!

Again.

She blinked against a spate of tears and told herself that all she had to do was step through the door and tell Hudson, who was waiting downstairs. He'd wished her luck as she'd hurried up the steps of her condo, pregnancy test kit tight in her hand.

If she figured right, the baby would be born in late November or early December. *A Christmas baby!*

"Stop it," she said, not wanting to get caught up in the host of fairy-tale dreams. It was too early for that. She'd been down that rocky road once before.

But it was time to inform Hudson that he would definitely be a father by the end of the year.

She stood up quickly and as she did, she felt the floor start to buckle beneath her feet. The walls closed in on her. A vision . . . Her head felt like it was splitting in two.

Oh, God, no! Not now!

Her vision fogged and she felt as if she were going to faint. She grabbed on to the sink for support, dropping the test. Head throbbing, she caught a glimpse of herself in the mirror only to have the image fade to watery waves. The smell of the sea was thick in the air, and in the glass she spied the same teenaged girl she'd seen before. Again on a rocky outcrop, the wind teasing her hair, her eyes, so like Becca's, wide with fear, her skin nearly translucent.

Dark clouds spun above her, the churning sea roiling far below.

"Jessie," Becca whispered as the girl looked at her and placed a finger to her lips.

But this time Jessie wasn't alone. This time there was someone else, a dark, faceless figure looming behind her, an evil presence of which Jessie appeared unaware. Becca cried out and the demon seemed to look straight at her, his eyes hidden, his nose tilting in the air, as if to smell the breeze.

Though she couldn't see his features, Becca knew deep in her heart that this monster was what Jessie had feared.

Her knees gave way, but she clung to the sink and realized there was something familiar about him, something bone deep and riddled with an evil as dark as all of Hades. "Jessie," she tried to cry again, in warning, but her voice failed her as she slid further downward.

Jessie was already dead. She knew that . . . didn't she? But this girl . . . she looked so much like Jessie.

This horrid creature, this malevolent force had already killed her. The girl on the cliff was only a spirit, a ghost of the girl who had been murdered and buried in the maze at St. Elizabeth's. Becca knew that.

So why was she here?

Why had Jessie returned to haunt her?

Not to haunt you . . . To warn you . . .

Had that thought come from her own mind, or had Jessie mouthed the words?

She couldn't tell, but the ominous figure in the dark cowl came closer, nose in the air, so close that surely Jessie sensed him. She had to feel the heat of his fetid breath against the back of her neck, yet she didn't move, not even when he raised a hand over her.

Watch out! Jessie, run! Run as fast and as far as you can!

She mouthed something to Becca, then glanced back at the monster.

Becca's heart was pounding, fear coursing through her bloodstream, but Jessie, facing into the wind, stood motionless. Didn't try to escape.

No!

The monster stopped. Hand raised, he drew a knife from deep within the folds of his cloak and stared over Jessie's shoulder straight at Becca.

Becca gasped. This was what had killed Jessie.

And it was coming for her.

Chapter Twenty-One

"Becca?"

She heard her name as if from a distance. It rolled inside her head, echoing.

"Becca!"

Hudson? It was Hudson's voice?

"I'm coming in."

She blinked, her eyes opening to the bright lights of her own bathroom. Her head ached dully and she was lying on the cool tile floor, her head inches from the bathtub, her feet nearly touching the tub. She remembered the demon in her vision, could almost smell the saltwater that had clung to him. Was he even real?

"Dear God," she whispered, thinking of her unborn child.

She lay motionless, trying to pull herself together, trying not to shiver from the coldness and the fear.

The bathroom door cracked opened and Hudson, all six feet of him, stepped inside. Seeing her on the floor, he went pale as death. "What happened?" He was at her side in an instant, dropping to his knees as she struggled to hers. "Are you all right? Becca!" Concerned eyes studied her, strong arms surrounded her.

Wincing against the pain, she remembered the pregnancy test. Where the hell had the wand rolled to?

"You had another vision," he realized, concern etched into his voice.

"Yes." She rubbed the back of her head where it had hit the floor. God, it hurt. "I'm fine, though."

"You need to see a doctor."

"No doctor. I'll be fine." She spied the pregnancy wand with its two vibrant lines announcing that she was pregnant. Corralling it with one hand, she wordlessly handed it to him.

He looked down at the two pink lines. "This means . . . ?"

"Positive. You're still okay with this?" she asked anxiously.

"I'd be better if you let me take you to a doctor. You're pregnant," he said, as if she needed to be reminded. "And these visions . . . I don't like them."

"I know, I know." Becca struggled to sit up. "But you're okay about the baby? I just need to know."

"Yes. More than okay. But we're going to the Laurelton Hospital ER." He pulled her, protesting, to her feet. "I want to make sure both you and the baby are okay. We'll make an appointment with your doctor later." He gave her a hard look. "You have a doctor?"

"Yes. But—"

"C'mon."

He shepherded her out to his truck, and despite her continual assertions that she was totally fine, they headed over to Laurelton Hospital, which hung on the edge of a hillside, making the third floor on one side, the first floor where the emergency vehicles entered.

Becca was surprised when Hudson insisted on going into the cubicle with her. "I can do this by myself," she said with a smile.

"I want to talk to the doctor about your visions."

"I've been through this with my parents. There was never anything wrong."

"You've never been pregnant before," he said, and her heart clutched. "You seem to be having them more now. Maybe it's connected. I don't know."

The doctor appeared, a young woman with her hair scraped into a ponytail and a stern expression that suggested she'd never suffered a moment of joy in her life. "You're here for a pregnancy test?"

"And an exam," Hudson said. "She's also been suffering severe headaches that seem to bring on delusions."

The doctor looked at Becca. "Are you having a headache now?"

"I just want to confirm my pregnancy," Becca said. "I'll make an appointment with my doctor."

"I can give you a cursory exam, but it sounds neurological. You might want to schedule further testing."

"I will." Becca was firm.

She gave Hudson a look and he seemed about to argue, but then let it go.

"I'll be in the waiting room," he said.

Twenty minutes later Becca came out of the room, a smile quivering on her lips. She started laughing as Hudson jumped to his feet and met her in front of the ER's sliding doors. "We're going to be parents," she said, and he hauled off and kissed her hard to a smattering of clapping from the other waiting-room attendees.

"I love you," he said, and she squeezed her eyes closed, holding on to the moment with all she had.

"I love you," she blurted.

Tears threatened and she laughed them away. And she didn't say the words that trembled on her tongue: *I always have.*

*   *   *

Mac should have felt elated that some of the pieces were falling into place. The Portland Police had Scott Pascal in custody, a confession signed. Two murders had been solved with the killer copping a plea.

But two more murders were still unresolved, and he was no closer to figuring out who was behind them, or even if they were linked, as it seemed they were. Renee was working on Jessie's story and someone had killed her. A case could be made that she'd learned something that implicated a killer who'd been waiting twenty years.

He was in the squad room, at his desk. Phones rang, a fax machine whirred, and there was light conversation between the cubicles, but Mac barely noticed. Nor could he concentrate on the report he should have been writing about a bar fight turned fatal. Or the domestic violence case where a kid had shot his father rather than accept another beating from the old man's belt. They were both in his computer, ready to be polished.

But what had Renee learned?

Or was he way off base, trying to make a connection that didn't exist simply because he wanted the Brentwood case solved? Tim Trudeau was certainly a possibility. His alibi—his cleaning woman had said he was definitely home the day of Renee's accident—might not prove true. When she'd been questioned, Aida Hernandez had hidden behind a language barrier that Mac wasn't certain existed. But her interpreter, Sergeant Delgado, had been adamant that Hernandez's words were the truth. "She's scared, but not of Tim," Anna Maria Delgado assured Mac. "Aida's very religious. She wouldn't lie easily." Delgado, whose own parents had been born in Mexico, was as smart as she was beautiful. Her word was usually golden with Mac, but Mac had done some checking on Trudeau and wasn't completely convinced of the guy's innocence.

Trudeau had financial motives. Though they were divorcing, at the time of her death Renee had yet to change her will.

Her ex would still get the proceeds of a hundred-thousand-dollar life insurance policy, the joint bank accounts worth twenty-three thousand dollars, Renee's small IRA, and the house she'd paid for and owned outright with the proceeds her brother, Hudson, had paid her for her share of their parents' ranch. All told: over half a million; closer to three-quarters.

Not a bad motive for murder.

"Damn." He scratched at the stubble on his chin and thought. Hard. Why did he feel he was missing something; something important, something right under the surface of his thoughts? He glanced at the computer screen. It was split between actual images of Jessie Brentwood at sixteen and the computer-generated one of her as well. Dead on.

No . . . it wasn't just coincidence that Renee Walker and Jezebel Brentwood were dead. He couldn't believe that. Logically, their murders were connected.

And he believed Scott Pascal. That man had been frantic to convince them he had nothing to do with Jessie Brentwood's and Renee Trudeau's deaths. His emphatic denial had rung with truth and indignation, as if it made any sense that he could feel self-righteous about *not* killing the women when he'd admitted to murdering the men—two of his best friends. And for what? Money. Debt.

Lost in thought, he picked up the smooth bit of oyster shell found near Jessie's grave between his forefinger and thumb. A piece of shell from an oyster found in the inlets and bays off the northern Oregon coast.

Everything led back to the beach.

Jessie Brentwood's parents owned a cabin overlooking the ocean in Deception Bay.

Jessie was known to have been hitchhiking on the road running from the ocean shore inland not long before she disappeared.

Renee Trudeau, doing research on a story about Jessie, had been killed on her way back from Deception Bay.

Mac glanced at the picture of Levi propped up on his

desk. Why not head to the beach, do a little poking around, see what was up. He could take Levi for the weekend, spend some father-son time at the beach while he explored the town of Deception Bay. He could check in with Tillamook County Sheriff's Department and see if they were any further in their search for the vehicle that had rammed Renee's. The biggest roadblock to that plan would be Connie, his ex. She seemed to think his time as a father should be spent in structured, planned activities all revolving around schoolwork. No wonder the kid was having problems. Connie was pretty insistent that Mac not retire, either, but then she had lots of ideas about how he should run his life; especially when it came to raising their boy, who, she sometimes conveniently forgot, was his as well as hers.

Schoolwork be damned, this weekend he and Levi were going to hang out at the beach. Maybe do some crabbing down on the docks at Deception Bay, watch basketball, play cards, reconnect.

And yeah, he'd do a little investigating as well.

He needed to put the murder of Jezebel Brentwood to bed.

Just like that, his life had changed irrevocably, Hudson thought as he drove to his ranch the next morning. He'd lost a sister and then learned he was going to be a father.

One life ended; another started.

It was a weird sensation.

Not that he ever thought he'd be a father; but this, an unplanned pregnancy, was a shock to his system and an out-and-out high. He hadn't suggested Becca marry him, wasn't rushing out to buy a diamond ring, it was all happening way too fast. But he couldn't imagine not living with her. He wanted to raise their son or daughter together and spend the rest of his life with her.

So marriage was definitely in his plans.

He just had to think things through.

Squinting against the harsh rays of sun that slipped through the clouds, he turned down the long drive to his house. More storms were predicted from the west. It was the end of March and winter would not let go of its grip.

But he was going to be a *father*!

Becca and he had talked. All yesterday afternoon and into the evening, and after spending the rest of the day and night together, they were on the same page about raising a kid, but it was a little early to ask her to move her things to the ranch. Hell, her little dog still wasn't certain Hudson wasn't an enemy. And there was something else, something he didn't really understand. A "feeling" that Becca wasn't being entirely honest with him—not about the pregnancy, he trusted her on that one, but there was something off about this whole vision thing. He felt she was holding back. He feared it was physical and that she was in denial, that something was causing these delusions.

Yet . . . her visions were strangely prophetic.

He parked near the garage and studied the old farmhouse with its mossy roof and often-repaired gutters. The windows needed replacing, a family room and third bath added. He had plans drawn nearly a year earlier but hadn't started the renovation. Now he'd give them to Becca, get her input, and adjust accordingly.

If she wants to move in with you.

She wasn't a hundred percent on that, now, was she?

They'd skirted the subject, each stopping short of saying, "Let's live together." He figured when the time was right, they'd move in or marry, didn't really matter which order it happened. They had more than a few emotional hurdles to leap over if they were ever going to find happiness, and a lot of those hurdles had to do with Jessie Brentwood and why she was killed.

With the weak sun warming his back he slid out of the Jeep, nearly whistled to Booker T., then stopped himself short. His dog was gone and he couldn't really see Ringo riding with him in the truck, trotting out to the barn to feed the stock, but then you never knew.

He headed alone down the path past the old pump house and willow tree where he was certain his twin sister had spied him and Becca making love years before. He felt more than a little pang of grief and anger when he thought of Renee. He missed her.

No two ways about it.

Sorrow surged but he tamped it back down, deciding to look to the future, and as he did, one side of his mouth lifted. In a few years he'd be walking down this path, a young son or daughter at his side.

You should have told him about your first pregnancy at the hospital. You had the opportunity. Why didn't you take it?

And why don't you tell him about the vision? He won't laugh at you. He's worried about you. You need to tell him how you were rammed off the road like Renee, that you lost the first baby—his baby, too!—because of it.

Becca gave herself a swift mental kick as she e-mailed changes to the latest spate of documents for an ongoing land trust dispute back to the offices of Bennett, Bretherton, and Pfeiffer. The television in the living room flickered in the corner, the volume on low. She absently listened to the weather report as she worked, learning that a new storm was forming in the Pacific, blowing inland.

"Great," she murmured, but as soon as the weather report was over she heard Scott Pascal's name mentioned. She looked up sharply to see an image of Scott in handcuffs, his face turned from the camera as he was led past a surge of reporters and helped into a patrol car. It was hard to believe. Everything that had happened seemed so surreal. The news reporter, an earnest-looking woman with dark hair and eyes, suggested that Scott, who had confessed to two killings, might be linked to more deaths. In an instant pictures of Jessie and Renee took the place of Scott's image: Jessie's from high school, Renee's head shot much more recent.

Becca located the remote, scooped it off the coffee table, and clicked off the television. The image of Hudson's twin disappeared.

She sank onto the couch and let out her breath.

Would it ever end?

She found it hard to fathom that Scott had killed Glenn and Mitch, but she really couldn't believe he'd murdered either Jessie or Renee.

Then who?

Touching her abdomen, she recalled her last vision, then thought about the baby and, of course, Hudson. Now was the time to be completely honest with him. She knew that. If they were ever going to have any relationship, they had to trust each other implicitly. No lies. No equivocations. No damned secrets.

"Come on," she said to the dog, and snapped on his leash. It was getting dark, the watery March sunshine fading into twilight. She let Ringo sniff each twig and branch as the sound of rush-hour traffic on the Pacific Highway only blocks from her condo reached her ears.

She gazed back at the condo. Was it all too soon? She'd lived here with Ben, hoped to have a family with him, but then that relationship had been based on lies. She wouldn't make the same mistake with Hudson. Maybe it was finally time to let go of the past and sell this condo. Time for a fresh start. With Hudson Walker.

He'd told her he loved her. Sure, it was in a moment of joy upon learning they would be new parents, but he'd meant it. And she'd certainly meant it when she'd told him back. And so he hadn't said it again. He'd shown her in a lot of other ways. And if they could ever learn what really happened to Jessie, she felt the last issues between them would be resolved.

Picking up her mail from the box, a fistful of bills, credit card offers, and advertisements, Becca waited for Ringo to do his business, then headed inside. Not for the first time, she wondered why her visions of Jessie were backdropped by the ocean—a stormy, raging sea where she could hear the roar of the surf, feel the tide pound the shore, taste the brine on her tongue.

The answer was somewhere in the cliffs overlooking the angry ocean, and Jessie was adamant that she tell no one about it. In her recent visions, Jessie had been warning her, shushing her. She wasn't supposed to tell anyone of her visions, that much was clear. But she'd already confided in Hudson.

That had probably been a mistake. Not only might he think her a nutcase, but she might have inadvertently put his life in danger. There was a chance that Jessie was warning her to be quiet for Hudson's safety.

Or her child's.

Either way, she felt, the answers to everything wouldn't be found in the soil, debris, or bones at St. Elizabeth's maze. The answers would be found somewhere on the Oregon coast, most likely in the town of Deception Bay.

Becca stood for a moment in the fading light, struck by the thought. What had taken her so long to recognize that? That's where Renee's research on Jessie had taken place. That's where the answers were.

Becca hurried Ringo along, back to the condo. Now that she'd made that decision, she wanted to go. It was early evening and it was a two-hour drive. She could be there by seven, or maybe eight, if it took her a while to pack.

"Ready for a ride?" she said to Ringo, who dogged her anxiously, sensing her new determination. She pulled her cell phone out of its charger and put a call in to Hudson.

As she waited for him to answer, she packed a few things into an overnight bag, then once her call was forwarded to his voicemail, left a quick message that she was heading out of town for the beach.

He called her back almost instantly. "I'm right on the way. Pick me up. I can be ready in twenty minutes."

"You want to go?"

"I want answers, too, Becca. And you're right, Renee was researching Jessie, following in her footsteps. Something happened, and I want to know what it was."

"Well, okay," she said. "I'm putting Ringo in the car and I'll be at your place in about half an hour depending on traffic."

"Lookin' forward to it."

I love you, she thought, but she didn't say it.

"I'm a coward," she told the dog as she settled him into his fuzzy car seat.

He looked at her and wagged his tail.

By the time Becca's car slid into his driveway, Hudson had cared for the horses and few head of cattle, called Emile Rodriguez to come by and feed and water the stock the following day, made arrangements for a place to stay at the beach online, showered and changed. He was just stuffing a change of clothes into an overnight bag when he spied her headlights against the trunks of the oak and fir trees near the mailbox.

He hurried downstairs and locked the door behind him just as she pulled to a stop near the front porch. Ringo, true to form, was barking his fool head off and wasn't all that happy to be relegated to the backseat as Hudson slid into the passenger seat.

"Sorry, bud," he said as the dog gave one final bark and settled into a tiny bed Becca had brought for him.

Becca was on the phone and held up a finger when he settled into the seat. "Yeah . . . sure . . . I'll call you if and when

I know anything else, but you're right. It's a shock." She looked at Hudson and mouthed, "Tamara." Hudson nodded. He'd already been fielding calls from The Third and Jarrett about Scott. No one would have pegged him for a murderer. Everyone was shocked. Jarrett wanted to believe that Scott had killed Jessie and Renee as well. Christopher Delacroix III didn't think so. Otherwise the cops would have booked him for all the murders already.

"It's a pisser," The Third had said when he'd called earlier. "A real pisser. Makes you wonder, doesn't it? How well you really know someone."

"You can never know everything," Hudson told him. "You get the public side, not the private."

"Do you think we're safe now?" The Third had asked him.

"Safe?"

"From whoever did this. If Scott really didn't kill your sister and Jessie, then who did? We're running out of friends. Either way, I've got a .357 magnum by my bed. No motherfucker's going to mess with me and not know it. I'll blow his fuckin' head off. Got another call coming in. Gotta run."

"Sure, I'll call," Becca was winding up her call. She fingered the ignition with her free hand, then cast a glance at Hudson. "Yeah, I know . . . Weird. When I get back into town, we'll get together. Bye." Becca disconnected and slid a glance at Hudson. "Tamara's having a tough time with this."

Hudson suddenly leaned over and kissed her, hard, on the lips and smiled at the scent and taste of her. God, he wanted to drag her out of the car this very second and take her upstairs. To lose himself in her for hours. To forget the hell they'd all lived with for the past couple of months. But like Becca, he wanted closure.

Becca wheeled the car around and drove down the lane. At the county road, she turned west toward the foothills of the Coast Range while Hudson fiddled with the radio and found a country station that he knew came in clear through most of the mountain range. A slice of moon was quickly being covered by clouds, only a few stars visible as the night thickened. Hudson leaned back in his seat. "I called the owner of the cabin where Renee usually stayed. It's owned by a friend of the family. The police are done with it and he said we could spend the night if we wanted. I said thanks, but no thanks."

Becca shivered.

He drew a long breath. "I made a reservation online for Cliffside, a B&B in Deception Bay. Great view of the ocean and dog-friendly. But I think we should go to Renee's cabin and look around."

"Oh, definitely."

She glanced in the rearview mirror, frowned, then stepped on the accelerator as the road widened to four lanes for a while and she was able to pass a white panel truck that was slowing with the incline.

A few minutes later, she looked in her rearview again, and Hudson twisted in his seat, peering through the foggy back window.

"Something back there?" he asked.

"No."

"Renee thought she was being followed," Hudson reminded her.

"And she didn't even have visions," Becca murmured.

Hudson gave her a long look. "What did you see? In your last one?"

"I haven't wanted to talk about it."

"That, I know."

Becca wanted to just forget, and he'd let her for a while. She didn't want to think about what she'd seen—some hooded being with evil intent. She wasn't convinced it was even real. But they were on the same path Jessie had taken, and Jessie was the reason she'd had the vision. And she was worried about what it meant for herself, for Hudson, and now for their unborn baby.

"I think the visions mean something," she said. "They

may have a physical cause that no one's found," she granted, shooting him a look, "but I believe they are some form of communication, even if it's only with my own subconscious."

"You saw Glenn's burning note," Hudson allowed.

"That's right. And I've had other visions in the past. But the ones that include Jessie? The ones I seem to be having more and more of? They're a warning. Jessie's at the beach and she's trying to warn me about something—or some-one—who wants to do me harm. She keeps saying something, then putting her finger over her lips. And in this last vision, there was a being behind her. In a hood. Dark. Angry. I could feel how much he hates me and my baby!" she added, her voice quivering a bit. "It's—real. I believe it's real. And Renee ran into him and it's what got her killed."

Hudson let that sink in for several miles. "You're sure it's a he?"

"Positive."

He sighed. "Maybe you do see things. Like Jessie, I guess," he said. "Everyone says she was precognitive."

"She knew something was after her," Becca said, with an-other glance in the rearview. "And I know something's after me."

Chapter Twenty-Two

Becca was letting her nerves get the better of her as she made the long drive through the canyons and ridges of the mountains. Tall evergreens, like an army of sentinels, rose into the thick dark sky. Sleet and misting clouds caused the winding, slick road to seem even more isolated and sinister than ever.

Whatever was after her felt very close.

But she was safe.

Hudson was at her side.

Ringo was in the damned car. Sleeping in the backseat.

Nonetheless, despite her internal pep talk, Becca felt the gloom of the night-dark forest closing in on her. And as she drove, listening to some obscure country song riddled with static, she thought of Jessie, who had traveled on this very same road so many times.

It seemed as if Jessie's spirit had infiltrated this stretch of road.

She told herself she was imagining things, that she couldn't "feel" Jessie or "sense" her ghost wandering through the rain, mossy, old-growth timber, and sharp canyons. Her mind was playing tricks on her.

She glanced at Hudson, whose eyes were trained on the road. His jaw was set, his expression harsh in the dim glare from the dash lights. He, too, was lost somewhere in his thoughts.

She drove across an icy bridge spanning a deep chasm and her heart seized when she recognized the area. Hadn't she herself been run off the road here on her way from Seaside sixteen years before?

The last time you were pregnant.

She slid another glance at Hudson, then stared through the windshield where condensation was fogging the glass. She felt as cold as death as she passed the mile post marker where her car had been forced off the road.

Nervously, she checked her rearview mirror, but the car that had been behind them for a while had lagged back, no headlights visible. Nothing but the frigid black night. Her teeth chattered and no amount of adjusting the temperature of the Jetta's heater could warm her.

"Cold?" Hudson asked, rousing from his thoughts.

She offered a weak smile as her fingers clenched the wheel. "It's supposed to be eighty in here."

"It is. At least."

Really? God, she was chilled to the marrow of her bones. "I guess it's just me."

"We could turn back," he said reluctantly.

She shook her head. He wanted to see this through as much as she did.

Should she admit why this stretch of 26 gave her the willies? Point out the place where she, like his sister, had been forced off the road? Admit that she'd been pregnant with his child and hadn't had the guts to tell him about it?

Now her hands were sweating. Though she felt chilled to her soul, her palms were damp. *You're a basket case. Just tell him. Let the chips fall where they may.*

A flash caught her attention and there in the rearview, she glimpsed twin headlights cutting through the night. Either the car that had been following at a distance had caught up, or someone else had passed the first vehicle and was bearing down on them.

Hudson's attention was on the radio. "I think we should be able to pick up a decent station from Astoria or Seaside," he said.

Becca kept her eye on the rearview. Why here? Why after all this time alone on the highway would a vehicle appear at this winding spot in the road, so close to where—

"Is he nuts?" she said as the beams bore down on her.

Just around the next bend, the highway widened, a passing lane over the summit, but the vehicle behind—a truck— didn't wait. In a rush, it swept by, sliding a little as it flew into the oncoming lane and roared past, no one visible through its foggy windows.

Hudson looked up sharply. "Damn idiot."

Becca hit the brakes, making room.

The big truck rocked, sliding into the right lane before thundering ahead, rushing into the night, taillights disappearing into the mist.

Becca's heart was pounding, her lungs tight, her nerves about to shatter.

Hudson glared through the glass. "That son of a bitch could have killed us. You know, it's one thing if he wants to play Russian roulette with his own damned life, but it's another thing to screw with my family."

His family.

From the backseat Ringo gave out a disgruntled woof, then stood on his back legs, nose to the glass of a rear window.

"You tell 'em," Becca encouraged him, finally relaxing a bit.

Swearing under his breath about brainless jerks with driver's licenses, Hudson continued his search for a radio station. The choice was a late-night sermon or songs from the "AWESOME sixties, seventies, and eighties." Hudson chose the music and Gloria Gaynor, in the middle of "I Will Survive," blasted through the speakers. He turned the volume down, though their conversation disintegrated to a few observations about the condition of the road or the distance left.

Becca hit ice a couple of times at the summit, but the Jetta's tires grabbed on. Still, as the car wound down the westerly slopes, she couldn't let go of the tightness in her chest, the eerie and growing sensation of doom chasing after her.

Whoever *he* was, he was sure working on her fears.

And it didn't ease up when they turned south on Highway 101, following the snakelike coastal highway. Through small towns, over deep chasms, and hugging the cliffs that rose from the ocean, Becca drove on, battling the wind and rain that slanted in from the Pacific.

A few miles north of Deception Bay, Hudson craned to look out the window. It was the cliff edge where Renee's car went over. "You want to stop?" she asked carefully.

"No. I've seen it."

They drove the remaining miles to Deception Bay in silence. It was dark and a sharp wind blew patchily as they entered the small coastal village that curved along a crescent-shaped shoreline. The town itself was wedged between the ocean and mountains with the highway separating the two. To the south was the bay, a freshwater body of water allowing fishing boats a gateway to the open sea.

Becca's heart began to race and she felt strange. She knew she'd never set foot in the town before and yet, as she turned one corner after the next, buildings illuminated by the watery glow of a few street lamps, she felt as if she'd walked these narrow streets. An eerie sense of déjà vu so real it chilled her to the bone enveloped her and she had to fight to keep her teeth from chattering. Even with the mist rising, the weathered storefronts and the fishing boats moored in the bay seemed like pictures from her childhood, though, of course, they couldn't be.

Not your childhood. Jessie's.

A chill whispered up her spine and she swallowed back her fear.

It's all in your mind. You've never been here before. You're letting your damned imagination run away with you.

"Becca?" Hudson said and she snapped out of it.

"What? Oh!" She realized she'd slowed to a stop and idled at an intersection controlled by a blinking red light, but she hadn't resumed driving, despite the fact that no other car was waiting. "Sorry."

"You were a million miles away," he said.

"I was thinking about—Jessie—and this town."

"Deception Bay?"

It's like I've been here before; not once, but several times. Had she dreamt of this place, had visions of the tiny fishing village that she couldn't consciously remember?

"Let's get something to eat before everything shuts down," he suggested, pointing to an establishment with a glowing "Open" sign in the window, and Becca headed into the parking lot. She had her pick of parking spots in front of a restaurant that still displayed its mid-century façade. The entire building appeared as if it hadn't been updated much since the early 1930s with its stone façade and rusting anchor mounted over the door.

Inside a heater blasted warm air around a near-empty cavernlike room with plank ceilings to match the floors and fishing nets filled with dusty glass balls and fake fish draped along walls paneled in rough wood. A couple of twenty-somethings in stocking caps played pool, an older man in a ski jacket and full graying beard nursed a drink at the end of a long, timeworn bar, and a middle-aged couple sat in a corner, drinking beer and staring at the big screen positioned over an area Becca assumed was sometimes used as a dance floor.

Becca and Hudson took seats opposite each other in a booth near the huge rock fireplace. Kindling had been lit and now hungry flames crackled and hissed over mossy chunks of oak and fir. A fading stuffed marlin leapt over a rough-hewn mantel, and wood smoke covered the scents of frying food and cigarette smoke drifting in whenever a side door opened.

Becca swabbed some crumbs from the table and noticed that it, secured into the wall, listed slightly. Soft music—some kind of nondescript jazz—played from speakers mounted on the walls, pool balls clicked, and the deep fryer sizzled, the scent of oil-fried food rising above the sound emanating from the kitchen.

Hudson ordered a microbrew to go with his Dungeness crab cakes while Becca settled for sparkling water to wash down the spicy clam chowder. They shared a small loaf of sourdough bread and lathered it in garlic butter, but Becca barely tasted any of the food.

What was it about this town that made her feel as if she'd been here before? Certainly not just because Jessie had spent time here. And not because Renee had visited. But something . . . something she didn't understand had infected her, made her think she'd peeked around the corners of Deception Bay.

The restaurant was warm enough that she shed her coat, but during the hour they spent over dinner, watching the few people enter and leave, making small talk, Becca never completely lost the chill that had burrowed into her spirit.

Hudson left bills on the table, helped Becca with her coat, then together they dashed the few steps through the lashing rain to the car. She switched on her wipers though they were nearly useless against the downpour and she drove slowly, creeping up the hill to the bed and breakfast, a two-storied rambling hundred-year-old manor with eight bedrooms and a panoramic view of the ocean, now dark as tar.

Hudson carried the bags and she shepherded Ringo into a wide foyer with an antique chandelier suspended from the ceiling that rose high over a sweeping staircase. Hudson had already paid for everything online, and they found their key in a lockbox just inside the door. With Ringo leading the way, they headed to the second floor and a cozy room complete with a glowing gas fireplace, canopied bed, and Victorian antiques. His and Hers robes were draped by a jetted tub behind an obscure shade.

"Nice," she murmured.

"Only the best."

"Or the only place available on short notice."

He smiled and she relaxed a bit as she stood at the window, looking out to where she knew the Pacific should be. With the ocean dark, no moon offering its glow, and rain peppering the glass, she couldn't see anything but her own pale reflection, a worried woman searching the storm.

As she stared at her own weak image she felt another pair of eyes, not Hudson's, who had opened his laptop and was struggling with a barely existent wi-fi connection. Nor did she feel Ringo's dark eyes upon her as he was sniffing the connecting rooms, hardly paying attention to her. Whoever was staring at her, she was certain, was on the other side of the glass, observing her through the shroud of the storm, following her every movement, reading her damned thoughts.

She snapped the blinds shut and turned around.

Hudson abandoned his computer and came around the desk to gather her in his arms. She snuggled into them gratefully. "You make me feel safe."

He kissed the top of her head. Then he tucked a finger under her chin, turning her face up to his. "You make me feel . . . something else," he said suggestively.

"Ahh . . ." she said, her mood lightening. And when he kissed her again, more passionately, she kissed him back with all her pent-up love and desire.

Nothing could hurt her and her baby as long as she was with Hudson.

From my lighthouse, I stare at the shoreline, barely visible through the night. But she's there. Becca. Close.

And rutting like a whore!

I feel my lip curl in disgust, though I shouldn't be surprised.

Isn't it what she does, what they all do?

Jezebel was the mistress of fornication.

Rebecca is no different.

Fingering the knife I stole from the cabin, I tamp down my frustration. I'd known she would come, of course, had felt her need as the sea pulled her. But I'd thought she would be alone.

Who is this man? This stud?

I push open the door and it's nearly ripped from its hinges with the force of the gale, the door thudding hard. The old metal walk is rusted, but I step outside naked, feeling the slap of the wind, hearing it howl and whistle as it whips the breakers into froths of whitecaps and swirls of angry foam.

I had to pass her in the mountains, take a chance and speed by her in an effort to outrun the storm and get to the lighthouse. As it was, I barely made the crossing, the waves washing over the sides of my craft, threatening to plunge it to the bottom of the ocean.

I will have to kill them both.

Once again, I'll need to attach the grill guard to my vehicle. Two bolts to secure the bars across the front of my truck and then I'll force them off the road as well. My truck will go unscarred, the grill guard hidden securely.

I finger the edge of the knife and wish I could use it as my weapon. Feel the lifeblood ooze out of Rebecca's body. Like it did with Jezebel. With a smile I remember her rounded eyes in the moonlight, her gasp of surprise. She, too, had been curious and, foolish girl, had thought she could better me, lure me to her and then stop me from my mission.

Talk me down?

Convince me of the sin of my ways?
Offer up sexual favors for me to ignore my duty?
Or did she really think she could kill me with her
tiny little knife, the one I turned on her?
She'd been shocked to know that she'd lost.
Jezebel who had always won.
And now it is time for another.
Rebecca needs to die.
And die soon.

"So you wanna watch a movie? There's a *Star Wars* mara-
thon running all night," Mac said to his son. Levi sat on the
edge of a plaid couch, his bare feet propped on the edge of a
metal and glass coffee table, his head bent over a handheld
computer game. "We missed the first one, but the second
comes on in twenty minutes."

"Okay." Levi's lack of enthusiasm was palpable.

"I picked up some microwave popcorn and red licorice."

Levi winced, but it was from missing something on his
game system. He hadn't heard a word Mac uttered. The kid
was placating him. They were stuck together in a small cabin
in a coastal town in the middle of nowhere, and Sam McNally
realized for the first time how little he knew his son.

"I'll put in a pizza."

"Yeah." Levi stopped and for once Mac thought he'd
caught the kid's attention until his boy picked up his cell
phone, read the display, and began texting like crazy. Mac
hadn't even heard the damned thing ring.

"Someone callin' ya?" Mac turned on the oven, preheat-
ing the ancient thing.

"No."

"But you saw a message."

"I texted Seth. No big deal." The phone either vibrated or
made some inaudible noise and Levi snapped his head into
the direction of the tiny screen. Once again his fingers flew
over the keypad.

"Seth must've had something pretty important to say."

"It wasn't Seth. Someone else."

"You can do two at once?" he asked and smelled old crud burning off the inside of the oven. This fleabag was the first place he'd tried when he called for a place to stay, and now he was second-guessing himself. He'd known as soon as he'd driven up and seen the rates for daily, weekly, or monthly that the units wouldn't be five-star. But he'd thought a fireplace and a cabin feel would be roomier and a little more relaxing than a sterile motel room with two matching beds, TV in an armoire, coffeepot, and maid service rapping on the door in the morning.

Now, looking at the sagging, scratched furniture and ancient paneling, he wasn't so sure. Even the plumbing at the Coastal Cove Cabins seemed suspect.

"It's easy to text a bunch of people," Levi told him disparagingly.

"If you say so." Mac slid the frozen meaty pizza out of the box. Hell, he could count the pieces of pepperoni and sausage on the thing on the fingers of one hand. He figured it didn't much matter. The oven reached the temperature and he placed the pie inside.

Levi had abandoned his game completely and now was texting faster than the best typist in the department.

"How many people are you talking to?"

"I dunno. Why? Oh. Don't worry, I've got unlimited texting. It's not costing you . . . er, Mom or Tom anything."

"Tom? Who's Tom?" he asked before he realized what he was saying.

"Mom's latest." For the first time Levi met his gaze.

"You don't like him."

A shrug. "He's okay."

"And he's paying your cell phone bill?" This was news to Mac, but then Connie only told him what she wanted to, when she wanted to.

"He added me to his plan. It doesn't cost much."

"But—"

"Mom's on it, too. Tom's moving in."

"How do you feel about that?"

Levi's phone zinged again and he looked away. "It's all right." He began texting again and Mac sensed the conversation was over. He'd known Connie was "involved" with someone, but he'd never heard his name and figured it would pass. In the years since they were separated and divorced, she'd dated a number of men. One guy, Laddie, had moved in with her twice, and twice she'd kicked the bum out. Now, it seemed, she was onto a new one.

Mac didn't begrudge her the new men in her life. He just hated that Levi had to be dragged along for the ride.

"You could move in with me," he suggested and Levi's head bobbed up as if it had been pulled by an invisible string.

"You're serious."

"Thinking about retiring."

Levi's eyebrows drew together. "You sure?"

"Yeah, why not?"

"I don't know . . ." He shook his head. "Mom wouldn't like it."

"We'd work something out."

"I don't think so. Mom, she says she and Tom are gonna move in together and get married. He's got a couple of daughters. They'll need a place to stay, so the den, that'll be their room when they come."

"How old are they?"

"Dunno." He thought. Scratched at his chin and Mac saw the first evidence of a beard, a few stray hairs on his chin.

At twelve? The kid was growing up. Fast.

"I guess they're five and eight maybe. Little kids."

"How do you feel about that?"

Levi was about to equivocate, to lie, and say it was "all right" or "not too bad." Instead, he scowled and yanked off his stocking cap. "It sucks. Big time."

"Then we should talk about you moving in with me."

He hesitated, then said, "Mom and I already talked about it."

"You did?" The first he'd heard anything like this.

"Mom told me to give it a chance, that Tom would make things . . . better. We would eventually get a bigger house, and, you know, I could go to a better school. Get ready for college." He forced a smile he didn't feel and in a falsetto mocked his mother's voice. "We'll be this one big happy family and everything will be just perfect."

"That what you want?" Mac asked, surprised that his kid was opening up. Connie hadn't said a word about the new guy, just that she was seeing someone and that Levi had a girlfriend. Mac couldn't remember the girl's name, but he'd bet his badge she was texting Levi up one side and down the other.

"I just want everyone to leave me alone," he muttered and picked up his phone again.

It ain't gonna happen, Mac thought, then waited as the pizza finished baking. When the timer dinged Mac found an old towel to drag the bubbling, half-burnt thin crust from the oven. He cut the pizza into pieces and Levi ate with him, only to slip into game mode again. Rather than bug the kid, he turned his attention back to the case. He was going to check in with the sheriff's department in the morning, see what, if anything, had developed on Renee's accident, then do a little reconnaissance around the cabin the Brentwoods had owned.

Afterward, weather permitting, he'd take Levi crabbing on the bay and talk some more.

He might just learn something about his own damned kid.

"Hey, Sleeping Beauty."

Becca opened a groggy eye. She'd slept like a rock after making love to Hudson, and sometime during that time, the storm had passed. Struggling to sit up, she found him at the foot of the bed dressed only in jeans, his hair dark from a shower, his torso as bare as his feet.

"Weather's better," she observed as sunlight streamed through the now unshuttered window.

"Don't count on it lasting. Supposed to get colder again. Maybe snow in the passes."

Becca groaned. "What time is it?"

"Nearly ten."

"Really?" She couldn't remember when she'd slept so late. She blinked and stretched as Hudson walked to the coffee-pot and poured some into a cup.

"Here, this is all that's left, but there's breakfast until eleven, so . . ."

"I'm up!" She rolled out of bed and padded to the bathroom where she got a glimpse of herself and cringed. Her hair was a tangle, her face still heavy with sleep, her makeup long gone. What had Hudson called her? Sleeping Beauty? A bad joke at best.

She showered, slicked her hair into a ponytail, applied minimal lipstick and mascara, then pulled on a pair of jeans and a sweatshirt. Hudson had already walked Ringo, so they, along with one other couple who looked to be in their seventies, ate a breakfast of a spinach quiche, fruit cup, and cinnamon rolls that, the owner of the establishment confided, were baked at the local bakery.

"You own this place long?" Hudson asked as the tall, lanky man brought them a new pot of coffee.

"Nearly twenty-five years. Will be this September. My wife and I decided to give up the rat race and move here from Chicago. This old house was for sale and we converted it to a B and B. We've never looked back."

At the next table, the woman waved her hand. "Is there any more orange juice?" she asked, and the owner/waiter hurried off to the kitchen. Becca looked out the window toward the ocean, now calm, beams of sunlight bouncing off the restless gray water.

The beach far below was littered with debris, driftwood, seaweed, the shells of dead clams and crabs. Seagulls wheeled and cawed above the small strip of sand. Waves came and went, lapping the shore and leaving bits of thick foam as they receded.

They finished their meal and then Hudson opened a thick sliding door and he and Becca stepped onto a deck that ran the length of the building. Despite the sun, the air was crisp and cold, and though there was no wind, the surf continued to echo against the cliffs. To the south was the bay, a few brave fishing vessels having already slipped over the bar and into the sea, and to the north was a curving peninsula of rocks and trees, a narrow cape stretching clawlike into the ocean. A few black rocks, islands unto themselves, protected the cape's shoreline. Farther out, atop a rocky mound, was a lighthouse, a tall spire rising into the heavens. Farther still, an island sat on the horizon, mist shrouded and about a half mile out.

Becca stared at the lighthouse and shivered against a sudden rush of cold air. She turned back inside.

They checked out of the bed and breakfast, packed up the car, then walked into town. It was nearly noon, a few people on the streets. Hudson had the address and knew where the key to the cabin where Renee had stayed was located. The yard was overgrown, the carport sagging a bit, but inside the cottage was cozy, though it seemed to Becca as if she'd stepped back in time at least twenty years. The futon had to have been built in the seventies, and the television was similar to one her parents had bought while she was in grade school.

She noticed the desk, imagined Renee working here, her near-black hair shiny under the tension lamp.

Unexpectedly, her throat thickened and tears burned the back of her eyes. She couldn't believe Renee was gone. Gone forever. She thought of Hudson's twin and wondered what Renee might have been doing.

"Feels odd," he said, his mood matching hers as he walked

through the few rooms, his footsteps creaking on the old floorboards.

"Yeah." Becca noted the faded pictures on a wall of a family decked out in yellow windbreakers while standing on the deck of a fishing vessel, the open sea swelling behind them.

"Okay, I think I've seen enough," Hudson said and they locked up the cabin and walked into the center of town, where, unlikely as it was, Becca felt that same chill deep in her soul, the one that had been with her since driving into the town. A few pedestrians littered the streets, a man walking his dog, a woman jogging behind a stroller, skateboarders weaving along the sidewalk, the hoods of their sweatshirts nearly hiding their faces as they flew past.

The Sands of Thyme bakery was filled with customers, a line for cinnamon bread that had just come out of the oven, the shop filled with the warm scents of spices. The pizza parlor had a sign that said it was closed for the winter and a kite shop, too, was locked up tight.

They bought coffee and walked along the waterfront where beachcombers searched the strand for treasures washed up by the storm.

On their way back to the car, while Hudson tied Ringo to a post outside, Becca wandered through the open door of a shop that smelled of soap and candles, where antique dressers, tables, and armoires displayed smaller items. Everything, including the hanging lights, had price tags attached.

The clerk, a prim woman in her sixties with straight white chin-length hair and a wary expression, sat on a stool near an antique cash register, a half-finished knitting project on a ledge near the window where a calico cat sat, tail curved under its body, as it basked in the sunlight streaming through the windowpanes.

There was one other customer in the shop, a stooped woman with iron-gray hair and gnarled hands who was interested in a case of antique buttons.

Her knitting forgotten, the tight-lipped clerk eyed the woman like a hawk, as if she suspected her of pocketing some of the merchandise.

The old woman was oblivious. "Aren't they pretty?" she said, looking up at Becca with flat eyes. She was fingering a mother-of-pearl button that glittered under the overhead lights.

Becca eyed the luminescent button. "Yes. Very."

"But only one . . . I need two."

"Can I help you with something, Madeline?" The clerk, obviously displeased, let out a put-upon sigh as she reluctantly slid off her stool, its legs scratching against the wood floor. The cat, disturbed, leapt onto a highboy from where it peered down imperiously.

Madeline? Becca stared at the old woman, who stared back. "You look like one of them," the old woman whispered.

"Madeline," the clerk reproved.

"One of who?" Hudson was just stepping through the front door.

Madeline's head snapped up and she viewed Hudson with a furtive glare as he wove his way between the displays to stand next to Becca.

"Siren Song," she whispered.

"Are you Madame Madeline?" Becca asked.

"Maddie!" The clerk was heading their way.

Instead of answering, Madeline placed her twisted fingers on Becca's abdomen, then shrank away, quickly sketching a sign of the cross over her chest, then shuffling to the door.

"Did she take that button? Damn it!" The clerk stamped a small booted foot. "She always does that!" She started for the door, but Madeline was gone, through the door and hurrying off. "I should call the police, but for the most part she's harmless."

Becca was unnerved that she'd touched her abdomen. "Who is she?"

"Oh, yeah, she calls herself Madame Madeline. She pretends to be a psychic. She's a town fixture, lived here all her life."

"And what did she mean by Siren Song?" Hudson asked.

"It's a tract of land run by . . . well, some locals. They mostly keep to themselves. The property is valuable, it stretches from the mountains on the east side of 101 and across the highway to the ocean. They're this clannish group, like a colony, some even say cultish. Different, you know. All related."

"Colony?" Hudson asked.

She smiled then and took a long look at Becca. "I see what Maddie means, though, you do resemble them . . . a little."

"Them?" Becca felt a little weak in the knees. What the hell was all this? Maddie placing her hand over Becca's stomach as if she *knew* she was pregnant, and then this talk of resembling members of a—cult?

"I'm not related," she said firmly.

The woman didn't argue with her, but did add, "This is the second time in the last few months that someone has asked about Siren Song. I've owned this shop for six and a half years. Before that I worked in one of the spas that closed, and I can go for months without anyone mentioning Siren Song, maybe years, but lately . . . Oh, well." She straightened the little case of buttons that Madeline had pawed through.

"Who asked about Siren Song?" Hudson wanted to know.

"A visitor in the town. Can't remember her name." The shopkeeper frowned, thinking hard, her fingers frozen over the buttons. "Oh. Yes. It was that dark-haired young woman. The one who was killed when her car went off the cliff just north of here."

"Renee Trudeau?" Hudson asked.

Becca's heart did a nosedive.

"Yes." The shopkeeper brightened, proud of herself. "That's her name!"

* * *

Mac had had enough of the beach. He'd spent the whole day trying to figure out what kind of "fun" thing he and his son could do together. They'd made an attempt at crabbing, but Levi wasn't really into it. Now the sun was sinking into the horizon and storm clouds were just about to block it out completely. A glacial wind was trying its best to rip his coat from him. Levi was bundled in a hat and coat and all Mac could see were his nose and mouth. They were both frozen and trying to act like they were having a good time.

The Tillamook County Sheriff's Department knew nothing more than they had the first time Mac had visited them. Mac got the feeling they wanted him to disappear and let them work their investigation in their own way. He didn't blame them. He didn't like interference, either.

So he'd taken the hint and brought Levi into Deception Bay with the thought of hanging out with his son, but the weather was sure as hell making that a dicey proposition. He was trying to think what he could come up with, some kind of entertainment they could both enjoy, when his cell phone buzzed. He saw it was Gretchen and was almost grateful for the intrusion.

"What's up?" he asked.

"A helluva lot, actually. Maybe you should leave town more often and let the rest of us do your work for you."

"Yeah, yeah, yeah. What is it?"

"You know the DNA you got back on the Preppy Pricks? And the girls, too?"

"That proved Zeke's paternity, yes." Mac was trying to be patient, but he could hear the edge of annoyance in his voice.

"You only asked to know the baby's paternity."

"Yeah?"

"Well, the tech found some other—unexpected—information in that DNA, and he called this morning to give you the news. I took the call."

"How long is this build-up gonna go?" Mac demanded.

"Ends right here, killjoy. Your little girlfriend's DNA matches one of the others. They're full-on siblings."

"What?"

"Rebecca Ryan Sutcliff is Jezebel Brentwood's sister," she said with relish.

Chapter Twenty-Three

Becca stood with Hudson outside their car, the wind slapping her hair around her face. They'd started driving toward the tract of land the locals called Siren Song when Becca had suddenly insisted they head away from Deception Bay and to a neighboring town to the south. Hudson hadn't asked her why at the time, but when she proceeded to waste away half the afternoon in studied silence, hugging her dog, he'd asked her what was wrong. She'd been incapable of telling him that she didn't want to go. After all this, she—didn't—want—to—go. It was laughable, really, as much as she'd insisted on learning the truth, an insistence that had sent them barreling toward the coast. But now, now that she was on the brink of real discovery, she was paralyzed with fear and she didn't know how to explain it.

"What's going on?" Hudson had finally asked in frustration when they turned the Jetta back toward Deception Bay. Becca shook her head and kept her eyes on the road, unable to verbalize the feelings tight within her. "Maybe I should drive," Hudson said, for about the fifth time.

"I'm fine."

"You're not acting fine."

"I'm just—thinking."

"Care to include me in that thinking?"

He sounded pissed and she didn't blame him, but she really didn't get it herself. She was running on emotion and sensation, and a deep fear for her baby's life that seemed to have taken control.

He wants to kill you. He wants to kill your baby. She'd repressed her last vision, but after learning from the shopkeeper that Renee had asked about Siren Song, it had come to the fore, frightening her anew. She was desperately afraid for her baby. Afraid for Hudson. Afraid for herself.

Now they were at a lookout, gazing over the darkening ocean, gathering their thoughts. The lighthouse sat on its rocky mound to the south, and the murky island beyond had disappeared behind a fog bank. Night would be upon them very soon.

"Madame Madeline knew I was pregnant," Becca said aloud. She'd said the same thing several times over the course of the afternoon.

"She seemed more like someone suffering from dementia than a 'seer,'" Hudson answered. He'd also said the same thing over the course of the afternoon.

"I know you want to go to Siren Song."

"I don't have any problem seeing Mad Maddie first, but we need to make some kind of decision soon." His eyes scanned the horizon.

"You don't think it's important," Becca accused him.

"Renee got spooked by her," Hudson allowed. "But she didn't really learn anything from her."

"Except that she was going to die."

Hudson shook his head, his jaw tight. "Someone killed my sister by running her off the road. Someone I'm going to find. I don't believe for a minute that Mad Maddie's prediction had anything to do with it. This was murder, premeditated, because Renee asked questions and somebody didn't like it."

Becca closed her eyes and let the wind throw a shiver of rain at her. It was freezing cold but it felt oddly cleansing. She heard Ringo barking from the car, scolding them for leaving him inside. "I don't want to go to Siren Song," she admitted.

"What is it that scares you?"

He's there, she thought. She wanted to say the words but couldn't form them.

"When Renee called me," Hudson said, "I think she'd just been there. Maybe she talked to them."

"The cult members."

He inclined his head. "She said something about colonies of people. She was excited. She meant Siren Song."

"And I look like them," Becca stated flatly.

"Yeah, well, that could mean next to nothing. I just want to talk to them. See if Renee asked them about Jessie, or maybe something else."

Becca felt ridiculous, being so stubborn, when she'd been so gung-ho earlier. But it was like Jessie's warning was playing over and over again in her head, an endless reel. Had that been what Jessie had been trying to tell her? Siren Song? But there were too many syllables in that message. Three, instead of two. So Jessie had to be trying to tell her something else, and Becca was sure it had to do with *him*.

Hudson pulled her into his arms. "I can go see them by myself."

She shook her head, unable to explain the depths of her fear. She wanted answers as much as he did, yet now, suddenly, she couldn't take the last few steps. She was profoundly frightened in a visceral, nonsensical way.

"I don't want anything to happen to our baby," she whispered.

"I won't let anything happen."

She didn't say it, but she wasn't sure he would be able to stop the cataclysm she sensed was coming for her.

Hudson suggested, "Let's get another night at the B and B. I'll take you there, then go see the people at Siren Song."

"No, I'm staying with you. Don't leave me."

"Would you feel safer back in Portland, or Laurelton?"

"Yes. No. I don't know." She turned toward him, burying her face in his jacket, clutching its leather folds with tense fingers. "I'll go," she said in a muffled voice against his chest. "I want to know, too. I'll go."

"What is it?" he asked again, holding her close. "Why now?"

"I can't explain it." She was torn between laughter and tears. "If I didn't already know I was pregnant I'd be wondering, because my emotions are all over the place. I just feel something bad is going to happen. Like we're prodding the beast. And though I want answers as much as you do, I'm afraid."

"Maybe we should just forget about this for now."

"No, you need to find out about Renee," she said, steeling her courage. "And I want to know if Jessie met with them, and if Renee followed her path."

He pulled back to look into her face, sweeping her wind-tossed hair from her eyes. "You sure?"

She nodded.

"Then we'll drive over there and see how it goes. If you don't feel safe, we'll leave."

"Okay."

"Want me to drive?"

"No, I'm okay," she said, turning toward the car. Ringo was standing on the front seat, his paws on the dashboard. He yipped at her and scratched at the dash.

"Sure?" Hudson asked.

She nodded tautly. "Sure."

* * *

Mac shoved his cell phone into his pocket and made a sound of frustration.

"Still can't get hold of her?" Levi asked.

Mac had made a half dozen calls to Becca's cell and home phone numbers, but there was no answer anywhere. Levi only knew that Mac was anxious to connect with the woman he'd been dialing for the past hour because of something that had come up at work. "I was hoping to get an answer before we start heading over the mountains and I lose the signal completely," Mac muttered.

Levi looked long-suffering. "I'm hungry. Is there anywhere to eat here? They got a Subway?"

"I doubt it."

"McDonald's?"

"We'd have to go to a bigger town."

"Then let's do it."

Mac considered. They could drive to Seaside, which had any number of fast-food restaurants, but it would be a good half hour out of their way. Still, it might give him just enough time to connect with Rebecca Sutcliff before he headed over the mountains.

And what was he going to tell her? *By the way, Becca, did you know that Jezebel Brentwood was your sister? Either good old Mom and Dad gave her up for adoption and kept you, or you were adopted out, too.* Was that the kind of news—the kind that created more questions than answered them—that you delivered over the phone?

"Let's go to Seaside," he said gruffly, and they both got into his Jeep.

Becca found the turnoff to Siren Song after passing the entrance twice. It was little more than an opening between hedges of laurel and sturdy grasses that led to two lines of gravel whose center was a tall strip of weeds. Rain drizzled down to be flung in sheets by sharp puffs of wind, making the entry look desolate and cold. Anyone could believe this road hadn't been driven on for months. Maybe Renee had been the colony's last visitor.

As soon as they turned off the highway onto its bumpy surface, Becca gripped the steering wheel with white knuckles, easing the Jetta along as its tires dipped and swayed through potholes filled with water. It was not an auspicious first impression, though Siren Song itself, the lodge, loomed large and imposing when viewed from Highway 101. This hidden, dreary access did not do the place justice, but maybe that's just what the secretive inhabitants within its walls wanted.

"This must be it," Hudson muttered.

"No other way to get to the lodge as far as I can see."

"They could use some signage."

They bumped and swayed along for over a quarter mile before the lane widened to provide a view to a tall stone fence that stretched east and west and a high wrought-iron gate with vicious-looking spikes whose double swinging gates provided a view into a grassy field where Siren Song stood. In the fading light its dark, cedar shakes and darker windows seemed to stare back at them.

Becca pulled to a stop in front of the gates, leaving the engine running. Both she and Hudson peered through the wrought-iron gate in silence. The gloom from the storm had deepened the shadows. Faintly, light shone from several windows on both the first and second floor. From a distance they heard the thud of a closing door.

"Someone's here," Hudson observed, reaching for the handle.

Becca began to shiver uncontrollably, but Hudson didn't notice as he climbed from the Jetta and walked to the gate, peering through the bars. Ringo whined from the backseat.

Who are you? Becca silently asked.

There was no answer. Not even a feeling that someone received her message.

Becca saw Hudson straighten. He glanced her way urgently and she slowly got out of the Jetta, hearing the car's door-ajar bell ding several times. The sounds were muffled by the wind, which was loudly shaking the trees, and something beyond the gate, maybe an unlatched shutter, was banging with surprising ferocity.

She moved in beside Hudson and with a distinct shock saw what had captured his attention. A young woman in a long dress standing beneath an umbrella. She was staring at them.

They stared back at her, and Becca's mouth opened in a silent scream.

She looked just like Jessie!

Hudson grabbed Becca by one arm as she started to go down. He caught her before she slid into a dark puddle and pulled her quaking body into his arms. Glancing back, he saw the brush of the woman's skirt as she entered through a side door of the building, heard the distinct *plok* of a thrown bolt.

"We have to go," Becca chattered. "We have to go."

"Wait."

"No!"

"Okay, okay."

"We have to go."

"Fine. Then I'm driving."

He helped her into the passenger side, alarmed at how white her face had become. Ringo, now in the back, bounced around wildly, scrabbling to reach Becca, but Hudson held up his hand to the dog. "Stay," he ordered.

"It was Jessie," Becca whispered. "You saw. It was Jessie, wasn't it? She's our age now." Becca's eyes fearfully peered through the windshield at the sudden driving rain. The lodge was barely visible. Faint smearings of light.

"It wasn't Jessie," Hudson said, though he'd had a moment of shock himself. "She was younger than we are."

"Who are these people? I don't look like them." She threw Hudson a panicked glance. "Do I?"

"Not—like that," he said.

"Not like Jessie, you mean?"

"We don't know what Jessie would look like now."

"She would look like *that*!" Becca flailed an arm in the girl's direction. "Please! I want to go. Now."

Hudson didn't hesitate further. He jerked on the wheel, turning the Jetta around in a tight space. Branches scratched against the sides of the car.

"Hurry," Becca said.

Her attitude worried him; he would have liked to stay and try to ask a few questions. But it was clear the woman in the dress had no interest in talking to them. It was not Jessie. He knew it wasn't.

But she'd been the spitting image.

The Jetta bumped, shimmied, and jostled as Hudson ran it faster than he should back down the rutted track. When they reached 101, Hudson turned the car's nose north and the wheels zinged along the wet pavement toward the turnoff to Highway 26.

Becca sat tensely for several miles, then said in a voice so low he could scarcely hear her, "In my vision, he was standing behind Jessie with a knife. He was going to stab her and then he looked at me. Hudson, he *knows* I'm pregnant!"

"Was he at Siren Song?" he asked carefully. He didn't know how far he believed in her ability to see the man who intended her harm, but her fear had infected him. She believed it, and that's what counted right now.

"I don't know," she said. "I thought so. Before we went. But then we saw the girl . . ."

"Woman."

"Yes, woman." She drew a hard breath. "Jessie was adopted.

Are these people . . . did she come from this *cult*? If that woman wasn't her, is she Jessie's sister?"

"Some kind of relative, maybe." Hudson didn't want to jump to conclusions, but Lord, there had been a resemblance.

He shot a glance Becca's way. In profile, she possessed a striking similarity as well. It had always been there, to some degree, but until he'd seen the Jessie lookalike, he'd never really taken it seriously.

"Jessie came to find them, but then she encountered him," Becca murmured, watching the rivulets of rain run down her side window.

"Who is he?"

"One of them? I don't know. But he hates me. I can feel it, and it's real."

"We'll go home," Hudson said grimly. "Make sure you and the baby are safe."

Something in his tone cued Becca to his unspoken thoughts. "You're going to come back here without me!"

"Not tonight. I want to get home. Safe. Have a late dinner. And think about this."

"I don't want you to come back here."

"I need to know what Renee learned."

"It's not safe."

"I don't believe we're marked for death," Hudson told her. "Mad Maddie's a demented old woman who believes in a psychic ability she doesn't possess."

"I know. I know." But she didn't sound like she believed it.

"I'll feel better knowing you're back in Portland, safe and sound, away from whoever killed my sister."

Becca didn't respond. She wanted to get back home and she wanted Hudson and Ringo with her.

They made the turnoff to Highway 26 in relative silence, each absorbed in their own thoughts. As they started into the Coast Range, the light drizzle turned into mixed rain and snow.

"Maybe we should call McNally." Becca broke into the

silence, watching the hypnotizing slap-slap-slap of the wipers.
"Send him to Siren Song. Let him take it from here." Without waiting for a response she dug in her purse for her phone
and made a sound of annoyance. "I switched it off last night
and never switched it back on."

"You're not going to get much reception now," Hudson
observed, but Becca pressed the green On button and hoped
for the best. The cell phone went through its waking-up routine, but the words "no service" filled the screen.

"When we get over the mountains," she said and settled
in to wait, her cell phone in her hand.

Snow fell in earnest as they reached the summit and started
down the other side, causing Hudson to take the Jetta down
to a slow creep. Almost immediately over the pass, however,
the snow turned to a mix, then the ever-present drizzle. It
was dark as pitch out. No illumination other than their own
headlights.

Becca realized they were only a few miles from where
she'd had her accident, and her right hand squeezed her cell
phone hard. Hudson was concentrating on the road. Visibil-
ity was less than perfect.

As they hit a longer, straight stretch, the forest dropping
off on either side of the blacktop, headlights came up behind
them, bright around a last curve. Their illumination scoured
the inside of the Jetta, throwing Hudson's profile into sharp
relief.

Becca half glanced around in fear. It wasn't him. It wasn't.
It was just her irrational terror. "He's awful close."

"For these road conditions, he sure is."

The vehicle pulled closer. A truck.

"Jesus," Hudson muttered. There was no shoulder. They
were driving on a ridge where the asphalt ended abruptly
and the land dropped away. Becca knew this section of the
highway well, and her heart began a deep, slow tattoo. "Pass,
you idiot!"

The truck rumbled loudly, shattering the night. Hudson

yanked the wheel, trying to pull over, but there was nowhere to go. Becca's phone flew from her hand. She scrambled for a hold.

Ram!

The truck hit them from behind, throwing Becca forward. "Shit!" Hudson yelled. The seat belt jerked Becca back. Ringo yelped and his toes scrabbled for purchase as he slammed into the back of the front seats.

"Christ!" Hudson muttered. He twirled the wheel the other way, turning into the spin, keeping the car on the road with everything he had.

"It's him," Becca moaned. "It's him."

She turned to gaze back, her face caught in the glare of his headlights. She saw the grill on the front of the vehicle. A truck.

Hudson hit the accelerator and the Jetta spurted forward, shimmying across the road, righting itself for a moment in the oncoming lane.

Ram!

The truck caught the Jetta on the driver's side, spinning it back. Hudson didn't wait. There was no more trying to stop. No searching for a place to land. He was going to have to outrun the bastard.

He punched the accelerator. The Jetta's wheels grabbed the pavement and lurched ahead of the truck with a jump. The truck's driver threw it into reverse, then ground the gears, readying for another assault. Hudson pressed the accelerator further and the Jetta charged forward, shaking like a rattletrap.

"The axle," Hudson muttered. "Shit."

"Hudson, he's coming!"

"Bastard."

He punched the Jetta. Shivering madly, the compact car ran forward like a runner fighting a limp.

The headlights pinned them. The truck's horn bellowed a

cry of war, then slammed them with enough force to slide the Jetta over the edge. One moment they were following the center line of the highway, the next they were plunging over an embankment into black nothingness.

Becca screamed. In her mind's eye she saw Hudson cold and bleeding. Eyes closed in death.

Blam! The Jetta hit the ground with force enough to break the axle entirely. Becca's teeth slammed together. The car surged through underbrush. Ringo yipped. Hudson swore and then suddenly the bole of the tree raced toward them.

The driver's side hit the tree dead on. Becca jerked into her seat belt again. The windshield shattered. Cold air and glass rained.

"Hudson! Hudson!"

Becca didn't immediately realize she was calling his name. She surfaced as if from a dream and saw something stuck into the arm of her jacket. A sharp chunk of wood. She reached for it and pulled it out, felt searing pain. It had been jabbed into her bicep. She yanked it out before any of that penetrated her brain and she felt the ooze of blood on her skin.

Hurry, she told herself. *Hurry!*

Her gaze shot to Hudson. He was slumped over the wheel. The area above his right ear was dark with blood. The steering wheel had pinned him to his seat. "Hudson," she said brokenly.

Steam sizzled into the cold night. Rain poured in through the half-missing windshield.

"Hudson," she whispered again. She tried to move forward but the seat belt held her fast. The dog whimpered and she glanced back. Ringo was trapped in the backseat. The car had folded inward on the driver's side and the dog was blocked from jumping to the front, but he appeared to be unhurt.

Hurry! He's coming back!

With dull fingers Becca unclasped her seat belt. It zipped

back as if the car were in perfect working order. She was having trouble getting her brain to command herself to move with urgency.

She pushed on her door and it groaned open with the sound of grinding metal. A frigid wind slapped her face.

The cell phone.

She glanced at Hudson again. He was pale and his breathing was labored. Was that the effect of being crushed by the steering wheel? *Please, God, let him be okay.*

Think.

The cell phone, yes.

She reached a hand around the floor of her seat, feeling dull and disconnected. Where was it? She couldn't find it.

Hudson kept his cell in his jacket.

Gently, she reached a hand in his right pocket, but it was empty. Making mewling sounds of distress, she reached over him, flashing anger at the steering wheel, throwing her shoulder against it as if that could help to release him.

She caught the other side of his jacket and hauled it up, heavy with his phone. She struggled to get it free and when she did, she flipped it open.

No service.

Tears squeezed from her eyes. Ringo was whining and whining and she gazed back at him. "Stay put, boy. It's okay. It's all right. We're okay." She glanced around and felt a zap of pain jump up her neck. Something twisted there. Muscle pain. Immediately her arms went to her abdomen, but she was fine. Her baby was fine.

Rage ran through her like wildfire, burning through her torpor.

Bastard. Murdering, killing bastard!

With new strength she pulled herself from the car, slipping in mud and fir chips and needles. Glass tinkled against itself and fell off her clothes as she hung on to the car. She could feel the pain in her left arm. The wrench of her neck. And there was something with her left hip—a deep bruise.

But her head was clearing rapidly. The rain was good for that, at least. She blinked against the drizzle and listened hard. No sound but the rain and the whoosh of an impish wind.

No engine. He had moved on. He had driven his truck far away.

Just like last time.

Her teeth started instantly chattering. She felt a headache building. From the accident? No! A vision. For the first time she welcomed it.

Please. Please, Jessie.

And suddenly there she was. Standing precariously on the headland. Alone.

Where was *he*?

Jessie mouthed the word to her. Two syllables. A warning.

Becca wanted to cry with frustration. "What is it?" she cried aloud.

"Justice," Jessie answered.

Becca came back to the moment as if someone had turned a switch. She turned her face to the high heavens and shrieked, wanting answers, not riddles.

And Hudson?

She had to get help.

Struggling, she grabbed on to exposed tree roots to help her scale the embankment back to the road above. She was glad for her beach clothes, her sneakers and jeans and jacket, but she still scrambled for purchase against the slippery mud.

Gasping for breath, she finally reached the top, hauling herself up with shaking arms onto the asphalt. She stared down the highway from where they'd come. No sound of an approaching vehicle. She glanced toward the east. The road curved toward the right. Nothing approaching from there, either.

She wanted to lie down and rest her head on the wet road. She needed . . . rest.

But Hudson needed help.

With an effort, she staggered to her feet. *You're unhurt,* she told herself. *You're okay.*

She was only a couple of miles from her first accident. Where someone had run her off the road. Where she'd lost her baby. Again, she cradled her abdomen.

Which way to go to find cell service? Toward Portland, or toward the beach?

A toss-up.

Becca chose Portland. She stumbled east. A car would come by soon. A good Samaritan. Hudson was okay. He wasn't in any immediate danger. He was okay. But tears formed in the corners of her eyes and she silently prayed for him as she trudged along the road.

She reached another curve of the road and trudged around it, looking through the rain ahead. Was that a car stopped on the road? To her shock, headlights suddenly blasted her in their bright glare. She saw the grill guard.

For the briefest of seconds Becca was paralyzed. Then she heard the door slam and a tall figure was backlit in the headlights. He held something in his hands. A knife.

She turned and fled like an Olympic runner, racing down the road away from him.

His footsteps slammed hard behind her.

Not toward Hudson, she thought. She had to lead him away. To the other side of the road.

She crossed the center line and zigzagged toward the opposite cliffside, sliding over the ledge on purpose, brushing a low Douglas fir branch, scratched by stickery limbs.

He was close. Breathing hard. He leapt down after her.

She was surprisingly coolheaded. She had to lead him away. Away. Away. From Hudson and Ringo. From her and her baby.

"Sister," he called softly. "You cannot hide."

Sister?

Becca stumbled, nearly fell.

"Spawn of Satan."

Becca struggled onward, hands outstretched, tearing as fast as she dared through the thick shrubbery and trees. But he was gaining. He was strong.

Who was he?

She came to a clearing. To the left and up was the highway. Straight ahead, an open gully with no protection. To the right, more woods and God knew what.

She had to get back to the highway. Help would come.

Moving more stealthily, Becca crept around the trees and shrubbery, farther into the woods. Her footsteps sounded loud to her ears, but the rain and wind were covers. He'd slowed down, too. He was listening. Struggling to keep track of her.

Then she saw the edge of the highway thirty feet above her. She hesitated, hating to make herself an open target. But there was no time. No time!

With a supreme effort she climbed up the bank, her fingernails scraping the bark on the tree boles, her hands clinging to stubborn vines.

She heard his breathing behind her.

With a sob of effort, she threw herself onto the empty road. Her hand closed over a rock the size of her fist. Snatching it up, she stumbled to her feet and ran west.

"I can smell you!" he roared, reaching the road behind her.

Her lungs burned and her legs were rubber. He ran after her. His breath came in excited gasps. His hands scrabbled for her, tangling in her hair. She yanked free and screamed for all she was worth.

And then Jessie was there. Beckoning her forward. Sobbing, Becca ran toward her. It took her several seconds to realize her attacker had slowed his pursuit.

She glanced back and saw his face. A shudder went through her. The same face she'd seen when she lost her baby. He was staring through dead eyes at—Jessie. Becca jerked her gaze from his back to Jessie, who was fading from sight.

"Justice," she said again.

Becca fearfully glanced back as her attacker threw back his head and roared. He came at Becca doubly hard. "Jezebel!" he called. "Rebecca!"

The rock felt heavy in her hand. She paused as his big body hurtled toward her, then she heaved her arm back and hurled the stone at him as hard as she could. It smashed into his forehead, knocking him off his stride.

"I am God's messenger!" he bellowed, staggering.

Becca turned and ran with renewed energy, tearing down the road, her lungs on fire, leg muscles burning.

Faintly, she saw the glow of headlights far ahead, somewhere through the trees. She cried out in desperation, staggering, running, near collapse. She ran toward the approaching vehicle, waving her arms, silently praying this wasn't some kind of backup for the sick monster chasing her.

The car, a Jeep, slowed to a halt and the driver got out. A man. Becca, muddy, blood-splattered, and sick with fear, shrank away from his stark headlights. When he suddenly ran toward her, her pulse spiked and she stumbled over her feet.

"Becca?" the voice called urgently. "My God, are you all right?"

She knew him. She knew that voice. She turned back, then shot her gaze in the direction of her attacker. The highway steamed in the glow of her savior's headlights but there was no one chasing her. No one there.

He was beside her now. She recognized him, but not her own shaking voice when she said, "Detective McNally?"

"I've been trying to reach you. What happened?"

She broke down, falling limply, but his reactions were swift and he grabbed her before her knees fully cracked against the blacktop. "Levi!" he called over his shoulder. "Get out here!"

The passenger's side of the Jeep opened and a man stepped out. He half loped, half walked their way, and then hung back. A boy, Becca realized belatedly. She could scarcely think. Her brain was muddled.

"Hudson's hurt," she burbled out. "We had an accident." She pointed behind her to the underbrush. "Down there. Back a ways. He was pushed off the road. The truck with the grill guard. He tried to kill us!"

"Where?" McNally demanded.

He helped Becca to her feet and she pointed in the direction the Jetta had careened off the road. McNally didn't waste time. He barked to the boy to get a flashlight while he asked Becca if she could stand on her own for a moment. She nodded and he raced back to the Jeep, pulling it farther off the road but leaving the lights on.

Then he came back and helped Becca lead the three of them in the right direction. It was easy to find. The crash through the underbrush had left branches torn, the bark gone, their exposed white interiors ghostly in the flashlight's beam.

Spying the back of the Jetta, McNally scrambled down the hill, yelling at the boy who was following a tad more slowly to keep the flashlight's beam ahead of him. Becca slid down the hill on shaking legs, scratching her hands and feeling mud slide into her shoes.

As soon as McNally saw Hudson he attempted to open the driver's door. It took several tries and a lot of swearing before it wrenched free with a scream of protest that sent Ringo into paroxysms of barking. The front side of the car was sprung sideways and Hudson was wedged firmly. Mc-Nally twisted the keys and the engine coughed and sputtered but didn't catch. He pulled the seat lever and moved the driver's seat backward a couple of inches. Hudson's body slipped forward over the wheel. He was free, but still unconscious.

McNally laid fingers against his throat. "Strong pulse." He checked his cell phone and swore softly. "Someone ran you off the road?"

"Yes."

"You think it's the same guy who rammed Renee Trudeau's car over the cliff?"

"Yes."

"We need cell service." He flipped his phone shut and stared hard at the boy Levi, who was talking to Ringo through the window. The little dog was torn between trying to reach Hudson and lick him and wanting to dig through the window. McNally fumbled with a button and the rear window slid downward and Ringo scrambled to get his head through. Levi petted and cooed to him, calming him down.

"Someone's got to drive back and call 911. We need an ambulance." McNally was looking at Becca.

"I can't leave Hudson," she chattered.

"I'll stay with them," Levi said soberly. "You go."

McNally wanted to protest. Becca could tell it was all he could do to leave them and go for help. But there was no choice. She couldn't go, and Levi was too young to drive. "As soon as I make contact, I'm driving right back here," he said tautly. He hesitated a moment, then withdrew a handgun from the inside of his coat. As if choreographed, Levi stepped up and took it from him. McNally looked like he wanted to argue about that, too, but he sent Becca a swift look, said, "Don't hesitate," then climbed back up the bank in record speed.

Levi switched off the beam of the flashlight, then removed the keys from the car, quietly petting Ringo's head, which strained out the window. "No need to advertise where we are," he said into the sudden dark.

Near exhaustion, Becca settled herself inside the driver's door next to Hudson. She found his hand and linked her fingers through his.

Spawn of Satan. I am God's messenger. Sister . . .

He'd seen Jessie. He'd shared Becca's vision.

He knew them both.

"He's still out there," she said. "He chased me. Through the woods."

Levi moved closer to Becca. She saw the gun was in his

hand. She heard a click and realized he'd removed the safety.
"You know about guns?" she asked him.

"No."

"You're not—McNally's son?"

"Yeah. I just don't know him that much."

"And you don't know about guns."

He was staring into the dark, not at her. "I know video games," he said, and for some reason that was enough to comfort Becca.

The rain eased up and finally quit. Becca kept feeling Hudson's pulse but it was strong and steady. Eventually, they heard a car approach and saw it was Mac's Jeep. He scrambled down the bank and took the gun from his son, resetting the safety. He assured them an ambulance was on its way. They would take Hudson back to Ocean Park Hospital. He felt Becca should be looked at, too, and had told the 911 operator there were two victims.

Ringo, who'd waited patiently till now, started renewed whining and bouncing in the backseat, so Levi pulled the dog from the car and held him while Ringo reached his tongue toward Becca. She leaned forward and let him wash her face, hugging him hard.

"Can I take him home?" Levi asked her. "I'll take good care of him for you."

Becca started crying in earnest. She couldn't stop. She nodded jerkily, and in the distance came the wail of a siren.

She gazed off in the opposite direction and wondered what had become of her assailant. "He had his truck around the corner," she told McNally.

"I'm going to find him," the detective told her with certainty.

Becca turned to Hudson. *Please be okay,* she prayed. *Please, please.*

And then the ambulance arrived in a blinding flash of red and white strobes and the welcome scream of its horn.

Chapter Twenty-Four

"Sister."

The word was a sibilant sound searing through Becca's mind.

"Sssssissssster."

Oh, God, no!

Becca's eyes flew open, the hiss of his voice still ringing in her ears. Her heart was pounding, her pulse racing from the terrifying nightmare. In the dark dream, she'd been running through rain and mud, vainly searching for Hudson, seeing the ghost of Jessie at every turn, feeling the hot breath of a nameless, twisted psychopath upon her neck.

Sister.

She blinked, but remnants of the dark nightmare persisted where a writhing wrought-iron fence separated her from hundreds of women, all with the same face. Jessie's face! And there had been a baby crying, its pitiful, frightened whimper nearly obscured by the roar of the sea and rush of wind. Panicked, knowing there was danger at every turn, Becca had been running, faster and faster through the forest, following the ever-shifting fence line, searching vainly for the baby and Hudson . . .

She shivered.

Forced the damned dream away and tried to think clearly.

She was in a hospital bed in a room with stainless steel fixtures and a table at her side. A single narrow window cut into the wall overlooked a near-empty parking lot where security lights offered weak illumination of the rain that poured in gusting sheets while the limbs of the already crooked pine trees twisted in the wind.

The accident. It flooded back in a flash of mental pictures.

Not an accident, though. It had been intentional. Someone had forced them off the road. She could scarcely remember the ambulance ride to Ocean Park Hospital. What had the doctor said about Hudson? "Concussion. Contusions. No broken bones . . ." That was right, wasn't it? Her memory was spotty, but she did recall she'd told the medical staff about her baby. Without thinking, she placed a protective hand over her abdomen and remembered the doctor saying there was no sign of miscarriage. *But where is Hudson now?*

Her heart was pounding irregularly, adrenaline and fear speeding through her bloodstream. She remembered well the feeling of doom that had been chasing her. The reason Renee had been killed was the same as the reason she and Hudson had been forced off the road.

Who is he? How am I connected to him?

She couldn't just lie here in bed.

He would never be stopped. Not if she didn't do it.

Though not a wimp, Becca had never been particularly brave, but now she felt a deep anger growing inside her. She had to thwart him. Stop him. Stop his murderous intent or he would eventually win—like he'd won with Jessie.

The answer lies at Siren Song. You know it. You felt it. That's why you didn't want to go.

The clock mounted on the wall said it was all of six-twenty in the morning, and from the sounds of rattling trays, carts, and gurneys coming from the hallway, the hospital was stirring. No time like the present.

She threw off the covers and sat up, pulling an IV taut in her wrist, one she hadn't noticed. Her head throbbed.

"Good morning." A woman's voice caught her attention and she looked toward the door. A nurse armed with a stethoscope and thermometer was entering the room. Her name tag read Nina Perez, R.N. Though her dark eyes were kind, there was a presence to her that suggested she was used to being the boss. "How're you feeling today?"

"I've been better."

"A little sore?"

More than a little. "I'm okay." Becca slid out of the bed, bare feet hitting the cool linoleum floor. "I need to find Hudson Walker," she explained. "I . . . I think he's here. A patient." Unless he was taken to another hospital. She had to find him. "He and I were in an accident. That's why I'm here and—"

"He's here. Recovering." Nurse Perez offered a steady, sincere smile and Becca felt a smidgen of relief. "You can see him soon."

"But I need to talk to him now." *To see for myself that he's really all right, that whatever horror I led him into, he's now safe.*

"You will. First let's take your vitals."

"No!" Becca snapped. "Really, I have—I have to see him."

"No problem." But, despite her words, Nurse Perez wasn't budging. "I just need to check your temp and BP. See if your pulse is normal."

Of course it's not normal! I've been through hell and back. Someone's trying to kill me, to kill my baby, to kill Hudson. There is no normal here. None at all!

"And . . . and the baby?" She needed to be reassured.

"You're still pregnant," the nurse said. "No sign of trauma. Your arm wound is the worst of your injuries."

Becca glanced at the bandage over her bicep. Her arm was sore.

"We do need to monitor you." Perez's voice was firm, her hand steady as she shepherded Becca back to the bed and inserted a thermometer under her tongue.

Becca didn't argue. She wasn't going to risk the baby's health, but she felt anxious. Edgy. "I need to see Hudson," she insisted once the nurse had read the thermometer, then taken her pulse.

"You will." She slid a blood pressure cuff onto Becca's uninjured arm. Once she was satisfied that she wasn't going to stroke out, she unwrapped the cuff, then removed her IV and said, "Okay. I'll see what I can do. But you have to be careful. A concussion isn't anything to take lightly."

Becca nodded, but as soon as the nurse slipped out the door, she searched for her shoes.

Her need to visit Hudson, to see for herself that he was all right, was pressing. She frowned at the state of her clothes, hung in a tiny closet, still damp and stained with mud and blood. Stripping off her hospital gown, she stepped gingerly into her grimy jeans.

But she had no purse.

No makeup.

No ID.

No credit cards.

No cash.

Not a damned thing.

Nurse Perez popped her head through the open door. "Mr. Walker is in room 212," she said, then eyeing Becca's outfit, frowned. "No other clothes came with you . . ."

"It's all right. But I do need my purse?"

"I think we have that in a locker. Got it from the sheriff's department early this morning. You can't leave the hospital until you're released. I just talked to the doctor and he'll be by in about an hour, but it looks like you'll be on your way. I've already ordered release papers."

"Thanks. 212?" she repeated and at the nurse's nod Becca hurried out, albeit a bit stiffly. Two orderlies pushing patients in wheelchairs were at the elevator, so she took the stairs, wound around the carpeted corridor, then found Hudson's room. She walked inside and saw him sleeping upon the bed. His head was bandaged, his face already bruising, an IV and some kind of monitor hooked up to him, snakelike tubes running in several directions at once.

"Can I help you?" a tall, lanky male nurse asked.

She introduced herself and explained that she'd been with Hudson in the accident. He took her at face value, giving out some basic information. None of Hudson's injuries appeared to be life-threatening, though he was still sedated and sleeping. Aside from bruised ribs, a slight concussion caused by the blow over his right ear, and a separated shoulder that had already been reset, Hudson, in time, would be fine. "It's best if he rests," the nurse concluded, so Becca only took the time to touch Hudson's hand and give it a squeeze before leaving the room. "Come back in a few hours."

"I will," she promised and, ignoring her own throbbing head, hurried to the discharge desk where she was reunited with her purse. When she asked about her overnight bag and clothes, she was told that everything in the car, aside from the purse, which the police had already looked through, was considered evidence. "I'm sure they'll get it back to you soon."

Becca wasn't about to wait. She couldn't.

And she wasn't about to leave Hudson. She pulled out her cell phone, realized it had been turned off, and checked for incoming messages. There were six. All from Detective Sam McNally, all asking her to call him. Vaguely she remembered him saying he'd been trying to reach her. She phoned him now but was sent directly to voicemail. She left a message, giving him the name of the motel she and Hudson had stayed at the last time she'd visited this hospital as to where he could find her. She trusted him now. Completely.

Funny how a few weeks and a couple of murders changed her perception.

She placed a few other calls, including a local rental car company advertising "cheap, slightly worn cars," her insurance agent, and her own answering machine at her house. Mac had called there once and Tamara had left a "Just checking in, call me," message.

Not now, Becca thought.

The rental car, an ancient dented Chevy, was delivered, thankfully, and she drove to the motel to secure her room, then to a local outlet mall where she picked up a change of clothes, some toiletries, PowerBars, and a six-pack of juice. Back at the motel she showered and changed into clean clothes, then downed one of the PowerBars and a couple of pain relievers and put together a pot of decaf coffee from the pre-measured packet provided by the management. Once fueled, she returned to the hospital, determined to run Hudson's doctor to the ground, but she was waylaid by two detectives, a man and a woman, from the Tillamook County Sheriff's Department, who also wanted to speak to him.

Hudson was still asleep, but the detectives, who were waiting at the door to his room, realized who she was and decided to interview her first. They'd gotten some information the night before, but they wanted something more to go on in order to find who had run her off the road, then chased her through the dark forest.

They all sat in a waiting area not far from the second-floor nurses' station and Hudson's room. Aside from a few scattered plastic chairs, a fake plant, and a coffee table littered with old magazines, the area was empty. As the woman detective, who introduced herself as Marcia Kirkpatrick, took a few notes and asked questions, her partner, a husky silver-haired cop in his fifties, Fred Clausen, studied her intently, only interjecting a few questions of his own for clarification.

"You didn't see your attacker?" Kirkpatrick asked. She was trim, fit, with sharp features and thin, unpainted lips.

"I saw him, or his form," Becca said, "but it was dark in the forest and raining, no moonlight. I caught a glimpse of him in the headlights once, but he was dressed in black or dark blue and wearing a hood." She thought about the image she'd seen in her visions, superimposed it over those of the man who had chased her to the ground the night before, and thought it was her assailant. But that picture was all in her mind and had no merit. She wasn't comfortable enough with these two cops to admit that she "saw" things. They'd dismiss her as a nutcase. Hands clasped between her knees, she said, "All I have are impressions."

"How tall is he?" Kirkpatrick asked.

"Six feet, maybe six-one. Big."

"Heavy? Slight?" Reddish eyebrows lifted as she skewered Becca with her gaze.

"Neither. I know that he was fit. Never seemed to get winded . . ." She called up his dogged pursuit, the cold terror that had consumed her. "It seemed that he was athletic. I can't tell you how old he was, but not a kid, nor an old guy. He moved too quickly. Was too strong." She remembered the pure hatred she felt emanating from him. "He wanted me dead."

"How do you know?" Clausen asked.

Her stomach roiled and she thought she might be sick. "Because I'm the target. This might sound like I'm reaching, but something like this happened a long time ago. About sixteen years ago, not far from the same place. I was forced off the road . . . I think it's the same man."

"You think the same guy was chasing you then, nearly twenty years ago, but you've been living in the Portland area ever since and he hasn't bothered you?" Kirkpatrick was understandably skeptical.

"He failed the first time."

Clausen exchanged a look with Kirkpatrick, who twisted her pen, then clicked it several times. "But he hasn't accosted you since."

"Not until last night. But that's because of Jessie."

"Who's Jessie?" Clausen asked.

"Jezebel Brentwood. She was a friend of mine in high school."

"The girl whose bones were just discovered," Clausen said, his interest piqued. "The one the Laurelton cop McNally was here asking about." He was nodding now. "McNally thinks there's a relationship between her death and Renee Trudeau's."

They were catching on quickly now.

"Renee is—was Hudson's sister." Becca hitched her chin toward the door to his room.

"If you're the target, then why kill her?"

"I don't know. I think . . . I think it has something to do with Jessie's murder." Becca went on to explain the links, as she saw them, that Renee was digging into the past and had riled up the murderer, who then focused on her.

It had sounded so much more solid before she said it aloud. It was impossible to explain.

"Back to last night," Kirkpatrick said, her eyes narrowing. "This guy who chased you, did he say anything to you?"

"He called me 'sister.' Said he was God's messenger."

"Hmmm. Maybe 'sister' as in the 'we're all sisters and brothers' communal sense?" the woman cop suggested.

"It seemed more personal, but . . ." She shrugged.

"He say anything else?" Clausen asked.

She closed her eyes, remembered. "He called me the 'Spawn of Satan,' I think, then later said 'Jezebel and Rebecca.' "

"Did any of it seem to make sense?" Kirkpatrick asked.

When Becca shook her head, Clausen said, "Sounds like he talks to God, or is doing the Big Guy's bidding." Clausen kept his expression neutral.

Kirkpatrick's eyes held Becca's. "Would you recognize his voice?"

"I don't know," she said, but as she remembered her struggle and panic, she nodded. "I couldn't pick him out of a lineup, but I think I would recognize his voice." And the thought of it made her shiver. She prayed she'd never see him again, never hear the horrid, snakelike sound of his whispered curses.

"But you don't remember anything that would make him identifiable? No tattoos or scars or facial characteristics."

Becca shook her head. "I didn't see him, but I do know that I knocked him good with that rock. He staggered and it gave me time to run. He may have some damage. A black eye or bruised forehead or something."

"Anything that would send him to seek medical attention?" the woman detective posed hopefully.

"No."

"Doesn't sound like that kind of guy, even if he needed it," Clausen agreed.

After a few more questions about her confrontation, hoping to learn something more about her attacker, anything that might help, they gave up. Clausen promised to return to speak with Hudson when he awoke. "If you think of anything else, call," Clausen insisted and handed her his card.

"I think you'd better see this." Gretchen, subdued for her, waved Mac over to her desk.

"Just a sec." He headed for the break room and a cup of coffee before wending his way back to Gretchen through the maze of desks where cops were already on phones, booking suspects, going over notes, and shuffling paperwork.

Even the Homicide Department was cranking it up. Aside from the regular caseload there had been a fight in one of the local watering holes. Another drug deal gone bad, and one twenty-three-year-old had been stabbed and died on the way to the hospital. Another couple of kids had been drag racing on 26. A bad accident, one kid in the hospital, not expected to make it, another dead. The driver, of course, suffered a few cuts and a broken leg.

Gretchen was seated at her desk, printouts spread upon the neat surface, her computer screen glowing.

"I'm not here long," he said, yawning, stopping close enough to look over her shoulder. He was driving back to the beach after a perfunctory appearance at the station. He'd been up half the night after dealing with Hudson and Becca's accident, and he'd been back and forth on the phone with the Tillamook County Sheriff's Department and rereading the notes he'd taken.

He'd dropped off Levi and Ringo with Connie on his way to work this morning and Connie, in her gracious way, had said, "This is emotional blackmail, telling Levi that he can keep the dog here when you know I'll be the one taking care of it."

"For a day. I should be back tonight."

"Should," she repeated. "I know you, Sam. You'll get caught up in this case, this same damned case involving that Brentwood girl, and you'll lose track of time, or have to go . . . investigate something somewhere and you'll leave me holding the bag again."

"One. One day. That's all." Over her shoulder he saw into her house, warm light glowing softly, the corner of a modern green couch, the smell of cinnamon and some other spices wafting from the kitchen. "You just have to keep the dog one day. He belongs to a victim. As soon as she's out of the hospital she'll want him back."

"Haven't you ever heard of the damned pound? Isn't that where strays are usually kept?"

"He's not a stray." Mac's patience was thinning.

"And one way or the other, I end up the bad guy. Damned

if I do, damned if I don't." Connie's face was getting redder by the second.

"I'll be back tonight."

"Tom's allergic," she said, folding her arms under her breasts and looking imperiously down from the doorway, but Mac was already halfway to his Jeep.

He'd known she would keep the dog. Not for him. But for Levi.

Now Gretchen pointed to one of the copies of documents she'd dug up. "You tell Rebecca Sutcliff that Jessie Brentwood's her sister?"

"Haven't had a chance yet."

She snorted. "Look at this. Rebecca Sutcliff . . . I've done a little digging on her. Remember that bone spur we found on Jezebel Brentwood's skeleton?"

"Yeah." He was interested.

"Rebecca Sutcliff has one, too."

"You have her medical records?"

"Ummm. You heard her tell the paramedics she was in an accident sixteen years ago. Same kind of thing, run off the road. Guess which road." She looked up at him.

He was lifting his cup to his lips but hesitated. "You're shittin' me." He knew what she was going to say before the words crossed her lips.

"I'm definitely not. She was run off the road not far from Elsie on Highway 26, but taken to a hospital in Portland."

"Ocean Park wasn't much then," he said, wired by the new information and looking closer as she moved from one computer screen to the next.

"Anyway, I got the medical report. She was relatively unhurt, but pregnant and lost the baby."

"Shit."

"And there was a report of a bone spur . . . same spot as Jezebel Brentwood's. And so I did a little more checking, pulled military records on her father, medical records on her mother, and here's the kicker. They both have O positive blood; Rebecca Ryan is B neg."

"They aren't her parents," he said flatly.

"Not biologically."

"So she and Jessie have the same parents, but they're not the Ryans."

"Both of 'em must have come through the same adoption agency, or attorney, or whatever."

"In Portland? How'd they both end up at St. Elizabeth's?" Mac wondered.

"Coincidence, maybe. Jessie was a runaway and had burned through a lot of schools by the time she was sent to St. Lizzie's."

"The Brentwoods don't like to talk about her. Don't want to mention her adoption or anything about it."

Gretchen gazed at him through her narrowed Siamese cat eyes. "Think the asswipe that ran Sutcliff and Walker off the road last night knows something about this?"

Mac actually grinned at her. "You're starting to think like me, Sandler. Making connections out of nothing."

"Not such a leap. You think he's the same guy who stabbed Jessie."

"He's certainly a person of interest."

As he headed for the door, she yelled, "Bring me back some saltwater taffy this time, cheap ass."

Becca hung around the hospital and waited. She'd just grabbed a cup of decaf tea and a newspaper at a kiosk in the lobby when her phone rang. She caught the glare of an older woman with a fluff of white hair piled high on her head who silently dared her to answer. The woman's gaze moved to a sign stating the hospital was a "cell phone free zone" and Becca took the hint as she checked Caller ID. Seeing the number was Sam McNally's, she answered as she walked across a carpeted hall and through the automatic doors of the main entrance to the outside.

She wasn't alone. Another man was nearly yelling into his phone while he paced back and forth and smoked.

"Hello?" she said. "Detective."

"How are you doing?"

"Okay, everything considered."

"And Hudson?"

"He's going to be fine. How's Ringo? And your son?"

McNally brought her up to date quickly on where Ringo was and how Levi had surprised him by rising to the "animal responsibility" level so fast. They were both with his ex-wife for the day. At least Ringo was safe, she thought as the rain slowly let up and the guy who'd been nearly screaming into his phone had walked back inside.

"Where are you?"

"Still at the hospital."

"Wait for me. Coming your direction. It won't be more than fifteen minutes."

"Sure."

She hung up and walked back in to check on Hudson, who was groggily coming to. He managed a faint grin at the sight of her. "You're okay?"

"Yeah."

"And—?" His gaze drifted to her abdomen.

"Baby's fine."

Some of the tension left his face and she wondered how she'd have broken the news to him if she'd lost their unborn child. *Like before. How will you ever tell him about the first baby? About the accident, so like this most recent one, that caused the miscarriage?*

She looked into his eyes, heavy with pain and medication, the scruffy stubble on his chin barely hiding bruises already forming. Today wasn't the day to bring up an old sadness.

"Hey," she said, leaning over and brushing her lips across his forehead.

Hudson reached a hand up and kept her close to him. "Did they find him?"

"I don't think so. Not yet. McNally was there."

"Where?"

"He was coming from the beach, and if he hadn't shown up, I don't know what would have happened." She filled him in on the events of the night before that he'd missed, brushing over some of her own terror, though the way his blue eyes bored into hers, she didn't think she was fooling him.

"I'm going to kill that son of a bitch. The next time he messes with us, I'm going to rip his damned head off."

"I think Jessie would agree with you," Becca said lightly. "That's what she's been trying to tell me: justice. She wants justice."

"You saw her?"

"And so did he. He called us by name, Jezebel and Rebecca."

"What the hell does that mean?"

She heard a soft cough behind her and turned to find the two detectives from the sheriff's department in the doorway. "Looks like you're wanted," she whispered. "I'll be back later."

While the detectives entered the room, she headed down the stairs. Her cell phone jangled and she picked up to hear Tamara's worried voice on the other end of the wireless connection.

"Are you all right? What about Hudson? O-my-gawd, I just heard about your accident on the news. That you were forced off the road. Just like Renee!"

"We're okay," Becca assured her and lingered in the hallway near a side door. "I mean, I am. Hudson's going to be out of commission for a bit." She sketched out the details of the last twenty-four hours, but she omitted the part about Siren Song; no need to go into that. She didn't even know what it meant yet herself.

Her one-sided conversation was interjected with Tamara's

remarks. "Are you kidding me . . . But who's after you . . . Do you think it has anything to do with Jessie . . . You know, she was right, there does seem to be a damned curse . . . Don't you need, like, police protection or something?"

"I just need to figure out what's going on," Rebecca said and thought about Siren Song. Her earlier fear and aversion to the place had been replaced by an overriding anger. Like Hudson, she wanted to nail the son of a bitch.

"Don't you think you should come back home?"

"Not without Hudson," she said and left it at that. She couldn't confide in Tamara, couldn't confide in anyone. Not until she had more answers.

She stepped through a side door where the wind tugged at her new hooded sweatshirt and the air was heavy with moisture. She was just wondering what was holding up McNally when she saw the detective heading toward the front door of the hospital. He veered toward her and they met on a cement path that led to an adjoining building that housed other clinics.

"Glad you showed up last night," she said seriously.

His hands were in his pockets and he looked as if he'd aged ten years in as many hours. Unshaven and rumpled, a bit of gray showing in his hair, dark smudges under his eyes—clearly he hadn't slept much. But then, neither had she. She wasn't too interested in holding a mirror up to her face.

"Look," he said, "is there somewhere we could go and talk privately?"

"There's a coffee kiosk in the lobby and some tables. I don't know how private it is . . ."

"It'll do."

They walked through a set of automatic glass doors behind a couple of nurses, heads bent against the wind, their uniforms visible beneath their coats, who were deep in conversation. "I'll buy," McNally said, and Becca asked for decaf black coffee.

A few minutes later he joined Becca at a table she'd chosen because it sat away from the rest a little bit. He handed her one of the paper cups and gazed at her soberly.

"What do you want to tell me?" she asked, suddenly scared. "Oh, God, did someone die? Another wreck?"

"Nothing like that, trust me, and your dog is fine. Getting excellent care." He paused, then said, "Tell me about your parents."

"My parents," she said blankly. "What do you want to know?"

He frowned. Hesitated, then looked her squarely in the eye. "Your blood type doesn't match to either Barbara Metzger Ryan or James Ryan. It would be impossible for you to be their biological child."

Rebecca just stared at him. "Where is this going?"

But she knew. She *knew.* She belonged with those people, as did Jessie. They were connected. Both of them. Connected to *him*!

Her mind spun backward to the night before. "Sister," the beast had called her. *Sister.* Had he meant it—literally?

She was trembling.

"You look like one of them," the old lady had said as she'd placed her gnarled fingers over Becca's flat abdomen. "Siren Song."

Chapter Twenty-Five

"Ms. Sutcliff? Becca?" McNally asked, seeing her face pale, her attention turn inward.

She pulled herself back with an effort. "You're saying I'm adopted."

"Yes."

She was related to the colony members at Siren Song. Related to that girl who looked so much like Jessie. A question trembled on her tongue. Something so bizarre, and yet it made a peculiar kind of sense.

Before she could ask it, however, McNally gave her the answer. "We have a DNA match," he said. He told her about the lab results, as well as the bone spur on her rib that was identical to Jessie's. "You're Jessie Brentwood's sister."

"A DNA match," she repeated.

"Your parents and Jessie's were the same two people," he added for clarification.

"How can this be?" Becca murmured, but the tumblers started clicking into place. She looked like Jessie in some ways. She shared a strange and troubling extra ability with her—her visions; Jessie's precognition. Jessie came to her in visions that were real enough to make her believe they were a message.

McNally was talking, saying Jessie might have come looking for Becca, that she was a runaway and had attended more schools than not around the Portland area, that she was maybe running to something, rather than away from it.

"No." Becca cut him off. "She was running from him."

"Him? The guy who ran you off the road last night?"

"Yes."

He nodded, watching her closely, as if he expected her to fall apart. "I've talked to the Brentwoods several times. They're not very forthcoming about Jessie's adoption."

"My parents never even told me." She made a sound of disbelief, then sank into another long silence while her mind rearranged pieces of her life like a jigsaw puzzle, trying it this way and that, discarding a piece, picking up another, moving it around.

"You do resemble her," McNally pointed out.

Is that why Hudson "loves" me? Is that what he sees in me? She'd always wondered, and now it seemed a likely bet.

DNA was irrefutable. She believed McNally.

She stared into her untouched cup of coffee and felt as if her life, everything she'd ever held to be true, was crumbling at her feet. Why had her parents lied to her?

"Jessie never knew," she said. *Until after her death.*

McNally nodded.

Becca swallowed. Hadn't she always known she was different? Suspected that because of her visions, there was something in her past she didn't know or understand?

Her hand tightened over her cup. Her whole life had been built on lies, and because of it she could not have predicted that this monster would relentlessly chase her down.

"He killed her," Becca said with certainty. "He had a knife last night. He wanted to kill me but then he saw her and it stopped him."

"Saw who?"

"Jessie. In a vision. Did I tell you I have visions? That I see Jessie standing on a cliff's edge, whispering to me? She wants justice, and I think she wants me to end it once and for all with this demon who won't let us be!"

"Let the police do their job," McNally said quickly, clearly thinking she was going to charge out on her own.

And wasn't she? Wasn't that what she was thinking? Didn't she feel the urgency inside her breast that was like an angry, living thing?

"We're looking for him. He drove off, but his vehicle had to sustain damage. I believe you said it was white or tan?"

"The grill guard," Becca said suddenly. "His truck had a grill guard."

"A grill guard," he repeated. "Maybe detachable, if he used the same vehicle to push Renee Trudeau's off the road."

"It was damaged. It was scraped."

"Do you remember anything else? Something else that might help? Any little thing?"

She gazed at him a long time. McNally waited, wondering what was coming down the pike now. At length, she said, "I think the answer is in Deception Bay. I think he lives there."

"Any particular reason?"

She almost told him about Siren Song. He hadn't blinked when she'd mentioned her visions, but that only meant he was just taking in information, it wasn't proof that he believed her. He could think she was the biggest nutcase in the world.

"There's one more thing," Mac said, drawing her back to the here and now. "You said this has happened before to you. That you were run off the road the last time you were pregnant."

Her head snapped up. He *knew*?

"You told the paramedics and I overheard," he explained, correctly guessing her feelings. "That accident was about sixteen years ago on the same stretch of road. My partner looked it up. Was Walker the father?"

She felt as if the life had been squeezed out of her. "Yes," she whispered, nodding, "but I've never told him. If you plan on breaking that news, I should do it first."

"If there's a pattern, he needs to know."

"There's a pattern."

"Then you need to tell him now."

Becca couldn't move for a moment. Every ache and pain sustained from the night before seemed to manifest itself ten times over. With the low-level energy of the elderly, she rose from her chair and headed back to Hudson's room.

Hudson ached all over.

When he shifted in the bed, there didn't seem to be an inch on his body that wasn't in pain. He looked at the chart next to his bed, a sequence of "happy" and "not-so-happy" faces indicating where his pain medications should keep him. He was supposed to be in the kinda happy zone, and he definitely was not. But the nurse had just been in and adjusted his IV drip, so things would improve. The detectives from the sheriff's department had already taken off as well.

It had been a frustrating interrogation. He'd learned little, and, he suspected, they'd learned less from him. A no-win/no-win situation, leaving both the cops and him discouraged.

He itched to get out of this place, to start looking for that unhinged jerk who had run them off the road and most probably killed Renee. But try as he might, he couldn't convince the doctor to release him. Whenever he asked a nurse or physician when he could be released, he'd been met with a "soon" or "possibly later today" or "probably tomorrow." He wanted out and he wanted out now. It worried him that Becca was still hanging out here, where all the trouble had started, where Renee had been investigating before she'd been killed, where the attacker had already tried once to kill them. What was to stop him now?

And what did it mean that both Becca *and* her attacker had seen a vision of Jessie?

Hudson cursed his luck, tried to move and felt another sharp pain slice through his shoulder. He forced his eyes closed so that he could think and plan. Somehow he had to nail the son of a bitch who'd attacked them before the lunatic got another shot.

The medication had just started to kick in when the door to his room opened and Becca let herself inside. He'd never been so glad to see anyone in his life. "Hey," he said, sliding over as best he could. "I think there's room for two up here."

"Yeah, right," she said and managed a bit of a smile.

"I'd make it worth your while."

"Must be the pain meds talking."

"Seriously."

"Well, that's just it," she said, her smile sliding away. "I do want to talk to you. Seriously."

He saw a shadow cross her eyes and wondered what was coming now. Something else had happened! Another one of their friends killed? Someone they knew?

Reading the alarm in his eyes, she grabbed his good hand and said, "It's not that bad. Relax." And then she told him about bone spurs and DNA and the fact that it looked like she'd been adopted, had never been told the truth, and had no idea who her biological parents were.

And she told him she and Jessie were sisters.

"What?" Hudson was stunned.

"We're both from Siren Song," she said. "Both of us. Those are our people, and they're his."

"I don't believe you," he declared, but he was lying.

"There's something else."

"Something else?" he asked in disbelief.

She took in a deep breath. "Something I should have told you a long, long time ago."

"Okay . . ." Her tone sharpened his attention.

"Remember the last time we were together? After high school?"

"Yeah," he said.

She was nodding and he saw a sheen in her eyes. Tears?

"We were together all the time," she said thickly.

He nodded.

She hesitated.

The hospital room seemed to close in on him and the noises from the hallway outside receded. "What, Becca?" he asked and realized she was squeezing his hand so hard he felt it through the smooth haze of whatever painkiller was seeping into his IV.

"I was pregnant," she said, her face white and twisted.

"What?"

"With your baby, Hudson. Just a few months, but very definitely pregnant."

He heard the thudding of his own heart and noticed that her fingers, where they were clenched to his, were sweating. "So what happened to the baby?" he asked, but he knew as surely as if he'd heard the words. The baby hadn't survived. He stared at her and felt a gnawing ache deep in his gut. Not for one second did he disbelieve her—all her raw emotions were etched across her skin.

"I'm sorry," she whispered, her nose red. "The baby died in a horrible car crash. An attack, really. I miscarried." She cleared her throat and blinked back tears. "I should have told you," she said in a whispered rush. "Before. Afterward . . . there didn't really seem any reason to."

"Didn't you think I'd want to know?"

"I wasn't sure what you wanted, Hudson," she admitted, looking toward the ceiling and blinking rapidly. "You were just so . . . distant. I thought you didn't want me and I was pretty sure you wouldn't want a baby."

Hudson closed his eyes. The roller-coaster ride of the past few months had just taken another dip. He'd thought Jessie had been pregnant with his child, and then that had proved untrue. But now to learn that Becca had been . . . and she hadn't trusted him enough to tell him?

You weren't exactly reliable in those days, Walker.

But his child—his kid—would be sixteen years old now, nearly graduated from high school, and he and Becca . . . who knew? It was true that he hadn't known what he'd wanted at that time in his life; that he was still messed up over Jessie. Still guilt-riddled for wanting Becca when Jessie had seemed to fall off the face of the earth.

"You were forced off the road, just like we were last night?" he asked.

"Yes."

"You think it's no coincidence."

"No." She was tense, her jaw tight. "He won't stop, Hudson. I'm sorry. I should have told you, but he's—"

Rap! Rap! Rap!

Becca turned toward the door just as it swung open and Hudson's gaze followed. He was frustrated. He needed to talk to her, and his frustration increased when he saw his friends Jarrett and The Third swing into the room.

"I thought since Scott was in jail all this life-threatening crap would quit," The Third said. "What the hell happened?"

"Trying to figure it out," Hudson said, looking at Becca.

She knew he needed to talk more to her, but then Zeke entered the room, looking as if he'd lost ten pounds and aged as many years, and the conversation took off.

Becca took the opportunity to extricate herself from Hudson. She'd given him a hell of a lot to think about, and she wanted to make up her own mind about what to do next without his cynosure. "I'll be back later," she said.

"When?" he demanded.

"Soon."

"And you're letting McNally handle things, right?"

"Right."

She slipped out of the room before he could protest, leav-

ing him with his friends and a thundercloud of frustration
darkening his expression.

Becca jogged across the parking lot to her beater of a
rental car while a million questions chased after her. Jessie's
family had lived here. Jessie had known she was adopted.
Jessie's adoptive parents had owned a second place in Deception Bay. The people at Siren Song resembled her and
were secretive. Renee had been killed for what she learned.

Becca climbed into the rental, jabbed her keys into the ignition, and took off through the puddles of the parking lot.
The rain had stopped but clouds covered the sky, melding to
the ocean and obscuring the horizon. She drove toward Deception Bay. That's where all the lies, deceit, and murder began.
In a sleepy little coastal village shrouded in secrets and lies.

She turned off 101 and drove down the desolate main
street of town. Could she really have been born here? Even
lived here in this tiny fishing village? A part of Siren Song.
She'd known it felt familiar.

She parked not far from the Sands of Thyme bakery,
which, like so many of the businesses, was closed. Climbing
from the rental, she noticed that for once not a breath of
breeze stirred through the streets, and the fog bank sitting
out to sea seemed to ride slowly inland on the back of the
swells.

Shivering inside, she pulled her sweatshirt more tightly
around her. *The calm before the storm.*

Cold dread climbed up her spine and she wondered if she
really wanted to uncover the truth, to pick apart its onion-
skin thin layers of lies. How many people had tried to keep
her from knowing the circumstances of her birth, and why
had it inflamed one maniac enough that he would kill and
kill again?

Was she related to him? Was he after both her and Jessie?
Were they both the spawn of Satan?

She walked toward the ocean and felt the oozing sensation of déjà vu slither through her mind. Could she really have lived here?

That's where the answers lay: Siren Song.

That's where she needed to go for answers.

She felt a sudden breath of icy air upon the back of her neck and turned to look over her shoulder.

He was there.

Dark, hidden in shadows, he stood with feet wide spread and looked into her mind.

"Hey!" a man's voice yelled and she turned. "Watch out!" A pickup was stopped at an intersection, ready to move forward, except that she was standing in the middle of the street, blocking the road. "Lady, are you okay?"

Her head cleared. "Sorry."

"Friggin' locals. All a bunch of whack jobs," the guy in the pickup said under his breath as he drove past.

If you only knew, Becca thought, still quaking inside as she looked toward the corner and the spruce tree where she'd seen the man she was certain had tried to take her life. "Brother," she said, and the word tasted foul.

Had she seen him? Had she? She'd certainly sensed his presence, but did that mean he was actually here?

Drawing a long breath, Becca shook it off. There was no time to waste. She needed to get to Siren Song and find the answers. Now.

The doctor wasn't going to release him, but Hudson couldn't stay cooped up another minute. He decided that he'd sign whatever releases he needed to, absolve the hospital, doctor, and any damned hospital worker who had stuck his or her head into the room of any liability, and walk out on his own two legs.

He'd already convinced Zeke to loan him his wheels.

Zeke had been reluctant, and though Hudson couldn't blame him, he was on a mission. And yes, he'd played on Zeke's guilt, so that his one-time friend had handed over the keys to his vintage Mustang to a man with one arm who was sporting a bad attitude and was loaded up on pain meds. The Third had told Zeke he was crazy, but Zeke had snapped back, "Just gimme a ride back, okay?"

"Vangie waiting for you at home?" Jarrett asked meanly.

"No."

Hudson hadn't wanted them to disintegrate into high school one-upmanship, so he'd stated firmly, "Zeke and Vangie are through. Nothing more to say about it."

And then he'd taken his request one step further, asking for Zeke's cell phone. "Mine was lost in the accident," Hudson explained, and Zeke slapped it into his hand, holding his gaze.

"We square, then?" Zeke asked.

There were a lot of things Hudson could have said, a lot more recriminations. But like Zeke and Vangie, it was time to simply move on. "We're good."

As soon as they were gone, he climbed from the bed. Pain shot up his arm and his head ached like a hammer was striking an anvil somewhere behind his eyes. Bad idea. And yet, the only idea. He didn't care how much it cost him, he needed to leave. He needed to find out if Becca was really depending on McNally, or if she'd taken matters into her own hands.

He was betting on the latter.

Filthy bitch!

I see her. Standing in the road. Now she turns away but rage boils my blood!

She must die. Now! I had planned to wait but that stupid old woman sped up the time line.

I cannot wait any longer.

Rebecca . . .

My head throbs like a heartbeat from the blow you gave me.

You will pay for that as well.

Bitch. Evil mother. I will kill you and your devil spawn.

I see you get in your car but you cannot escape your destiny.

But I must lay the trap.

You will come to me.

Very, very soon.

Becca drove toward Siren Song. She didn't have much of a game plan but seeing her nemesis—whether real or imagined—had spurred her on. She'd face the son of a bitch. Track him down. It was time for the hunter to be the prey.

If only Hudson were with her—but she didn't want him to be drawn into *her* battle. She'd already risked his life. He was lying in a hospital bed because of it.

The afternoon was dark enough to seem like night. For a moment she considered calling McNally. She reached for her purse and her cell phone, but then hesitated.

And what're you going to tell him? That you feel *him?*

She would seem as crazy as Mad Maddie. More so.

Gritting her teeth, Becca bumped up the pothole-riddled land to the gates of Siren Song.

Where Renee had sought information on Jessie's past.

Where it had all begun.

The wrought-iron barrier was closed, of course, and, as it was getting dark, she couldn't see much beyond the outline of the lodge. She climbed out of the rental and stepped to the gates. "Hello?" she yelled. "Anyone there?"

She waited, yelled again, then waited some more. After twenty minutes, she went back to the rental. There was no daylight left now, so she switched on her headlights, pointing them through the black fencing as the mist rose and swirled in the twin beams that cut through the tall fencing. The side door and a stone path were illuminated and the arms of surrounding trees seemed to reach inward in long fingers.

She honked the horn of her car, and it sounded like the pathetic bleat of a dying lamb over the dull roar of the Pacific, which could be heard as if it were right next door.

Should she try and scale the fence with its pointed arrow-like spikes piercing upward? She honked again and this time there was movement, a flash of color in her headlights.

What if it's him?

You didn't think of that, did you?

What if you've walked into a trap? You have no weapon, nothing to protect yourself.

She started the car, but as she did, she saw the same girl who had been at the gate before appear in her headlights. Tonight she was wearing a long coat with a hood. She stared at Becca with wide eyes. Jessie's eyes.

Becca clambered out of the rental and approached the gate.

"You need to leave," the girl said in a quiet voice.

"I can't."

"Drive away. Now."

"Jessie Brentwood came here years ago, and someone else just recently, a reporter. With dark, short hair. Renee Trudeau. She wanted information on Jessie."

"She did not come in."

"You didn't let her in," Becca realized.

"It wasn't safe."

"But she knew this is where Jessie came from. I think I came from here, too." The girl gazed at Becca soulfully. Becca had no idea what she was thinking. "Can't I come in?" Becca cajoled. "I just have so many questions."

"It's not safe for you, either."

"Do you know who I am?"

She glanced behind her, then down at her feet. "Rebecca . . ."

Becca's pulse jumped. "Look, I think . . . I think I might

be related to someone here and it's very important that I find him."

Jessie saw the girl's eyes dilate, the pupils making her eyes two black orbs with the faintest halo of color around them. "You won't find him here," she said.

"You know who I'm talking about?"

The girl hesitated. "You've met Madeline?"

"Yes," Becca said, surprised by the non sequitur. "But I'm looking for someone else and it's really important. People have died. I need to find him."

She half turned away.

"No, wait!" Becca called, but she was already leaving.

She stopped when she was about thirty feet away. "Whoever you're looking for is not here."

"How do you know?"

"Because you asked for 'him,' " she said without inflection. "There are no men at Siren Song."

Chapter Twenty-Six

Hudson stared at the pimply-faced clerk on the other side of the faux-wood counter in the lobby of the tired-looking motel where he, Becca, and Ringo had stayed only a few short weeks ago. A striped yellow tabby viewed the interplay with utter disdain from the back of a worn couch as the clerk, who was all of fourteen or so, gazed at him in consternation.

"I—I—can't talk about our guests. It's, um, the privacy policy." The kid kept looking over his shoulder, hoping someone would come to the rescue while the cat yawned and stretched his legs.

"I'm her fiancé," Hudson tried. A stretch maybe, but close enough, and the next time he saw her, he damned well was going to ask her to marry him. He'd spent too many hours in the hospital wondering about her, worrying about her, loving her, to let her go again.

"Do you, like, have some kind of proof or somethin'?" The kid's gaze slid to the sling supporting Hudson's left arm, and Hudson realized he looked like hell in his filthy clothes, disheveled hair, and scruffy beard. He probably appeared to the kid to be one of those loner, killer types from the movies.

But Hudson was too panicked, too sick with worry to go into it or explain anything. Time was running out. "Just tell me what unit she's in."

"Grandpa?" the boy called nervously over his shoulder to the open door at the back.

"What?" a male voice bellowed.

"I, uh, could use a little help out here."

With a huge sigh, "Grandpa," a large man built like Humpty Dumpty, shuffled into view. Suspenders looped from his faded denim pants, doing nothing as they dangled uselessly from his waist. A thin, tank-style T-shirt was half covered by an open flannel shirt. He peered over the tops of half-glasses. "What's the problem?"

Irritated, Hudson repeated his request. "My fiancée checked in earlier. I'm supposed to meet her, but I don't know what room she's in."

The man swiped a hand over the graying stubble on his jaw, started to argue, then said, "Oh, forget it. A woman checked into unit seven today. I can't let you in, but I can go there myself. You can come along." He glanced out the window. "But I'd bet Butterfinger over there," he said, nodding to the orange tabby, "that she's not in. Her car's missing. No lights on. No television, either."

The kid walked over to pick up the cat, stroking its head.

Butterfinger snuggled up to the boy, his long tail twitching as he, too, gave Grandpa Humpty the evil eye. Gramps found a baseball cap and jacket, then, with a jangling set of keys, waddled toward unit seven.

It was all Hudson could do not to run in front of him. The fact that Becca wasn't here made him crazy. Where was she? God, what was she doing? He had a deep, driving fear that she might be out baiting the madman. As they crossed the seedy parking lot, he tried her cell phone again.

Humpty cast him a look. "Cell service ain't great around here."

So get into the twenty-first century! But the man was right. He couldn't connect. Not with Becca and not with Mac, as he didn't have the detective's number on Zeke's phone.

The big man knocked on the door, and when no one answered, rapped again and said, "Hello? Ms. Sutcliff?" He opened the door, and the minute it swung inward Hudson could tell that Becca hadn't been in the room in a while. Packages were strewn on the bed, bags from a local all-in-one market. Her dirty clothes from the night before were stacked on a chair near the television stand. Grandpa Humpty nodded to himself as if he'd been an ace detective. "Whaddid I tell ya?" He looked over his shoulder at Hudson. "Maybe you should find yerself a new fiancée."

Hudson didn't stick around to listen. He was jogging across the parking lot, his shoulder screaming in pain, his jaw set. Once in Zeke's Mustang, he found his vial of pain pills, tossed a couple into his mouth, and swallowed them whole. He found the card the two detectives from the sheriff's department had given him, and dialed. They would have Mac's number or, if not, they could damned well help him themselves.

He had no proof.

They would have to take his word for it.

But Hudson was damned sure Becca was heading for trouble.

Trouble . . . Jessie's word.

The thought sent ice running through his veins.

What *was* Siren Song? Becca asked herself as she drove back toward Deception Bay proper. Her birthplace? A cult?

She eased the old Chevy through the streets of this sleepy little town where traffic was sparse. The wind, which hadn't existed a few hours earlier, was beginning to pick up, sharp gusts stirring the branches of trees and pushing litter and debris inland. Night had fallen in earnest and the few street-lights' bluish lights cast a pool of illumination down the main street.

But Becca was on her way to see Mad Maddie. The young woman at Siren Song had mentioned her name, almost like a direction to what Becca sought. And Renee had talked about the sometime psychic who'd warned her that she was marked for death. Becca herself had wanted to see her, but then had gotten sidetracked by the cult at Siren Song.

She turned her car northward. Driving mostly by instinct, she headed for the cliff area and the area she suspected was the old woman's home. She'd never been to Maddie's before but knew it was on the sea, so she only had to follow the road running along the shoreline. The beachfront road turned inland for a bit as it climbed away from the downtown area and the sandy crescent that was connected to the bay at the south end of town.

She recognized the old motel the minute she turned the corner, so she eased the car onto the pockmarked gravel lot. A few lights were shining on the long, low building, an old motel, situated on a ridge overlooking the dark, whitecapped ocean. Another storm was in full force now, wind screaming, rain on its way.

Becca wasn't sure what she was going to say to the old woman. Something about "Mad Maddie" was definitely off. But Mad Maddie had first mentioned Siren Song to Becca, so the connection between her and the cult members existed.

From one end of the building, a light glowed. Or was it illumination from a television? A silvery blue flickering patch of light came from the window of the end unit. The manager's home, if the battered vacancy sign was to be believed. The other apartments, eight or ten "homey cottages with cable TV," were connected by vacant carports that were dilapidated and weathered and worn. Peeling gray paint covered rusted gutters that had worked themselves loose and swung and groaned in the wind that rose above the sea. The motel was untended and unkempt. Tall beach grass and berry vines encroached, the concrete was cracked and fissured, the gravel pounded into potholes, a sorry-looking picket fence undulating and bent from age and rot.

But it wasn't the ramshackle buildings that caught Becca's attention. No. As she sat in the car, her windshield wipers clapping away the gathering mist, she stared through the streaky glass to the cliff beyond.

So familiar.

So like that rocky outcropping where she saw Jessie in her visions, where she'd witnessed the embodiment of evil, the murderous bastard who had loomed over Jessie in her visions.

This was the scene of those visions, not Siren Song.

"Dear God," she whispered, her throat tightening.

Her cell phone jangled and she jumped, then realized that it hadn't actually rung, but that a message had been left on her voicemail. She punched buttons to retrieve it and heard, over the pounding of the surf far below, Hudson's worried voice. He asked her to call, to meet him at the motel as he was checking himself out of the hospital. And she was to call Zeke's number, as Hudson was using his friend's phone. He signed off with a quick "love you," which nearly brought tears to her eyes. He'd forgive her for keeping the secret about the baby. Maybe he really did love her. Maybe it wasn't all about Jessie.

She tried to call him back, once, twice, three times, and three times she failed.

"Damn," she whispered as she climbed out of the car and the wind, fierce now, tore at her clothes and hair. She considered leaving, driving into cell phone range and calling Hudson, but she didn't want to take the time.

Not when she had the overwhelming sensation that time was running out, faster and faster, grains of sand slipping through the hourglass that was her life.

But she tried to call Hudson one more time and failed again, the call never going through. Swearing softly, she tucked the phone into her pocket and started up the broken flagstones to the "office" door. Glancing around the side of the building to the open sea, she hesitated briefly. Darkness made it hard to see the shifting gray waters of the Pacific, but she could hear the waves pounding the base of the cliffs, spraying upward while the wind wailed.

Spiderwebs of realization brushed up her arms.

She had been here before. She was certain of it. What was it about this place? Nervous, she walked along the exterior of the decaying motel, barely noticing that some of the glass panes of the windows had been replaced with plywood, the plywood having grayed and buckled over the years. When she reached the back of the motel she stopped short.

"Jessie," she whispered as her hair whipped over her face.

This narrow point of land on which she now stood was the ridge in her visions, the one in which Jessie was poised over the angry, rushing sea. It had to be. She felt familiar here, and she thought for just an instant that the girl she'd seen in her trancelike state hadn't been Jessie at all, but herself. Hadn't people said they resembled each other?

But, no, the girl she'd seen had been Jessie. Jessie, trying to tell her to get justice from the man who'd murdered her. Becca recalled suddenly that Jessie had told Renee when she was sixteen, "It's all about justice," which made Becca wonder if Jessie had seen her own death approaching.

She shivered, then gazed at the surrounding cliffs, seeing the dark shape of the lighthouse on its rocky mound and the island farther out, barely distinguishable tonight in shades of black and gray.

How many times had she witnessed just this view? How many times had it terrified her? "No more," she vowed as her sweatshirt flapped around her. "Jessie?" Becca called. "Tell me what to do." She closed her eyes for just a second, willing the dead girl, her newfound sister, to enter her mind. If the dark figure, the image of the killer, joined the ghost of Jessie, so be it. "Come on, come on," she said, feeling the cold from the ever-changing Pacific seep through her skin and burrow into her heart.

But nothing came to her.

Just as she had in life, Jezebel Brentwood played by her own rules, stubbornly refused to bend to anyone else's whims.

Becca opened her eyes. It was dark and she was alone. Alone and on her own.

Backtracking to the front of the motel, Becca walked up a couple of steps to a sagging porch and pressed the doorbell. Over the keening howl of the wind, she heard the faint sound of a buzzer and then nothing. No footsteps. Maybe the old gal had fallen asleep in front of the television. Or maybe she wasn't home. Becca rang again, heard the buzzer, but no other sound.

"Maddie?" she called loudly. "Madame Madeline? It's me, Rebecca Sutcliff. Ryan. We met at the antique store?" She started to pound on the door only to have it creak open. She froze, arm raised to beat on the weathered panels again. "Maddie?"

From within came a low, pain-filled moan.

Becca's heart dropped through the rotted floorboards of the porch. She thrust open the door and stepped inside to the smell of fried fish and ashes from a wood stove and something else. Something metallic and out of place. "Maddie?" she called again and was already extracting her cell phone from her pocket. The living room with its flickering television screen was empty, the worn recliner sitting near a TV tray with a plate of food—tater tots, cole slaw, and fish sticks— half eaten. A fork with some white sauce still globbed on its tines had clattered to the floor. A cigarette burned in an ashtray.

And stains on the floor? Dark red stains. Blood . . . ?

Oh, dear God, what was this?

The hairs at Becca's nape stood on end. She speed-dialed Mac, but the call didn't go through. She should turn back now, drive into town, call the police . . .

Another groan emanated from a doorway at the back of the house.

Carefully, her pulse racing, her nerves wound tight as watch springs, Becca peeked around the corner to a bedroom where Madame Madeline lay slumped on the floor, blood pouring from her abdomen, a pistol in one hand.

"Maddie!" Becca said, trying to remain calm, not knowing what the wounded, crazed woman would do. Maddie looked up, her bloody fingers wrapped around the butt of the gun. "Justice," she whispered and leveled the barrel of the pistol straight at Becca's heart.

Mac took the call, a patch in through the sheriff's department, and he couldn't make out much, mostly static that the detectives had to repeat. The upshot was that Hudson Walker had checked himself out of the hospital against doctor's orders and now he was worried sick that Rebecca Sutcliff might've taken off after the killer—the same sicko that so far had eluded capture by all the authorities in Tillamook County. Hudson was certain Becca had gone back to Siren Song—a place Detective Clausen informed Mac was a cult.

"What the hell's she doing?" Mac growled as he noticed a turnout in the road and pulled a quick U-turn. "Son of a goddamned bitch."

"Don't shoot," Becca said as calmly as she could, though her heart rate was zooming wildly. "Don't shoot. Please . . ."

"Justice!" Maddie cried again, her face ashen, her eyes round with terror, the gun wobbling in her hands.

"You'll get justice, I swear, but now we need to get you to

a hospital. Drop the gun," Becca said, terror striking deep in her heart. She thought of Hudson, of their unborn child, and she knew she couldn't die. Heart jack-hammering, she stepped out of the gun's sights, and miraculously, the old woman didn't train the muzzle on Becca's moving form, just kept the barrel pointed at the doorway. "It's all right," Becca lied, a wary eye on the weapon and the heavy-knuckled fingers curled possessively over it. "It's all right," she said softly, again.

She moved closer to one side and eased the pistol away from Maddie's nerveless fingers. Quickly, she retrieved her phone with the other and dialed Mac again. Maddie's eyes closed. She was bleeding profusely from a wound in her abdomen. Self-inflicted? Or . . . what . . . ? She set the gun down, put the phone on speaker, and tried to stanch the flow of dark blood with some of the old woman's clothing. "Don't move," she said, "I'll get help." But there was so much blood, so damned much blood. "Hang in there."

This time, the call went straight to voicemail, and snagging up the cell, she sputtered off where she was and that she needed an ambulance and that she was going to call 911—when he stepped from the shadows, from the hallway.

Becca froze, eyes wide. For the first time she got a good, hard look at this psycho who had been chasing her down, for that's who he was. She nearly crumpled when she recognized his features, so like Jessie's, so like her own. He was an older, stronger, male version of Jezebel Brentwood. And he was related to Becca in some way, as well.

"Sister," he snarled, smiling and showing strong white teeth as he realized she recognized him for the monster he was, a murderer who was blood kin. He lifted a hand. In his fingers was a long-bladed knife. Blood dripped from its cruel razor edge.

"Why?" she whispered, gesturing vaguely toward Maddie's crumpled form.

"Her time came."

She saw the deadly intent in his hazel eyes as the wind raged around the cliffs, rattling the eaves, screaming over the thunder of the tides. "Why? Why are you doing all of this?"

"You are Satan's spawn, witch." His nostrils flared. "And you carry a new evil."

"Bastard!" she screamed.

His heartless leer chilled her to the bottom of her soul. "If you only knew."

The gun was only a few feet away. If she jumped to the left . . .

"At last, your blood will spill," he taunted. "Your time has come, too."

"Justice," Maddie whispered, glaring up at him, tears streaking down her wrinkled cheeks. "Run, girl."

Justice. His *name* was Justice. He'd attacked Maddie with the knife and hidden upon hearing Becca arrive. The gun was her defense, and Becca had taken it from her.

And now he was back to finish the job.

Take not only Madeline's life, but hers as well.

No way!

Becca lunged for the gun but he was quick, anticipating. His knife whizzed through the air, sliced into her arm. She cried out but her fingers found the handle of the gun. She grabbed it, flung her arm around, aiming the barrel his way, finger on the trigger.

He yelled at the same moment she screamed.

BAM!

The pistol kicked, but he'd expected the shot as he threw himself sideways, rolling out of harm's way. Becca scrambled to fire a second shot.

BAM!

The bullet slammed into the side of the wall, kicking up sheet rock and bits of wood. He ducked sideways, then quickly out of the way, around the corner.

Becca's pulse deafened her. "Leave before I blow you away!" she yelled, but heard nothing save her own ragged breathing, the shriek of the wind, and Maddie's slow moans. Becca's hands were shaking, but she forced them steady, training her aim on the doorway. If the son of a bitch stepped one foot into the open area, she'd pull the trigger again. Her arm hurt and she saw blood soak her sleeve. The useless cell phone was still within reach, but surely the shabby motel had a landline . . . She glanced around the room, searching for a receiver. A shadow streaked across the window.

He was outside!

She turned toward the sagging window where the panes rattled and cold air hissed into the room. But she was mistaken. The moving umbra she'd seen wasn't this monster of a man, but merely a branch being tossed in the wind. From the corner of her eye, she saw movement in the hallway.

What?

She whirled as he flew through the door, his knife raised. She shot again, the bullet zinging into his shoulder. *Again!* Her fingers tightened over the trigger, but he was on her, the weight of his body, toppling her to the floor. She screamed and they fell on the near-dead woman and she groaned painfully.

The demon-man's breath was hot against her, his body all muscle and sinew as they struggled. Becca slapped at him, tried to claw his face, attempted to shoot the damned gun again, but as she did, he wrestled her arm behind her back.

Pain shot through her shoulder and she dropped the gun, heard it hit the floor. No! Oh, God, no!

"Finally, sister," he growled. "Finally."

"No way in hell," she threw back at him and he cinched her arm up a little higher. She screamed in pain and he, lying atop her, pinned her to the floor, said, "Scream all you want, Rebecca. No one will hear you out here."

He was right. Even on a day when the wind was still and

the surf quiet, this old ruin was so isolated, a scream would never carry to another human's ears.

"By the light of the moon," Maddie whispered. "When the demons of the earth arise, then will you be taken, son, to the world from where you came. I curse you this day and the day of your birth. *You, Justice,* are the true spawn of Lucifer."

Becca felt the man atop her tense. This monster was Mad Maddie's son?

"You curse me?" he demanded, looking up and glaring at his dying mother. "*You* curse *me*? When I'm God's messenger? Sent here to right all the wrongs of Siren Song?"

Becca didn't move, didn't want to distract him. He was on his knees now, all of his attention focused on the woman who had borne him.

"I'm the only reason there are not more of *them.* I'm the only one who can cleanse the earth of their evil." He was moving now, closer to his mother, no longer straddling Becca.

It took all of Becca's willpower not to move, to feign unconsciousness, to draw no attention to herself.

"You are as bad as the rest, old hag."

Maddie gurgled and rasped, "Go to hell."

Becca's eyes darted around the room. The window.

She didn't wait. In one motion, she scrambled to her feet, hurtled herself through the rotting pane, tucking and rolling as glass shattered and crackled around her. She hit the sandy ground outside, sprang to her feet, and took off screaming at a dead run.

"Whore!" I bellow, jumping toward the window.

Behind me the old woman makes a sound of glee. I whirl back on her.

"You cannot kill them all," she says.

"I can. I will."

"God will save them . . ."

It's all I can do to keep from strangling her right

*there. But it's what she wants. To deter me from my
goal. To hold me with her. To protect them!*

*"I'm coming back for you," I whisper. "Wait for
me."*

*Terror fills those old eyes and I grin as I leap
through the window after the evil one. She is just
ahead of me. I have wounded her. Her blood will spill
and I will have her very, very soon.*

Mac was hauling ass to Siren Song. At the local Safeway
store he'd picked up Hudson Walker who'd tersely told him
the way. Walker had been hell-bent to storm the gates of the
cult, but Mac had been able to calm him down, insist that
they leave the sports car and drive together.

". . . but when we get there, you stay in the car. We have
to wait for a search warrant anyway, but the sheriff's department thinks they can get one."

"We don't have much time." Walker was ashen, one knee
jiggling nervously, his arm in a sling, and probably on some
kind of pain medication. Useless, Mac realized. Worse than
useless. A liability.

"So here's how it's going to go down. We wait until we
hear, then you stay in the vehicle while I—"

"I'm *not* staying in the vehicle."

"You'll stay or we won't go."

"I can't, Mac, you know that."

"And I can't have you—wait a sec." His cell phone was
ringing, the tone indicating he had a voicemail message.
"The phone never rang," he said. "Fuckin' coastal service."
He listened to the terrified message from Becca Sutcliff. As
he did, his heart plummeted and at the next wide spot in the
road, he executed a police U-turn.

Hudson grabbed on to the dash, his seat belt tightening,
his injuries screaming at him.

"She's not at Siren Song," Mac informed him tersely as
he hung up.

"Where is she?"

"Mad Maddie's motel? Know where that is? She said it was north of Deception Bay on a ridge."

"I got a good idea," Hudson said tersely.

"Lead the way," Mac muttered, phoning for backup and praying the damn cell phone would make a connection.

Her screams useless, Becca ran as fast as she could around the building toward the rental car. Her keys were still in the ignition and if . . .

Oh, God, she heard his footsteps pounding behind her. He was running fast, gaining on her.

Heavy footsteps chased her down.

Closer.

Faster.

Oh, dear God, help me! Help my baby!

She willed her legs to move, but she was losing ground. She'd been crazy to come looking for him, should have known he'd get the upper hand. *You're not dead yet,* she told herself and saw the fence in front of her. With missing pickets, like a gap-tooth smile, it was still a barrier. Could she vault over it or would she have to find the gate? Where was the damned opening?

She spied a break in the graying pickets and turned.

Too late!

He leapt through the air, his heavy body catching her and driving her to the ground. She hit hard, her jaw banging into the sand, grit on her lips and tongue. "Stupid woman," he snarled, yanking her to her feet.

She was a rag doll in his arms, head lolling, blood staining her sleeve a dark red.

He shook her. Hard. Lips pulled back in a triumphant grin.

"Finally! Finally, I have you!"

Becca couldn't move. She felt played out. Spent. Done.

His evil face glared into hers. "Nothing to say, bitch?" He hauled his right hand back and slapped her.

My baby, she thought. *My baby. Have to save my baby . . .*

As if reading her mind, he snarled, "That abomination will die before it is born. You will all die. I've been waiting. Waiting! And now the time is right."

"Please . . ."

"That's right. Beg. It will do you no good. The devil's own will be returned to him. Now!"

No way was Hudson going to sit in the car like a trained dog while Becca's life was in danger. No effin' way!

Nor was Mac waiting for backup. He parked his Jeep on a stretch of road less than a quarter of a mile from the cabins, and with strict instructions for Hudson to wait for the sheriff's department, he slid into the night.

Hudson gave him thirty seconds, then checked the glove box and lo and behold, there was Mac's backup weapon. Perfect. He checked the chamber. It was loaded.

He wasn't going to wait for the damned backup.

Not with Becca's life in danger.

Not with his unborn kid's life at risk.

Sliding the heavy sidearm into his waistband, he stole into the night, circling around the north end of the property, spying Mac, barely discernible in the security lights near the front porch.

He crouched along a broken fence line, his finger on the trigger. Tonight, that son of a bitch who'd been terrorizing Becca was going to die.

She had to move. Had to! The knife was still in his hand though he seemed intent on shaking some truth from her.

He glared down at her, enjoying the capture. "Nothing to say?" he whispered.

She flung herself forward, intending to bite him but he held her back, then turned her roughly around, pressing her back against him, the knife blade cutting into her throat. "You couldn't help yourself, could you, slut? I knew you'd come. Just like Jezebel. You're so much the same."

Terrified, she tried to think of a way to escape, any avenue that would set her free.

"Have you learned the truth yet?" he hissed in her ear. "Like she did? That she came from incest. Father and daughter! You, too, fucking whore!"

Becca tried to speak but she felt the knife at her throat break skin. A thin trickle of blood ran down her neck.

He was holding her fast to him, his chest pressed hard to her back. She hardly dared breathe, couldn't risk moving as they stood on the cliff face, the piercing wind whirling and yowling around them, the black ocean frothing and raging below. *Just as it was in your visions. As if this is your destiny.*

"She was pregnant with her vile child, just as you are," he whispered.

His enjoyment sent rage flowing through her, but she needed to keep him talking.

"Renee?" she managed.

"That slut was asking questions around town, a tell-all book about the sickness at Siren Song."

"What sickness?" The blade pressed, cold on her throat.

"You know, whore. You know."

She shuddered. It was as if she were being held by the devil himself. "No . . . truly . . . I don't know."

"Jezebel and Rebecca are the most foul," he intoned, as if it were a litany he said to himself often. "They can never be allowed to breed, to continue the cycle. Jezebel came to Siren Song and learned. That's how I found her. I smelled the fetus within her. That's why she had to die."

Becca was shivering, the wind slapping at them, the salt

in the air sticking to her skin. "You killed her in the maze," she said unevenly.

"Jezebel thought she had me, but I had planned to kill her all along and leave her at the base of the statue that bears her abominable mother's name."

"Mary?"

"She could see things," he said with the faintest hint of admiration. "So can you."

"So can you," Becca said, recalling how he'd seen Jessie's vision on the road.

"It won't work," he suddenly said. He leaned closer and licked the inside of her ear. "It never does, sister, I *always* win."

Her stomach convulsed and she nearly threw up.

But then he shifted slightly, the knife slipping just a fraction. Becca's fury took over. She kicked backward as hard as she could, then reached behind her and wrenched his balls in a death squeeze.

"Bitch!" he howled in surprise, his grip loosening. He doubled over in pain.

Hudson counted the seconds. *One . . . two . . . three . . .* Sweat was building on his back beneath his jacket. He had to get to Becca. Had to save her and their child. They were all he had. All he wanted and if this prick so much as harmed one hair on her head.

But he was scared to his soul. This madman was relentless and focused on Becca.

"Bitch!"

The shout roared through the night.

Mac yelled something but Hudson didn't hear. He jumped to his feet and ran blindly forward, hand hard on the gun.

He was gonna blow the sucker away.

*   *   *

Becca clung to Justice but he beat on her with his fists. She couldn't breathe. Had to let go. He was swearing and flinging his arms. His knife slammed downward, gouging into her thigh. She cried out.

Bang!

A shot shattered the night.

Justice, with a scream louder than the wind, fell to the ground, writhing.

What? Oh, God, what's happening?

Becca spun, her leg burning. She was staring straight at Hudson, one arm in a sling, a large pistol in his right hand. He walked forward quickly, the nose of the gun aimed directly at Justice's slithering and twisting form. Hudson's face was a mask of fury, his eyes dark with murder, as if he intended to empty every round in the gun into the man who had nearly killed Becca.

"Don't!" she warned as sirens screamed over the wind and Mac burst out of the end unit of the motel. "Hudson, don't!"

Mac screamed, "Put the gun down, Walker! Now!" His sidearm was aimed not at Hudson, but the wounded man. "We want this fucker alive. He's got a lot of explaining to do, and he can start with Jessie Brentwood."

Hudson lowered his gun and Becca nearly collapsed against him. "It's over," she whispered as his good arm held her tight. "It's finally over."

The sheriff's department seemed to appear by magic. One moment Hudson was holding Becca and Mac was staring down the writhing monster on the ground, gun aimed at the man's chest, the next a swarm of armed men were running across the grounds.

Becca pressed her face into Hudson's chest. She heard him swear softly. "We need to take you back to the hospital," he said.

"I never want to go there again."

"You're hurt."

"But alive. He didn't hurt our baby. He wanted to. He wanted to hurt our baby."

"He's sick."

"It's something to do with Siren Song, Hudson. He wanted to kill everyone from Siren Song."

Her teeth were chattering. Hudson didn't wait any longer. He led her toward Mac's Jeep. "Gotta get you help," he murmured.

Mac materialized out of the gloom. "I'll call an ambulance," he said, glancing at Becca. "We're ordering one for the woman in the cabin."

"Madeline? She's alive?" Becca turned toward him.

"Barely. But she's breathing okay."

"I can go in the Jeep," she assured him.

Hudson said to Mac, "You want to stay, I can drive."

Mac nodded and handed him the keys.

"Thank you," Becca said to him, heartfelt.

Mac paused. "I should be thanking you. I put you all through hell for a long, long time. And none of you were responsible for Jessie's death."

"Becca and my baby are alive, in part because of you," Hudson said, helping Becca into the passenger seat. "We're all even."

With that Hudson slid in the driver's seat and turned away from the motel and Deception Bay and toward Ocean Park Hospital once more.

"I love you," he said into the sudden quiet. "I love you so much."

"I love you," she breathed.

"You don't have to answer now, but I want you to know, I plan to marry you."

She almost smiled.

"What?" he asked, and she could tell he was glancing at her with concern in the darkness of the Jeep's interior.

"I've been planning to marry you since high school. I just didn't think it would ever happen." She felt him relax a little. "You're sure you want me? With my visions and physical anomalies and possible 'cult' connections?"

"I want you," he said, and it was decided.

Chapter Twenty-Seven

Becca stood in the hot July sun, staring through the wrought-iron gates of Siren Song. It was the third day in a row she'd kept up the vigil, and she knew the reclusive residents had seen her. She brushed her hair away from her face, feeling heat burn into her scalp. Hot for the beach. Blistering, really.

Her belly had grown. There was no hiding the fact that she was pregnant, and her joy showed on her face. That pregnancy glow. She had it in spades.

Hudson had told her so the morning that she'd left for the beach. "I love you," he'd said. "You've never looked more beautiful." Becca had curved into his arms and kissed him deeply, bursting inside, loving him with everything she had.

They'd been standing outside the barn, watching the new colt kick up its heels. It ran from one side of the field to the other, zigzagging in front of his mother, never getting too far away.

New life. New love. Four months ago it had seemed an impossibility.

She wrapped her hands around the bars of the gate; they

were almost too hot to touch. She wasn't going to give up. She had questions. She deserved answers, and when she'd told Hudson what she planned to do, though she knew he wanted to keep her safe with him, he'd reluctantly allowed her to go.

"I'll go with you," he invited himself, but she'd shaken her head.

"I'll have a better chance by myself. They're secretive and suspicious, but I am one of them."

He wanted to argue, but she pointed out what he already knew: The Colony members at Siren Song were no threat to her. Justice Turnbull—Madeline Turnbull's son—was the threat and he was in custody, locked up under heavy guard, preparing for a transfer to a mental facility for the criminally insane. Justice's wild ramblings had assured that conviction.

In the wake of the events at Mad Maddie's motel, the authorities had swarmed over his life. His strange lighthouse lair had revealed torn notes and scribbled writings about his obsession over the colony; a cache of weaponry was discovered, notably knives, and a tan truck with a removed front grill guard was parked at the side of the motel under a dark gray tarp. There was a sense that he'd killed other colony members besides Jessie, but without the colony's cooperation it was all conjecture, and the women at Siren Song were collectively unhelpful. McNally had tried to interview the members but they would not open their gates. Justice's ramblings didn't offer enough evidence for a search warrant. Half of what he said was delusional fabrications. He insisted that Jessie and Becca were the devil's spawn and they must be sent back to hell. It was his mission.

Then with continued digging a story had emerged, one that was recorded by a Deception Bay pseudo-historian who'd written down an undocumented account of The Colony's founders. It had found its way into the hands of a Dr. Parnell Loman, who'd fallen to his death from his cliffside home into the Pacific some fifteen years earlier. This was the same

Dr. Loman who'd signed both Jessie's and Becca's birth certificates and facilitated their adoptions.

The account talked about the area's early inhabitants, and there was mention of women arriving from the east—witches—and how they'd mingled with the local Indians and created their own colony. A shaman "wed" one of the women, and the children from that union were unusually perceptive in "odd and repellant" ways. For reasons unknown, those children, the ones that survived, were mostly female. The few males born died early.

How Justice fit in was a bit murky. The written account ended with the birth of Mary Durant and Catherine Rutledge, sisters whose mother, Grace Fitzhugh, had married first Richard Durant, then John Rutledge, having a daughter by each. Dr. Loman had added several paragraphs that indicated Madeline Abernathy Turnbull was part of the family as well, some distant relative of Mary and Catherine, who both still lived at Siren Song as of Dr. Loman's writings.

But one thing was clear: Justice believed in his mission totally. He had to rid the world of the cursed offspring of colony members. Did that make Becca Mary's daughter? Justice seemed to think so. Or was it all a fabrication of his depraved mind? His accusations of incest could not be corroborated, but he clearly felt he'd been scorned by the colony women, and in the twisted soup of his beliefs, which combined witchcraft, native lore, and a fear of the wrath of God, he was determined to send as many members as he could back to the depths of hell from where they'd come. They were children of lust, incest, and the devil's design. They must be killed.

Becca shivered despite the beating sun. She was thirsty. If they didn't come soon, if she failed to make contact again, she might have to abandon this quest for now. Releasing her fingers from the bars, she gazed up at the heavens to a pale blue sky and white, burning sun.

A flicker of movement brought her attention back to the

colony grounds. To her surprise, a middle-aged woman in a long gray dress was walking toward her. Finally!

Becca straightened. The woman's hair was steel gray and wrapped into a bun at her nape. Her dress was from another era.

She came directly to the gate and Becca took a step back. They stared at each other.

"I will not open the gates," she said.

"I could probably sneak in. I've seen the truck that goes into town for deliveries," Becca informed her.

"What do you want?"

"My name is Rebecca. I was adopted into the Ryan family. Dr. Loman signed the certificate. My deceased sister was Jezebel. She was also adopted out. I believe we're both related and that's why Justice killed Jessie and came after me."

Her gaze dropped to Becca's burgeoning stomach. She said with a spurt of emotion, "You're having a girl."

"Yes." Becca was momentarily thrown, but she was determined to glean as much information as possible. "Are you Catherine? Or Mary?"

"Catherine. Mary's dead."

"Oh. Was Mary my mother?" Becca held her breath.

Catherine's gaze scoured the hillsides surrounding the compound, as if searching for an answer. Long moments passed, and then she said, "We didn't want you to know. We sent you away to protect you because Justice was already attacking us. We were forced to build the wall, but he found Jezebel, didn't he? She came here looking for answers and we gladly gave them to her. We welcomed her and in welcoming her, sealed her death. We want you to stay away."

"I've seen a woman . . ." Becca gestured past Catherine to the lodge. "Someone closer to my age."

"The less you know, the safer you are."

"Justice is in custody. He can't hurt anyone anymore."

"Are you so sure?"

Becca stared into Catherine's pale blue eyes—eyes the

color of the sky—and felt a deep frisson of fear slide down her back.

"Go back to your husband."

"We're not married yet," Becca said.

"You will be. You will live on his farm and raise horses and children. But be vigilant, my dear. Be vigilant."

"How do you know my future?"

"I see things," she said. "Like Jezebel."

And then she turned and walked away.

Epilogue

The van bobbed along. A jerky ride. Justice sat on one of the bench seats and examined the other passengers with a cool eye. They were criminals. Animals. He was God's messenger.

The shackles at his wrists glowed like silvery rings. Fools. They could not contain him forever. His mission wasn't over. He'd found Jessie years ago and his abilities had led him to Rebecca, twice. Catherine, the filthy witch, kept a close watch on the whores within Siren Song's walls. He could only get to them when she made a mistake.

But he was God's messenger and God wants retribution. *The colony whores are gifted with dark and dangerous abilities, and God wants them stopped!* He caught a whiff of Jessie twenty years ago, when she showed up at Siren Song. How they welcomed her home, with her incubus inside her. He found her then and ended her life. *Now Rebecca knows about them. She won't be able to stay away.*

She is doomed. Like her sister.

Twisting his wrists, he thought how easily he could choke a man with these chains. Sure, they were strung through a loop at his waist, but there was enough room. The faintest of smiles touched his lips. The guards were stupid and lazy. They did their job by rote. They had no brains.

These shackles were a momentary delay. Soon, he would be free again. Free to find Rebecca. Didn't he find her once before, long ago, when she was pregnant? Didn't he take care of that unborn scourge? He was infuriated that she lived after that accident. Lived! And he lost track of her for sixteen long years.

But now she's pregnant again.

When they're pregnant, they're easy to smell.

That is his gift.

He is the tracker. He will eventually find them all. One by one. When he escapes—and he will—he'll run them to ground and send their evil souls back into the fires of hell.

It is his mission.

IF AT FIRST YOU DON'T SUCCEED . . .
For two years, Justice Turnbull has paced his room at Halo
Valley Security Hospital, planning to escape. Justice has a
mission—one that began with a vicious murder two
decades ago. And there are so many others who must be
sent back to the hell that spawned them . . .

KILL . . .
Laura Adderley didn't plan to get pregnant by her soon-to-
be ex-husband, though she'll do anything to protect her
baby. But now reporter Harrison Frost is asking questions
about the mysterious group of women who live at Siren
Song lodge. Harrison hasn't figured out Laura's connection
to the story yet. But Justice knows. And he is coming . . .

THEN KILL AGAIN . . .
All her life, Laura has been able to sense approaching evil.
But that won't stop a psychopath bent on destroying her.
Justice has been unleashed, and this time, there will be no
place safe to hide . . .

**Please turn the page for an exciting sneak peek of
Lisa Jackson and Nancy Bush's
WICKED LIES,
on sale in June 2011!**

CHAPTER 1

I can smell her!

Another one whose scent betrays her!

Even inside my cell, I can smell her sickness. Her filth. Her lust.

There have been others, too, while I've languished here. Others who need to be avenged. Others who, with their devil's issue, must be driven back to the deadly fires from which they were spawned!

Oh, sick women with your uncontrollable needs.

I am coming for you. . . .

Laura Adderley leaned a hand against the bathroom stall, clutching the home pregnancy test in her other fist, unable to look. She didn't want this. Not when her marriage was newly finished—a divorce she'd wanted as much as her newly minted ex, maybe more. Byron had already taken up residence with another woman, and he would undoubtedly cheat on her as much as he'd cheated on Laura. It didn't matter. Their marriage had been ill-conceived from the beginning; it had just taken Laura three years to recognize that fact.

Ill-conceived . . .

Grabbing on to her courage, she slowly unfurled her fist, staring down at the two glaring pink lines of the home pregnancy test.

Positive.

She'd known it would be.

Oh, God . . .

Squeezing her eyes closed, Laura inhaled a deep, calming breath. She'd ignored the signs for as long as she could, but there was no keeping her head in the sand any longer. She was pregnant. With her ex-husband's child. They'd signed the papers that very week, though Byron had tried to stall because he simply didn't want to give Laura what she wanted: freedom from lies and tyranny.

But now what?

Dr. Byron Adderley was an orthopedic surgeon at Ocean Park Hospital, and she, Laura, was a floor nurse. They'd moved to this smaller facility along the Oregon coast about a year earlier, leaving one of Portland's largest and most prestigious hospitals for a slower-paced life. Laura hadn't wanted the move, had been adamantly against it. For reasons she didn't want to tell Byron, she wanted, needed, to stay far, far away from Ocean Park and the surrounding hamlet of Deception Bay.

But as if he'd somehow divined her secrets, he'd announced he'd taken a position at the smaller hospital and they were up and moving. Laura had been stunned. Had told him she wasn't going. Simply was not going. But in the end he'd gotten his way, and though she'd dragged her feet, she'd reluctantly made this move in the vain hope that she could get her dying marriage off life support, though she knew she no longer loved him, maybe never really had. But with a new start, it was possible something could change. Maybe her heart could be rewon. Maybe Byron would want just her. Maybe everything would be . . . better.

Then he was discovered groping one of the Ocean Park nurses in an empty hospital room. The hospital tried to chastise Byron Adderley, but he wasn't the kind of man to be chastised. The nurse was summarily dismissed and the incident swept under the hospital rugs . . . and Laura filed for divorce.

At first he'd argued with her. Not that he wanted her; it just wasn't his decision and so therefore it couldn't *be*. She didn't listen and he changed tactics, humbly begging for a second chance. Laura was suspicious of his motives, aware he might be acting. But she looked down the road of her own future; and it was decidedly bleak and lonely; and one night, three months ago, he'd sworn that he loved her, that he would never cheat on her again, that he would seek help for past mistakes. She had wanted to believe him so much. Needed to. Shut the clamoring voice in her head that warned her to be smart, and one thing led to another and they ended up making desperate love together. A second chance, maybe a last chance that Laura had to take.

And then another nurse came forward, complaining that Dr. Adderley had made inappropriate advances toward her. Byron vehemently denied the charge, but Laura, who had abilities that he didn't understand—some she didn't understand herself—knew without a doubt that he was lying through his miserable white teeth.

She let the divorce proceedings run their course, and being Byron, he took up with another woman. This time Laura didn't look back. She was through with Byron Adderley, and until today, she'd been determined to move back to Portland and find employment far, far away from Ocean Park and Deception Bay.

But now . . .

The door to the bathroom opened. "Laura?" Nurse Perez called.

"I'll be out in a minute," Laura said, flushing the toilet and wrapping the telltale wand in toilet paper and shoving it in her purse.

"We need help in the ER. We've got a head trauma coming in."

"Okay."

She heard the door close and let herself out of the bathroom. Washing her hands, she looked hard at her reflection in the mirror. Serious blue-gray eyes stared back at her; and she could see the beginning of her own dishwater blond hair reappearing at her hairline, the longer, darker tresses trying to escape their ponytail and curl under her chin, a strong chin, she'd been told, that, along with high cheekbones and thick lashes, gave her a slightly aristocratic look, something far from what she really was.

A familiar pressure built inside her head, and she mentally pushed it back, visualizing a twenty-foot-high iron gate to withstand the force coming at her. This was an automatic response that clicked in almost unconsciously when particularly strong, unwanted—*bad*—thoughts attacked her. For years she thought everyone had this ability but then slowly realized that it was unique to her alone. It was like someone, or ones, was knocking at her brain, trying to get inside, and she would push up a mental wall to keep them out. But this time was different; there was more urgency and determination. As if this someone were pounding a metal hammer at her wall. At her brain.

Sisssterrrr!

Laura jerked to attention and glanced around, half expecting to see who had spoken. But there was no one. Nary a soul. And the voice had been decidedly male.

Her eyes widened; she watched the autonomic response happen in the mirror as realization dawned, a realization she wanted desperately to deny. He was back.

Shutting her lids tightly, she squeezed at her brain, holding the wall firm until the hammering turned into a tinny, lit-tle *ping, ping, ping* and was gone.

By the time she reached the ER, the ambulance was screaming up the drive. It was 8:30 p.m. Late June, so it was still light out, though she could see the shadows forming be-neath the gnarled branches of the scrub pine that lined the asphalt. Red and white lights flashed in opposite rotation and the *woo*-woo . . . *woo*-woo . . . *woo*-woo of the shriek-ing siren seemed to vibrate the very air.

With a squeal of brakes the ambulance jumped to a halt. EMTs leapt out and ran to the back of the vehicle. Doors flew open, and a victim was rushed in on a gurney, head sur-rounded by a white bandage that was dark red with blood.

One of the residents sucked in a breath. "Jesus, it's Con-rad!"

"Conrad?" Laura repeated in shock, gazing down at one of Ocean Park's security guards: Conrad Weiser.

"What happened?" one of the trauma surgeons de-manded.

"Attacked at Halo Valley," the EMT responded. "He was on the way there to pick up a patient, and one of the crazies beat the hell out of him and escaped."

"Halo Valley?" Laura repeated through lips that barely moved.

"Yeah, the mental hospital," Dylan, the EMT, clarified soberly.

"Let's get him in here," the trauma surgeon ordered as a second victim on a gurney was off-loaded from the ambu-lance.

"You okay?" Dylan asked, frowning at Laura.

"Fine."

Bringing herself back to the present, Laura helped guide the second wounded man's gurney into the ER. He was awake but his throat was wrapped and he clearly couldn't speak. His dark eyes glared at her, and Dylan said, almost in an aside, giving her a second shock, "This is Dr. Maurice Zellman from Halo Valley. He was stabbed in the throat."

"Also by the escapee?" she asked.

"Looks like it."

She watched as Zellman was hurriedly wheeled through the double doors to the ER as well, and was unable to control a full-body shivering that emanated from her very soul.

Halo Valley. The mental hospital for the criminally insane.

He was there.

Wasn't he?

Or, was that why he'd just tried to breach the wall in her mind? He'd escaped!

And he was coming after her.

Oh, God, no! Not now! She thought of the baby and her heart nearly stopped. Fear crawled up her spine and nestled in her brain. *No, no, no!*

Blindly, pushing back that horrid snaking fear, she turned to one of the other nurses. "Who did this?" she asked.

"Don't you wish we could ask Zellman and find out?" Nurse Carlita Solano answered flatly. "Some nut job, for sure."

Please, God, don't let it be him.

But she knew it was. Justice Turnbull had escaped the walls of Halo Valley Security Hospital, and he was free to take up his murdering ways.

Laura watched the doors behind the injured doctor slowly close with a soft hiss and wondered how this had happened.

The day had started out like many others.

Dr. Maurice Zellman, one of Halo Valley Security Hospital's premier psychiatrists . . . maybe the premier psychiatrist, if you'd asked him . . . had begun his morning with a piece of dry wheat toast, a soft-boiled egg, and a slice of cantaloupe before driving to the hospital and arriving punctually at 7:15 a.m. He had several consults before lunch, called his wife, Patricia, at noon and learned that their sixteen-year-old son, Brandt, had gotten in some kind of trouble at school and was facing detention for the rest of the week. With a snort of disgust, Zellman told Patricia that Brandt would be facing some serious punishment from his father as well, and then, ruffled, he visited a number of his patients in their rooms—cells, really, though no one referred to them as such—throughout the rest of the afternoon, his mind on other things.

By six o'clock he was finished with work, except that he hadn't yet visited with his most notorious patient: Justice Turnbull, a psychotic killer who had tried to kill his own mother and had proven to be obsessed with murdering the group of women who lived together in a lodge called Siren Song along the Oregon coast. These women were whispered about by the locals as members of a cult dubbed the Colony and were reclusive, brooding, and odd. What Justice's personal beef was with them remained a mystery, one Zellman had sought to crack in the over two years of Justice's incarceration but hadn't quite managed yet. Justice was also responsible for several other murders and was an odd bird by anyone's definition.

No one at Halo Valley knew what to make of him, and they certainly didn't know how to treat him. The other doctors just didn't have it, as far as Zellman was concerned. They were adequate, in their way, whereas he, Maurice Zellman, was extraordinary. He actually *cured* patients instead of resorting to mere behavioral modifications.

And Justice . . . well . . . Maurice had made significant progress with him. Significant. Yes, the man was still obsessed with the Siren Song women, but that was because Justice was apparently related to them in some way. At least he thought he was, though that had yet to be proven. Maybe the women were a cult; maybe they weren't. They were certainly paranoically reclusive and, in appearance, looked as if they came from another century. Zellman was inclined to think they should be left alone to their own devices. Everyone found a way to live in this world and there was no right way or wrong way, although getting Justice to see that point was a work in progress. For reasons of his own, Justice Turnbull seemed determined to snuff them all out.

But . . . there had been progress, Zellman reminded himself with a mental pat on the back. Initially, when Justice had first been incarcerated at Halo Valley, he'd bellowed long and loud that he would kill them all and their devil's issue! The staff hadn't known whom he meant, at first, but he made it clear that he wanted to wipe out all the *ssissterrss* at Siren Song. With the help of time and antipsychotics, he'd all but recanted this mission. He still was agitated about them; he couldn't completely disguise it when Zellman would mention the women of the lodge, just to see. But Justice wasn't nearly as single-minded as he had been at first. Was he cured? No. Would he ever be? In Justice Turnbull's case, unlikely, though Dr. Maurice Zellman was definitely the man for the job if there was a chance.

And Maurice understood Justice was tortured by demons of his own making, which didn't matter to his colleagues one whit. They had locked the man away for the next few decades with no chance of getting released. Paranoid schizophrenic. Sociopath. Psychopath. Homicidal maniac . . . Justice Turnbull might be a little of all, but he was still a patient in need of care.

With a glance at his watch, Zellman noted the time: 6:45 p.m. He had a surprise for Justice, one Justice had been asking for and Zellman had finally been able to put together, though not without much resistance. With a satisfied smile on his face, he headed for Justice's room. It was at the end of the hall by design as no one wanted to visit him. In fact, no one ever did, outside of hospital personnel. He was considered weird by the other inmates, which was saying a lot, as they were criminally insane themselves, every last one. But every group had a pecking order, and Halo Valley Security Hospital was no exception. As one of the hospital's leading physicians treating some of the most notorious patients— killers, sadists, rapists, to name a few—Maurice Zellman was intimately aware of how mentally unstable and deranged the men and women were on this side of the hospital, the side that housed those convicted of serious crimes. They might be excused from regular prison by reason of insanity, but it didn't mean they weren't the worst kind of criminals. That was why they were housed on Side B, as this sterile section of the hospital was euphemistically called. Side B. The side for the irredeemable. Connected to Side A, where the mentally ill without criminal tendencies were lodged, by a skyway, surrounded by a tall chain-link fence and razor wire, which were partially hidden by a laurel hedge, all the better to make everyone think the hospital was a warm and cozy place. In truth, Side B was little more than a prison for the criminally insane.

Dr. Zellman was high in the pecking order of the specialists on Side B. He understood the criminal mind in a way that both fascinated and horrified the less imaginative doctors. Well, that was their problem, wasn't it? he thought with a sniff. Dr. Maurice Zellman did his job. And he did it very, very well.

With a tightening of his lips, he picked up his pace. He was running late, and checking on Turnbull was going to make him later still, but he really had no choice as Justice was his patient and was patently feared by the rest of the staff. This fact half amused Zellman, who'd worked with the strange man ever since he'd been brought to Side B, because Justice was really no more frightening than any other psychotic. He was just a little more directionally motivated, focused on women, specifically these Colony women.

Just as Zellman reached Justice's room, the door flew open and Bill Merkely, one of the guards, practically leapt into the hall. Merkely didn't immediately see Zellman, as he was looking back into Justice's room. "So long, schizo!" he yelled harshly, his beefy face red. He yanked the door shut and checked the automatic lock as Zellman cleared his throat behind him. Merkely jumped as if prodded with a hot poker, his already red face turning magenta. "Fucker told me I was going to die!" he cried as an excuse.

"You can't listen to him."

"I don't. But he sure as hell predicts a whole lot of shit!"

"What were you doing in his room?"

"Picking up his tray. But I had to leave it in there. Hope the food rots!"

He stomped off toward the guards' station, which divided Halo Valley Security Hospital's Side B from Side A, the gentler section, which housed patients who weren't considered a serious threat to society. Zellman thought of Side A as an Alzheimer's wing, though he would never say so aloud as they considered themselves to be a helluva lot more than institutional caretakers. He shook his head at the lot of them. Perception. So many people just didn't get it.

He had a key to Justice's room himself, and he cautiously unlocked the door. Justice had never attacked him; he'd never attacked anyone since he'd been brought to the hospital, but the man had a history, oh, yes, indeedy he did.

Now the patient stood on the far side of the room, disengaged from whatever little drama had occurred between him and Merkely. Justice was tall, dusty blond, and slim, almost skinny, but hard and tough as rawhide. He didn't make eye contact as Zellman entered, but he flicked a look toward the meal tray, which had been untouched except for the apple.

"That man is afraid of me," Justice said, now in his sibilant voice. Always a faint hiss to his words. *An affectation,* Zellman thought.

"Yes, he is."

"He always leaves the tray."

Zellman had a clipboard with a pen attached shoved under one arm. There were cameras in Justice's one-room cell, tracking his every move. Zellman didn't need to watch reams of film to remind himself of the content of each of their meetings. He wrote himself copious notes and typed up reports, which he suspected no one ever read. They all wanted to forget Justice Turnbull and his strangeness. When first brought to Halo Valley, he'd referred to the women he sought to harm as "Sister," in his hissing way. *"Sssiissterrrs . . . ,"* he would rasp. *"Have to kill them all!"* he'd warned. But a lot of that dramatic act had disappeared over time.

Not that he wasn't dangerous. Before his incarceration he'd killed and terrorized a number of women. He had also cut a swath through some peripheral people and had nearly slain his own mentally ill mother. She now lay in a twilight state in a care facility with no memory of the attack and not a lot of connection with the real world.

"Justice," Maurice Zellman said now in a stern, yet friendly, voice, one he'd cultivated over the years. "You've finally got clearance to have those medical tests run at Ocean Park Hospital. The van's on its way here now. I'm warning you, though. If this stomach problem proves to be just a means to get out of Halo Valley, you'll be further restricted. No more walks in the yard. No being outside and staring toward the sea." Zellman heard his faintly mocking voice and clamped down on that. "No privileges."

Justice turned to look at him through clear blue eyes that were almost translucent. He was extraordinarily good-looking except . . . there was just something unnatural about him that made one hesitate upon meeting him. A reaction to something he emanated that Zellman had never quite put his finger on. Now his mouth was turned down at the corners and he winced slightly, as if he were in pain.

Over time and in-depth sessions with him, Zellman had come to realize that some of Justice's deeply rooted problems were because he'd been rejected and scorned. Rejected and scorned by women. Maybe even his own mother. The women of the Colony particularly bothered him. They might not be his sisters, per se, but he seemed to think they were. Was there any shared genetic makeup between them? Zellman thought it unlikely. Justice's world was all of his own making.

Still, Justice definitely believed the Siren Song occupants were the Chosen Ones, while he was kept outside the gates. Locked out. Barred. Left with a mother who had been spiraling into mental illness most of her adult life, Zellman guessed. Who knew about his father? Certainly not Justice or anyone Zellman had ever talked to.

Not a great childhood by any stretch of the imagination.

"Can we go now?" Justice stared at him hard.

Zellman nodded. Justice wore loose gray pants and a white shirt, the regulated outfit for the patients on Side B. "I need to get the handcuffs, first. Sorry."

Justice asked softly, "From the guard?"

"Yes."

"I won't try to escape."

"It's hospital policy."

A spasm crossed his face, and he clutched a palm to his stomach. "This pain is killing me."

Zellman considered the man. Inside the van Justice would be chained around the waist and locked to the side of the vehicle for the ride to Ocean Park. The handcuffs were merely an extra precaution. Sure, it would be against protocol to give him this small freedom as they made their way to the van—against the most basic rule of the hospital. But the stomach pain Justice had been complaining of was definitely worsening, and anyway, Zellman knew when someone was telling the truth and when they were lying. It was just . . . his gift. Justice was telling the truth.

It would take time to get the damned handcuffs, time and effort. And Maurice disliked Bill Merkely almost as much as Justice did. "Come on, then," he said. "Hurry up."

Justice's expression brightened a little, the most anyone could ever scare out of him. He was in gray felt slippers, and he eagerly walked through the door ahead of Zellman. There were precautions overhead in the hall: big, glossy, mirrored half circles that housed hidden cameras. Justice looked up at them as they passed, and Zellman smiled to himself. There would be hell to pay later when the handcuff protocol breach was noticed. Dr. Jean Dayton, a mild-mannered little brown bird with a permanent scowl, would scream her pinched-tight ass off.

They walked along the hall together and, side by side, clambered up the utilitarian metal stairway that led to the ground level. At the top it was a short walk toward a set of gunmetal gray, locked double doors with small windows filled with wire netting—doors that led to the outside. They stood together just inside, looking through the windows, waiting while a white hospital van with the Ocean Park logo pulled under the portico beyond. Daylight was disappearing, the fading sun fingering stripes of dark gold along the grass that fanned out on the far side of the portico, night still an hour or so away.

As Zellman watched, the driver, an orderly from Ocean Park, jumped from the van. The man would be expecting Justice to be handcuffed, and with a faint feather of remorse touching his skin, Zellman turned to Justice and opened his mouth to . . . what? Ask him to be good?

Swift as lightning, Justice snatched Zellman's clipboard and pen away from him. The clipboard clattered to the floor, and while Zellman goggled in surprise, Justice jammed the pen deep into Zellman's throat and out again. Twice.

Blood spurted in a geyser.

"Wha? Wha? Wha?" Zellman burbled.

The door opened and the driver stepped in. Justice grabbed the man by his head and slammed it into the metal door. Once, twice, three times. More blood. Pints of it.

"Keys," Justice demanded.

"Van . . . van," the man mumbled, his eyes rolling around in his head.

And like that, Justice was gone.

Shoved aside and tossed to the floor like a rag doll, Zellman clutched at his throat helplessly, blood squeezing through his fingers. Shocked and outraged that Justice had lied. About the stomach pain. About needing to go to the hospital. About *every damned thing!*

And he, Dr. Maurice Zellman, a doctor of psychiatry, a member of Mensa, had believed him. Worse than the sting of pain at his throat, the bite of his own damned pen, was the knowledge that he, Dr. Maurice Zellman, had been wrong, after all.

CHAPTER 2

Sssisssterrr . . .

Whore . . . !

With Satan's evil incubus growing inside you . . . !

The voice rasped against Laura's brain again. She flinched and nearly stumbled as she thrust up the mental wall against him again on her way to surgery to check on Conrad's condition. But her worst fears were confirmed: it *was* Justice.

And he knew she was pregnant??? How?

The frisson that shivered down her spine was an old friend. She'd felt it before many times, but not since Justice Turnbull had been captured, convicted, and locked away. Not like this. Not with this harsh hammering into her thoughts.

Outside the doors to the surgical ward she glanced around, always a bit uncertain that someone else couldn't hear him as well, though she knew from experience she was the only one. She could block him from digging into her thoughts and feelings, but she could not prevent her own mental receptors from hearing him.

He was a devil. A scourge. A sickness that frightened them all. He was—

"Laura?" Her ex, Byron Adderley, broke into her thoughts, causing her to jerk as if goosed. "What's wrong with you?" he demanded instantly. Frowning, he stripped a pair of surgical gloves from his hands and tossed them into a trash receptacle. His eyebrows rose, as if he were waiting for her to answer.

Like an obedient puppy, she thought sourly.

He'd just come from surgery, she realized. Of course she would run into him. Of course. Murphy's Law. Pulling herself together, she ignored his question. "How's Conrad? Do you know?"

"Who? Oh. That security guard?" He shoved a thinning shock of coffee-dark hair from his eyes. "We drilled into his head to relieve the pressure in case of a subdural hematoma. Hope he has a brain left. Someone beat him half to death." He actually smiled, as if he'd said something clever. "That what you wanted to know?"

"I was just concerned."

His smile fell away and Byron gazed at her hard. "You like him?"

"I barely know him," she shot back. "I just want to make sure he's okay."

"Yeah, well. 'Okay' is maybe not the word for it." Byron yawned. He stretched his arms over his head in a move she remembered, one she'd once thought was sexy. No longer. "God, I gotta get some sleep," he admitted. "I was out late last night, and this morning came early."

Like she cared.

"What about Dr. Zellman?" Being a floor nurse, and not part of the surgical team, Laura was forced to get information secondhand.

"Jesus. He's lucky to be alive! That fuckin' psychotic stabbed Zellman, too. Got his voice box but good." Byron actually sounded a little concerned. "Could be, Zellman never speaks again."

"Oh, I hope you're wrong." She glanced past him toward

the double doors that led into surgery. "That's what they're saying?" she asked.

He shrugged. "Too early to tell."

"The psychotic who did this . . . ?"

"No surprise there. You remember the one. Justice Turnbull." Byron shook his head, his unruly forelock falling forward again. "A whole new kind of crazy." He stifled another yawn. "Think Turnbull'll come back to his old stomping grounds and go after those cult freaks again?"

Laura went completely still. Tried not to look as if his remark had hit a nerve. "The sheriff's department will find him," she said with an effort.

"Oh, yeah." He barked out a laugh. "Count on them."

Ever the cynic.

Laura had heard enough. "I've gotta get back to work." She turned on her heel.

"Hey. Laura." She didn't so much as look over her shoulder and set her jaw. How had she ever found him attractive, and why the hell had she married him? Her thoughts strayed to the child growing within her, *his* child, the baby that Justice seemed to sense, and her insides went numb. "When are you going to stop dyeing your hair?" Byron called after.

She ground her teeth together, angry at him and herself for ever thinking they could build a life together. She'd known he wasn't her kind of man from the get-go, hadn't she? She'd suspected he was self-centered and narcissistic. How had she let him convince her to leave Portland for this stretch of coastline and Ocean Park Hospital, when she'd known it might not be safe? God, she'd been a fool to let him talk her into anything so idiotic. She hadn't wanted to move. She certainly hadn't wanted to relocate *here,* of all places. The house they'd rented together in Deception Bay, about six miles down Highway 101, until he'd moved out wasn't much to write home about, and the apartment he'd subsequently moved into was even less impressive, but that was just icing on the cake of her unhappiness.

Why did you marry him?

At a corner, she hazarded a quick glance over her shoulder, but Byron had already turned away. He couldn't really care less about the horrific events that had taken place at Halo Valley. If he wasn't the center of the universe, then the universe itself didn't matter.

Because I wanted to believe someone loved me.

And she'd been stupid enough to buy into his good looks, his easy charm, his success . . . what a fool she'd been and now . . . Automatically her hand strayed to her abdomen and the life beginning to pulse within her. She couldn't keep this baby. Byron's baby. She couldn't. Yet, it was a child . . . *her* child. . . .

Nurse Baransky, middle-aged, brusque, was coming down the hall toward her. "Are you checking on Mrs. Shields?" she asked.

"I'm on my way to her room now." Laura tried not to appear like she was hurrying, but inside she was running, running, *running*. From Byron, from her marriage, from the strangeness of her childhood, from Justice . . . *from the truth* . . .

"Were you at the ER?" Baransky asked.

"Just coming from outside surgery. No word yet on Conrad or Dr. Zellman."

Baransky nodded. "It was that madman who escaped, wasn't it? The one they captured in the shootout at the motel a few years back? Can't think of his name. Justin something?"

"Justice," Laura reminded carefully, the taste of his name on her tongue bitter, the sound of it striking a chord of terror that shuddered through her. *Sssiissssttterrr.* His hiss echoed through her brain. Dear God.

"They were bringing him here for testing because he was complaining of stomach pain off and on, apparently."

"He was faking," Laura said automatically.

"They told you that?"

Laura nearly bit her tongue trying to take the words back and was instantly sorry that she'd blurted out something she didn't really want to discuss. "I'm just going on an assumption," she backtracked as a patient, a thick-in-the-middle woman with a wan expression, walked tentatively down the hall. Her plump fingers were clenched tight around the pole of a rolling IV stand.

"You need help?" Baransky asked, and the woman offered the ghost of a smile as she shook her head, determined to walk on her own. "You said that Justice Turnbull was faking his illness?" Baransky asked, turning her attention back to Laura.

She didn't know how to answer that she knew Justice was faking. She sure as hell wouldn't be able to explain that Justice had started banging against her brain, something that had begun when she was young, though its strength had waxed and waned over the years, and had practically been nonexistent since he'd been incarcerated, had come back with a vengeance. That she still could manage to hold him out, but there was always a tiny iota of time before she could effectively throw up her mental wall, an infinitesimal moment where he left traces of his own thoughts, scraps that were available to her. So, yes, she knew he'd faked the stomach pain because, in effect, he'd told her as much. More like an overall realization than the needle-sharp words he sent to her.

And she also knew he'd been planning this escape a long time.

And she knew that he was hunting her now. . . .

How does he know about the baby?

"Laura?" Baransky suddenly demanded, eyeing her closely. She had a big voice and little or no tolerance for anything she deemed to be nonsense.

Laura could tell her face had lost color. "I'm just overly tired. Didn't get good sleep last night."

"Maybe you should sit down. I can check on Mrs. Shields."

"No, no. I'm okay."

Laura forced out a smile as she walked past her. She was feeling nauseous, but it was less about the pregnancy and more about the realization that Justice Turnbull had escaped. When the events of his rampage had taken place a few years earlier, she'd kept the wall against his thoughts up solidly high. Before then, he'd never been seen as a serious threat to her and the others he'd targeted by either herself or her family. But then suddenly he was after them all! Threatening the very foundation of her family, her ancestors, anyone even remotely related to her, all those who lived at the huge lodge shielded from the world by massive iron gates. Her sisters.

Sissterr . . . How he'd given the word a horrid sound. Her flesh crawled as she remembered the sibilant sound of his voice, a hiss that grated, like talons running down a blackboard.

Justice was bent on destruction and chaos and killing, and though she hadn't been before, Laura, within the sterile hospital walls, sensed she was definitely in his sights now.

Mrs. Shields was sitting up in bed, her beady, dark eyes regarding Laura with avid curiosity as she walked into the room. She was in her fifties and had been through knee replacement surgery. "How many times do I have to push this button?" she demanded. "I need painkillers, Nurse Adderley. Where's your husband?"

"My ex-husband," Laura said for about the tenth time.

"I need more pain medication. I'm supposed to keep 'on top of the pain,' that's what I was told, to be at a 'ten on the chart,' right?" She was referring to the pain management chart that had been pinned to her wall, a row of smiley faces where the smile disintegrated to a frown as the level of pain increased. Zero was pain free; ten was excruciating, the face on the chart twisted in serious agony, a far cry from Mrs. Shields's primarily ticked-off expression. "Right now, I'm at about a level twenty!" she insisted and, when Laura didn't respond quickly enough, added, "I need *Dr.* Adderley . . . stat!"

"You're on the medication levels he prescribed," Laura said calmly as she tried to take the woman's temperature.

"It's not enough!" Mrs. Shields said, around the thermometer.

Her voice had risen, and it brought Nurse Nina Perez to the doorway. Nina, an attractive woman in her forties, was Laura's immediate boss, and she was fiercely devoted to her job. She also was fair and could assess a situation quickly. "Everything all right in here?"

"No!" Mrs. Shields had been scheduled to leave earlier in the day, but she was one of those rare patients who wanted to stay in the hospital as long as possible. She was an attention seeker who had bullied her husband for so long that he seemed to have no identity and no ability to make decisions.

"I need more painkillers," Mrs. Shields declared as Laura removed the thermometer and noted a reading of 98.6. Perfectly normal. "And here. Fill this up." Mrs. Shields thrust her water glass at Laura, who took it from her hand. Laura's fingers brushed hers, and a tingle fled up Laura's nerves to her brain.

Pancreas.

The word pulsed across her mind. Vivid. Red.

She nearly dropped the glass.

Laura knew, with certainty, that Mrs. Shields would contract pancreatic cancer at some future point and that the disease would ultimately lead to her death. Laura received these messages from time to time when she touched another human's flesh, and it was this odd ability that had first steered her toward a career in medicine. She couldn't tell anyone about it, just as she couldn't tell anyone about her private communication with Justice Turnbull, but she trusted it implicitly.

"Let me see," Nurse Perez said. She turned toward the

woman's IV and examined the drip. Laura suspected that it was all an act for the bristling Mrs. Shields. The woman was being given the proper amount of medication.

Laura asked her casually, "Does cancer run in your family?"

"No. Why?" She was suspicious.

"I thought I saw it in your medical file." She poured water into the glass from a near empty pitcher on Mrs. Shields's tray near her bed, then noted how much fluid the patient was taking in.

The older woman harrumphed, then admitted, "My father had cancer of the pancreas. Killed him in his fifties."

Nina Perez gave Laura a searching look; it wasn't usual for the floor nurses to pore over their patients' medical history. The doctors ordered the protocol, and the nurses followed through.

Laura, offering a smile she didn't really feel, said, "With all the tests you've had for this surgery, I'm sure you've checked that, too."

"I'm not sure of anything!" Mrs. Shields declared. Her nostrils flared slightly, and there was a definite purse to her lips. "Tell your husband to check on that, too!"

My ex, Laura thought, but nodded on her way out. She was grateful to Nina Perez for not questioning her too closely, but now that she'd "heard" this information, she wanted to follow through. So thinking, she had to search out Byron, catching him coming out of the staff room. That boyish smile she'd once found charming curved his lips, and his eyes definitely sparked as he joked with one of the nurse's aides—a girl with round doe eyes, pert nose, and was probably just into her twenties. Her face was bright and flushed as she looked up at him with an adoration she didn't bother to hide.

Laura didn't know whether she was disgusted or amused.

Byron's latest woman—definitely not this girl—wasn't the kind to take his flirting with a forgiving attitude.

Spying his ex-wife out of the corner of his eye, Byron stopped short, as if caught in a nefarious act.

Serves you right, Laura thought as the clueless aide wandered away, gazing back at Byron longingly and even waving her fingers coquettishly before catching a glimpse of Laura, frowning slightly, then rounding the corner to disappear.

A ninny, Laura thought, but bit her tongue. Who cared? It was surprising to find that she didn't.

But you're pregnant. With his child.

Ignoring that persistent and irritating voice in her head, she said, "I was checking on Mrs. Shields. She told me her father died of pancreatic cancer in his fifties, about the age she is now."

"I know her history," he bit out, obviously irritated. "Why?"

"I don't know. I just thought maybe it was something to recheck."

"What? Why?" he demanded, affronted.

"Due diligence."

"So now *you're* the doctor?"

She wasn't going there, wasn't going to be drawn into a no-win discussion, and Byron's pager erupted, anyway, and he stormed off. Fortunately, in the direction of Mrs. Shields's room. Good. He could deal with her.

She walked the other direction but felt him glance over his shoulder and give her an assessing look. The way he always did when she became a puzzle, something he couldn't begin to understand. His ex-wife just wasn't a square peg that fit snugly into the square hole he'd wanted to force her into.

Not that it mattered any longer.

Laura pushed aside all thoughts of him and, for now, her unexpected pregnancy. For now, she concentrated on doing her job and keeping Justice, the monster, at bay.

Thankfully, the rest of her shift was uneventful, but as

she was driving to her house, her senses were on high alert. She hoped to hell they'd caught Justice already, but she suspected that hope was unlikely. If he were captured, she believed he would blast out a raging message to her, and since that last sibilant *ssssisterrrr,* he'd been quiet.

The house she and Byron had rented was a two-bedroom with white trim and gray shingles. One bathroom. Built in the fifties, renovated in the seventies, left to disintegrate over time. She and Byron had bought a condo in downtown Portland, and then the housing market had tumbled and they'd sold for a small loss. It had soured Byron on real estate; he hated losing anything. So, they'd chosen this rental for its proximity to the hospital and signed a six-month lease, which had turned into month-to-month as time had marched on. Once Byron had moved out, Laura was grateful for the cheap rent, even if it did come with a leaky bathroom faucet.

Pulling up to the back porch, she cut the engine and climbed from her Subaru. Byron drove a black Porsche, but Laura had preferred her dark green Outback. The Porsche was leased and Byron's affair; Laura owned the Outback in her own name. Another blessing.

Hurrying past the rhododendrons long past blooming, she heard the rumble of the Pacific Ocean and smelled the thick, damp scent of the sea as she walked along the cement walk to her porch. The neighbor's black cat slid under the porch as she climbed the two steps and unlocked the back door.

Once inside the small kitchen, she snapped on the lights, then dropped her purse and coat on the counter. Its chipped Formica had been scrubbed to a shine when Laura moved in, and she'd repainted all the interior cabinets, trim, and walls herself. Tired it might be, but it was bright and white.

And home.

Her sanctuary.

She'd thought that she might feel a bit of nostalgia, a

loss, when Byron had moved out, but all she'd really experienced was relief, a quiet peace.

Until today.

When Justice had reached out to her and reminded her that she was different. Growing up at Siren Song had made her so. Now she was vulnerable . . . so very vulnerable. Sighing, she sat down in one of the two café chairs surrounding the small glass table, put her elbows against the surface, and buried her face in her hands.

The baby . . . a baby . . .

She should go to the lodge and talk to Aunt Catherine, tell her that Cassandra's prediction had come true. But Justice was out there. Loose. Waiting for someone to make a move. And she, being outside the gates, was the logical choice.

Oh, dear God.

She shuddered. She'd never told Byron about her past. She'd simply said she was estranged from her mother and she'd never known her father. She'd been in her second year of nursing at the hospital where he'd been a resident when they met, and he'd just become a full-fledged osteopath when they'd started dating. She'd been starry-eyed and too eager, and he'd been intrigued by her ability to understand, practically diagnose, underlying problems with his patients that had nothing to do with the broken bones he corrected. He called it her instinct, and they both let it be an understood, and basically untouched, thing between them. Now she knew it was what had set her apart from the other young nurses and medical staff that cast admiring glances in his direction. When he'd casually suggested marriage, she'd jumped at the chance. She'd ignored his selfish traits. She simply hadn't cared. She'd wanted the whole picture: the house with the picket fence, 2.5 children, a dog, and a husband. She'd suspected Byron wasn't as deep as she was. The fact that he hadn't been all that interested in her family had been one clue, but she'd thought it wouldn't matter if she was more in love than he.

On that, she'd been wrong.

So wrong.

He was not only shallow, but he was unfaithful. And uncaring. And unrepentant. He'd wanted her for his wife. He was intrigued with her "instinct," but he wasn't going to be monogamous for anyone. That was simply the way it was. She'd tried to accept the rules but been unable. She'd tried once to make believe they could work their way back together, and that was a complete failure, for which she now was pregnant.

With Byron's child. For so long she'd wanted a baby, hoped for a child, and now . . . oh, God, now she felt a fierce love for this baby but didn't kid herself that raising the child—Byron's child—alone would be easy.

She sat at the table a long time, finally got up and heated water in the microwave and, when the timer dinged, dipped a packet of decaf tea into the steaming cup. As the fragrant tea steeped, she turned on the television and caught breaking news.

Her heart nearly stopped.

The narrow face of Channel Seven's Pauline Kirby, her short, slick dark hair blowing a bit in the evening breeze, was reporting that Justice Turnbull, a known murderer, had escaped from Halo Valley Security Hospital. Two men had been critically injured. One was fighting for his life.

"Oh, dear God." Laura stared at the screen.

"A madman is loose," Pauline was saying, and Laura recognized the redwood and stone facade of the mental hospital in the background, filmed earlier this evening, and shivered to her toes.

Her tea forgotten, she watched the rest of the short report while her heart drummed in her chest and her worst fears were confirmed.

She wished suddenly, mightily, that there was someone out there who could find Justice Turnbull, dig him out from under whatever rock he chose to hide, expose him, and make sure he was locked away so deep that he could never hurt her or the new life growing inside her, a life she was already bonding with.